Midnight kiss

New Year

Fantastic stories from favourite authors
Robyn Grady, Anna DePalo and
Shirley Jump

Escape for New Year

ROBYN GRADY
ANNA DE PALO
SHIRLEY JUMP

MILLS & BOON

DID YOU PURCHASE THIS BOOK WITHOUT A COVER?
If you did, you should be aware it is **stolen property** as it was reported *unsold and destroyed* by a retailer. Neither the author nor the publisher has received any payment for this book.

All the characters in this book have no existence outside the imagination of the author, and have no relation whatsoever to anyone bearing the same name or names. They are not even distantly inspired by any individual known or unknown to the author, and all the incidents are pure invention.

All Rights Reserved including the right of reproduction in whole or in part in any form. This edition is published by arrangement with Harlequin Enterprises II B.V./S.à.r.l. The text of this publication or any part thereof may not be reproduced or transmitted in any form or by any means, electronic or mechanical, including photocopying, recording, storage in an information retrieval system, or otherwise, without the written permission of the publisher.

This book is sold subject to the condition that it shall not, by way of trade or otherwise, be lent, resold, hired out or otherwise circulated without the prior consent of the publisher in any form of binding or cover other than that in which it is published and without a similar condition including this condition being imposed on the subsequent purchaser.

® and ™ are trademarks owned and used by the trademark owner and/or its licensee. Trademarks marked with ® are registered with the United Kingdom Patent Office and/or the Office for Harmonisation in the Internal Market and in other countries.

Mills & Boon, an imprint of Harlequin (UK) Limited, Eton House, 18-24 Paradise Road, Richmond, Surrey TW9 1SR

ESCAPE FOR NEW YEAR
© Harlequin Enterprises II B.V./S.à.r.l. 2012

Amnesiac Ex, Unforgettable Vows © Robyn Grady 2011
One Night with Prince Charming © Anna DePalo 2011
Midnight Kiss, New Year Wish © Shirley Jump 2011

ISBN: 978 0 263 89663 3

010-0112

Harlequin (UK) policy is to use papers that are natural, renewable and recyclable products and made from wood grown in sustainable forests. The logging and manufacturing processes conform to the legal environmental regulations of the country of origin.

Printed and bound in Spain
by Blackprint CPI, Barcelona

AMNESIAC EX, UNFORGETTABLE VOWS

ROBYN GRADY

Award-winning author **Robyn Grady** left a fifteen-year career in television production knowing that the time was right to pursue her dream of writing romance. She adores cats, clever movies and spending time with her wonderful husband and their three precious daughters. Living on Australia's glorious Sunshine Coast, she says her perfect day includes a beach, a book and no laundry when she gets home. Robyn loves to hear from readers. You can contact her at www.robyngrady.com.

This book is for my fellow
Romance Writers of Australia
Romantic Book of the Year finalists.
Couldn't have wished for better company!

One

A muffled conversation, barely audible, filtered in through the closed hospital room door. Laura Bishop raised her bandaged head off the pillows and, concentrating, pricked her ears. One voice was female, the other distinctly male—her fiery sister and equally passionate husband. Laura rolled her teeth over her bottom lip and strained to make out the words. No luck.

But neither Grace nor Bishop sounded pleased.

When Laura had taken a tumble at her home this morning, Grace, who was visiting, had insisted they have the bump on her head checked out. Waiting to see a doctor in a cell phone-free waiting room, Laura had asked Grace to contact Bishop at his Sydney office. She hated to bother him but stints at Casualty could wind on forever, and she didn't want her husband coming home to an empty house and worrying.

Besides, Bishop would want to be informed. He was a protective man…at times, overly so. With her congenital heart condition—and his own family history—Laura supposed he had good reason to be.

The door clicked. When it cracked open an inch, Laura propped up on her elbows.

"I won't have her upset," Laura heard Grace hiss from the corridor.

Laura's husband growled back. "I haven't the least intention of upsetting her."

Wincing, Laura eased back down. How she wished the two people she cared about most could get along, but Grace seemed to be the one woman on earth who was immune to Samuel Bishop's compelling brand of charm. Laura, on the other hand, had been smitten by his sizzling charisma and smoldering good looks from the moment they'd met. Even so...

Lately she'd begun to wonder.

She loved Bishop so very much. She was certain he loved her, too, but given what she'd rediscovered about herself this past week...was it possible they'd jumped the gun and had married too soon?

The door fanned wider. As that familiar athletic frame entered the room, their eyes connected, locked, and suddenly Laura felt dizzier than she had all day. After six months together, Bishop still stirred in her this breathtaking, toe-curling effect, the kind of reaction that flooded her core with want and left her quivering like a half-set jelly.

He looked as magnificent in that dark, custom-made suit as he had that first night, decked out in an impeccable tuxedo, a wicked gleam igniting his entrancing blue eyes when he'd affected a bow and had asked her to dance. Today his eyes were hooded in that same heart-pumping way, but his gaze didn't glow with anything close to desire. In fact, his eyes seemed to reflect no emotion at all.

A shiver crept over Laura's skin.

He was always so caring and attentive. Was he annoyed that she'd slipped? That she'd pulled him away from his work? Shaking herself, Laura broke the spell and touched the square bandage that sat above her left temple. She gave a sheepish smile.

"Apparently I fell."

His dark brows swooped together then his head slowly cocked. "Apparently?"

She hesitated at his single word reply and cast her mind back. "I...I can't remember it now. The doctor said that's not unusual. A person has a fall, knocks their head and they can't recall the incident."

He was unbuttoning his suit jacket, running a deliberate palm down his crimson silk tie. His fingers were long and lean. His hands, large and skilled. She loved his hands. Loved the way they knew precisely where, and precisely how, to please.

"So what *do* you recall?"

Her gaze bounced back to his questioning expression and she examined the sterile but comfortable private room.

"I remember arriving at the hospital. Meeting the doctor. Having a scan...and other tests."

Bishop's mirror blue eyes narrowed.

He wasn't fond of tests, as she'd found out two months into their relationship—the night he'd proposed. He'd presented a dazzling white diamond ring and, overwhelmed with surprise and new love, she'd instantly agreed. Later that evening, curled up in his strong arms in his penthouse's sumptuous bed, she'd told her fiancé about her heart condition—hypertrophic cardiomyopathy. Never one for attention or pity, she normally kept that information to herself. But if they were to be married, of course Bishop needed to know.

"Grace said she saw you when she was driving up the path to the house," Bishop said now, flicking back his jacket to slide his hands into his trouser pockets. "She saw you tumbling from the garden's footbridge."

Laura nodded. A drop of around six feet. "That's what she told me, too." Like she'd said. She couldn't remember.

A pulse pumped once along the dark shadow of his jaw.

"Grace also said you're feeling fuzzy. That you seem… uncertain about some other things, too."

"I'm clear on everything else." She pulled herself higher on the bank of pillows at her back. "In fact, I feel clearer today than I have in a long while."

His eyes flashed. She knew he'd heard the backbone in her tone, but he didn't probe. More tellingly, he didn't come near, gather her up and comfort her, the way he had that evening after he'd proposed.

That night, when she'd confided in him about her illness, he'd drawn her extra close, had brushed his lips tenderly over her brow then had asked about the odds of any offspring inheriting her disorder. She'd done lots of research. Statistics attested to the fact that a baby could inherit the condition as she had done, however, screening precautions were available. An early termination, due to medical considerations, could be performed. Thankfully, from the hard set of his jaw, she'd gleaned he was as uncomfortable with that scenario as she was. But neither was he convinced that they should take a gamble and simply hope for the best.

In the quiet of the hospital room now, Bishop's head angled and he continued to study her as if he wasn't certain who she was. As if she were some new and curious anomaly. Laura's nerves frayed more and she thrust her hand out, beckoning. She couldn't stand the distance a moment more.

"Bishop, please come over here. We need to talk."

The ledge of his shoulders went back and, as an almost suspicious expression darkened his face, her stomach knotted more. When his eyes skimmed her brow, her cheek, her lips, her skin heated, and not in a pleasant way. The vibes he gave off…

If she hadn't known better, she'd think he disliked her.

Finally he came forward, but his gait was guarded, as though he expected to be ambushed at any moment. Had the doctor spoken to him about more than her fall? If not, she'd better tell him now, herself, before someone else could. How would he react when she told him that, no more than an hour ago, she'd taken a pregnancy test?

Pulling herself up, she swung her feet onto the floor so that they could sit side by side. Bishop cut the remaining distance separating them in three purposeful strides. Her stomach jumped when, in a commanding gesture, he cast the covers back more. Avoiding her gaze, he tipped his head at the sheets and a lock of his immaculately groomed hair fell over his brow.

"Get back in bed."

She contained the inappropriate urge to laugh. This was absurd.

"Bishop, I'm fine."

His gaze slid to hers and his brows lifted. "You are?"

"Perfectly."

"Do you know where you are?"

She suppressed a sigh. What was it with a knock on the head and endless questions? She'd been barraged by them half the day.

"I've been through this already with the doctor." As well as Grace and a handful of nurses. But when his implacable look held, she exhaled and supplied the name of the hospital and added, "Which is west of Sydney and east of the Blue Mountains." Where they lived.

"What's my name?"

She tacked on a smug smile and crossed her legs prettily. "Winston Churchill."

Familiar warmth rose up in his eyes—a comfortable, sensual glow that left her aching to reach for him. But then that serious line cut between his brows again and he cleared his throat like he did whenever he was uneasy.

"No games."

She almost rolled her eyes. But anyone who knew Bishop knew his stubborn streak. The sooner this was over and he was assured, the sooner she could get her change of heart out in the open, the sooner they could work this issue through, and the sooner they could get on with their life together.

God willing.

"Your name is Samuel Coal Bishop," she stated. "You enjoy reading the Financial Review cover to cover, long distance running and the occasional good bottle of wine. Furthermore, tonight you're celebrating an anniversary." She smiled... soft, inviting. "Three months ago today, you and I were married."

Her words hit Bishop squarely in the chest, knocking him completely off balance. It was all he could manage not to cough up his lungs and reel back from the blow. Instead he ran a rather unsteady hand through his hair.

Good God in Heaven. She'd lost her mind.

Grace, the nurse...they'd said Laura had hit her head and was a little hazy. No one told him that she'd lost two years of her life! That she thought they were still *married*. As for falling off that same footbridge...

Bishop hid a cringe. Was this some kind of sick joke? Would the host of a lame candid-camera show jump out, sock him on the arm and point out a hidden lens?

But looking into Laura's unsuspecting emerald eyes now, Bishop knew she was deadly serious. Gazing up at him, with such unabashed innocence and adoration, was the face of the fair-haired angel he'd married. He hadn't been able to figure out why he'd been asked to come here today. Now Laura's request for her sister to call him made sense. So did Grace's inability to look him in the eye when he'd hammered her for details a few minutes ago.

Bishop resisted the urge to drop his head into his hands and groan out loud. He should have insisted on seeing a doctor. He'd been set up. He knew by whom and he could sure as hell guess why.

Laura's sister set the blame for their marriage's breakdown solely upon his shoulders. Chances were that Grace had hoped when Laura laid eyes upon the fiend who'd deserted her, a deluge of sordid memories would come flooding back. Laura's memory would be restored. Once again, *Belligerent Bishop* would be the bad guy and control freak Grace would be number one in her little sister's life. If he'd had a low opinion of Grace before, this took the cake. He'd deserved to know the facts.

Laura had deserved that courtesy, too.

After so long of a silence, worry began to cloud Laura's eyes. His brow damp, Bishop adjusted the crimson knot at his throat and scanned through the maze in his mind. But the harder and longer he searched, the more dead-ends hit him in the face.

Only two things were certain. He couldn't throw up his hands, walk out and leave her here, wondering. Neither could he callously dump the truth of recent events on her. He and Laura might have said goodbye under less than amicable terms—downright hostile, actually—but now she was ill.

And, dammit, he'd loved her once. Deeply. She may or may not thank him for it later, but he had to make an effort to ease her though this…reunion.

He found a small, amiable smile. "Laura, you're not well. You need to stay overnight. I'll speak with the doctor and—" He stopped. Blinked.

And *what*?

He cleared his throat. "And we'll go from there."

She uncrossed her legs only to ravel hers arms over her waist and ease up her chin.

"No."

He frowned. "What do you mean, no?"

Her arms unwound and, her expression imploring now, she reached for him.

Bishop froze. He should pull back. Crush any possibility of

physical contact. He'd never been able to resist her whenever they'd touched.

But the last time they'd been anything close to intimate was well over a year ago. Perhaps that part of him—that primal, perpetually hungry part—was largely buried, along with the love they'd once known.

And so, to curb her suspicions—to keep her calm—he reached out, too, and allowed her delicate fingers to lace through his. Instantly his blood began to stir, and when her sparkling eyes looked into his, the awareness he saw there delivered a pleasure-pain jolt that pierced his ribs and stole his breath.

"Darling," she murmured, "I've spent enough of my life in hospital rooms. I know you mean well, but I don't need to be wrapped in cotton wool. I'm not a child. I have my own mind and I know I'm okay."

Swallowing the dry brick lodged in his throat, Bishop eased his hand from hers, slid a foot back and, determined, injected a take-no-prisoners tone into his voice.

"I'm afraid you're not in a position to object."

Her eyes darkened and her lovely mouth turned slowly down. "I didn't give up my rights when I married you—"

Stopping mid-sentence, her head went back and she flinched, as if someone had slapped her. Gradually her dazed expression faded and her face filled with all shades of remorse.

"Bishop...oh, God. I'm sorry." Confusion swam in her glistening eyes. "I didn't mean that. Not a word."

Bishop let go of the breath he'd been holding. Apparently, a lack of memory couldn't suppress her true, less than charitable feelings toward him. The person who'd challenged him a second ago had sounded like the Laura who'd glared at him when she'd told him to get out. The Laura who had mailed divorce papers a year to the day after that.

Laura was the one who'd ended their marriage. Of course

he'd been upset. Hell, he'd been wounded to his core. But he'd never hated her. He didn't hate her now. Nor did her love her. Which should make this situation easier than it was.

He nodded to the bed. "You need to lie down."

"I need to *talk* to you."

He held the cover back again. "Lie down."

When she stood up, refusing, he fought the urge to force her to act in her own best interests and do as she was told. But that was out of the question, for more reasons than one. She was still a beautiful woman...more beautiful than he even remembered. As much as his brain knew they couldn't live together, his physiology understood only that she was uniquely, tormentingly desirable.

How easy it would be even now to sweep her up, whisk her away and take shameful advantage of this situation. So easy... And more destructive than any act that had ever come before.

He loosened the knot at his throat. He'd try to reason with her one more time.

"You might think you're all right, but—"

"I thought we were pregnant."

The back of his knees caved in. Tipping sideways, Bishop propped his shoulder against the wall then, mind spinning, slid to sit on the bed. His ears were ringing. He felt as if a bomb had exploded inches from his face. Holding his brow, he waited for the stars to fade then finally found the wherewithal to question his ex-wife.

His voice was a croak.

"You thought...*what?*"

She folded down beside him and held his hand as she beseeched him with her eyes. "I was so happy. And worried. Worried about what you would say."

His chest squeezed around a deep ache at the same time a horrible emptiness welled up inside of him. He felt ransacked. As if his insides had been ripped out and thrown on the floor.

He couldn't go through this again, not for anything. Not even that trusting, desperate look on Laura's face.

He turned more toward her, willed the truth to show in his eyes. "Listen to me...you *couldn't* be."

"I know we use protection," she countered, "but nothing's a hundred percent."

The breath Bishop held burned in his chest. This was worse than he'd thought. Was now the time to serve it to her cold? If he were in her shoes, he'd prefer it that way. He wouldn't want to feel like a fool later on. Laura wouldn't, either. They weren't married anymore, much less pregnant.

Her green eyes glistened over at him and as her fingers kneaded his, unbidden brush fires began to heat and lick familiar pathways through his veins. Closing his eyes, he worked to kill the desire to take her in his arms and comfort her as a devoted husband would. So vivid, so hauntingly clear...it all might have happened yesterday. Their meeting, the wedding, the honeymoon, that fall from the northern footbridge, then the slow agonizing death of "them."

"You are *not* pregnant." His words were strained, controlled. *Or, if you are, I'm not the father.*

Her slim nostrils flared with quiet courage and she nodded. "The doctor told me. I was mistaken." That hope-filled light came back up in her eyes. "But when I thought I had a baby growing inside of me, a tiny new life that *we'd* created, it made me realize..."

Her gaze grew strangely distant and yet somehow stronger. Then her shoulders rolled back and a fire lit her cheeks.

"My illness won't make a difference to how I feel," she told him. "I know there's a risk, but I want a baby, Bishop. *Our* baby." She held his hand tighter, angled her head and brought his fingers to her hot cheek. "We just need to have faith."

Bishop closed his eyes as a scolding, prickling sensation crawled up his spine. They'd already had this conversation.

Going on two years ago. It had been the beginning of the end…a long, drawn out, bitter affair.

Laura's broken voice cut through the haze.

"I'm sorry. I shouldn't have blurted it out like that."

Again Bishop tugged the Windsor knot at his throat and, finding it increasingly difficult to breathe, lengthened his neck. Other than Laura's light floral scent, the air in here seemed stale. He needed some space to try and work out how to diffuse this crazy situation before it got any worse.

Winding his hand out of hers, he found his feet and an impassive voice.

"Is there anything I can get you? Anything you need?" Three fingers of scotch sat at the top of *his* wish list.

"There is one thing." She stood, too, leaned closer and placed a warm palm on his chest. Unbidden flames ignited in his sternum as her slightly parted mouth came near. "I need for you to kiss me."

Two

In her eyes—in his heart—Bishop understood that today Laura loved him. He also understood she was far from her true state of mind. Fighting the raw ache in his throat, he found his ex-wife's arms and urged her gently away.

Refusing her affection was one of the most difficult things he'd ever had to do; toward the end of their marriage he'd have given anything to have had her show him love again. But while his hardening body whispered for him to accept what she offered now, his conscience said a resounding no. Laura was far from well, and no man for any reason needed to take advantage of that.

But he had to be careful how he handled this problem. He didn't want to tip her over whatever mental precipice she so obviously teetered on.

He put a calming note into his voice. "Laura, this isn't the time."

"Not the time?" Her face pinched. Then she blinked several times. "I don't understand. We're husband and wife. We always kiss."

His heart lurched but he wouldn't let that twist of emotion show. How in God's name would he ever navigate through this mess? He felt as if he'd been thrown into the mouth of an active volcano. Everywhere he stepped he got burned. A lot like their marriage, really.

But information was power. He'd get the facts, a professional's opinion and see what was what.

Laura was still looking at him, confusion and hurt brimming in her eyes. In the first three months of their marriage, he hadn't been able to keep his hands off her, and vice versa.

Even now…

Needing to reassure her, he relented and let one palm slide down her arm. Immediately, that minimal contact sent up a flare and a throb that echoed like a warning bell through his blood. Setting his jaw, he put up both his hands and took a resolute step back.

"I'll go speak to a doctor."

"About the pregnancy test."

His gut knotted and jaw tightened more.

"Yes. About that."

He left her standing in a white hospital gown, uncertain, beside the bed. In the corridor, he took a moment to orient himself and order his blood pressure to drop. Laura might be the one who'd had a fall and lost her memory but he was the one feeling off balance. Still, there must be a rational, safe way to maneuver through this hopscotch of emotional landmines. And damned if he wouldn't find it, and find it fast.

At the nurses' station, Bishop made an inquiry and a man in a white coat studying a file down the hall was pointed out. He sped off.

"Doctor—" Bishop glanced at the name tag as he came to a stop "—Stokes, I'm Samuel Bishop. I was told you examined Laura Bishop earlier."

The middle-aged doctor peered over his bifocals and set aside the folder. "You're Mrs. Bishop's husband?"

"In a manner of speaking."

The doctor gave a knowing grin and they crossed the room, away from others' earshot.

"Head trauma," Doctor Stokes summed up. "Retrograde memory loss."

Bishop nodded. "How long will it last?"

"Usually in these cases, memory returns gradually over the following days. It can take longer. In some rare instances it never returns."

Bishop's head began to tingle. He needed to clarify. "In *rare* instances?"

"Initial tests were free of fractures or contusions. She could stay overnight but, as long as she takes it easy and you keep an eye on her, there's no reason she can't go home. When she sleeps, wake her every three to four hours and ask those same simple questions—name, address—to be sure she's stable. You can see your own GP for a follow-up."

Take her *home*...?

Bishop scratched his temple. "Thing is, Doc, we're not married anymore."

One of the doctor's eyebrows lifted. "Your sister-in-law hinted as much."

"Ex-sister-in-law."

The older man's eyes conveyed his sympathies for the situation before he slotted his hands into his coat pockets. "Subtle jogging of the memory. Perhaps photos when you think she's ready. When she's in familiar surroundings, I'm sure more recent events will resurface soon enough." Doctor Stokes seemed about to say more but then he merely tipped his head. "Good luck, Mr. Bishop."

As the doctor moved off, Bishop fell back into a nearby chair. He'd need a whole lot more than luck.

His cell phone vibrated against his hip and he scanned the text from his second-in-charge, Willis McKee.

Where are you? A buyer's on the line. Wants to speak with you ASAP.

Bishop's jaw shifted. Already?

He'd listed Bishop Scaffolds and Building Equipment, the

business he'd built to a multimillion dollar entity, only last week. At the price he'd set, he'd never expected such a quick response, and he wasn't certain how he felt about it.

Over these past few months, since the finality of the separation had sunk in, he'd felt a certain restlessness. One chapter of his personal life had closed and he'd begun to wonder whether he needed a new challenge in his professional life, as well. But he hadn't given a lot of thought as to which direction he should take.

Still, he was pleased he'd taken the initiative to move forward. He'd been seeing a nice woman for just over a month, too. Nothing serious; he wasn't certain he'd ever do serious again. But he enjoyed Annabelle's company. She wasn't high maintenance. Didn't ask the impossible.

Bishop snapped the cell shut.

And now Laura was back in his life, and given the doc's opinion, who knew for how long? What the hell was he going to do? He couldn't simply walk away. Then again, how could he stay? He was stuck like a bug under a shoe.

A tap on the shoulder brought him back and his head snapped up. When he saw Grace poised beside him, he groaned. At this moment, she was his least favorite person. What was new?

Grace made herself comfortable in a seat alongside him and laced her peach-tipped nails on her crisp linen lap.

"So now you know."

He slid her a bland look. "Thanks for the heads-up."

"She didn't remember?"

"Laura thinks today is our three-month anniversary."

"How are you celebrating?"

He pushed to his feet. "Don't be smart, Grace." He set off toward Laura's room. He'd have to speak with this woman again and soon, but right now he didn't trust himself to keep his hands from circling her throat. He didn't care how much she disapproved of him; he should have been warned.

The only good thing to come from his and Laura's bust up was getting rid of one very toxic influence in his life. Always sticking her nose in, stirring up trouble. Laura had defended her sister, but he wondered if deep down she wondered if she'd picked the short straw in the sister pool of life. Grace was one hell of a control freak.

Of course, he'd heard people say the same about him, but that was different. He had a business to run. People who relied on him to get things done right, and that meant the first time.

"I still think you could have saved the marriage."

Grace's silky words hit his back and, temper spiking, Bishop edged around. He set his hands on his hips to keep from making fists.

"First, redundant observation, Grace. There isn't a marriage anymore. Second—" steam rising from his collar, he strode back "—are you trying to have me think you want Laura and me to get back together? Because I'd sooner believe in the Easter Bunny."

Fingers unlacing, Grace found her feet, too. She always came across as so damn perfect—hair, nails, prissy platinum blond French roll. He'd love to rattle her cage, but this wasn't the place. Already, interested people were staring.

"You're wrong," Grace said, "if you think I want to see Laura unhappy."

Grace wasn't interested in anything but being right. "You never wanted us married."

"I didn't want you to marry so soon. You both needed time to think things through. You didn't give yourselves a decent chance."

"And you've been gloating about that ever since."

Her head tilted as her gaze searched his. "Have you considered using this time in a positive way? This might be an opportunity to do things differently. To listen to her this time. Try to understand."

Bishop only glared. Even now she was trying to manipulate. Grace knew nothing. She hadn't lived in their home during that turbulent time. He'd done his best. From the start, when Laura had said she'd changed her mind and wanted to have a baby of their own rather than adopt, he'd tried to understand. Their downfall wasn't due to his behavior but to Laura's conscience; she'd made the wrong decision and had never gotten over it.

Her hopeful look dissolving, Grace sighed.

"I've said goodbye to Laura." She collected her handbag and headed toward the wing's exit. "Take good care of her."

He almost called out; where the hell did she think she was going? Grace had always been so ready to ingratiate her presence into Laura's life before. Now, when Laura really needed her, she was walking out? But the question marks on their curious audience's faces roped back any choice words. As uncomfortable as this would be with his ex, having Grace around would only make the situation ten times more difficult. If Laura's parents were alive, he was certain they would step up, but both her mother and father had died long before Laura met him.

Like it or not, this was his problem, as well as Laura's, to work through.

Resigned, Bishop returned to the private hospital room. When he entered, Laura was standing by the window, her arms wrapped around her middle. She rotated back. Her delicate face was pale. Clearly she wanted to go to him, but after his earlier reticence, she hesitated.

"I spoke with the doctor," he said.

"And?"

Bishop considered his reply. He thought about Grace's opinion—a second chance—then the doctor's remark regarding *rare instances*. Might Laura never regain her memory? Could this accident give them another shot at their relationship? After all the anguish, a full year apart, was there any piece of him that even wanted that? He didn't love her. Not anymore. Too much water under that bridge. For now, however, he could only take one step at a time.

Willing the bite of tension away from between his shoulders, he came to her, offered his hand, and innocent hope flickered bright in her eyes.

"Get dressed," he said with a small but encouraging smile. "The doctor says we can go home."

An hour later, as Bishop steered up that familiar spiraling mountain road, Laura gazed out the window, a warm smile tugging her lips. She wanted to roll down the window and enjoy a good long lungful of that fresh, clean air. The glorious cloud-wisped sky, those endless forests of eucalypt and pine, so many colorful birds swooping between branches... Everything looked somehow brighter.

She'd loved this part of the Blue Mountains countryside from the moment Bishop had first driven her to his estate two weeks after they'd met. Now, almost six months on, she couldn't imagine living anywhere else. Or being with, and loving, anyone else. Although...

Laura stole a curious look at the driver.

Bishop looked somehow different this afternoon. Tired from a busy week at the office most likely. Worried about her, of course. But she hadn't noticed those fine lines branching from his eyes before. And he'd seemed so distant all the drive here. She didn't need to be Einstein to know he was avoiding the subject she'd brought up in the hospital. He didn't want to discuss the possibility of renegotiating what they'd decided upon before taking their vows.

That night four months ago, when he'd suggested adoption as their safest bet, a rush of emotion had stung her eyes and hurt-filled tears had brimmed. But he'd assured her that he was only being practical. Sensible. Yes, he understood that her own condition was easily managed, but there was no guarantee that a child might not inherit a more severe form of cardio impairment. Surely the most important thing, he'd said, was to be together and raise a healthy baby. An adopted child.

She'd respected his concerns—still did—but she'd come to realize that he needed to respect her feelings, too. Feelings that weren't about to go away. From as far back as she could recall, she'd wanted her own family, particularly in her late teens after her parents had passed away. She had her Arts History and Literature degree—her parents had been big on education—but her dream was to be a homemaker, a good wife and great mother. She wasn't career-minded in the twenty-first century sense, and she didn't care who knew it. She wanted to bestow upon her children the same kind of love and support she'd known and valued growing up. Never had she considered the possibility of raising another woman's child.

But she *did* want a healthy baby, and she most certainly wanted to marry Bishop, so she'd agreed to his suggestion. Over these past months, however, the weight of that decision had pressed on her heart like a stone. More and more she'd begun to believe there must be a thing as being *too* cautious. It was far from certain that any child they conceived would inherit her disorder. And there was always medication and a simple operation to implant a defibrillator to regulate the heartbeat if need be. Of course, if a child were severely affected, more involved surgery might be needed. A pacemaker. Even a transplant.

But in this age of high technology and information, parents-to-be were aware of so many frightening things that could go wrong in vitro. Then there were the concerns surrounding keeping a child safe later on, from disease and accidents and predators. But most people didn't let those fears beat them. A husband and wife hoped for the best, knowing they'd be there for one another, no matter what.

As long as she was fertile—and there was no reason to believe that she wasn't—she wanted to try. The reward would be well worth the risk. Was she wrong to want what so many women longed for?

A child of her blood. A child of her own.

Deep in thought, Laura absently ran a hand over the car's armrest, and then something odd struck her. She'd been so caught up in memories and today's events, she hadn't noticed until now.

"You didn't mention you were getting a new car."

Bishop's eyes, beneath their aviator sunglasses, didn't leave the road. "Willis negotiated a good lease on the Land Rover."

Her mind wound back but didn't hook onto anything. She shrugged. "Willis who? I don't remember you mentioning that name before."

"Haven't I? He's my assistant. New assistant."

"What happened to Cecil Clark? I thought you said he did a good job. He seemed nice enough at that charity dinner we went to last month."

"He…got another offer."

"You should have matched it."

His voice dropped. "Sometimes you just have to let people go."

Four-wheel drive tires crunched as he braked at the top of their lengthy gravel drive. Rather than one of the four garages, he'd parked in front of the house, a sprawling ranch-style dwelling cut into the hillside. Both inside and out, the house combined tasteful luxury with a homey rural feel—enormous individually crafted open fireplaces, large yet cozy bedrooms, two massive home offices, a fully equipped gym with sauna and indoor pool for laps.

On Sundays, Laura served eggs Benedict on the eastern porch and together they would watch the southern hemisphere sun climb higher toward the far-stretching haze of mountains to the west. Even more she loved what came after coffee… returning to bed to savor her delectable, insatiable husband.

Touching the small bandage above her temple, Laura frowned and thought back. Had they enjoyed their ritual this Sunday past? She couldn't remember.

Bishop swung out of the driver's side and performed his usual courtesy of opening her door. Together they moved up the slate-paved steps that led to the lofty teak and glass paneled entry door. Halfway up, he paused to clear his throat and rattle the keys awkwardly in his palm.

"My, uh, house key must be on my other set."

"I have mine." She didn't recall grabbing her bag before leaving for the hospital—silly, but she couldn't even remember this bag. Still she dug in, rummaged around, fished out a set of keys...but then her eyes rounded and she froze.

Horror slow-dripping through her veins, she rotated her left hand one way, then the other as panic fisted tight and fierce inside of her.

"My rings," she got out. "The nurse must have taken them off before the scan."

Common sense said her diamond-studded wedding band and magnificent princess-cut engagement ring must be filed away at the hospital somewhere safe. Clearly it was an oversight that they hadn't been returned before they'd left. But the staff would have records. There was no reason to believe she wouldn't get them back. Still she couldn't loosen the suffocating knot in her chest. She felt naked without them. Somehow so vulnerable.

Standing on the expansive veranda, with the sun arcing toward the towering eucalypt trees behind, Bishop took a step closer. "Don't worry. I'll take care of it. You need to rest."

He'd said it kindly enough but it was on the tip of her tongue to tell him that she'd been resting all day. Still, the truth was that suddenly she did feel tired, and a few degrees off balance. Maybe she should swallow her pride and do as he asked. Lie down.

But not alone.

She twined their fingers and tugged until the back of his hand pressed against her heart. She hoped her teasing grin was persuasive.

"You look like you could use a rest, too."

Emotion flared in his eyes, hot and cold at the same time. "I didn't have a fall today," he reminded her. "You did."

Her heart dropped. He sounded so...detached. But unlike earlier in hospital, this time she knew why. Of course he wanted to be with her. Of course he wanted to caress and kiss her. But safety-first Bishop was determined not to go against professional advice. During the drive home, he'd made a point of repeating the doctor's instructions that she ought to take things easy for a day or two. Still...

"You know something?" She moved closer until their hands lay flat between them like pressed flowers. "I can't think of a better way to relax than making love with my husband."

As if infused by a sudden rush of blood, a cord rose and pulsed down one side of his throat. His chest expanded on a giant breath and that odd emotion in his eyes flared again.

"We'll go inside." His free hand opened the door. "I'll fix you something to drink."

"Champagne?" she asked, trying hard not to sound hurt by his flat tone as he herded her in. "It's our anniversary, after all."

"Tea, iced or hot." He shut the door and walked past. "In a couple of days we'll see if you still want champagne."

Three

When Laura relented and took herself off to bed, Bishop sent up a silent prayer of thanks.

She'd tried to corner him into joining her in the bedroom, but he'd dodged another bullet, albeit with a minimum of skill. He only hoped his ex-wife's memory returned before either of them had to endure that kind of farce again.

In her mind, they were married. Married couples enjoyed conjugal intimacies, and he and Laura had been intimate often. What bothered Bishop most now was how strongly his body responded to the possibility of holding Laura close. Naked. Loving. His again.

As she disappeared down the wide hardwood hall, gait slow, head down, Bishop shoveled a hand through his hair and threw a glance around. Same furniture, same stunning yet homey fireplace. How many times had they made love before the flames he'd stoked there?

After several moments remembering back...wishing something, somewhere, had turned out differently...he bit down and wheeled toward the door.

His hands bunched at his sides. The urge to walk out was overwhelming; he could only see this ending badly. But he couldn't leave. At least not yet. If Laura's inability to remember lasted beyond Sunday, however, he'd fabricate a business trip and organize assistance…a nurse perhaps. Or Grace would need to make arrangements. Until then, he was stuck.

But he wouldn't sit around twiddling his thumbs. He might be away from the office, his apartment, but he could still get some work done.

He brought his laptop in from the car and without much thought, moved into his former home office. He let his eye linger over the heavy rosewood furniture, the maroon couch, his Rubik's Cube and the framed photograph of Laura that, remarkably, still sat on the polished desk. He moved forward and let a fingertip trail the cool silver frame.

Hell, he thought she'd have demolished this room and every reminder in it the first chance she'd got. Which led him to thoughts of her "lost" wedding rings.

They weren't at the hospital. She'd probably flushed them or tossed them in the fireplace, as he'd done with his band a raging moment before he'd slammed the door shut on this place forever. Or believed that he had. But his stay here this time would be short-term. After the long drawn-out business that had led to their separation, the shorter the better.

Settling into his chair, he connected with Bishop Scaffolds' server and brought up some recent specs. New dies were under discussion but he wouldn't commit until he was certain the designs were exactly right.

With a background in engineering, he'd always enjoyed a natural affinity with machinery. Routinely he checked presses, calibrations and product tolerances. It wasn't unusual to find the boss manning equipment should a worker be called away or need a few minutes off. This past week, after listing the company, he'd spent more time than usual in the factory where equipment was manufactured, stored and dispatched. He considered himself as much a part of the working machine, a cog in the wheel, as his employees, every one handpicked and valued.

But maintaining a manufacturing presence in Australia was a tricky ball to juggle. The uncertain slope of the Aussie dollar against other currencies, the force of reduced labor prices in neighboring countries, plus the quality versus cheaper options argument kept Bishop on his toes. The threat of any company folding to the sum of those pressures was real.

When he'd lost a couple of key contracts not long after his and Laura's split, an unsettling sense of doubt had clung to him. He'd never failed at anything of real consequence, but if he could fail at something as important as his marriage, might he not fail in business, too? If he began second guessing himself, losing his edge, maybe it was time to get out and hand over the business to someone who had the mind-set to keep it strong. He wanted to be that man, but then he'd also wanted to keep his marriage solid.

He went into a few emails but found he couldn't focus. Visions of Laura's toned form, tucked under a light cover in the bed they'd once shared, had seeped into his mind and now he couldn't shift them. Images of her chest softly rising and falling and the way her hair splayed over her pillow while she slept were glued in his mind. He thought of how perfectly her mouth had fit under his—how everything had seemed to fit—and for one frightening moment, he battled a tidal wave urge to stride down the hall and join her.

Growling, he pushed back his laptop and glared at the ceiling. Dammit, he'd never wanted his marriage to end. He'd fought to save it. But no matter what Grace thought about second chances, he'd be an idiot to entertain such a crazy idea. He was here because he had no choice. Laura would get her memory back and then they could each forget this episode and get on with their individual lives.

Laura woke with her heart hammering in her chest. The room was quiet, the walls stenciled with soft-edged shadows. The green numerals on the side table read 2:04.

Shivering and feeling inexplicably alone, she tugged the covers higher. Then she remembered Bishop and her smile warmed her right through. Carefully, she rolled over, reached out in the darkness...and that warmth dropped away.

The space beside her was cold and empty. Why hadn't Bishop joined her? Because he worried about her bandaged head? Didn't he know that his embrace was the only medicine she needed?

Well, if he didn't know, she'd simply have to go and tell him.

After wrapping up in a long, soft robe, she padded out into the hall. Outside Bishop's office, a wedge of light shone on the timber floor. Frowning, she huddled into the robe's warmth more. He was working at two in the morning?

She headed off but stopped in the doorway, her heart melting at the sight. Bishop was sprawled out on his Chesterfield couch, an ankle hung over the far armrest, one foot on the floor, his left forearm draped over his eyes. He'd taken off his shoes and trousers, and his white business shirt was undone to his navel. The steady rise and fall of his beautiful big chest told her he was sleeping soundly. Familiar heat sizzled through her. God, how she loved him. How dearly she wanted him. And there was another feeling swirling through her blood... one that was strangely difficult to pinpoint or analyze.

She *missed* him. Missed him like she hadn't seen him in years. The knowledge left her with a hollow ache in her chest. A chunk cut out of her heart. But she surrendered to a self-deprecating smile. He'd been away from their bed half a night. How would she cope if he left her for a week? A month?

She wriggled her toes on the cool floor. She wanted to go to him, wrap him up under her robe, rub her leg over the hard length and rouse him. Despite doctor's orders not to overdo it, if her hands were to knead his body and she poured words of love in his ear, surely he'd relent and make love.

Or would he be unhappy with her? He worried so much about her health.

She was still making up her mind when the ridges of his six-pack suddenly crunched and Bishop woke with a start. Driving back a breath, he sat bolt upright as if a monster had chased him out of a dream. His gaze shot to the doorway, to where she stood. His dark hair was mussed and his bronzed legs beneath the white shirt looked as strong as steel pylons. The tips of Laura's breasts hardened against the gentle fabric of her robe. How she longed to trail her fingers up over that steel, every blessed inch of it.

His blue eyes focused then narrowed slightly as they raked the lines of her body. A pulse began to beat in his jaw at the same time his eyes grew lidded and she knew he was visualizing the curves and valleys he loved to touch and taste.

Then he scrubbed a hand over his face and, shaking himself, sat straighter. His voice was thick from sleep.

"It's late. Go back to bed."

"If you come with me."

He held her gaze then looked to his desk. "In a few minutes. I have some things to wrap up."

She crossed the room, sat down beside him and gave him a level look.

"We can't avoid it, you know."

He leaned back the barest amount. "Avoid…what?"

"We need to talk."

She put her hand on his thigh. He promptly removed it.

"Not in the middle of the night." He pushed to his feet and, grabbing his hand, she pulled him back. He had the strength to resist, but a yielding expression touched his mouth, his eyes, and slowly he lowered back down.

"When I was old enough to understand about my condition," she began, "that I would need to be careful about overexertion and such—I felt…different. My parents made sure every teacher knew which activities I could or could not do. Once, when we were short on numbers, Mrs. Carols insisted I moved off the sideline and team up for the 500m relay. When he found out, my dad hit the roof. He threatened the principal's job and demanded an apology from Mrs. Carols as well as from the school."

Bishop's brows had knitted. "Why are you telling me this now?"

"Because I want you to understand that I know better than anyone what I'm asking of you, of myself and of any children we have."

As if he were considering her words, his gaze lowered. He saw his buttons undone and, deep in thought, he began to rebutton. "Laura, it must be close to three o'clock—"

"Junior school was lonely sometimes," she plowed on. She didn't care about the time. She needed to say this and he needed to hear it. "I couldn't do cross-country or horse riding at camp. Kids can be cruel and some laughed behind my back. A couple even called me a cripple."

Redoing the final button, his hands fisted in his shirt. "I wish I'd been there."

"I had good friends too, though. We ignored the girls who needed to make themselves feel taller by bringing someone else down. Then university happened and the entire world didn't need to know anymore. I was just like everyone else. A year after graduation, I met you."

A small smile hooked one side of his mouth. "That night I kept you up talking till dawn."

Smiling, too, she turned more toward him. "Eight weeks and one day later, you proposed. When you still wanted to marry me after you learned about my secret, I didn't think anyone could be more lucky…or more in love…" Her gaze dipped before finding his again. "Even if you didn't quite understand how deeply I felt about conceiving and having our own child. After I agreed we would adopt, I tried to deny it to myself."

He broke their intense gaze and cleared his throat. "We'll talk about it in the morning."

She touched the square bandage on her head. Feeling a faint throb coming on, she surrendered with a nod. It was enough for now that she'd opened that door a little wider. Tomorrow they would talk more, and when he realized how much carrying and giving life to her own child meant to her—when he accepted that history didn't need to repeat itself, hers or his—he'd come around. He loved her, and love could surmount any obstacle.

She found her feet and put out her hand. "Coming?" His gaze slid to her bandage and she grinned. If he thought he'd get away with another excuse, he was mistaken. "Or we can stay up and finish this conversation now?"

He stood. "You win. But remember, you're taking it easy."

She looped her arm through his and guided him toward the door, toward their bedroom.

Beside the bed, she slipped out of her robe while he unbuttoned his shirt again, which seemed to take an inordinately long time. When she slid between the covers, feeling sexy in the lacy negligee she'd donned when she'd first lain down, she watched as his gaze filtered over her in the golden glow of lamplight. Snuggling into the pillows, she slipped back his side of the covers.

"On my honor," she said, half-serious, "I promise not to ravage you."

A moment later, the mattress dipped as he moved in beside her. Lying on his side, resting on an elbow, he searched her eyes. Then he brushed a curl from her brow and said, "I promise the same."

The next morning, a world of birds' calls dragged Bishop from a deep sleep. Groaning, he rubbed his eyes, but before he could piece together the previous day's events, he recognized the room, the unmistakable crisp smell of mountain air. He also recognized the angelic form asleep beside him.

Laura lay on her back, her silky hair splayed around her head like a halo. One thin black strap had fallen off her shoulder. Beneath the lace bodice, he saw the rosy tips of her breasts.

Desire—thick, fierce and hot—plunged through his system, from the soles of his feet to the hair on his head and most definitely everywhere in between. On reflex, he reached to cup her flawless cheek but thankfully in time he set his jaw and forced his hand away. It was bad enough that they'd slept in the same bed last night. When he'd promised not to take her, Laura had no idea how serious he'd been. But when she'd curled into him, how could he stop her? Or the acute physical arousal that had kicked in.

Clamping his eyes shut, he'd forced himself to think of anything other than her faint jasmine scent and the satin feel of her negligee…of her skin. He had no idea how long he'd lain awake, forcing himself not to stroke her back or brush his lips over hers.

Now he was fighting the same merciless war. The urgent pulsing in his groin said to forget honor and let his palm slide over all those gorgeous contours. The arousal fueling his erection demanded that his mouth glide down and taste her breasts, her hips, the honey between her legs. He imagined her dreamy sigh as she woke slowly, then her fingers winding through his hair as her hips arced and the trapped pounding in his blood found its release. He thought of her climaxing once, twice, and the possibility of them spending all day in bed.

Hardening more, Bishop swallowed a tortured groan. He'd better get out of this room before he convinced himself what he wanted was not only natural and necessary, but appropriate.

Quietly, he eased up and pushed to his feet. He slipped

his arms into the sleeves of his shirt, which brought another problem to mind. What would he wear over the weekend? Perhaps a quick trip into Burniedale, the nearest township, was in order.

He glanced at his watch.

The shops were two hours from opening yet.

Behind him, Laura stirred but when he turned to study her, she didn't look uncomfortable. In fact, the corners of her too-kissable mouth were curved into a heavenly smile. The doctor had suggested he wake her every few hours and ask routine questions, but she'd been fine four hours ago. She looked so peaceful now, perfectly healthy but for that small bandage above her temple. He wouldn't disturb her. Besides, when she was asleep he wasn't walking on eggshells, wondering when and how the memory pennies would begin to fall.

A few minutes later, he stood in his office, collecting his BlackBerry off the desk. He checked his messages and found another from Willis.

Where the hell are you?

Bishop headed outside. Where was he? Living in a time warp where the woman he'd once loved—who had once loved him—couldn't remember that she didn't want him in this house, let alone in her bed. The bigger, far more dangerous issue was, as difficult as it was proving to be, he needed to remember that, too.

Moving out onto the eastern porch, he siphoned in a lungful of the fresh morning air. The birds were deafening. Living in the city heart this past year he'd forgotten how loud they could be. But it was a relaxing and at the same time invigorating noise. Another thing he'd missed. Something else he'd tried to forget.

He thumbed in Willis's quick dial and, phone to ear, waited for the call to connect. He'd swung a hip over the wood railing, was watching a hand-size echidna and its porcupine quills trudge into the brush, when Willis picked up.

"Are you in the office already?"

Bishop's gaze skimmed the dense forest of gum trees. "I'm nowhere near the office."

"Did you take care of whatever it was that dragged you away early yesterday?"

"It'll be sorted by Monday."

"Good, because I promised these potential buyers you'd speak with them then. I'll get a confidentiality agreement then talk to Saed about putting together the documents they'll want to see."

Bishop listened to Willis's plans while he examined the weathered stump he'd once used to chop logs for the fire. When Willis finished, Bishop absently agreed. "Sounds good."

Two beats of silence echoed down the line. "You don't sound as pumped as I thought you'd be."

"I'm pumped," Bishop argued. "I just didn't think we'd get any nibbles this soon."

"This isn't a nibble, Sam. It's a walloping great bite. The agent said the interested party is none other than Clancy Enterprises."

Bishop let out a long low whistle. "They own half the companies on the east coast." Manufacturing as well as retail.

"We're talking serious money and, if we can go by their track record, we don't have a whole lot of lead time. These guys move fast."

A family of wild ducks, two adults, four chicks, waddled out from behind a boulder. Bishop shifted his position on the rail. "How fast?"

"Just sign the on the dotted line fast."

A touch on his shoulder sent Bishop's heart lurching to his throat. Jumping off the railing, he spun around. Laura stood before him, wrapped up in that fluffy pink robe, the tip of her nose already red from the morning air's cool kiss.

Her gaze homed in on his phone and she stepped back, whispering, "Sorry, I didn't realize."

As if calling from another world, Bishop heard Willis's voice coming down the line. "Sam? You there?"

"That's okay," he said to Laura, thinking how young and fresh she looked, the same age she'd looked when they'd married. The bitterness he'd seen a year ago seemed to have left her face completely. "I was finishing up." He set the phone back to his ear. "We'll talk later."

Willis didn't ask questions, which was part of the reason he was paid so well. Willis knew when to push. He also knew when to back off.

Laura hunched and hugged herself, snuggling into her robe. It might be spring but up here the mornings still got mighty chilly.

"Must have been something urgent to be calling at this time?" she asked.

"Nothing for you to worry about."

But a line had formed between her brows and her gaze had gone from his face to his chest and lower. She shook her head slowly and Bishop braced himself. Something had clicked. Perhaps the fact she hadn't seen him on this porch in over a year. Or something he'd said, or his tone, had set off a memory. If it all came flooding back, he could be gone in two minutes. He'd simply find his shoes and be on his way. He had no desire to hang around and argue, which seemed to be all he and Laura had done those last few months.

Her head slanted to one side. "Why are you wearing yesterday's shirt?" Her frown eased into a reproving grin. "Anyone would think you don't have a change of clothes."

What could he say? He didn't live here anymore. He wouldn't find any clothes in what had once been his wardrobe. If he'd gotten to the shops in time and had bought a couple of shirts...

But this kind of thing was bound to happen. He wouldn't

try to explain. He'd simply show her his empty wardrobe and let her memory take it from there.

So they walked back inside the house, down the hall, back into the bedroom, and while she pulled up the sheets to make the bed, he stood before his former wardrobe doors. Holding himself firm, he eased out a long breath.

Do it. Just do it.

His fingers curled around the knob. And pulled.

What he found inside left his legs feeling like rubber. His jaw dropped, and he stepped closer.

Clothes hung from the rails. But not just anyone's clothes. *His* clothes. Suits and shirts, trousers and jeans. He held his brow. This didn't make sense. Yes, he'd left everything behind. He'd had clothes enough back at the Darling Harbor apartment. He didn't need anything here. Didn't need anything to remind him.

But he'd assumed that once he'd gone Laura would have bundled up his clothes and shipped them off to charity. Or burned them. Why hadn't she gotten rid of all this like she'd gotten rid of him?

"Need some help?"

Her voice, coming from directly behind, found a way through the fog. A moment later, her palms were sculpting over his shoulders and arms. As the contact lit fires all through his body, instinctively he leaned back into her touch. She pressed a kiss between his shoulder blades and as her grip hardened on his upper arms, he closed his eyes and tried to stay lucid.

"Of course, we don't have to wear anything at all," she purred, and her hands filed down his arms, arrowing over his hips, finally finding and wrapping around the weight confined beneath his trousers.

A whirlwind of darkest desire spiraled through him. His hand covered hers and pressed in as his mind went deliciously blank but for the need to have her again. To drown in her kisses and fill her with his—

Coming to with a jolt, Bishop pried her hand away. Clamping down on the frenzied heat racing through his veins, he turned to her and forced his mouth to curve into a breezy smile.

"You're certainly persuasive."

"And you are dying to say yes." Her gaze heavy with want, she reached up on tiptoe and tugged his bottom lip with her teeth.

A fireball shot to the top of his inner thighs and ignited a very short fuse. When she drew a line around his unshaven jaw and her mouth opened over his, Bishop shuddered and leaned into her kiss. With lava flooding his veins, every cell in his body cried out for more. Then her mouth opened wider, inviting him in deeper. Wanting to possess her, his hands found her shoulders and drew them in.

She tasted the same. Felt the same. And now he knew he was the same hungry man who craved to be with his wife.

She hummed in her throat and the vibration released bright-tipped sparks in his belly that unleashed an inferno a few inches below that. Instinctively, one hand left her shoulder and searched out her breast. As his touch grazed the soft, pert mound, his tongue dipped deeper, running over hers, and any sense of right or wrong vanished beneath the blistering force of mutual need.

Her hands were fanning beneath his shirt, but when he rolled her nipple between finger and thumb, she found his other hand and set it low on her belly. His fingers speared down. She wore no panties. He felt her damp and ready beneath the satin of her negligee. Pushed to his limits, he groaned against her lips.

"This always felt so right."

"Make love to me, Bishop," she murmured back.

"You don't know how much I want to."

"Oh, but I do."

He felt her grin against his lips as her palm slid down his side and the pressure built to flashpoint.

He was ready to forget that this wasn't real...was ready to drop her back onto the bed and enjoy what she offered in a very real way. And yet...

Still holding her, he sucked down a breath and, struggling, got his thoughts together.

"I...think we should stop."

Her tongue ran along his bottom lip. "Don't think."

Good God, but someone had to.

Gritting his teeth, he pried her a little away. "The doctor said—"

"I don't care what the doctor said."

"Listen to me," he growled. "We aren't doing this."

Her head came back and she probed his eyes for a long searching moment. "Is it because you think I'll ask you not to use protection? That I want us to make a baby now?"

Well, that was as good an excuse as any. Rolling back his shoulders, he lifted his chin. "Let's cool down, have a shower—"

Her eyes flashed. "Fabulous idea!"

"—*alone*. We'll have something to eat. You must be hungry. And later..." Later? He promised, "We'll discuss it."

And they would. If any conversation could bring her around—bring them *both* around—it'd be one highlighting the risks associated with her falling pregnant.

Four

Thirty minutes later, Laura's high-pitched cry, coming from the bedroom, sent the hairs on Bishop's scalp standing on end and his feet hurling him out of his chair. His heart belting against his ribs, he tore through the open glass sliders, slammed through the main sitting room and bolted down the hall.

What the hell had happened?

When Bishop had stepped out of the shower earlier, he'd heard the main bedroom pipes still running. Laura loved her baths; she'd be a little longer yet. He'd thought about jumping back on his laptop and sorting out a few budget discrepancies but had opted for checking around the house instead, seeing if the outdoor pool and gutters were free for starters.

After finding the net in the pool house, he'd skimmed the outside pool assured in knowing that Laura would have someone coming out once a fortnight or so to keep an eye on its upkeep. Money wasn't a problem. After their parents' deaths, both Laura and Grace had received a good inheritance, and after the split he'd also passed on a generous monthly allowance. Lawyers had advised him to wait until after the divorce when a settlement could be drawn up, but he wanted to contribute. Last month, however, the divorce became final and the settlement was, well, settled. He'd given her this house and land. Knowing that he'd see ghosts in every corner, he would only have sold it anyway no matter how much he loved the area. Neither of them had been overly concerned about snakes or spiders, poisonous though many of them might be. After hearing Laura's cry now, Bishop wondered if he needed to reconsider.

Had a deadly Brown crowded her into a corner? Had she fallen somehow again? Of course there was also the chance she'd gotten her memory back and, realizing she wanted to kill him for letting her make a fool of herself yesterday, had screamed out in blind rage.

Outside his home office, they collided. Her face was flushed, her legs temptingly long and tanned in a pair of white tennis shorts. She waved her hand in front of his face and squealed again. Not scared, not angry but rather...*excited*.

"They're here!" She bounced on her toes. "They were here all along."

He held her arms to steady her. "Hey, slow down. What's here?"

"These."

She wiggled a set of fingers. The gold and diamonds he'd slid onto her third finger two years ago sparkled in ribbons of morning light that streamed through the floor-to-ceiling eastern arch window.

"I must have taken them off before going to the hospital," she told him. "I'm not sure why. I can't remember any of it."

He eased out the breath he'd been holding. No falls. No bites. Thank God. If she couldn't remember taking her wedding rings off...

"It doesn't matter now," he muttered.

But, of course, it *did*. The doctor had said that with gentle prodding her memory should return. To his mind, bringing her back here to the scene of the crime ought to have been prodding enough. After a final argument, they'd barely exchanged a word for over a week until they'd run into each other on this very spot. After an awkward moment, he'd said he had work to do and pushed by. She'd told him he might as well *live* in the office—his office in town. Then she'd hiccupped back a sob and said that she meant it. That he could pack his things and leave. Leave *now*. She couldn't take this anymore and neither could he.

"Now it's the weekend you can wear yours, too," she was saying.

He came back to the present and his frown deepened. She was talking about *his* wedding ring?

"I understand you can't wear it during the week," she went on. "I know how you like to keep your hand in at the factory and accidents can happen. Rings can get caught. But on the weekends..." She bounced up and snatched a kiss from his cheek. "It's only you and me."

Over a year ago, he'd left his wedding band here. Actually, he'd thrown it in the fireplace before he'd stomped off. He'd always imagined that she'd built a roaring fire and had happily watched the gold circle melt into a shapeless blob. So how was he supposed to assure her that he'd wear it now?

But then her other hand came out, fist closed, palm up. When her fingers peeled back, the gold band he'd tossed into the fireplace a year ago gleamed up.

His heart lurched up the back of his throat. Dumbfounded, he shook his head. It couldn't be.

Carefully, he collected the ring and inspected the inscription inside. *Always and Forever.*

His voice sounded as if it'd been dragged through molasses. "Where did you find them?"

"Where I always put them," she said, studying both her rings and the gold band lying in the centre of her palm. "In my jewelry box."

His stunned gaze went from the ring to his wife's—his *ex*-wife's face. Her jewelry box? Had she dug the ring out of the fireplace after he'd gone? There was no other explanation. And yet whenever he thought about the hurt and frustration, how he'd believed every loaded word that she'd said—

"Aren't you going to put it on?" she asked.

Bishop opened his mouth, ready to say no way. The divorce was done and dusted, no matter what she might think. But for the life of him, he couldn't come up with a way out. He could hedge but what would that accomplish? Only suspicion on her part. Agitation on his.

She'd remember soon enough. Until then…

He gave a stilted nod, lifted his left hand and Laura held the band over his fingertip, ready to push it on. For a moment his thoughts wavered. *What does it matter?* Then, *This has gone far enough.* But then the ring pushed up over his knuckle and Laura's eyes were sparkling all the more.

Grace had implied this might be a second chance. The idea had seemed absurd yesterday, particularly coming from his arch nemesis. And yet this morning, being back in this house, spending the night in that bed, having this ring on his finger…

Bishop shook himself.

No. It was crazy. Not possible.

Not happening.

"What would you like to do today?"

His gaze jumped from his finger to her beautiful animated face. The lilac-colored top she wore was cut tastefully but, to his current way of thinking, provocatively low.

He swallowed deeply. "What did you have in mind?"

"Want to teach me to play chess? You said you would."

He'd already taught her and she'd proven a quick study. He'd thought about letting her win a couple of times, but she was too clever to fool that way. She'd vowed that she'd beat him fair and square one day. If they sat down at that chessboard now, would she remember the moves he'd taught her, or had that part of her memory been wiped clean, too?

He ushered her into his office, to the chess set he'd left behind. "What do you know about the game?"

"There are bishops."

He gave a soft laugh. "Right."

"White moves first."

"Right again."

Maybe she did subconsciously remember their lessons, which, most likely, meant she would remember more. And that was good, right?

He twirled that band around his finger—still a perfect fit—and sat behind the black. She took the chair behind the white.

He tapped the piece sitting directly in front of the black king. "This is a pawn."

"They move one space at a time."

"Only forward."

"Except when taking a piece, then they move diagonally."

"Perhaps we should do away with the lesson and start a game."

She laughed and the sound tinkled through him. "Oh, Bishop, everyone knows that."

"What else do you know?"

"I know the castle—"

"Rook."

"—gets to move across and up and down. That the horse is the prettiest piece and the queen is the most powerful."

He relaxed back in his seat. That was more like it. "That doesn't sound very technical."

"Tell me…is it as difficult to play as everyone says?"

"Only if you can't guess the other person's move before they make it."

He knew what came next in *their* game…every step, every misfire, after she'd let him know she'd changed her mind and wanted to conceive their own child, irrespective of any health concerns.

No matter the challenge he'd met it head-on, strategized, worked out the kinks and had always stayed one step ahead. Except where their marriage had been concerned. And that black mark had always stung. Always would.

Unless...

Puzzled, Laura was looking over the board. "Know the person's move before they make it? How are you supposed to do that?"

He shaped two fingers down the sides of the black queen. "By skill," he said, "and luck. And sometimes even by accident."

When Bishop had to take a phone call midway through their first chess lesson, Laura decided to stretch her legs. She headed off to the kitchen, poured a drink and told herself that getting a handle on the basics of the game shouldn't be too difficult. And once she was up to speed, no doubt Bishop would enjoy the competition.

She'd spent time playing cards whenever she'd been in the hospital in the cardio ward—sometimes with the nurses if she couldn't sleep, more often with the other kids. But, before yesterday's incident, she hadn't spent time in a hospital bed in years. She'd had a defibrillator fitted and was on a low dosage medication, which kept her well.

The condition had been passed on through her mother's side. An aunt had died unexpectedly in her teens and that's when the family had been tested and the condition diagnosed. But Laura suspected that Bishop's own family history had as much, if not more, to do with his pro-adoption stand.

He'd been the twin who'd survived and she didn't need to ask if he felt guilty about it. Bishop had told her briefly about the story surrounding his birth and the subsequent death of his baby brother. When she'd tried to delve deeper, he'd withdrawn, other than to say he'd heard enough about it from his parents growing up. Laura had envisaged a boy fighting not to be overshadowed by his mother's and father's ongoing grief. But Arlene and George Bishop had seemed pleasant enough, even welcoming, at their wedding. They'd said how proud they were of their only son and that they wished they lived closer; they'd moved clear across the country to Perth five years ago. But they intended to keep in touch and had asked that the newlyweds do the same. Laura got the impression there wasn't so much of a rift between parents and son as a gradual drifting apart that had, over time, come to be accepted.

Conversely, she and Grace had been so very close, to each other and to their parents. The sisters were devastated when first their father had died in a vehicle accident then cancer had taken their mum—a melanoma discovered too late. But as much as the sisters still figured in each other's lives, it was no secret that Bishop thought Grace wielded too big of an influence over Laura.

But what was too much? They were close, always had been. Grace had her own family—a four-year-old boy and a three-year-old girl—but she'd always let Laura know she was welcome in her home at any time for any reason. If Grace had been a little outspoken about her concerns before the wedding, it was because she believed no one loved and cared for her sister more than she did.

If Bishop's twin had lived, perhaps Bishop would better understand the sisters' situation. They said twins shared a special connection. Maybe Bishop was somehow aware of that connection and missed it more than he knew.

When she'd finished her ice water and Bishop was still on the phone, talking about the sale of something or other, Laura decided to take in some fresh air. She'd had enough of chess for one day.

Outside, the sun spread a warm golden hue over the spires of the eucalypts and pines. She peeled off her cardigan and, marveling at their balance, studied a koala and her baby dozing high up in the fork of a tree. Beyond that clump of gray-green trees lay the rock bricks and planks that made up the northern footbridge.

Her stomach gave a mighty kick. She winced and slid her foot back.

The fall—before and after—she couldn't recall, but it'd be a long while before she crossed that bridge again. Had she been trying to see something over the edge? Had a lizard scuttled up and scared her from behind? Had she slipped on the dew—

A flash—a fuzzy freeze frame—flicked on in her mind. The image... She couldn't hold on to it long enough, but the residue of the pain hit her first in the lungs and then lower. Holding her belly, she flinched. When she opened her eyes, her brow was damp with perspiration. She eyed the bridge, shuddered to her toes, and promptly set off in the other direction.

She was headed toward the gazebo when Bishop caught up. The planes of his face were hard in their naturally attractive way, but his blue eyes shone with relief. His hands caught her bare shoulders and urged her near. The heat of his touch, the sincerity in his eyes, left her feeling warm and loved all over.

"I couldn't find you," he said in a low, graveled voice. "I was worried."

"It looked so beautiful out here and I didn't know how long you'd be on that call. It sounded important."

His hands slid down her arms then dropped away altogether. A muscle ticked in his jaw before he answered. "I'm thinking of selling the company."

Laura's breath caught. She couldn't believe what she'd heard. He was so proud of what he'd built from scratch. He had plans to expand even more.

"When did this happen?"

"I've been mulling over it for a while."

But selling his company was *unthinkable*. He was so capable and responsible…still she had to ask the obvious question. "Are you in financial trouble?"

He began walking down a slate path lined with gold and lavender wild flowers. "Just thinking I might want to try something new."

"Do you think you'd be away from home more often? Not that it would matter," she added quickly. "I'd be okay. It's just if you were…well, I've been thinking about getting a dog. Someone to keep me company through the day."

He nodded slowly, considering. "I think a dog is a good idea."

"Really?"

He smiled. His eyes were so bright in the spring sunshine, they glittered like a pair of cut jewels. "We'll do some research."

The urge overtook her. She threw her arms around him and kissed his bristled cheek. She loved his weekend shadow, the sexy roughness against her lips, the graze when he gifted her one of his delectable morning kisses.

"For some reason I thought you'd say no."

"What will you call him?" he asked, slipping his hands into his trouser pockets as they continued down the sweet-smelling path that led to the gazebo. The white lattice was patterned with a riot of cardinal creeper blooms, deep vibrant scarlet in color. Beautifully fragrant, too.

"I'd have to see him, or her, first," she told him. "I've never thought you could name a member of the family until it arrived."

On their way up to the gazebo platform, his step faltered and Laura gnawed her lip. As lead-ins went, it'd been a clumsy one, but they had to talk about it sometime.

When he sat down on the surrounding bench, she positioned

herself close beside him and folded a fallen lock away from his brow.

"I don't want us to be afraid of what might go wrong," she said, "when it has to be better to think about everything that can go right."

When he only looked away, Laura chewed her bottom lip again. After considering her next words, she delivered them as carefully as she could.

"I know it must have been hard when your brother died."

"We were newborns," he said, his brow creasing as he found her gaze. "And that has nothing to do with us."

"I was only trying to talk—" But the line of his jaw was drawn so tight, his eyes suddenly looked so shuttered. Knowing when to back off, she ordered her locked muscles to relax. "I know you don't like talking about it. I shouldn't have brought it up."

Bishop drove a hand through his hair and groaned. She was dead-on. He didn't like discussing his twin. It dredged up feelings he'd rather not entertain. Feelings of guilt and helplessness and, the real kicker, loss.

But looking at Laura and her bowed head now, Bishop felt something inside of him shift. They'd never really talked about it during their marriage. If she wanted to discuss it now, hell, maybe he ought to. Perhaps something would tip off her memory and he would be on his way—out of the damnable bittersweet mess.

"We were identical," he began, letting his threaded hands fall between his open thighs. "I got most of the nourishment before we were born. The other twin—"

"Your brother."

"—died four days later."

"And you feel bad about that."

He felt an urge to explain that it wasn't his fault. That was life and his parents had never held it against him. But they had been the half truths he'd told her the first time.

Hell, his parents had made him live through that time every birthday, every Christmas, first day of school, on Easter egg hunts, at graduation. *If only your brother were here. How sad your twin isn't at your side today.*

Okay. He got it. He respected their regrets and dedication to the son they'd lost. But just for once in his life he'd have liked to achieve and be noticed without mention of that incident.

He blew out a breath and admitted, "Yeah. If ever I think about it, I feel…bad."

Laura was nodding. "My mother felt bad about passing on her heart condition. Until I told her I was so grateful she had me and if the price was having a metal bit in my chest and taking some medication, that wasn't too high."

"But when you were conceived your mother didn't know the risk." He and Laura had been aware. Therefore they'd had a duty to act responsibly.

"I'm glad my mother didn't know about her condition," Laura said. "And she admitted she was glad she didn't, either. She always said her children were her life."

A smile tugged at his mouth. What mother wouldn't be proud to have such a beautiful daughter? And Grace? Well, Grace might be a witch but, after her comment yesterday about second chances, the vote was out. Even if it was too little too late. He wished they'd had her support when it mattered.

"And all this," he said, getting to the heart of the matter, "is leading up to the fact that you want to have a family the old-fashioned way."

Her eyes glistened with innocent hope. "I really do."

The last time they'd had this conversation almost two years ago, he'd agreed. Laura had been thrilled and within weeks had confirmed her pregnancy. It should have been all rainbows and happy families from there on in.

Far from it.

He didn't know which had been worse. Watching his mother trying to hide her pain for years after his brother had died, or going through Laura's pain after her miscarriage. If he'd stuck to his guns and had said it was adoption or nothing, would she have told him to go? Or would they be happy now with a healthy baby, a healthy past, present and, hopefully, future?

"So...what do you think?" she asked.

He opened his mouth to shut down the conversation once and for all, but then he saw the hope swimming in her eyes and the steam went out of his argument. He held his breath, considered the options.

There weren't any.

"I think..."

Her lips curved up. "Yes?"

"I think we need to think about it more," he ended.

Her smile wavered and her eyes dulled over, but then the disappointment faded from her expression, replaced by the inherent optimism he'd always loved.

She pointed her white-sandaled toes out and flipped them prettily in the air.

"*The Nutcracker*'s playing in town," she said, changing the subject. "Tonight would be sold out but I wonder if we could get tickets for tomorrow."

The *ballet?*

The last time they'd gone they'd had an argument. One of his more notable clients and his wife had witnessed the scene. Bishop wasn't a fan of tutus and tights at the best of times. After that night he'd sworn never to sit through another *Fouetté en tournant* as long as he lived.

Sensing his reluctance, Laura let her toes drift down. "I know ballet's not your thing..."

"No, it's not. But it is yours," he added.

Going to Sydney tomorrow evening would leave them with another twenty-four hours in this environment. If a few lightbulbs went off...if he were lucky... Hell, they might not get to the ballet at all.

Five

Before Bishop drove off to the nearest shops to get a few provisions, Laura had sussed out whether he needed condoms. She'd already checked the bedside drawer where he always kept them, and he didn't need to stock up. There was plenty of contraception on hand.

That was okay. She'd only broached the subject of them falling pregnant yesterday. Getting her husband to come around to her way of thinking—the way that put faith ahead of doom and gloom—might take a little doing. She could wait. She and Bishop had too much going for them to let this difference get in the way.

She baked some pastries and had sat down at her laptop in her office when Bishop returned. She swung around in her high-backed chair as he moved up and lifted her face to him, waiting for a kiss hello. He searched her eyes for a long, heartfelt moment, then lowered his head and dropped a chaste kiss on her cheek.

A band around her chest pulled tight. He'd avoided kissing yesterday, last night. But for that peck, he hadn't kissed her at all today, and she wasn't happy about it. Rather than sounding testy or upset, however, she thought she'd go for teasing.

"Hey, I didn't hurt my lips when I fell."

Before he could see it coming, she caught him around the neck and brought him back down. Her mouth zeroed in on his with the precision of a ballistic missile. His lips were slightly parted, and she made certain to take advantage of that, too.

She aimed to kiss him swiftly but thoroughly, and as her mouth moved over his, her fingers kneaded the back of his strong, hot neck. There was a second of resistance on his part when she thought he might jerk away. But then a growl rumbled from his chest up his throat. The vibration tingled over his lips, ran over her tongue, then he was kissing her back.

The connection didn't last long enough. Just when she was thinking a trip to the bedroom might be in order, his hands found her shoulders and he pushed himself away. Before he could prattle on about doctor's orders again, she spoke up.

"I had it wrong," she told him.

An emotion she couldn't name darkened his eyes as he slowly straightened and those broad shoulders rotated back. "What have you got wrong?"

"*The Nutcracker*'s not playing. It's *Swan Lake*."

That emotion flickered again and then his brow furrowed and his voice deepened more. *"Swan Lake."*

Understanding his tone, she tilted her head. "We don't have to go." Frankly, after that kiss she'd be more than content to stay in. But he surprised her.

"No, we'll go," he said, his gaze shifting from hers to the computer screen. "I'll never forget the last time we went."

Laura cast her mind back. "We've only been together once. Just before we were married."

"I could've sworn we'd gone again after that."

He looked so earnest, she coughed out a laugh. "Was it that bad? Sounds like you had nightmares about men coming after you in tights."

His gaze dipped to her lips and he smiled softly. "Yeah.

Maybe that's it." He thrust his chin at her chair. "Shift and I'll book."

"What? My Amex card isn't as good as yours?"

"Just trying to do the gentlemanly thing and pick up the tab."

As if he ever let her pay for a thing.

Lifting out of the chair, she thought about kissing him again. But she'd let him book and then they could get back to…business.

"In that case, guess I'll go occupy myself in the kitchen."

Deciding on which outfit to wear to the ballet—her Lisa Ho cream wraparound or that new season black sequined jacket with a classic little black dress—Laura hummed as she made her way down the wide central hall and into the well-equipped kitchen.

She liked to cook—roasts, Thai, experimental appetizers, mouth-watering desserts. Her mother had always said the way to a man's heart was through his stomach. Laura could vouch that her husband certainly enjoyed his home-cooked meals—almost as much as he enjoyed making love.

And after dinner she would remove the bandage from her head and persuade her husband that tonight the doctor didn't know best. She'd rested long enough.

Entering the kitchen, she was a little taken aback at how many grocery bags lay on the counters. Seemed Bishop had stocked up. He usually left the major shopping to her. She stacked the fridge and the pantry then flicked on the oven to warm half a dozen bakery scones. Tomorrow she'd whip up a fresh batch herself.

She slid open the cake tin drawer, dug in to select a tray but, as she reached down, her mind went strangely blank. After a moment, she remembered what she was after and shuffled again through the pans. But where was her favorite heating tray? Straightening, she stuck her hands on her hips and glanced around the timber cupboard doors. Where on earth had she put it?

Of course it was no big deal. Definitely no need to worry Bishop with the fact that her memory was foggier than she'd first realized. Just little things, like wondering at the unfamiliar brand of toothpaste in the attached bath, or pondering over leftovers in the fridge that she had no recollection of cooking.

A rational explanation existed for it all, Laura surmised, wiggling out a different tray for the scones from under the hot plates. Things were a little jumbled, but they'd sort themselves out soon enough.

When she arrived back at her office, brandishing two cups of steaming coffee—one black, one white—Bishop had a different webpage open. She caught a glimpse of the images—bundles of fur with cute black noses and gorgeous take-me-home eyes. She gave a little excited jump and coffee splashed onto the tray.

"Puppies!" Eyes glued to the screen, she set down the tray on a corner of the desk and dragged in a chair. "I was thinking maybe a cocker spaniel."

Elbow on the desk, he held his jaw while scanning a page displaying a selection of breeds. He grunted. "Aren't they dopey?"

"They're soft and gentle and a thousand times cuddly."

"Maybe something bigger."

"You mean tougher."

He collected his mug and blew off the steam. "You haven't got too many neighbors around here," he said and then sipped.

"*We* haven't got too many neighbors," she corrected. What was with this *you* business?

He set down the mug, turned back to the screen and clicked a few more searches. "Maybe a Doberman."

"I'm sure they're lovely, but I can't imagine snuggling up

into a powerhouse of muscle and aggression." She ran a hand down his arm. "Present company excluded."

"They're supposed to be very loyal," he said, as if he hadn't noticed her compliment, and pictures of dogs with gleaming black coats, pointed ears and superkeen eyes blinked onto the screen. Laura's mouth pulled to one side. Sorry. Just not her.

"Did you have a dog growing up?"

He clicked on a link and a list of breeders flashed up. "A golden retriever."

"Guide dogs."

"One of the breeds used, yes."

"Can you tap that in?"

A few seconds later, images of the cutest, most playful puppies on the planet graced the screen and childlike delight rippled over her. Her hand landed over his on the mouse and she scrolled down for more information. Nothing she read or saw turned her off.

"They're so adorable," she said as Bishop slipped his hand from beneath hers and covered his mouth as he cleared his throat. "They look like they're smiling, don't you think? I can definitely see us with one of those."

"Good family dog," he read from the blurb. "Gentle temperament. Prone to overeating, shedding and joint problems." Obviously uneasy, he shifted in his seat. "One of my foremen spent over two grand getting his cat's broken leg fixed. Bad joints mean huge vet bills." He clicked the previous page back. "Let's look at Rottweilers."

She grinned. It wasn't about money. "I don't want a guard dog. I want a companion. A personality that will become part of our family." And would eagerly welcome new members in. "Just tell me…do you still like retrievers?"

"Of course."

"Then if we both want a retriever and somewhere down the track he needs some medical attention, wouldn't you rather have what we really want than settle on something which may or may not have other problems? There are risks everywhere, Bishop. Risks in everything."

His jaw jutted, but the dark slashes of his eyebrow quirked. While he considered, Laura folded her hands in her lap. She'd made her point. She was talking about far more than which dog to buy.

"But we don't have to make a decision today," she ended in a placating tone. "There's no hurry."

"You're right." He clicked on the top right-hand X and the puppies disappeared. "No hurry at all."

The phone rang. Not his cell phone this time. Which meant there was a good chance the call wasn't about business. Maybe Kathy from the library. They'd been talking about starting a literacy program for over-fifties.

Trying to recall what their last discussion had outlined, Laura pushed back her chair but Bishop was already up.

The *bbbbrrr*-ring of the phone ripped through to his bones, as unsettling as a bank alarm. Moving quick, his hand landed on the extension.

During his drive to the shops earlier, he'd considered the phone and the problems surprise calls could cause. If one of Laura's friends contacted her, it wouldn't take long for inconsistencies to rise and questions to flare in both parties' minds. Laura didn't need to be backed into a corner, faced with a reality that seemed Hitchcock-esque given what she could and could not remember. Prodding was far different to someone knocking you for a complete loop during a phone call.

Driving back, he'd decided to intercept calls, not to keep Laura from her friends and others who cared, but to forewarn of the situation and ask that they tread lightly for now. Eventually, Laura would check emails. Oddities like *Swan Lake* playing rather than *The Nutcracker* would become more obvious. Dates wouldn't mesh, like the dates he worried she might see on the web when trying to book those tickets. Soon there'd be questions. Ultimately, as she needed to know and was ready to hear, there'd be answers.

But for now...

His hand still on the receiver, he said, "I'm expecting a call." Then to divert her, "Is that scones I smell warming?"

Leaping up, she cursed and sprinted out. "I forgot."

Waiting until her padding down the hall quieted, he answered the call. He should've known who it would be.

"How are things going?"

He exhaled and a measure of his tension dissolved. *Grace*.

He ran a finger over a tiny crystal clock. "Not as bad as I thought."

"She hasn't remembered?"

"Not a thing that I can tell."

"I should probably come up and see her."

Or not.

"That's up to you."

"But you'd rather I stay away."

Smirking, he pushed the clock back. "You can read me like a book." He liked as much distance between himself and Grace as possible.

"But she's happy?"

He imagined Laura in the kitchen she loved, drawing the scones from the oven then finding those special little spoons she saved for serving jam. She made the best jam.

He surrendered to a smile. "Very happy."

There was a long pause. Bishop could imagine Grace smoothing her French roll. "I hope she'll understand when this is all over."

"Depends on who ends up sticking around. This Laura or the one who couldn't wait to see the back of me."

"Did I hear my name mentioned?"

Bishop's heart squeezed to his throat and he spun around.

Laura held a tray with scones, whipped butter, jam and those tiny silver spoons. From the open look on her face, she hadn't heard too much.

He hoped his smile didn't look manufactured. "Your sister."

Her eyes rounded playfully and she stage whispered, "You're having a conversation with *Grace?*"

"About your condition."

"My fall?" He nodded. "If it gets you two talking at last, it was worth it." Setting the tray down, she accepted the phone. "Hey, Grace. How're you doing? Oh, I'm fine." She gave Bishop a wink and angled toward the window view. "Better than fine."

Unable to pass, he dabbed some homemade jam on a scone and bit into the doughy sweetness. Grace would keep Laura on the phone for a while. He didn't need to listen in.

He wandered out from her office, his gaze skimming the same surrealist paintings that had frequented the hallway walls when he'd left. Further on, he took stock of the kitchen, its polished granite benches and gleaming utensils that Laura had taken such pride in when making those superb dinners she whipped up seemingly out of thin air.

He stopped beneath the ornate arch that led to the main living room. Same chintz couches, crafted timber furniture and grand fireplace, which they'd spent so many evenings cuddled up in front of, she reading a bestseller, he browsing over papers from work. In the beginning they'd felt so relaxed together and yet the steady thrum of excitement had always been there, too. A buzz that not only connected them, but drew them irreversibly, magnetically near.

Those were the best days of his life.

His gaze inched along the knickknacks on the marble mantelpiece...silver candlesticks, some ballerina figurines, a cup she must have accidentally left there. His eye line drifted higher. Then his heart stopped beating.

Their wedding photo was gone.

And why wouldn't it be? This was her house. They'd lived separate lives for over a year. His bet was she'd used the photograph as fuel for the fire. But then she'd kept his clothes and wedding ring. Maybe the photo was stored away, too.

More immediately, what would *this* Laura say when she realized the picture she adored was missing?

He swung an urgent glance around. Should he hunt in some cupboards, try to find and hang it back up before she noticed? Or would seeing the photo missing press a necessary button to jump-start her memory?

Although what had just happened between them should have sent up some flags.

The inevitable had happened. He'd kissed her. Or rather she'd kissed him. And he hadn't stopped her. But for a brief moment of "what the hell?" he hadn't even tried.

He'd mulled over how it would feel should he relent. Strange? Pleasant? Knock-your-socks-off fantastic? Check box three. And now, God help him, he couldn't help thinking about later, because Laura was going to want far more than lip service tonight.

"I was thinking I might come up and see you tomorrow," Grace said down the line while Laura made herself comfortable in one of the winged armchairs positioned beside a window view in her office.

"I'd like that, Grace, but Bishop and I are going into Sydney. The ballet's on."

"You're going out? Do you think that's wise?"

"Oh, Gracie, not you, too!" How many times did she need to tell people she was fine? A bit of a foggy memory didn't count.

"Learn to live with it," Grace returned. "I care about you."

Laura laughed softly. "I got that."

"Will Bishop be staying in town?"

"Tomorrow night? Why do you ask?"

"He's a busy man. I thought he might want to stay down rather than drive out again Monday morning to the office."

"I don't think so." Laura concentrated on the chess piece, thinking back. No, she was certain. "He didn't say he would."

"How is Bishop?"

Laura put on a suspicious tone. "Why this interest in Bishop all of a sudden?"

"Just making sure he's treating my little sister right."

"Always and always."

"Really?"

A prickle of annoyance rolled up Laura's spine and she held the receiver tighter. "Grace, I know you thought we married too soon. And maybe you were right," she admitted, knowing she'd thought the same herself yesterday in the hospital. "Maybe we should have waited a little longer to iron things out. But we love each other. That's what gets a couple through."

"I take it you're going to tell him you don't want to adopt?"

"I brought it up yesterday." And again today. "We're going to work it out, Grace."

Her sister sighed down the line. "Oh, sweetheart, I hope you're right."

Six

Laura cooked a roast dinner with all the trimmings and rosemary cream gravy. When Bishop took himself off to his office after dessert, Laura steeled herself against disappointment. He was avoiding her. Or, rather, avoiding that touchy subject.

But as she finished packing the dishwasher and headed off for a shower before bed, she put herself in her husband's shoes. Analytical. Methodical. He was divorcing himself from her until he thought she was completely well, as well as settle in his own mind the conundrum of adoption versus conception. If he thought she needed rest and he needed to be left alone, she would accommodate his wishes.

Up to a point.

As she'd told Grace, they were going to work this problem out. And if he didn't want to talk... Well, she'd simply have to grab and hold his attention some other way.

Before her shower, Laura removed the bandage from her head. She fingered the raise and shadow of a bruise in the gilt-framed vanity mirror. Barely a scratch. No sign of a headache. Quite honestly, she thought she ought to have done more damage given the six-foot distance off the bridge to the river rocks she must have landed on.

After a long, hot shower, she took care drying off, dabbing Bishop's favorite talc powder in all the right places, then slipping into the negligee she'd worn on their honeymoon in Greece. She mustn't have worn it since then. She'd found the mauve silk pushed to the back of her drawer behind other negligees.

Moving into the bedroom, she glanced at the clock: 8:43. She filled her lungs and, confident, sashayed down the hall.

But a few moments later she discovered that Bishop wasn't in his office. She found him out on the eastern porch, leaning against a column, seemingly counting the stars, and given tonight's luminous night sky, there must be more than a trillion.

Crossing to stand behind him, she filed her hands around his waist and set her cheek against the broad expanse of his back. His unique scent filled her lungs, burrowed under her skin. Her eyes drifting shut, she circled her nose over his shirt between his shoulder blades and imprinted the smell…the moment…onto her memory forever.

He must have heard her coming. He didn't move when she embraced him. Now, however, as her fingers trailed up his shirtfront and her palms ironed over his ribs, his hands covered hers and tightened around them.

"It's chilly out here," he said in that rich, smooth voice she loved.

She grinned against his back. "I hadn't noticed." Then she twined around and stood between her husband and the view of slumbering mountains. He opened his mouth, but she cut him off by placing a finger to his lips. "I don't want to hear about doctor's orders. I'm not cold." She threaded her arms around his middle. "Not while you're near."

As a breeze rustled through the leaves, in the shadows he focused on her brow. "You've taken your bandage off."

"I'm hoping to take off more than that." She found his hand and shaped his palm over her shoulder until the strap of her negligee slipped down. Then she angled her head to press a lingering kiss on the underside of his wrist. "I love you so much, Bishop," she whispered as her lips brushed his flesh. "So much…sometimes it hurts." She dropped tender kisses on his palm then on each fingertip in turn. "How long has it been since we made love?"

He exhaled. "Too long," he said.

Arching her neck back, still holding his hand, she skimmed his fingers down her throat. "I feel as if you haven't held me in an age."

Without her help, his hand continued over her shoulder then down the line of her back until it reached the rise of her behind. Laura sighed as the million sparks zapping through her blood caught light. Humming out a smile she grazed her lips over the hot hollow at the base of his throat and placed his other hand on her breast.

"Bishop, take me to bed."

As she pressed softly into him, familiar, simmering heat condensed high in his thighs.

Bishop grit his teeth but, although he knew what he ought to do, he didn't release her. His hold—on her breasts, on her behind—only increased while in his gut he felt an almighty battle raging, a war so fierce, the pull of yes-no threatened to tear him apart. If he did as she asked…if he took her to bed…they would each win and both lose. They wanted this, they'd always been electric together in the bedroom, but this time there'd be a heavy price to pay.

Unless her memories of that time before were lost forever.

His heartbeat pounding in his ears, Bishop searched her eyes and challenged himself again to do what Laura would want him to if she could only remember. But all he could see was pure clean love glistening in her eyes, pouring from her face. At this moment, she truly loved and believed in him. If he made an excuse this time it would only hurt her. And yet, if he complied...

Breaking, Bishop groaned and brought her closer.

What the hell. If she got her memory back during the night, she could hang him in the morning.

His head dropped lower and as his mouth claimed hers, he swept her up in his arms and headed inside. When he reached the foot of their bed, he released her lips and set her gently on her feet. While his pulse hammered through his veins, his gaze drank in the heavenly sight of her standing in the moonlight flooding in through the bedroom's ten-foot-high windows.

She raised her arms and, understanding, he folded the light fabric up in his hands and eased the negligee over her head. Before the silk and lace hit the floor, his head had lowered over hers again. He felt her dissolve in his arms as she happily, completely surrendered.

Laura trembled inside and out as her hands wandered over the granite of his chest and muscled sides. Then, only half aware, lost in the kiss, she was helping him tug the shirttails from his belt, unbuttoning the front, winding the fabric off his shoulders, down his arms. His kiss was so skillful, thoughtful, and at the same time, demanding. An avalanche of stirring sensations...of memories...rained down and filtered through her. When his mouth left hers to feather a tingling path over the sensitive curve that joined shoulder to neck, the energy, already so strong, multiplied. Intensified.

Laura's head rocked back.

She reveled in the feel of him. Her senses reeled at his clean male scent. As her palms sculpted over his shoulders and biceps, her mind visualized those hot mounds of steely flesh—how she loved to cling to them when he thrust above her—and she smiled.

His thumbs rubbed mesmerizing deep circles high on her arms as his mouth trailed her collarbone then dipped lower until the warm wet sweep of his tongue twirled and teased one nipple. Every atom of oxygen in her lungs evaporated. Gasping back air, she drove her fingers through his hair while tiny brush fires flashed and ignited through her veins. And the slow burn only grew, second by second, with every heartbeat and breathtaking loop of his tongue.

Light-headed, she tugged at his belt and murmured into the shadows, "We don't do this enough." His teeth nipped and tugged the bead at the tip of her breast and she sighed. "In the beginning we'd spend entire weekends in bed."

"I remember," he groaned, then drew her deeply into his mouth.

He'd heeled off his shoes. Now he tugged and stepped out of his trousers. When he hooked her under each arm and laid her upon the bed, she moaned with barely contained anticipation and delight. Like a big cat on the prowl, on all fours he edged up until he hovered over her. His head slowly dipped to kiss her mouth, her brow, the shell of her ear, as her back arched higher and his erection throbbed and grew.

"Should we flick back the quilt?" she asked between breathless kisses and running her leg over his. "Get beneath the covers?"

His palm, large and slightly rough, scooped under her hip. In a slow, languid movement, his muscular body grazed up against hers, drawing an urgent gasp of want from her lips. His knees nudged between hers. When his tip found her moist…silky, swollen and ready…he grinned against her parted lips.

"I'm good," he said, and eased in more. "How about you?"

In answer, her pelvis tilted up at the same time his came down and he drove three parts in. The thrust hit a hot spot so bright she gasped for air. Her nails dragged up over rippling tendons as she swallowed loving words from his mouth.

Making love with Bishop had always been wonderful, but this time...

This time was something *beyond* incredible. With the iron ruts of his abdomen grinding against her, his mouth sipping from her throat and strong fingers curling through her hair she felt consumed by a blanket of heat. The burn lifted her to a place no woman had ever flown to before. He felt so deliciously heavy on top her...so delectably, alarmingly male.

Smiling into the shadows, Laura held tight to the feeling.

He still wanted her. Of course he did. The same insatiable way she wanted him.

The slow, steady friction soon turned to leaping flame. As the energy—the raw imploding power—built and pulsed, she clung to his arms as her muscles contracted around him and every particle shivered, focusing on the indescribable magic awaiting her only a heartbeat away.

Perspiration slicked his skin; he slid and ground against her, making her burn wherever they touched. A rumbling groan sounded in his chest and in the shadows she saw him set his jaw. And then, without warning, he rolled away.

Working for breath, it took a few seconds for her to realize he wasn't coming back. She pushed up onto her elbows, worried.

"What's wrong?"

Stretched out on his back, out of breath, he laced his fingers over his brow. "We need protection."

Protection?

Laura fell back. She wanted to say just this once, couldn't they forget it? But there wasn't a chance he'd listen to that. Unprotected sex could result in an unwanted pregnancy. Unwanted on his part, anyway.

So she waited for Bishop's side drawer to open, for her husband to reach in and fish out a foiled packet from the place he always kept them. But he didn't move. Not an inch. And as the stillness eked out, the cool in the room compressed and settled upon her.

He'd been so insistent. After being concerned about her welfare last night and today, finally he hadn't wanted to stop long enough to pull back the covers. And yet now...

She pushed higher. "Bishop, what's the matter? They're in the drawer, right there beside you."

Another few seconds ticked by before he rolled onto his side away from her. Laura watched the long powerful line of his silhouette moving, heard the drawer slide open then his grunt.

She sat up a little. "What's wrong?"

"Condoms. They're there. A whole pack."

Grinning, she brushed her lips against his shoulder. "We don't have to use them all in one night."

"I just..." He shrugged and exhaled. "Never mind." She heard him remove one before he turned back. Once again his mouth slanted over hers and instantly any chill was gone, replaced by the heat he so effortlessly brought out in her. The embrace intensified, the kiss deepened and the need to join in the most fundamental way grew again. When her palm filed down the hard trunk of his thigh, his own hand mimicked her move, curving down her spine then sliding between her legs. He began to stroke her, tease her, and as he kissed her thoroughly she knew this night wouldn't end without that ticking bomb deep inside of her exploding at least once.

Teetering on the edge, she murmured against his lips, "I love when you kiss me. Anywhere. Everywhere."

As if she'd given the golden command, he began moving down, his mouth roaming, suctioning here and there, over her ribs, her belly, around the ticklish dip of her navel. And every kiss took her that much higher, drew her that much nearer. Had her falling that much more in love.

* * *

In the dark recesses of his mind, Bishop knew he'd lost the plot. When he'd found a box of sealed condoms in the drawer where he'd always kept them, he'd sent up a prayer of thanks then had plowed on. He'd expected Laura to have ditched the contraceptives long ago, but like the wedding photo and rings, she'd left them alone. Because she couldn't bear to touch them? Because she'd secretly wished for her husband back?

Hell, at this precise moment in time, he was way too pumped to wonder.

He'd succumbed to Laura's wiles and, God help him, he couldn't regret it. Particularly now as his mouth trailed an unerring course over her flat stomach and lower. When he reached those soft, moist curls, his brain stopped working altogether.

While her hips slowly rotated, he nuzzled down. After dropping a few barely there kisses on her inner thighs, he got more comfortable and, using his fingers and his tongue, exposed more of her. Her sigh of pure pleasure heightened his own, and as he made love to her with his mouth—with everything he was or had ever been—he understood that this time was beyond compare. Because it was forbidden? Or because they'd denied each other for too long? He only knew she'd never tasted sweeter and his desire for her had never been stronger.

It seemed like he'd only begun when he sensed the intensity building inside of her. Wanting to give her an experience without equal, he held her hips while his mouth covered her and he did what he knew she liked best. Her spine pushed down and she trembled, barely noticeably at first. But as the rolls of energy grew, she began to shudder and moan.

He stayed with her, adoring her fingers bunched in his hair and the series of contractions that urged him not to stop. When she was still floating down, he moved away just enough to open that foil wrapper and rolled down their protection.

When he joined her again, her eyes were closed, her head was slanted to one side and a fan of fair hair was flung over her face. Sighing, she clung to him as he eased in.

With one arm curled over her head, he gazed down at her face, more beautiful than any woman's alive. As he moved above her, found just the right rhythm, he wanted to tell himself to go slow. Make this last. Tomorrow he might not be welcome in Laura's life much less her bed.

As the heat of the inferno licking through his veins intensified, so too did his pace. Still, as his lips traced down her cheek and he stole another penetrating kiss, he was certain he could hold out. This was simply too good to let go yet. But then she quieted and a heartbeat later bucked beneath him, peaking again and riding another orgasmic curl. The push was too much.

Murmuring her name, concentrating on the delicious burn and how glorious she felt surrounding him, he drove in again and jumped off into the firestorm that consumed him inside and out. As white-hot flames swirled though him, Bishop held on tighter and for the first time hoped she didn't remember too soon.

The next morning Bishop sat on the eastern porch, gazing blindly out over the hills, listening to the early morning laughter of kookaburras and wondering what the hell had possessed him last night.

What had he been thinking? Sleeping with Laura once had been a bad idea. Sleeping with her again, and again, had to be moronic. Sure, it'd felt great. Unbelievably fantastic! But that wouldn't save him when her memory returned and she demanded to know why he'd taken advantage of the situation like he had. Never mind that she'd as good as drugged him with her words and her touches and her smiles. When the real Laura returned she wouldn't listen to a word of it. *That* Laura wasn't in love.

No more than he was.

Nothing could obliterate the words they'd exchanged during their roughest patch. The things they'd said to each other would crush the worthiest of loves. It had certainly killed his.

But love aside, clearly he still had feelings for her. He was still smitten by her scent, her voice, the cute sway of her hips whenever she walked. Laura affected him at his most basic primal level. Even when he'd sworn he never wanted to clap eyes on her again, he'd been on the verge of forcing her to hush by kissing her senseless. There'd been a time after they'd split when he thought he never wanted to sleep with another woman, the tough times had affected him that much. Truth was, until last night, he hadn't broken the drought. Although, he'd been heading that way with Annabelle.

His elbow on the outside chair armrest, he held his brow and rubbed his temple.

What was he going to do about that? He and Annabelle weren't in a relationship, as such. They'd seen each other a few times. They seemed to like the same things, got each other's humor and respected each other's space. But after what had happened between him and Laura last night...

His hand dropping from his brow, he blew out a breath.

Clearly, he wasn't anywhere near ready to even think about getting involved with Annabelle or any other woman.

Shifting his hip, he dug the cell out of his back pocket. A moment later the recipient's soft voice drifted down the line.

He straightened in his chair. "Annabelle. It's Samuel."

"Sam? I was hoping you'd phone this weekend. You've been busy?"

"You could say that."

As usual, she was understanding. "There's still most of Sunday left."

He cursed himself. He'd never felt more like a heel, but there was no way around it.

"Look, this is probably not a conversation we should have over the phone. But..." His gaze wandered over the bush, the gazebo, the setting that used to be so much a part of his life and seemed to be again for however long. "I'm afraid this can't wait."

"Something's wrong?"

"I told you I'd been married."

"Yes...you said it ended badly."

"Thing is, Laura, my ex, had an accident Friday."

He imagined Annabelle's long dark lashes batting as she took that in and then her eyes widening as she made a likely assumption. "You're with her now?"

"I took her home from the hospital."

"You're...patching things up?"

"It's complicated." He rubbed his brow. *Really, really complicated.*

"But you're together?" Her tone was less fragile now.

He answered as honestly as he could. In a sense... "Yes."

He waited as Annabelle no doubt composed herself. But she sounded calm when she spoke. Understanding, even. She'd make someone a great wife someday.

"Then I guess there's nothing more to say."

"Except, I'm sorry."

"Can I ask you not to lose my number, you know, in case things don't work out?"

"Sure. I'll do that."

But as he hung up, Bishop knew he wouldn't contact Annabelle again. Not because things would work out between him and Laura; he was damn close to certain it wouldn't. But because if they saw each other again, Annabelle would always wonder whether he was thinking about his ex. If he were in her position he might do the same.

Besides, Annabelle deserved someone who could offer

her a future and Bishop hadn't been after commitment even before Friday's incident.

And so another short chapter in his life was closed, while the case of the amnesiac ex was still wide-open.

As he slotted the phone away, his nose picked up on an aroma that came from the kitchen. Butter melting in a pan.

It was Sunday. Tradition decreed they have brunch on this porch. Hash browns and bacon, pancakes and maple syrup, or their old favorite, eggs Benedict? No matter which, from experience he knew the meal would be mouth-watering.

Bishop moved inside, thinking how easy it'd be to slip back into this lifestyle...*if* Laura remained this Laura and they could work their issues out. But it was dangerous to think that way. Yes, he'd had the best sex *ever* last night with his ex. He knew no complaints would be coming from her quarter. But relationships were about a whole lot more than physical attraction and sexual gratification. If he'd understood that over two years ago, he'd have held off asking Laura to marry him.

He hated to admit it, but snooty Grace was right. He'd fallen in love so hard and so fast he hadn't spared the time to think things through. Amazing, given his stellar track record regarding decision making.

He moved down the hall and as that delicious hot butter smell grew, so did his concern.

In sleeping with Laura last night he'd set a precedent. This afternoon they were off to Sydney, and she would expect them to make love again tonight. And he couldn't deny that he wanted to do just that. More to the point, if she didn't get her memory back between now and then, he knew that he would.

Seven

"Sam Bishop? Is that you?"

In response to the male voice at their backs, Laura pulled up at the same time Bishop swung around. A smile breaking on his face, Bishop offered his hand to the jovial-looking man striding up.

"Robert Harrington." Bishop shook the man's hand. "It's been a while."

Mr. Harrington, a rotund man in an extralarge dinner suit, arched a wry brow. "Enjoying the ballet, son?"

Bishop tugged an ear. "It's…lively."

The man chuckled as if to say he understood. Obviously, Robert Harrington wasn't a *Swan Lake* fan, either.

Earlier, on the heels of their Sunday morning eggs Benedict tradition, she and Bishop had journeyed to Sydney and, after strolling around the Rocks, one of Sydney's most historic harbor-side suburbs, had checked into their Darling Harbor residence, a five-star-hotel three-bedroom penthouse Bishop used if business kept him in the city during the week. Soaking up the sunshine on the balcony and watching the boat activity on the sparkling blue waters below had absorbed the rest of their lazy afternoon. They'd arrived at the Opera House with barely enough time to be seated. Five minutes ago they'd joined the rest of the Opera Theater's glittering crowd to partake of refreshments during intermission.

Their seats could have been better, but Laura wouldn't complain. It was the thrill of the experience she adored. Her mother had introduced her to the theater, in all its guises, at an early age. She'd dreamed of perfecting pointe work and pirouettes and one day starring in the Australian Ballet. But professional ballerinas were superb athletes; heart conditions, even mild ones, weren't the norm. So Laura, along with Grace on occasion, had been content to enjoy a number of magical performances as enthusiastic spectators.

Laura wished Bishop shared her love of the art form, but she was only grateful he hadn't bleated on about coming along; a lot of men might suggest their wives take a friend while they chilled out at a football match or poker game. But Bishop was one of the most supportive people she'd ever known.

That's why she was certain they could work out this difference regarding how to start their family. When he truly understood how important having her own child was to her—when he evaluated the risks from a less, well, paranoid point of view—he would come around. He'd support her, as he always had. This time next year, they might even be singing lullabies to their firstborn.

Boy or girl, she'd be beyond happy with either. Or both.

Laura put those thoughts aside as she smiled a greeting at this middle-aged couple. Wherever they went, it seemed Bishop bumped into someone he knew. Why should a night at the Opera House be any different?

"You haven't met my wife." Robert Harrington turned to a lithe, graceful-looking woman. "Shontelle, this is Samuel Bishop. We had business dealings a year back."

"Pleased to meet you, Samuel." Shontelle's pearl-and-diamond necklace sparkled under the lights as the chattering crowd wove around them. Laura waited. Bishop was usually prompt with introductions but, for once, he missed a beat.

Taking the initiative, she introduced herself. "Pleased to meet you, Robert, Shontelle. I'm Laura."

While Shontelle returned the greeting, Robert scratched his receding hairline. "Laura... Sam, wasn't that your wife's name?"

Her cheeks pinking up, Shontelle delivered her husband's ribs a silencing nudge.

But Laura only laughed. "Not was. *Is.*"

Robert's eyebrows shot up and his smile returned. "Well, that's great." He clapped Bishop's tuxedo-clad shoulder heartily. "Great to see you together."

The two couples bantered on a few minutes more, then went their separate ways. She and Bishop found a relatively quiet corner in the bustling room, away from the heart of the glitter and constant clink of glasses.

Laura spoke over the rim of her champagne flute before she sipped. "That was strange."

"Strange?"

She imitated Robert Harrington's baritone. "*Wasn't that your wife's name?* Didn't you think that was odd?"

Bishop raised his glass in a salute. "Guess we should get out more often."

"You know what else is strange? I've lost weight. I've been the same weight for years but now this dress is big on me."

"It looks beautiful on you. You probably just haven't worn it for a while."

She examined the fall of her red evening dress. The bodice was highlighted by black lace inlays and the back decorated with multiple ribbon crisscross ties, which she'd drawn tightly to compensate for her leaner figure.

"I wore it a month ago to that business dinner in Melbourne, remember?"

His chin lifted the barest amount. She could have sworn his eyes narrowed as his gaze roamed her face.

"What else do you remember?"

He hadn't finished the sentence before that northern footbridge flashed to mind. Then she remembered the hospital, thinking that she was pregnant. She remembered the doctor, the test, the tears—

Laura sucked back a quick breath then, blinking into her champagne flute, frowned.

There hadn't been any tears. She'd been disappointed that the pregnancy test was negative, but also grateful she hadn't risked a baby's well-being when she'd taken her tumble. She remembered being so happy to see her husband and wondering at his odd behavior…that Bishop hadn't come and embraced her straight away. It had taken a little while for him to thaw, even when they'd gotten home. But last night, he'd been as loving as ever.

So why this gnawing, niggling feeling at the back of her brain all of a sudden? A wavering sense that something, somewhere, between them was missing? Robert Harrington's curious comment hadn't helped.

Wasn't that your wife's name?

"Laura, are you okay?"

Bishop's deep voice hauled her back. He was looking at her intently, his brows drawn. And the bell was ringing, calling them back to their seats. Feeling off balance, she slid her flute onto a nearby ledge.

Was she okay?

Willing the faint dizziness away, she pinned up her smile. "Absolutely fine. I'm looking forward to seeing the rest of the ballet."

As they moved back through the crowd, the bell ringing low and persistent, Bishop threaded his jacketed arm through hers. She always felt so proud walking beside him. People noticed her husband—not only his movie star looks, but that unconscious quality that radiated off him like crackling heat off a fire…a vibrant warmth that was inviting and yet also potentially dangerous. Instinct told people you didn't want to get on the wrong side of Samuel Bishop. Not that *they* would ever be on opposing sides. Their difference of opinion on how to start a family didn't count. As she'd told Grace, they'd work that out.

"You didn't have much for dinner," he said as they climbed the carpeted stairs behind the slow-shifting throng. "We'll order some supper when we get in."

One part of her wanted to go straight back to the apartment, make love and then order a cheese platter and a fruity wine to savor throughout the night. Another part wanted to eke out as much of this dazzling evening as she could. Bishop was right. They did need to get out more.

"Let's walk back to the apartment," she suggested as they arrived at their gate. "We can stop for a bite on the way."

He flicked a suspect glance at her red high heels. "In those shoes?"

Teasing, she bumped her hip to his. "These shoes deserve to be shown off."

The corners of his eyes crinkled as he smiled, the bell stopped ringing and the theater lights dimmed. "Then shown off they shall be."

Laura didn't want to tell Bishop she hadn't remembered buying the shoes…like that handbag…like forgetting she'd slipped off her rings before Grace had driven her to hospital. In hindsight, she probably shouldn't have mentioned she thought she'd lost weight. But they were trivial bits and pieces that would filter back in time. And when they did, no doubt this annoying niggling—that *there's something missing feeling*—would up and fly away.

After the curtain had dropped and thunderous applause faded, he and Laura left the theater to stroll down the many Opera House steps, then along the boardwalk.

The night was mild and still bubbling with life—buskers strumming, tourists milling, night owls taking advantage of the round-the-clock restaurants. Laura was praising the prima ballerina's performance in the last act when Bishop's step slowed out front of an open-air café. Cozy tables dotted a timber deck that overlooked dark harbor waters awash with milky ribbons of moonlight. The coffee smelled out-of-this-world good.

"How are the heels holding up?" he asked. "Your feet need a rest?"

"I vote chocolate cheesecake."

His gaze flicked from the dessert display window to her knowing eyes, and he laughed softly. She was well aware of his sweet tooth and he was aware of hers.

"With two scoops of ice cream?" he suggested.

Her hand in his, she tugged him toward the tables. "Done."

He pulled out a chair for her by a roped railing, and a waitress took their orders.

"What time do you have to be at work tomorrow?" Laura asked casually as she skimmed the ballet's keepsake program for the tenth time. But despite the casual tone, Bishop knew she was already wishing the morning away. He'd worked long hours when they'd been married. Still did. She'd always dreaded Monday mornings when he left her to travel to his office in the city.

"Actually, I'm having a couple of days off."

Her eyes popped. "You *never* have time off."

"I'm sure I had time off for our honeymoon." A glorious week cruising the Greek islands. Santorini, Mykonos. The days had been brilliant. The nights were even better.

"Honeymoons are compulsory as far as vacations are concerned." Her finger, trailing his left jacket sleeve, ended its journey by circling that shiny gold band. Her voice took on a note of doubt. "Are you sure the company's not in any trouble?"

"If it were, I'd be chained to my desk." He poured two

glasses from the water carafe. "Trust me, Bishop Scaffolds is stronger than ever."

The worry, pinching her brows, eased and she raised her water glass. "Well, then, here's to a good long sleep in."

While she sighed over how romantic the twinkling bridge looked with a full yellow moon crowning its arch, Bishop made a mental note to text Willis; the boss wouldn't be in until at least Tuesday. From there he'd take each day as it came. Willis was more than competent to handle the day-to-day grind. As for the parties who were inquiring about purchasing the company...

Bishop flicked out his napkin as the cake arrived.

If the potential buyers were keen, they'd wait a few days.

They'd each enjoyed a first succulent taste of slow baked heaven when an elderly gentleman sporting an olive green beret presented himself with a flourishing bow at their table. He carried a battered easel. Two pencils sat balanced behind one ear.

"Would your wife care for a portrait?" the gentleman asked with a heavy French accent.

Bishop smiled dismissively. He liked his privacy.

"I don't think—"

"She'd *love* one," Laura piped up, before sucking chocolate sauce off her thumb and sitting straighter. "She'd love one of the both of us."

Out the side of his mouth, Bishop countered, "Do you really feel like posing for half an hour?"

"No posing," Frenchie said, flicking out his squeaky easel and wedging the legs into the planks. "Eat, talk. Reminisce. While I—" he whipped a pencil out with a magician's finesse *"—create."*

"I know what we can reminisce about." Laura's foot under the table curled around his pant leg. Bishop imagined her red painted toes as they slid up his calf. "Those amazing days we spent together sailing the Aegean."

He angled slightly down. Out of sight, his hand caught her foot and he tickled her instep. "How about that unbelievable night on Naxos?"

"Please, please. Sit closer." Frenchie feathered a pencil over the paper then stepped back to inspect his work so far. "This, I know, will be *magnifique*."

Bishop reveled in the sweetness of chocolate and honey vanilla while listening to Laura's recollections of their honeymoon…what they'd eaten and when, the people they'd met, their private dance on their private balcony in the moonlight that last night. Curious that she'd forgotten their divorce yet could remember every sensual detail of the time directly after their wedding as if it were yesterday. While the Mediterranean breeze and their lovemaking had kept them warm, she'd whispered in his ear and made him promise to take her on a cruise every year.

In between mouthfuls of cake, they talked and laughed. Bishop was so engrossed in their memories of Greece that he'd almost forgotten about the portrait until Frenchie set aside his pencil and announced, "It is done!"

Now, in the shadow of the Opera House's enormous shells, he dragged himself back to the present and reached for his inside jacket pocket.

"How much do I owe?"

Frenchie waved a blasé hand. "Your choice." Then, obviously proud, he pivoted the easel around.

Laura's hands went to her mouth as she gasped. "Oh, Bishop, it's *perfect*."

Bishop had to agree. It captured not only their images but the gay atmosphere of the night as well as their obvious affection for each other. It was like looking back in time.

"It was a pleasure to work with a couple so very much in love." Frenchie beamed.

Laura's eyes glittered in the flickering candlelight. "Does it show?"

"Like a comet," Frenchie enthused with a grand sweeping gesture, "illuminating a velvet night sky."

Laura's expression melted and Bishop slid out a large bill. Frenchie might be a bit of a poet, but his description wasn't much of an exaggeration. That's how they must appear to others tonight. Head-over-heels newlyweds in love. While they'd talked and shared desserts it had felt that way, too. He would've liked nothing better to have sat here, like this, all night.

By the time they finished up, it was late, so Bishop hailed a cab and her feet in their gorgeous heels got to rest.

As they crossed beneath the crystal chandelier of their hotel's grand marble foyer, the efficient-looking concierge—a different man from the one earlier today—glanced up from checking something behind his desk. A big grin etched across his face and he fairly clicked his heels.

On their way to the lifts, Laura commented, "Very friendly staff they have here. You should tip that guy for that special welcome home."

His step faltered the barest amount before he slid over a smile. "It's because you look stunning tonight." With the portrait in its cardboard sheath under his arm, Bishop stopped before the bank of lifts and thumbed a key. "You're glowing."

The lift arrived and she moved inside, smiling at his compliment, but deep down holding herself against a faint stab. *Glowing* was a term often bestowed upon pregnant women. Before that doctor at the hospital on Friday had informed her that she was mistaken—that she wasn't pregnant—she'd actually *felt* as if she were glowing, even with that scrape and bump on her head.

But she could well be glowing tonight. They'd had a wonderful evening out, and with Bishop playing hooky from office duties tomorrow, there were many more hours of "wonderful" ahead.

As the car whirred up to the penthouse floor, she leaned on Bishop to balance as she eased off one four-inch heel then the other.

Bishop took note. "You've shown them off enough for one night?"

Performing, she twirled a shoe around her finger. "Oh, this is only the beginning."

His brows hitched and pupils dilated until the crystalline blue of his eyes was near swallowed by black. When the metallic door slid open, she sashayed out ahead, sandals draped provocatively over one shoulder. She heard his footfalls on the marble tiles behind her.

"Guess you're not tired," he said.

"You guessed right."

They entered the suite, a vast cream, black and crimson expanse, furnished with clean lines and minimalist finesse. She cast her shoes aside. Unable to hold back a moment longer, she coiled her arms around his neck and tipped her mouth up to meet his.

The ballet had kept her occupied earlier, but when they'd sat by those sparkling harbor waters tonight, eating their cake and reliving those fantastic few days abroad after their wedding, there were times Laura had needed to bunch her hand in her lap to divert the energy she'd felt pulling her toward him. It was as if she were hooked on an invisible line and desperately wanting to be wound in…to let him kiss her with all the heat of emotion both their hearts could give.

In the cab home, crossing the hotel foyer, riding the lift, she'd wanted to do exactly this…let him know with a touch of her hand, the stroke of her tongue, that she couldn't live without him. With his breathing deepening now, his bristled chin grazing rhythmically against her cheek and his arms locked around her, the hot need inside of her only grew. Like a bulb without spring sunshine, she could survive without Bishop, but she would never know such true warmth.

Such real love.

That would never change. No matter what challenges they faced, they would always have this. An insatiable, natural need to be close.

When he grudgingly released her, her heart was pounding so hard that the vibration hummed through her body all the way to her fingers and toes. Her hand filed up through the back of his hair as she breathed in the glorious scent he left on his pillow each morning.

"Know what I want to do?"

"How many guesses do I get?" His voice was low and husky with desire, his eyes lidded with want.

"How many do you need?"

"I'll take one."

Her palms splayed over the broad ledge of his jacketed shoulders as she pressed in against him. "What if you're wrong?"

A lazy grin hooked one side of his mouth. "I'm not wrong."

"So I don't need to give you a hint?"

That lazy grin widened. "Hints are always welcome."

"Well, then, first we need to take this off."

She dipped beneath his lapels and scooped the jacket off his shoulders. His lidded eyes holding hers, he tossed the coat aside. She assumed a speculative look as her palms ironed up the steamy front of his shirt.

"And that tie needs to go, too," she decided, tugging the black length free from beneath its collar.

Bishop asked, "What about cuff links?"

"Cuff links are definitely out."

He managed the links while she saw to his dress shirt studs. When the last button was released, her touch fanned the steely ruts of his naked abdomen then arced up through the dark, coarse hair on his chest. She let out a sigh as her nails trailed his pecs before catching the shirt and peeling the sleeves slowly down.

Anticipating the moment, she quivered inside as she lightly pressed her lips below the hollow of his throat; the pulse she found there matched the throb tripping a delicious beat at her core. A cord ran down one side of his tanned neck. When the tip of her tongue tasted a trail up the salty ridge, his erection, behind its zipper, grew and pushed against her belly. Growing warmer by the second, she blew a gentle stream of air against the trail her tongue had left.

"Do you remember what we were wearing on the balcony that night on the ship?"

His hands were kneading her behind, rotating her hips to fit against his as he attentively nipped the shell of her ear.

"I remember what we *weren't* wearing." Cooler air brushed her back as he tugged on a ribboned bow and her bodice loosened. "Would you like to slow dance on this balcony tonight?"

Sighing, she ground against him. "I thought you'd never ask."

A knock sounded at the door, then a call. "Room service!"

Laura's stomach jumped while Bishop's chin went down. He searched her eyes.

"We haven't ordered anything, have we?"

"It's a mistake." Slipping back into the mood, she wove a hand up over the hot dome of one shoulder. "Ignore it."

"It might be important."

"Not as important as this."

Falling back into the magic, she drew his head down and kissed him more thoroughly than the first time.

But the call came again. "Mr. Bishop, room service, sir."

Groaning, Bishop unraveled her arms and headed for the

door. "Remind me to hang the sign up as soon as he's gone. *Do. Not. Disturb.*"

A bellboy with a sun-bleached surfer's mop stood behind the door. He didn't raise a brow at Bishop's state of half dress but merely handed over a shiny silver bucket, its sides frosty and the well filled with an impressive-looking bottle as well as two chilling glasses.

"Compliments of the house, sir," the young man said, then spun on his spit-polished heel with a cheerful, "Good night."

As Bishop hung the sign then closed the door, Laura crossed over and read the note, penned on hotel stationery.

"Welcome back, Mrs. Bishop." She shook off a laugh. "I was here just a couple of weeks ago, and a week before that." Staring at the note, she cast her mind back then set the note down on the teak hallstand ledge. "We should send this back. They've made some sort of mistake."

"Have they?"

She shot him a questioning look then shrugged. "There's no other explanation."

"Maybe there is."

As he held her gaze, she sent him a dry grin. "Then I'd like to hear it."

"Would you?"

Her jaw tightened and she crossed her arms. "Don't do that, Bishop."

"Do what?"

"*That.* Answer everything with a question."

As Bishop's eyes hardened—or was that glazed over?—an icy shiver chased up her spine. Feeling bad, *foolish,* she pressed her lips together. Her tone had been brittle. She hadn't meant it to be. It was just that...

Well, first there'd been that Robert Harrington and his odd comment, then the concierge's almost surprised reaction at seeing them, now this offering from the hotel management as if she'd been gone for years.

It didn't make sense.

But she was aware of the look on Bishop's face. Removed? Concerned? He thought she'd overreacted and he was right. Management had sent champagne. He was suggesting there was some good reason. Which was feasible. And unimportant. She was making more of this than she needed to. She was curious—puzzled—that's all.

Pasting on a smile, willing the flush from her cheeks, she nodded at the bottle.

"Either way, it's a nice gesture. We should thank them in the morning."

Bishop moved past and carefully set the bucket on the coffee table. If Laura thought she was confused, he hadn't a *clue* what he was doing or what he planned to do next.

Every step he'd taken since Friday afternoon had led to precisely this moment. Logical steps. Steps that had made sense at the time. Even making love last night. In his defense, he could put up a good argument for that. What man in his right mind could've refused? Particularly when it was this man with that woman.

When she'd waxed on tonight about how unbelievable their honeymoon had been, recreating all those images and feelings while they'd nibbled on cake, she'd accomplished something he would never have dreamed possible. She'd taken him back—*really* back—in time. He'd looked into her eyes, so animated and thirsty for life—for him—and, God help him, he'd only wanted to stay.

And that awareness made this situation—where they stood now—different than it had been last night, or this morning.

He hadn't wanted to force any recollections back too fast, too soon. He'd tread lightly, initially, because he hadn't known how to go about it, then because he'd liked to see her happy. Ultimately he'd liked feeling happy again, too.

He'd been very happy tonight.

Before the champagne had arrived, they'd been on the brink, about to make love again, and yet when she'd looked so frustrated and confused just now, he'd tried to force that memory door open again, and more than a crack. He'd pushed to try to make her remember. And he'd done it for a reason. A selfish reason.

If this happened—if they had sex, made love, came apart in each other's arms—he wanted it to be real. Maybe if she remembered the past, the ugly breakup, while she was feeling the way she did about him now, the anger and pain would pale enough for them to be able to work something out. That's all he'd ever wanted.

To work things out.

He folded down into the circular leather lounge, smoothed back his hair with both hands then found her eyes again.

"Laura, come here. We need to talk."

"About what?" She crossed and sat close to him, her beautiful face wan, her emerald eyes glistening with questions.

"We need to make an appointment."

"An appointment for what?"

"A follow-up. To get you checked out."

She blinked several times then tipped away. Even laughed a little. "I'm fine."

"Are you?" She went to object and he held up his hands. "Okay. No more questions. Except one. And I want you to think about it before you answer."

She searched his eyes and eventually nodded. "All right."

"At the hospital, you said you thought you were pregnant. It is possible you were mixed up? That maybe…"

Not wanting to say it but needing to, he exhaled and reached for her hand. Gripped it tight.

"That maybe you'd been pregnant before?"

Her expression cracked—half amused, half insulted. As if she'd been burned, she pried her hand away.

"That's ridiculous. For God's sake, Bishop, I'd know if I'd been pregnant before."

So adamant. *Too* adamant.

He swallowed against the ache blocking his throat. Out of anything he could have asked her—anything that would have set off a battery of alarm bells—that question had to have been it. And yet the only reaction he got was a disgusted look as if he'd called her a name. If he bit the bullet, went further and tried to explain about their discussions two years ago, how she'd been so happy with his decision to try to conceive, then ultimately so crushed...

Her eyes glistened more. A hint of panic hid behind the sheen. But her voice was hauntingly level when she spoke.

"Why are you looking at me like that?"

His midsection clenched and his gaze dropped away.

He'd had no illusions, but this was way harder than he'd thought. Near impossible.

He believed he'd asked the right question, but there was another. And now that he'd come this far, he had to ask it, for both their sakes.

After finding her gaze again, he lowered his voice. "Laura, how do you think you'd handle losing a child?"

She let out a breath. And smiled. Hell, she looked relieved.

"Is that what all this is about?" She leaned nearer and braced his thigh. "Nothing bad will happen. We have to believe that. I know everything will be all right. Have faith. Have faith in us." She squeezed his leg. "I do."

The emotion clogging his throat drifted higher and stung behind his nose. How could he respond to that? He had nothing. Then a crazy notion hit. So crazy, he wanted to laugh.

Wouldn't it be something if she fell pregnant again and this time everything worked out? If she didn't get her memory back, what man would convict him? She'd be happy. His soul would be redeemed. Or, if she fell pregnant before her memory returned, couldn't they work through to reinvent the happy ending they'd both deserved the first time around? Was that too crazy to hope for? Another chance?

Her hand left his thigh. "You mentioned something about a slow dance on the balcony."

Before he could respond, she stood and held out her hand. He looked at her for a long, tormented moment. There was no right or wrong. No win or lose. No way to predict how this would end. Or *if* it would.

His fingers curling around hers, he found his feet and led her out onto the balcony.

A cool harbor breeze filed through their hair as he cradled her close and she rested her cheek against his fast-beating heart. With the distant hum of traffic for music, he began to rock her gently around. After a few moments she murmured, so softly he barely heard.

"I love you, Bishop."

High in his gut that tight ball contracted more and time wound down to a standstill. The decision was instinctive.

He put aside the man he was now, the man whose heart had been mangled and who had vowed to never marry again. He tamped down the voice that said not to lie. That cried out what he planned was unforgivable. Instead, he assumed the mask of a man just three months married. A man who knew he should let go of the guilt over surviving his brother and forego the fear of "what ifs" in the womb and beyond. A man who wanted their own child as much as Laura did, no matter what.

No matter what.

He brushed the hair from her cheek, whispered her name then, willing himself to believe it, said, "I love you, too."

Eight

The next morning, in their Darling Harbor penthouse, Laura had trouble getting out of bed.

She wasn't sick. She'd never felt healthier. Or happier. After the hours she and Bishop had spent writhing in each other's arms, she only wanted to stay there, close to her incredible husband, soaking up his magnificent heat, reveling in the way he fulfilled her, each and every time. In the broader scheme of things, they hadn't known each other long, but she couldn't imagine these intense emotions ever waning. The texture of his hair, the sound of his rich, smooth voice, the intoxicating scent she inhaled whenever her nose brushed his chest.

She only hoped he never tired of her. She might have been dealt a bad card—her heart condition—but that was little or no problem now. And fate had more than compensated by gifting her the love of an extraordinary man like Samuel Bishop.

At around nine, while Bishop made some calls, she slid into the bathroom to shower. As she lathered her hair, she smiled, remembering how he'd mentioned during the night that he had a surprise for her this morning. It couldn't be jewelry. He'd already given her enough to weigh down a queen. Perhaps after their reminiscing, he was going to book another cruise.

Laura dried off, knowing that whatever he had planned

she would love. She wouldn't let her mind wander so far as to consider he might want to window-shop for baby things. Furniture, pink or blue jumpsuits, high chairs, stencils for a nursery wall. And she wanted to buy one of those faith, hope and love trinkets. She'd adored the idea of those symbols, and their meanings, since knowing a friend in primary school who had worn them around her neck on a thin gold chain. If she and Bishop had a girl, the heart, anchor and cross would go onto a bracelet; if a boy, she'd attach them to the cot.

Laura stopped to gaze at her pensive reflection in the fogged up mirror.

With so much to organize, perhaps they *should* start looking now.

But as she slipped the light butter-colored dress over her head, Laura berated herself. They hadn't agreed to fall pregnant. Not yet. It was an important and delicate matter, one they both felt strongly about. Still, perhaps she ought to bring it up again sometime today. Logically, she knew they had oodles of time to start a family; she was young and, at thirty, so was he. But that didn't quell the awareness she felt building every day. More and more she noticed mothers with prams, baby commercials on TV, schools and parks with swings and kids laughing and chasing each other around like mad things.

After applying a lick of mascara and lip gloss, she set a brush to her towel-dried hair. Her thoughts wandered more, to places they'd never traveled before, and the brush strokes petered out.

Frowning at her reflection, she shook her head. No. She would never do it. Even if there were a way. Bishop used protection; his nature was to be cautious, to think before he leaped. Still...

How would he react if she accidentally fell pregnant? Last week she'd honestly believed that she had. She hadn't planned it. Starting a family was a decision both people in a relationship needed to agree upon.

She started brushing again.

Definitely not. She would never intentionally, accidentally fall pregnant. Bishop would come around soon enough and then they could both go into this next important phase of their lives confident and with a clear conscience.

When she emerged from the bedroom, she found Bishop standing by the wall-to-wall windows that overlooked Darling Harbor's sun-kissed sights. But he wasn't interested in the view…traffic on the water, the busy restaurants, the fanfare facade of the Maritime Museum. Bishop being Bishop, he was still on the phone.

He caught sight of her, smiled, then obviously needing to concentrate, angled a little away. After the dinner suit he'd worn last night, those dark blue jeans, zipper at half-mast, were a different but still ultra-sexy look. No doubt he'd team it with a brand-name polo shirt. But for her part, she could gobble up the sight of that magnificently sculpted chest all day long. Every drool-worthy muscle was perfectly defined. The angle of those quarterback shoulders might have been crafted by Michelangelo.

He often stood with his weight favoring one leg. That unconscious pose now, in those heaven-sent jeans, gave him a too-hot-to-handle, rebel's air that left her mouth dry. Still focused on the call, he shoveled a hand through his shower damp black hair and Laura's pelvic floor muscles squeezed around a particularly pleasant pulse. With his fingers lodged in his hair, that bicep on display…

Laura fought not to fan herself. She only wished she had a camera to capture the moment and remember exactly how heart-poundingly handsome he was right now.

He disconnected and swung back to face her. Graceful, fluid… He didn't *walk* so much as *prowl*. And the quiet throb, ticking at every erogenous zone in her body, said she wanted very badly to be caught.

Joining her, he dropped a kiss on the side of her neck and lingered to hum appreciatively against her throat.

"You smell almost too good to eat."

Smiling, she dissolved against him. "*Almost* too good?"

His big hands measured her waist then slid higher. They didn't stop until long lean fingers were splashed over her back and a thumb rested beneath the fall of each breast. His head angled more. She shivered uncontrollably as his teeth nipped the sensitive sweep of her throat. The pads of his thumbs grazed her nipples as he murmured, low and deep, against her skin.

"You heard me."

That syrupy I-can't-get-enough-of-you feeling sizzled like sparking gunpowder through her system. Her knees threatened to buckle and her lungs labored, unable to get enough air. When her hand drove up his arm, over the sinewy rock of one shoulder, her eyes drifting closed, she sighed as he nipped and his morning beard grazed.

"Are you suggesting we stay in today?" she asked, sounding drugged and feeling that way, too.

"I'm saying you can make me lose my mind."

"That can't be a bad thing."

His face tipped up. His eyes were so hooded, she could barely see the blue.

He blinked once then asked, "Promise?"

She laughed. It was meant to be light, but he'd said that word with such earnestness…she wasn't certain how to respond.

For once too overwhelmed by his intensity, she touched a kiss to his cheek and, winding out of his hold, moved to the galley kitchen. There were times she felt completely consumed by him. That wasn't a complaint, but she wondered whether another woman might be able to handle his brute magnetism better. She didn't see his innate power ever diminishing.

She didn't want it to.

"I had blueberry pancakes sent up," he said, reaching for a casual shirt resting on the back of the lounge.

Her gaze darted to the meals area and her previously distracted senses picked up on the smell. Feeling guilty after that slab of cheesecake last night, she held her stomach.

"You're trying to make me fat."

"Fat, thin…" He strolled to the table to remove the silver dome. "I'll take you any way you come."

Inhaling again, eyeing the fluffy discs dotted with berries and dusted with icing sugar, she conceded. She had lost some weight, after all.

Joining him, she collected a fork, cut a portion off the top offering and slid the cake into her mouth. She chewed slowly, savoring the divine butter and fruit textures and flavors. Swallowing, she groaned with appreciation as well as disappointment.

"I wish mine turned out as good as this."

"Have I ever complained about your cooking?"

She gave a coy grin. "Never."

"The benefit with room service is…" He curled over her and stole a kiss from her ice-sugared lips. "More time for us."

More than tempted, she touched her lips where he'd tasted hers as she sliced off a little more cake. "You really do want to stay in, don't you?"

"That's a given. But there's also that surprise I had planned."

Her mouth was full again but, needing to know, she talked almost incoherently around it. "Wha ith it?"

He laughed and pulled out her chair. "Finish your breakfast and you'll find out."

* * *

Ten minutes later, he and Laura were walking through the hotel lobby. He had the ticket out, ready for the concierge to retrieve his car, when he recognized a figure standing in front of the lofty automatic glass doors.

Bishop's step faltered.

What was Willis doing here?

When his second-in-charge recognized him too, he waved and came forward. Bishop slid a sidelong glance at Laura. He and Willis were friends. Willis knew he'd been married and how badly it had ended. But he didn't want to explain this to the younger man here or now.

As Willis joined them, Bishop made succinct introductions. "Willis McKee, this is Laura."

Willis took her hand. "Pleased to meet you."

"Bishop tells me you're his new assistant," Laura inquired.

Willis cocked a brow. "I wouldn't have said *new*."

"Willis and I have known each other a while now," Bishop chipped in. "Laura, can you excuse us for a minute?" Taking Willis's elbow, he led him off to a quiet corner.

When they were alone, Bishop's no-problem exterior cracked. He never had a day off. Now he was being hounded by the man he knew could handle the job, and for more than twenty-four hours. Nothing could be this important.

"What are you doing here?"

"You didn't answer your phone or emails last night," Willis replied, no sign of a tail between his legs. "And these guys are keen, Sam. Dead keen. They've been on the phone yesterday and already this morning. They want to look at the books as soon as possible." Willis's eyes narrowed and he crossed his arms. "You're still interested, right? I mean, I understand—" he flicked a glance Laura's way "—you're busy. But *Laura?* I thought you were seeing an Annabelle."

"Laura's my wife. Ex-wife to be precise."

Willis's jaw hit the ground. "Your *what?* From what you'd told me, I got the impression there was more chance of a blizzard descending on the Simpson than you two getting back together."

Bishop rubbed the back of his neck. "Yeah, well, it's complicated."

"If you don't mind me saying, the vibes I get are more of the plain and simple variety."

"Laura had an accident Friday," he explained. "That's why I left early."

Willis took another longer look. "She seems fine now."

"She's great...except for the fact that two years of her life have been erased."

Willis took a moment. "You mean amnesia? And she thinks you and she..." Groaning, Willis held his brow. "Oh, man."

Bishop nodded. "Complicated."

"What're you going to do?"

"I went along at first because I didn't have much choice. Laura thought we were still married. The doctor said if I kept a close eye on her, she could go home. So we spent some time together, and as the hours and days went on..." He rolled back his shoulders, forming the words carefully in his mind before uttering a one. "I'm wondering whether we might not be able to save what we had."

Bishop respected this man; they were friends, but this was extremely private. Should he have been this open? It wasn't usually his style. Still, now the words were out, he knew he'd needed to say them out loud. Maybe then he'd be able to see how ridiculous this all was.

"Save your marriage?" Willis's hands dug into his pockets. "That would be if she remembers, or if she doesn't?"

"That part's a little up in the air."

"It's none of my business, and you probably don't need me to tell you, but you should tread carefully. If you decide to go that way, the road will be full of potholes, deep and wide."

Bishop grunted. *No kidding.*

"I'm going to book her in to see a neurologist midweek. See what can be done. In the meantime—"

"You have a beautiful bride who's all doe-eyed for you, but deep down hates your guts. Talk about being between a rock and a hard place. What a temptation."

Feeling his gills heat up, Bishop lowered his gaze and shuffled his feet.

Willis did a double take, then swore. "Oh, no...Sam, you *haven't*. She locked you out a year ago and now that she can't remember the bad times, you've *slept* with her?"

Bishop growled, "I don't need anyone beating on my conscience about it." His tone dropped. "I've been doing enough of that myself."

"Look on the bright side. Things couldn't get any worse the second time around."

"At least I know what to expect."

"With a woman?" Willis coughed out a laugh. "You're fooling yourself." He drew up to his full height and got back on track. "What do you want me to do about those buyers?"

"Tell them I'm unavailable. We'll get back to them later in the week." He'd thought he was ready to sell. Move on. Now he wasn't so sure. He did know that he didn't want any reminders of his failed marriage, and every time he walked into that office, talked to his team or went on location, he remembered how he'd buried himself in his work during those hard times. In truth, perhaps those memories had more to do with his desire to sell than feeling stale at work.

Either way, he didn't need to make a snap decision. He'd see how he felt in a day or two—in a week—about everything and decide then.

They returned to Laura, and Willis nodded his farewell. "Good meeting you, Mrs. Bishop."

"You'll have to come up to our place in the mountains for dinner one evening," she said. "Bring your wife, of course."

"I'm sure she'd like that. She loves the mountains."

Laura beamed. "Me, too." She looked to Bishop then back at Willis. "Why don't we make it this weekend?"

"This weekend we're having that get-together for my birthday, remember—" Willis stopped.

Bishop was glaring at him.

She's not ready for big groups yet.

The consummate hostess, Laura patched up the awkward moment. "Oh, well, if you have a party on, we'll make it another time."

Bishop quietly exhaled. Ah, what the hell. It would either be a disaster with everyone asking the wrong questions, or they'd have a great time. If her memory returned before then, it'd be a moot point.

"We're invited, Laura." He shrugged, offered a smile. "It slipped my mind."

Laura's eyes lit up. "That's wonderful." She spoke to Willis. "I suppose I'll see you next week then."

"I know my wife will enjoy meeting you." Turning to the doors, Willis sent Bishop a wink. "We'll talk."

He and Laura headed for the concierge's desk. The fellow from last night, Herb, was still on. After the ticket was handed over and pleasantries exchanged, he asked, "Did you receive the champagne?"

Laura spoke for them both. "That was so thoughtful. And unnecessary. But thank you so much."

"You were always so kind, Mrs. Bishop," the older man said. "It's good to have you back."

Looking touched as well as bemused, Laura patted her hair uncertainly then tacked up her smile. "It's good to be back."

They headed out through the doors and, between two soaring forecourt columns, waited for his car to arrive. Hanging on tenterhooks, Bishop knew Laura would mention Herb's comment. *Good to have you back*. She might think it was weird, but Herb hadn't seen Laura in eighteen months, and yes, she had always been kind. She was kind to everyone. The last months of their marriage, with regard to him, didn't count.

But rather than Herb, Laura brought up that other subject.

"Was Willis here about the sale of the company?"

"Yes, he was."

"So you're going in to the office later today?"

"No."

Her eyes rounded as she turned to him. "You're still taking the day off to be with me?"

She looked so innocent, so radiant, he couldn't help but smile. "Don't sound so amazed."

Clearly self-conscious now, she bowed her head. "I know you love me—" she met his eyes again "—but I never imagined you'd take time off when you have such important business to sort out."

The car rolled up. He opened the passenger-side door, thinking that he would never have imagined it, either. What an eye-opener. He hadn't analyzed the dichotomy before, but it was true. He *had* put business first. When they'd been married, the company was still climbing and he'd had no choice but to put in the hard yards. Or that's what he'd told himself. Truth was when things started to slide between him and Laura, he'd hid behind his job, used it as an excuse not to face his problems at home.

He slid in behind the wheel.

How often had he said to himself, *If I had my time again?* Now it seemed he had.

Thirty minutes later, the car slowed down and Laura brought the dented fingernail out from between her teeth.

"I'm nervous."

Bishop swung the Land Rover to the curb. "If you don't like any of them, we're under no obligation."

"I'm worried I'll like them *all*. What do you think? A girl or a boy?"

The engine shut down. "Your choice."

"A girl, I think. Maybe we could get a friend for her later on."

"I'd better watch out or we'll be taking all four home."

On the drive, Bishop had let the cat—or dog, as it happened—out of the bag. Laura had been beside herself, she was so excited to be actually looking at puppies. Now, as a tall, wiry lady answered the door of a pristine suburban cottage, Laura held Bishop's hand tight. The woman introduced herself as Sandra Knightly then ushered them around the back to where a silky coated retriever lay in a comfortable enclosure, nursing four adorable pups.

"As I told you on the phone earlier, Mr. Bishop," Sandra said, "we have three males, one female."

Besotted already, Laura hunkered down. "Only one girl?"

"Right there." Sandra pointed out the smallest. "She's the quiet one. They're six weeks old. They'll be ready to go to their new homes in a couple of weeks."

"Will their mother miss them when they go?" Laura asked.

"Think of it as your own children leaving for college," Sandra replied.

"I don't know that I'd ever like them to go." Laura reached out a hand then drew it back.

She looked up and Sandra asked, "Would you like to hold her?"

Laura's face lit up. "Can I?"

"Of course. It's good to have human contact at this age."

Sandra scooped up the female puppy and laid her in the cup of Laura's palms. She snuggled the sleepy baby close and brushed her cheek along the pale gold fur. The puppy turned her head and nudged her nose against Laura's.

"Oh, my." Her sigh was heartfelt. "She smells so... puppyish."

Standing again, Sandra laughed. "Would you like me to put her aside for you?"

"Not yet." Bishop stepped forward.

And Laura's head snapped up.

"Why not?" Hearing her own tone, more a bark, she bit her lip.

She'd only meant that she knew this puppy was the one. They could look at a dozen more, but she would always come back to this darling. If they didn't put something down to keep her, she'd be snapped up by someone else. She even had a name picked out.

Looking to Sandra, Bishop rolled back his shoulders. "We'd like to discuss it."

"It's a big decision," Sandra agreed. "All the relevant information is on the website where you found me. But feel free to call if you have any questions."

Hating to leave, Laura kissed her puppy between her floppy ears. "You stay put, little one," she murmured against the downy fur. "I don't want to lose you."

Two minutes later they were back in the car, buckling up. So happy and anxious and excited, Laura felt as if she could burst. She gave her thighs a hyped up little drum. "She's totally perfect, isn't she?"

He put on sunglasses. "She's a cute pup."

"So we can get her?"

"I'd like to be thorough. We want to make sure."

Laura clenched her jaw and held back a groan. Why must everything be put through the Samuel Bishop tenth degree decision sieve? For once, couldn't he say, "Yeah. Let's do it!"

"I don't care if she isn't from a long line of champions or if she'll need a hip replaced when she's twelve," she told him. "I'd want her anyway."

"And you wouldn't be crushed if down the road we found out she had a problem…that we might lose her?"

"Of course I'd be crushed. But I wouldn't love her any less, and I wouldn't blame anyone. I certainly wouldn't blame you."

"You wouldn't, huh?"

"I know you want to protect me, Bishop. You don't want anything bad to ever happen. And I love you all the more for it. We can plan and hope and dream our lives will turn out a certain way. We can care for each other and pray that nothing goes wrong. But no one's immune. If we put ourselves out there, sometimes we're going to get hurt. The alternative is to hide away. Wrap ourselves in cotton wool. I would never hold you back from your dreams. If you want to build Bishop Scaffolds into a multinational corporation, I'm one hundred percent behind you. If you want to sell to pursue another venture, I'll support you there. I know you'll support me in my dreams, too."

She was talking about more than buying a puppy, and he knew it.

He searched her eyes for the longest time. She saw the battle going on inside of him. Bishop was a man who made precise moves. He needed to anticipate, to strategize and arrive at the best possible solution to advance. As a wife, his process could be frustrating; *impulsiveness* didn't feature in Bishop's personal dictionary. But he wasn't indecisive. Quite the opposite. When he made up his mind, that conviction was set in cement. But he had to be sure…as sure as he'd been when he'd asked her to be his partner in life.

A deep line formed between his brows as he frowned and he thought. Behind his sunglasses, he was looking deeply into her eyes, but she knew he was envisaging the future…. Her concern if the puppy developed joint problems, her misery should she be struck by a snake or get lost in the bush. He wanted to shield her from pain. That was noble. But Laura wanted to feel, to *love,* and if that meant a possibility she might lose, then she was prepared to accept that, too.

He flicked a glance back at Sandra's house and, after another long moment, nodded once.

"It'll be two weeks before we can collect her."

A yip of happiness escaped and Laura flung her arms around him. He'd agreed they should get a puppy, *this* puppy, but in her heart she suspected she'd broken down a wall and he was agreeing to more.

At least she prayed that he was.

Nine

Bishop put a deposit down on the pup and Laura gave her furry baby another big cuddle goodbye. She spoke of little else all the way to the Darling Harbor apartment or on the way home to the Blue Mountains. Bishop couldn't decide if he felt relieved or ridden with guilt that he'd agreed to her getting a dog.

This time two years ago they'd had very near the same conversation. He'd stuck to his guns about checking out potential pets yet had agreed a short time later to Laura falling pregnant. He knew why he'd made that call. Laura would be able to abide by the logic behind checking out a dog's pedigree, but despite his own reservations, in his heart he understood, now more than ever, that Laura would never forget about conceiving and having her own child. Clearly, regardless of everything they'd gone through—everything *she'd* gone through—Laura hadn't put aside her deeper feelings.

Had he been wrong to expect such a sacrifice on her part in the first place? Had his insecurities been more important than her desire to be a mother in the truest sense? He'd thought he was merely being cautious, a responsible parent-to-be, but perhaps he'd simply been selfish putting his wishes above hers.

After he swung the Land Rover into the garage, he removed the luggage from the trunk, recalling how he'd rationalized this all the first time, when they'd been three months married. If Laura was willing to take the risk, he'd come to the conclusion that he could do little other than support her choice. It wasn't about courage or recklessness or defeat on his part. Back then it had been about love and, initially, she'd understood that. The here and now was about seeing if there was any chance they might get that love back.

When he'd married Laura he'd believed to his soul that she would be his wife for life. Divorce papers and living apart hadn't changed that ingrained perception, which was only one of the reasons he would never marry again. Beneath all the murk of the breakup, behind the smoke and mirrors of her amnesia, did Laura feel the same way? Reasonably, why else would her mind wind back to this precise point in her life, in their relationship, if not for some deep desire to change the misfortune that had come before? Statistics said her memory would return over time. When it did, she could tell him whether he'd taken advantage of the situation or if this time he'd been the one who'd taken a risk that might pay off.

When Bishop moved inside with their luggage, Laura was standing in front of the fireplace, peering up at their wedding portrait, her head tilted to one side as if something wasn't quite right.

While she'd chatted to Grace Saturday morning, he'd found their wedding photograph stashed at the back of a wardrobe in the adjacent guest room. His heart had thudded the entire time he'd perched atop a stepladder and rehung the print, but he had an excuse handy should she walk in. A spider's web had spread across one corner, he'd decided to say, and he'd taken the print down to see if the culprit was living behind the frame.

But she'd stayed on the phone a half hour and hadn't noticed the portrait either way after that. As he watched her now, inching closer to the fireplace, examining the print as though it were a newly discovered Picasso, he considered the other discrepancies she might wonder about now that they were home again. Things that didn't quite fit.

He'd bat the questions back as they came and tomorrow he'd get her into a general practitioner who could give them a referral to a specialist. Until then he'd wing it and let the pieces fall as they may.

Still engrossed in the photograph, she tapped a finger at the air, obviously finally figuring out what was wrong.

"It's crooked," she announced.

After lowering the luggage, he retrieved the stepladder, which was still handy. As he set it up before the fireplace, ready to straighten the frame, Laura continued to analyze.

"It seems so long ago," she said, "and yet…" She released a breath she must have been holding and a short laugh slipped out. "Can you believe we've been married a whole three months?"

He grinned back. "Seems longer."

He straightened the frame. She took in the angle, then nodded. "Perfect."

On his way down the ladder, he remembered the sketch lying on the car's backseat. "Have you thought where you might hang the other one?"

"Mr. Frenchie's? We'll need to get it framed first. Something modern, slim-lined, fresh!"

She was headed toward the phone extension. As she collected the receiver, Bishop's pulse rate jackknifed and he strode over. When he took the receiver from her, her chin pulled in.

Hoping unease didn't show in his eyes, he found an excuse.

"We've only just come home." He set the receiver back in

its cradle. "Don't you want to unpack, have a coffee, before we let the outside world in?"

"I was expecting Kathy to leave a message about the library. I told you about the literacy program we want to set up. We usually get together Wednesdays if there's anything to discuss."

She waited for him to back down, to say, of course, call your friend. But if he did that, Kathy would likely ask what on earth Laura was rabbiting on about. Laura would expand and not clued in, Kathy would laugh, perhaps a little uneasily, and say that her friend was living in the past. That what Laura was talking about happened two years ago.

Should he protect her from such a harsh jolt or hand the phone over and let friend Kathy help unravel this tangle of yarn? He'd been prepared to field any blow when last night he'd questioned her about losing a baby, so what was different now? Other than the fact that he wouldn't have control over how this conversation wound out. No control at all.

He glanced over the luggage by the door then their wedding portrait, rehung on that wall. Were they home again or should he have kept the engine running?

Resigned, he stepped back.

"I won't be on the phone all day," she said, guessing at his problem. She could talk under water once she got started. "I just promised Kathy I'd call her early in the week to check."

"Take as long as you like."

He moved down the hall, feeling as if he were walking the corridor of a listing ship...as if he were traveling back, deeper and deeper through time. If he walked far enough, fast enough, maybe Kathy wouldn't ask questions and the present, and its regurgitated disappointments, wouldn't catch up...at least not today.

He ended up out on the eastern balcony. For what seemed like a lifetime, he absorbed the warm afternoon sun and soothing noise of the bush...the click of beetles, the far-off cry of a curlew. To his left, a couple of wallabies were perched on a monstrous black rock. They chewed rhythmically and occasionally scratched a soft gray ear. Their manner was lazy, instinctive, as it had been for many thousands of years. Bishop breathed in, and the strong scent of pine and eucalypt filled his lungs. As fervently as he'd wanted to leave here a year ago, he'd missed this place.

Hell, he'd missed this life.

But with Laura talking to that friend inside, he felt the cool edge of an axe resting at the back of his neck. Would it fall now? Tomorrow? Next week? How in God's name would this end?

Laura's footfalls sounded on the Brush Box timber floor behind him and the hairs on Bishop's nape stood up. But he was ready for the attack. Like Willis had said, it couldn't get any worse than the first time.

He angled around. Laura was striding out onto the porch but he couldn't read her expression.

"Kathy was home," she told him.

He folded down into a chair. "Uh-huh."

"But her daughter and grandbabies were over. She said there was no meeting this week."

The sick ache high in his stomach eased slightly and he sat straighter. "She did?"

That was it?

"She said she'd call back, but I said not to worry. We'd just got back from the city and had unpacking to do."

We?

He threaded his hands and, elbows on armrests, steepled two fingers under his chin.

"What did Kathy say to that?"

"The baby started to cry so she had to go."

Even more relieved, he exhaled slowly. One massive pothole avoided. Although, sure bet, there'd be more—and soon.

He'd tried being subtle as a brick with his prodding last night. The questions he'd asked about possible pregnancies hadn't ignited any sparks. Rather than approaching this dilemma at ramming speed, perhaps he ought to take this opportunity to scratch around and sprinkle a few seeds—ask some casual questions—that would grow in her mind day-to-day.

He lowered his hands. "How old is Kathy's grandbaby?"

Laura spotted the wallabies. A brisk mountain breeze combing her hair, she moved toward the railing for a better look. "Oh, three or four months, I suppose."

"Kathy has more than one grandchild?"

"Just the one."

And yet she'd said grandbabies, plural, earlier. An unconscious lapse to the present?

"What's the baby's name?"

Her gaze skated away from the bush and she lifted a wry brow. "I think it might be Twenty Questions." Then her grip on the railing slackened off and she gave a quick laugh. "Since when did you get so interested in the local librarian's grandchildren?"

"I'm interested in *you*."

Thinking how the afternoon light glistened like threads of golden copper through her hair, he found his feet and joined her.

Her smile turned sultry as she traced a fingertip down his arm. "How interested?"

"Interested enough."

"Enough to take another day off?"

He focused on her lips.

"Too easy."

The brightest smile he'd ever seen graced her face. But a heartbeat later the joy slipped away and some other emotion flared in her eyes. A cagey, almost frightened look, and he wondered what he'd said. But she didn't say a word, although he could tell from the questions in her eyes that she wanted to.

His hands found her shoulders. "What is it? What's wrong?"

Tell me what you're thinking.

"I—I'm not sure. I guess I'm not used to you taking time off. Not that I don't want you to. It's just…"

He dug a little more. "What?"

Her gaze darted around his face. The color had drained from her cheeks and some of the trust in her eyes had fallen away.

"Bishop…I have to ask." She stopped. Swallowed. Wet her lips. "Is there something you're not telling me?"

She'd just had the strangest feeling. More than a feeling. That niggling again, which, rather than waning, had grown, and a lot. Still, she couldn't put a precise finger on where, or what or who was behind it. She only knew it had been there in the way his assistant Willis had looked at her when he and Bishop had returned from their talk in the hotel lobby. There again when she'd examined their wedding picture after they'd arrived home and just now…some gesture, some word, had brought that awareness shooting like a cork to the surface of her consciousness. It was like a runaway thought she couldn't quite catch…a dream she couldn't quite remember. A moment ago Bishop had asked some everyday questions about a friend and yet, standing on this spot, with those wallabies on that rock and the sun at precisely this angle…

A hot pin had wedged under her ribs and, try as she might, she couldn't remove it. What had happened—what had been said—to make her feel as if she'd crashed into a ten-foot high brick wall at warp speed?

She focused on his eyes. *What aren't you telling me?*

"There is…something," he said.

The hot pin slid out and, breathing again, she leaned back, letting the railing catch her weight.

So it *hadn't* been her imagination. For a second she'd thought she might be going mad! But whatever it was nagging, there was a reason and Bishop was about to tell her.

"I haven't told you…" he began haltingly "…not enough anyway…how much you meant to me."

Like a well filling, her relief rose higher, but then that niggling pricked again and she frowned. What he'd said didn't quite make sense. The tense was wrong. *I haven't told you how much you* meant *to me?*

"You mean, you haven't told me how much I *mean* to you."

"I want you to know it now."

His tone was so grave and his expression… He looked almost sad.

Her heart melting, she found his hand and pressed it to her cheek as a lump of emotion fisted in her throat. Her husband loved her. *Really* loved her. She was so lucky. So much luckier than most.

"I know, darling," she murmured. "I feel the same way."

He seemed to consider his next words. She could almost see him lining them up in his mind.

"I was taken aback when I saw you lying in that hospital bed."

She thought that through and came to a conclusion.

"You thought something was wrong with my heart?" Oh, no! She wanted to hug him so tight. Reassure him everything was all right. "I would've been in a cardio ward. Besides, that's all under control." She turned her head to kiss his palm. "Easy."

That pin jabbed again, deeper and sharper this time and her heart missed a beat at the same instant her gaze trailed away and she tried to grasp on to and hold that elusive, annoying thought.

"I wasn't sure what to expect," he was saying.

Drifting back, she found his gaze again. "That's why you acted so strangely?"

He nodded. "I'd seen you in hospital before."

She narrowed her eyes, thinking back. She'd been in hospital in her younger years, but…

Certain beyond doubt, she shook her head. "I don't think so."

"No?"

The pin stabbed again, so deep it made her flinch. She held her chest and, a knee-jerk reaction, wound away from him. At the same time, a noise—a crunching kind of rattle—echoed to her left. Her gaze shot over. She expected to see—

She held her brow.

—she couldn't think what.

She concentrated to form a picture in her mind, but she only saw those wallabies bounding off; they must have pushed loose gravel over the side. Now their boomerang tails and strong hind legs were catapulting them away, farther into the brush.

Here one minute. Gone the next.

Gone for good.

Those words looped around in her mind. She shivered and hugged herself tight. Her mind was playing tricks. Tricks that were seriously doing her head in. But she had a remedy.

Shaky inside, she feigned a smile. She hated to sound fragile, but she needed to lie down.

"Bishop, do you mind if I take myself off to bed early? Our late night must be catching up."

"You have another headache."

"No. Just…tired." Taking her elbow, he ushered her inside. "Wake me up when you come to bed?" she asked.

As if to confirm it, he dropped a kiss on her crown. As

they moved down the hall, she felt compelled to ask him to promise. That's what a newly married bride would do, no matter how tired, right?

But the words didn't come. And as that pin pricked again—niggling, enflaming—she only wished she knew why.

Ten

The following day, Bishop accompanied Laura into the office of a local GP.

Colorful children's drawings hung on a corkboard, but Bishop's attention was drawn to the top of a filing cabinet and a Hamlet-type skull, only this skull exposed the complicated mass that made up the mysterious chambers of a human brain. A little creepy but, in this instance, rather fitting.

Dr. Chatwin, a woman in her thirties, gestured to a pair of chairs.

"Please take a seat, Mrs. Bishop. Mr. Bishop." While they made themselves comfortable, the doctor swept aside her long brunette ponytail and pulled in her chair. "Your husband spoke with me briefly this morning, Mrs. Bishop."

Dressed in a pale pink linen dress Bishop had always loved to see her in, Laura crossed her legs and held her knees. "Please, call me, Laura."

Dr. Chatwin returned the smile. "You hit your head last week and are experiencing some difficulties, is that right?"

"I wouldn't say that." Laura's clasped hands moved from her knees to her lap. "Not...*difficulties*."

The doctor's brows lifted and she leaned back in her chair. "Some issues with memory?"

Laura froze before her slender shoulders hitched back. "Some things have seemed...a little foggy."

Swinging back around, the doctor tapped a few words on her keyboard. "Any headaches, dizziness, sleeplessness, nausea?"

"One headache."

"Irritability, confusion?"

"I suppose some."

While Bishop stretched his legs and crossed his ankles, happy to let a professional take charge, the doctor performed the usual tests with her stethoscope then checked for uneven dilation of the pupils. She asked a few simple questions. What suburb they were in. Laura's full name. The date. She gave no outward sign of surprise when Laura announced a year two years past.

After tapping in a few notes, the doctor addressed them both. "You'd like to be referred to a specialist, is that right?"

Bishop replied. "Thank you. Yes."

Without argument, the doctor began writing the referral. "Dr. Stanza is considered the best neuro specialist in Sydney. This isn't an urgent case, however, so expect a wait."

Bishop straightened. "How long of a wait?"

"Call his practice," the doctor said, finishing the note. "They'll book you into his first available slot." After sliding the letter into an envelope, she scribbled the specialist's name on the front. "As you're both no doubt aware, there are instances of memory impairment associated with head trauma due to a fall. The doctor last week would've told you recollections usually return over time, although it's not unusual for the events leading up to the incident, the incident itself and directly after to be lost permanently." The doctor pushed back her chair and stood. "You're not presenting with any physical concerns, Laura." Her warm brown eyes shining, she handed the envelope to Bishop and finished with a sincere smile. "I'm sure you'll be fine, particularly with your husband taking such good care of you."

Five minutes later, Laura slid into the car, feeling tense and knowing that it showed, while Bishop reclined behind the wheel, ignited the engine, then slipped her a curious look.

"Something wrong?"

Laura didn't like to complain. Bishop was simply making certain she was cared for. As she'd told the doctor, she had felt irritable on occasion. Some things were a little confusing… clothes she couldn't remember in the wardrobe, a new potted plant in the kitchen…that truly odd feeling she'd had yesterday on the eastern porch when those wallabies had bounded away. But the doctor hadn't seemed concerned. She'd indicated that the missing bits and pieces would fall into place soon enough.

The broad ledge of Bishop's shoulders angled toward her. "Laura, tell me."

"I don't need to go to a specialist," she blurted out before she could stop herself. "You heard Dr. Chatwin. No physical problems. Nothing urgent. I don't want to waste a specialist's time. It'll probably cost a mortgage payment just to walk through the door."

A corner of his mouth curved up. "We don't have a mortgage."

"That's not the point. Dr. Chatwin said she was sure I'd be okay."

"I'm sure you will be, too. But we'll make an appointment with the specialist and if we don't need it, we'll cancel."

She crossed her arms. "It's a waste of everyone's time."

"If it is, then there's no harm done." His voice lowered and he shifted the car into Drive. "But you're going."

She stared, not pleased, out the window as they swerved onto the road that would take them home. She loved that

Bishop was a leader, that he wanted to protect and care for her. But she didn't need to be bossed around. She hated visiting doctors and hospitals. How many times did she have to say she was okay?

She stole a glance at his profile, the hawkish nose and proud jutting chin and her arms slowly unraveled.

And another thing...he hadn't come to bed last night. When she'd woken, his side hadn't been slept in. Seeing the covers still drawn, the pillow still plump, had put an unsettling feeling in her stomach, as if she'd already foreseen or had dreamed that he wouldn't be there when she woke. Not that she'd tell Bishop that. He'd blow it way out of proportion. She didn't need to be asked more questions.

But perhaps Bishop needed the green flag from this specialist before giving his consent to her falling pregnant. He liked to have all the pegs lined up before going forward with anything. And he took the whole becoming a father thing ultraseriously which, on a baser level, she was grateful for.

So she would grit her teeth, visit this specialist, get the all clear, and once she had a clean bill of health, there should be absolutely nothing to stand in their way.

Three days later, splitting wood for the fireplace, Bishop set another log on the chopping block and, running a hand up over the smooth handle, raised his axe. The blade came down with a whoosh and a *thunk* that echoed through the surrounding forest of trees.

He'd taken the rest of the week off, and every minute since that doctor's visit, he'd waited, wondering if this would be the day when his metaphorical axe would fall. Every minute inhabiting that house, sharing that bed, he was conscious of living out the mother of all deceptions.

But, if he were being manipulative, it was with good reason. He was a man stuck in the middle of a particularly difficult set of circumstances...locked in a game of nerves where he could anticipate the moves and yet still had little control over how this rematch would end.

Grinding his teeth, Bishop set another log on the block. He was about to bring the axe down when Laura appeared, carrying his cell phone, traversing the half dozen back stairs and crossing the lawn to where he waited near a yellow clump of melaleuca. With her, she brought the floral scent of her perfume as well as the aromas of the casserole and chocolate sponge dessert she was preparing. He'd missed her home-cooked meals more than he'd realized. Hell, he'd missed a lot of things.

"It's Willis." After handing over his phone, she dropped a kiss on his cheek then inspected the blemish-free sky. A frown creased her brow. "You should put a hat on." She headed off with a skip. "I'll bring you one."

He was about to call out *don't bother,* but he liked her looking after him. The meals, the smiles. The love.

His attention on the sexy bounce of her step, Bishop put the phone to his ear. On the other end of the line, Willis didn't beat around the bush.

"I don't know how much longer I can put them off," Willis said, referring to the potential buyers of Bishop Scaffolds. "They want to speak with you, Sam."

Having set the axe down, Bishop wiped sweat from his brow with his forearm. Laura was right. He should wear a hat.

He moved into the shade. "Not this week, Willis."

"Early next week then."

"I'll let you know." He tipped his nose in the direction of the kitchen and inhaled. "Laura's doing beef Stroganoff. You should smell it."

Willis stayed on track. "I've given them as much as I can with regard to figures and projections. But the guy keeps calling. You should at least give him ten minutes on the phone. It's only good business."

Bishop understood Willis's point. He should phone, but he wasn't in the right frame of mind. He was anxious about when, or if, Laura's memory would return, but on another level he was feeling, in a strange sense, settled; he worried he'd tell the buyers he was no longer interested and later regret that he hadn't moved on the opportunity. So it was better, for now, to wait and see what transpired.

Bishop swapped the phone to the other ear. "I'll call him next week."

A long silence echoed down the line. Bishop dug a booted toe in the black soil while he waited for Willis to spit out whatever else was bothering him.

"You want me to be frank, Sam?"

"That's what I pay you for."

"Laura still hasn't got her memory back?"

"Correct."

"I know you want to help, but there's a good chance the past will all come back and you'll be in the doghouse again. Even if those memories don't return, you're still going to have to tell her the truth." When Bishop only stared into the sun, scrubbing his jaw, Willis prodded. "You know that, right?"

"It's not that simple."

"I don't imagine it is. That's why you need to be doubly cautious."

Hell, cautious was his middle name.

But Willis was right. He was getting carried away. Getting tangled up between past, present and possible future. One of them needed to keep their feet firmly planted on the ground.

Willis changed the subject. "Are you coming tomorrow night?"

To his birthday bash? Bishop moved back to the axe he'd left leaning beside the block. There'd be people there from work. People who knew about his divorce. He doubted anyone would have the guts to ask either him or Laura directly about that, or the fact that they looked to be together again. If anyone did...

With his free hand, he swung up the axe and inspected the blade. The sharp edge gleamed in the sunlight.

Bottom line, he wanted to help her remember, right? If things got interesting tomorrow evening and she started to come around too quickly, he'd whisk her away and begin explaining. Not a moment he looked forward to.

But Willis had hit the proverbial nail. He and Laura couldn't live in the past. Not indefinitely, anyway.

"We'll be there," Bishop said. "Laura's excited about it."

"Great. We'll find a few minutes to talk then."

Bishop was signing off when Laura strolled out again, Akubra in hand. She stuck it on his head and told him to leave it there.

Grinning, he tipped the rim. "Yes, ma'am."

"Is everything okay at the office?"

"Everything's good."

"It's been wonderful having you home this week, but if you need to go in, don't stay because you're worried about me." When he only looked at her, she set her hands on her hips. "I feel great, Bishop." Then, shading her eyes from the sun, she asked, "What will we give Willis for his birthday? Is he interested in chess?"

"Not that I know of."

"You've never asked?"

"It's never come up."

"But you have a chessboard in your office. The one I gave you as a wedding gift."

Twenty-four karat gold and pewter pieces. It was the most exquisite set he'd ever seen. But something in her tone set his antenna quivering. These past days they'd spent so much time together, taking walks, enjoying picnics, at other times staying indoors to ponder over the chessboard. Laura had been testy when they'd left Dr. Chatwin's office on Tuesday;

she didn't want to see a specialist. And she'd seemed so off balance that evening on the porch—Monday. But since that time she hadn't shown any obvious signs of feeling foggy, as she called it, or agitated. Quite the opposite. She'd seemed particularly breezy.

And yet subtle things she'd say or do let him know that some connections, or at least curiosities, were still clicking. The thing that struck him most was that, despite whatever connections she might secretly be making, Laura didn't seem any the less in love with him. In fact, her love seemed to grow every day.

As for him...

Laura's next question took him by surprise.

"Have you heard from your parents lately?"

He gave the obvious reply. "They live in Perth."

"I know that, silly. But there is such a thing as a phone."

Some years ago, his parents had moved to Western Australia, a six-hour flight from Sydney. They'd flown back for his wedding and had approved of Laura in every way. He only wished his mother hadn't cried so much during the ceremony. Without asking he knew she was wishing that his brother had been there; she'd made sure to tell him later. Bishop understood the emotion—he felt it, too. But on that one day, Lord knows he hadn't needed it.

He'd vowed if anything so tragic ever happened to him—if, God forbid, he lost a child—he'd keep the memories, the pain and regrets—to himself. But in hindsight, he should have been more open about his feelings after Laura's miscarriage rather than building that wall...pretending it hadn't hurt as much as it had. As Laura stood here now, the mountains a dramatic backdrop and the sun lighting her hair, he knew he ought to have shared more of himself, particularly when she'd stayed shut down.

She'd needed comfort then, not steel.

"Maybe we should invite them out for a couple of weeks,"

Laura went on. "Your mother seems so sweet. It'd be nice to get to know her more."

"I'm sure she'd like that, too."

"You could call your folks tonight after dinner."

"I could do that." But he wouldn't.

"I should probably start getting the guest wing ready."

"Laura, my parents travel a lot. They might not even be home."

And as they walked arm in arm back to the house, she leaning her head against his shoulder and a palm folded over the hand he had resting on her waist, Bishop decided that was the excuse he'd give after pretending to call.

The following evening, he and Laura arrived in Sydney for Willis's birthday bash forty minutes late. For a present, they decided on a dinner voucher at one of Sydney's most exclusive restaurants. As Bishop slid out from the car now, the lights and sound coming from the party venue descended upon him. He'd tried to stay optimistic, but he couldn't see tonight working out well. Someone was bound to say something that would trip a switch and Laura would naturally want to know more. Most likely she'd grow suspicious. Agitated. There could be a highly embarrassing scene.

It wasn't too late to back out.

Instead, Bishop sucked it up, swung around the back of the car and opened Laura's door.

"Willis knows a lot of people," Laura said, surveying the elite restaurant as she slid out. Through the generous bank of streetfront windows, a throng of people could be seen milling, talking and generally having a good time. Wringing her pocketbook under her chin, Laura hesitated.

Bishop's palm settled on her back. "We don't have to go in if you'd rather not."

The pocketbook lowered, her shoulders squared, and she pinned on a smile. He guessed that at some deeper hidden level where memories waited to be restored, she was as worried about this evening as he was.

"I want to go in," she told him, but then rolled her teeth over her bottom lip. "I'm just a little anxious. I don't know many of the people you work with."

Bishop straightened his tie. She'd know fewer of them tonight.

They climbed the stairs, entering through tall timber paneled doors decorated with colorful leadlight, and a DJ's music, underlined with general chatter, grew louder. There must've been a hundred people talking, drinking, laughing at anecdotes and discussing politics or the latest Hollywood gossip. Bishop's gaze swept over the group. No Willis in sight. In fact, he couldn't see anyone he knew. But then a familiar, animated face emerged from the crowd.

Ava Prynne worked in Bishop Scaffolds's administrative section. Tonight she wore her platinum-blond hair in cascading ringlets that bobbed past the shoulders of a snug-fitting aqua-blue dress that barely covered her thighs. When she saw him, Ava, champagne glass in manicured hand, sashayed over.

"Mr. Bishop! I was hoping you'd come."

"I've said before, Ava, call me Sam."

He didn't agree with those formalities in the office.

Ava's gray eyes sparkled beneath the chandelier light and she breathed out his name. "Sam."

Bishop cleared his throat. He hadn't been aware that Miss Prynne had a crush on him until this moment.

Laura leaned across and introduced herself. "Do you work at my husband's company, Ava?"

The blonde's gaze slid across. Her smile disappeared at the same time Bishop's stomach kicked and he bit his inside cheek. *Already it begins.*

Ava looked Laura up and down. "Husband?"

Bishop waited for the answer, then the next question, then

the next. He might feel sick to his gut, but what else could he do?

But before Laura could speak and confirm that the man to whom this woman was so obviously attracted had been married three months, a uniformed waiter with a tray appeared.

"Drink, sir, madam?"

Thankful for the intervention, Bishop grabbed a juice—he was driving back—and collected a champagne cocktail for Laura.

He nodded at Ava Prynne's glass. "Top up?"

Ava's curious gaze, swinging from Laura back to her boss, lightened a little. "Uh, no, thank you...*Sam*." But the smile she had for him fell as she looked back to Laura, then she manufactured an excuse to leave behind an awkward situation. "Katrina from accounts has just walked in. I'll see you both later." Ava and her blue micro dress hurried off.

Laura's brow quirked at an amused angle. "Lucky I'm not a jealous woman."

"You have nothing to be jealous of."

He'd said the words before he'd thought, but it was true. Laura had never had reason to think he had eyes for anyone but her. She still didn't. Ava Prynne, Annabelle...no one compared.

Tables set with gleaming cutlery and fragrant multicolored centerpieces occupied the far end of the room. To their left, waitstaff manned a line of bains-marie filled with steaming dishes. The tantalizing aromas of roast beef, mornay and Chinese cuisine seeped into his lungs.

Ready to set off toward the food and avoid any more awkward introductions for the moment, he tipped his chin at the spread. "The buffet's out."

Her nose wrinkled. "I'm not that hungry yet. Are you?"

"I can wait." In fact, he could wait until they got home. He'd thought they could handle whatever came from tonight but now, whether it might seem rude or strange, God how he wanted to leave. But he could delay…keep them alone and together for a time.

"Would you like to dance?"

Laura's emerald eyes lit up. "You recognize it, too."

"Recognize what?"

"That song." She sidled up to him, toying with the silk knot at his throat. "It's our bridal waltz."

He concentrated and the memories the tune stirred left a warm place in his chest. He cast a glance around for a dance floor, but couldn't find one.

Laura craned to peer over the heads of the crowd. "There's a courtyard through those French doors."

Bishop smiled. More private than he'd hoped.

"In that case," he offered his arm, "may I have this dance?"

They cut a path through the pack and emerged in a private courtyard. Over the fainter music drifting out, the nearby trickling of a fountain could be heard. Above them, the moon was a pale yellow claw hanging amid a quiet tapestry of twinkling lights. Feeling as if they were the only couple on earth, he brought her to the center of the cobblestoned area, instinctively immersed himself in her eyes, gathered her in his arms and began to slow dance.

She rested her cheek against his shoulder. The floral scent that was so distinctly Laura wrapped itself around him. His eyes drifting shut, he grazed his jaw over her crown, soaking up the magic that was "them" again for however long it lasted.

Moving against him, she looked up. Her eyes were dreamy, her lips moist and slightly parted.

From his heart he said, "You look incredible tonight."

She wore a black evening dress, low at the back, with a high halter neck, the ties of which were studded with glittering diamantés. But Laura looked as breathtaking in a pair of tatty weekend shorts as an evening gown. In *anything*. Or nothing.

She was the kind of woman who could never lose her beauty. It was far more than classic bone structure and those large well-lashed eyes. Laura had a quality that defied and superseded simple beauty. No matter how old, she would always glow and turn heads.

"So," she said, with that seductress's smile, "you're not sorry you married me?"

She'd said it teasingly, but a certain light in her eyes hinted that she was digging and not simply for compliments.

Holding his easy expression, he rocked her gently around. "Why would you say that?"

"There're a lot of beautiful women in there."

"The most beautiful is dancing with me."

Happiness radiated from her every pore. It hadn't been empty flattery. He'd meant every word.

Leaning her cheek against his shoulder, she gazed up at the stars.

"Have you ever thought what we'd be doing ten years from now? Twenty?"

He gave an honest answer. "I'm more focused on tonight."

"I wonder how much of the world we'll have seen together. How many different celebrations we'll have had." Her gaze lowered from the stars and met his. "I wonder if we'll be as in love as we are now."

His heart thumped harder. He didn't answer. Hell, didn't know what to say. So, with the slightest pinch between her brows, she rested her cheek against his lapel again.

After an uncertain silence, she asked in a soft, curious voice, "Are you happy, Bishop?"

He fought not to stiffen or clear his throat.

"Don't I look happy?"

She peered up again and warm trust filled her eyes. "Yes. And we'll always be." Her hand tightened slightly on his. "I was thinking, after I see that specialist next week, after he gives me the all clear—"

"Let's get there first," he cut in.

But she plowed on. "I thought we could talk more about having a baby."

His jaw tensing, he looked away. But he'd known that request had been waiting in the wings. Given this romantic setting, how close they felt right now, he shouldn't have been surprised that she'd brought it up.

His palm moved to stroke the smooth dip low on her back. "We'll talk about it when we get home."

"I don't want to stir anything up," she added, "but we need to talk about it again sometime."

He cocked a brow. Was she going to push it now? "Laura, this isn't the place."

She flinched and he cursed himself. He'd sounded dismissive, patronizing, when he knew full well how much having a baby meant to her, probably better than *she* did at this point. He was only trying to delay. Delay long enough for all her memories to return.

Or to consider more that other idea...half-baked and brainless though it was. What would happen if Laura fell pregnant again only this time she went full-term and gave birth to a healthy child? Given her condition, he was well aware the notion was appalling. While they slow danced beneath this moon and he thought about taking her home, however, it was also dangerously appealing.

He'd never wanted a divorce. He should never have left that day.

The music faded and inside someone took a mic.

"Everyone, it's time for the cake!"

Stepping back, Laura toyed with one diamond drop earring, his wedding gift to her two years ago. "Guess that's our cue."

"We'll talk later. Promise."

She gave a wan smile that said she'd like to believe him.

Back inside the crowd was congregating at the far end of the room. A massive cake was displayed on a round table, its decorated top ablaze with candles.

A heckler called out, "Blow 'em out, Willis, or the place'll burn down."

Dressed in a tux, Willis laughed along.

Someone hollered, "Speech!"

The man of the hour held up his hands and eventually everyone quieted.

"First I want to thank you all for coming tonight," Willis said. "The big three-oh is certainly a milestone. But I've enjoyed every step along the way. Best one being the day I met my wife." He held out a hand and the lady in question joined him, her face stained with a blush. "Life wasn't complete until I met you." He brought his wife close and gifted her with a heartfelt kiss.

Someone called out, "You're getting soppy in your old age, Will."

"I'll get soppier still," he called back. "I have an announcement." Oozing love and commitment, he brought his petite wife closer. "Hayley and I are having a baby."

A hoot went up. Glasses clicked while Willis and Hayley embraced like the young lovers they were, with all their future ahead of them.

His heart sinking to his knees, Bishop dared a sidelong look at Laura.

Her eyes glistened with unshed tears. When she caught him studying her, she forced a carefree laugh.

"I'm so happy for them." When she lowered her head, he read her thoughts. *I want us to be that happy.*

Bishop ran a hand down her back. They'd come tonight, had a nice dance. Now, after that announcement, it was past time to leave.

He was about to say they'd go home when Willis appeared

before them, surrounded by well-wishers raising their glasses.

Willis nodded to them both. "Glad you could make it. Laura, you look wonderful."

Faultless in company, Laura resurrected her smile. "Congratulations." She came forward and pressed a light kiss on his cheek. "You and your wife must be so happy."

"We've been trying for a while so, yes, we're both over the moon."

Having received dozens of congratulatory hugs, Hayley joined them. Her face shone like Laura's had when she'd known she was carrying their child—the same rosy tint to her cheeks, the same exuberant confidence knowing that soon she would be the mother of a healthy, beautiful babe.

Willis brought his wife close again. "Hayley, you remember Sam Bishop. And this is Laura."

Bishop held his breath and his gaze darted around at the faces of onlookers. Some murmured behind their hands. Others, less discreet, openly gaped at the boss's stunning companion. He guessed the women might have glimpsed the wedding bands on both their hands.

"I've heard so much about you," Hayley said.

"I'm looking forward to getting to know you and your husband better. He's only started at Bishop Scaffolds recently?"

Bishop held himself taut, but Hayley showed no sign of inappropriate curiosity and only smiled. Obviously, Willis had clued his wife in.

"Willis said you invited us to your home in the Blue Mountains. I'll look forward to it."

"You might be showing by then."

Hayley beamed and touched her belly. "I'm only twelve weeks. The doctor said another month or so before I feel him move."

"You want a boy?"

"I'd be happy with either—" she sent her husband a knowing grin "—but I think Willis would like a son."

Willis's hand covered his wife's where it rested. "What man doesn't?"

Bishop felt Laura's gaze edge over to him and his neck burned. Yes, he'd wanted a son. He'd wanted a family. Still did.

But he hadn't let himself think that way for so long.

Hayley dropped a kiss on her husband's cheek. "I'm going to serve the cake. Would you like some?" she asked them both.

"None for me," Bishop answered.

At the same time Laura said, "I'm good."

And Bishop stopped and thought, *This must be the first time either of us have passed on dessert.*

As Willis and his wife moved away, Bishop found and held Laura's hand. "Would you like to stay?"

"Actually, would you mind if we go?"

She was looking at her shoes and he suspected those tears had welled in her eyes again. She might be happy for Hayley, but she was also envious, and hurting because of it. Her logical side would be assuring her that her husband would agree they should try to conceive while her subconscious might be reliving the miscarriage and heartache that followed. That would explain why she felt so fragile. So ready to break.

Only Laura didn't know that.

"I'll take you home." He threaded his arm through hers and added, "We'll talk."

He couldn't wait for the specialist's appointment. She needed to be told and she needed to hear it from him, no matter the consequences. No matter if she slapped his face and called him every name invented.

But as he began to lead her out she stopped. Her glistening lashes lifted and her needful eyes found his.

"I don't want to talk. Bishop, I want to make a baby. I want to make one tonight."

Eleven

During the drive home, she and Bishop didn't discuss her no-frills request. She'd said she wanted to make a baby...not sometime in the future or next month, but tonight!

Rather he turned on a CD, and when the road didn't demand two on the wheel, held her hand, his thumb grazing the back of her fingers. She wanted to speak with him more about it. It was one thing to insist and another to have her husband's blessing.

The reality was that they'd only been married a short time. They didn't need to leap into this, particularly given the roadblocks Bishop perceived to be in their way—her heart condition, his fear of losing a child. But when Willis had made his announcement tonight, something greater than logic or fear had whispered in her ear. Spoken to her heart. Some inner deliberate voice had embraced her and stated, *Now is the time.*

Call it women's intuition or blind faith. As weird as it sounded, she only knew she had to act.

Their baby would start off smaller than a pinhead but from the moment of conception, the life growing inside of her would be a person with a soul, already loved, so very much longed for. When the good news was confirmed, Bishop would overcome his concerns because, as Willis and Hayley's joy had proven tonight, hearing that you were soon to be parents must be the very best feeling in the world. She couldn't wait to know it herself.

As they moved from the garage into the living room, Bishop took her hand, ready to lead her to the bedroom, she guessed, but she pulled back. Already in her mind she knew how this scene should play out, how and where she wanted to fall pregnant. In the quiet of the shadows, she reached behind, tugged the bow at her nape, and the black evening dress rustled into a silky puddle on the rug at her feet.

Bishop's hot gaze raked her body, drinking in every line, every curve she knew that he admired and loved. In that moment, she felt the heat in the room, in their blood, grow and thicken and beat. Tossing back hair fallen over her eyes, she tried to make out his expression in the shadows. She wanted to know what he was feeling other than fast-rising physical arousal.

Was he concerned? Feeling trapped?

"I'd like to stay out here by the fire," she said.

Bishop lobbed his jacket at a chair while his gaze skimmed over her tingling breasts then dropped to take in her quivering belly and the black silk triangle covering the apex at her thighs. As she stood before him, trembling, anticipating, he removed his tie, purposefully flicked open each button then rolled his shoulders out of the shirt.

Gloriously naked from the belt up, he moved forward and, in the gray darkness of the room, their eyes connected. He reached for her. Warm palms shaped down the column of her throat before arcing out over her shoulders and upper arms. His grip tightened slightly. She heard the groaning rumble in his chest as his fingers fanned to curve around the outside of her breasts.

He stepped closer and then his face was hovering over hers, so close their noses touched. His voice was deep and husky.

"You want that fire now?"

That's what she'd asked for, and yet now that his hands were upon her, she didn't want him to leave, not even to build that fire. She wanted to say they could create their own. Already, flames were licking a blistering causeway through her veins.

But then she glimpsed a vision of Bishop prodding the kindling, a theater of light and shadow rippling over his perfect torso, shoulders and arms. She smiled into his eyes.

"A fire would be good."

His thumbs slid up the underside of her breasts, brushing the aching tips and making her light-headed before his hands slipped away and he moved toward the fireplace. While he collected small logs from the stack, Laura heeled off her shoes and hunted down blankets and pillows. When she returned, Bishop didn't turn or acknowledge her, even as she made their campout bed. As she spread a blanket out over the large center rug, she studied his broad back and her stomach began to churn.

He wanted to make love, she was certain, but was he that agitated over what she'd asked of him tonight? She'd been firm about what she'd wanted. He hadn't said no. She knew he was way less than one hundred percent comfortable with this. She hated the thought of him being angry with her then having that anger linger and, perhaps, burrow deeper and spread. She would hate that at any time, but particularly if she were to fall pregnant.

A shiver scuttled over her skin and she held the second blanket to her chest.

Maybe she should tell him that she knew she was pushing; they had plenty of time yet. Having a child—her own flesh-and-blood child—was important to her. But so important she was willing to risk her relationship with her husband? Risk their marriage? Still, she couldn't agree to adoption when there was every reason to believe she was fertile, and Bishop, too.

Another shiver—more a chill—racked her body. As the warm feeling in her tummy began to wane, she wrapped the blanket around her shoulders. She was about to tell Bishop to forget the fire, that they should head off to the bedroom, or perhaps not make love at all. Earlier he'd said they should talk.

But then he turned to face her.

Balanced on haunches, he smiled, the kind of smile that left her blissfully warm all over. An expression that, in an instant, touched and reassured her like nothing else could.

He wasn't angry. She'd let her imagination run away on her. He loved and supported her in everything, just as she loved and supported him.

He noticed the blanket cloaked around her.

"I didn't realize you were that cool," he said. "I'll get this heat turned up."

Laura slid down onto their "bed" and let the cover slip from one shoulder. Hugging her knees, she soaked up every smoldering movement he made. Arranging the logs, seeing to the kindling. After pushing to his feet and scouting down matches on the mantel, he struck one. A flare went up, illuminating the dramatic angle of his jaw, the *GQ* dimensions of that chest.

Bishop was classically handsome with the rugged features Australian men were famous for. He possessed an air of confidence that was innate but never overstated. She loved the way he laughed and moved and smelled and felt. What would have become of her life if they hadn't met and fallen so instantly, deeply in love…if he ever truly turned his back on her and left?

Her gaze drifted up to their wedding picture. The frame was glowing in the firelight, but the photo itself was dark. She could still make out the happy couple, one dressed in black, the other in white.

Making herself comfortable, she lay back on the pillows.

She was a homebody where Bishop was a highflyer. One was step-by-step cautious, the other more casual. But she didn't see herself and Bishop as different so much as complementary. Perfect foils.

Ideal as man and wife.

When orange flames curled high behind the grill and the logs were crackling nicely, Bishop rotated back. His eyes glued to hers, he heeled off his shoes, unbuckled his leather belt with one deft pull, and stepped from the rest of his clothes. She reached out and he moved closer, kneeling beside her carefully, as if she were a bubble that might burst at any time. His face in the flickering light appeared both tender and intense, the prisms of his eyes black but for the occasional sparkling flash of blue.

With a fluid movement, he spread out beside her. The masculine breadth of his chest rose and fell in a regular hypnotic rhythm. His body radiated its own perfect heat. Cords, ridging his biceps, wound down to his equally strong lower arms. Still lower, his heavy erection demanded relief.

When he reached for her, drew her close, she swallowed a short breath. They'd made love before, this past week so many times, but what was unfolding here, the prize this particular union might bring, left her giddy.

Her mouth welcomed his and he gathered her close. His hand smoothed over her hair, trailed her cheeks then lifted her chin high so that his kiss could penetrate deeper. For an endless moment, she reveled in the feel of his chest pushing against her breasts, the way he moved enough for the friction and simmering tension to build naturally. Swiftly.

As the kiss eased, she drove down a breath and her arms came from around his neck. Cupping the sandpaper roughness of his jaw, she spoke to his eyes. From her heart.

"Know what?"

"What?"

"I'll love you forever."

Beneath the shifting shadows of his eyes, a fire ignited. Then he grinned, a slow slant of a smile.

"Forever," he said. "Is that a promise?"

"On my soul."

That fire blazed again then his mouth covered hers, possessing her, thrilling her, filling her with a desire that was rare and precious and all theirs alone.

If two people were ever meant to be together, it was them. One wasn't complete without the other, and having a child could only make that need stronger. Nothing would go wrong. Not when everything about them…about this…felt so right.

Reluctantly, his mouth broke from hers. She sighed to her bones as his tongue trailed down between her breasts and his thumb and forefinger toyed with a nipple until liquid heat pooled at her center and her hips tipped invitingly up. He dropped loving kisses over her breasts, his head tilting this way then that as his tongue and teeth worked to create a cadence that set fireworks off in her head.

Her touch wandered down, over the superb landscape of his chest and abdomen, then lower until her fingertips combed through strong, dark hair and curled around a shaft that felt too hard to be human. Savoring the heat and the rock, she gripped him low. As his tongue flicked and teased, she dragged her hand up, the pressure unforgivably firm the way he liked it. On reflex, his teeth tightened and her hips bucked while her nipple burned and cried out for more.

"Do it, Bishop." Already, his skin was deliciously damp. She tried to slip beneath him at the same time she whispered in his ear, "I've never wanted you more."

Every muscle in his body seemed to lock. She ran her hand down his side and her fingers came away wet. As he moved above her, her head rocked back. Mind and body, she was more than ready.

He kissed her thoroughly, a caress that made her tremble so badly, her core throb so much, she worried she might climax then and there. His palm slid from her hip to the mound at the top of her inner thighs. His touch curled between, slid over that most sensitive spot, and she gasped, clinging on and concentrating on the purest of energies smoldering there. His touch swam up, circled around, and again. Laura ground against him as the pulse inside of her beat faster.

He nuzzled her neck. "You want to do this?"

Make a baby? "Yes. Do you?"

He took less time to answer than she expected.

"I do."

He scooped up her hip, captured her mouth with his, and as her leg wound around his thigh, he nudged in, naked and hot. A blissful goose-tingly shudder rolled through her. She bit down on her lower lip and moved beneath him, willing him deeper inside, feeling the ceiling beginning to lift as his concentrated rhythm bit by bit increased.

She was vaguely aware of the hiss and crackle of the fire… the smell of wood and passion smoking. Then the pulsing and glowing deep in her womb was absorbing all her attention. As he murmured her name and his thrusts became urgent, she clenched her inner muscles, clung to his arms, and sent up a prayer that this would all turn out well.

A heartbeat later, the blast went off, and fire and ecstasy consumed them both.

The next morning, rubbing his eyes, Bishop rolled over and stared at the empty space beside him. After they'd made love last night in front of the fire, they'd shifted into her bedroom. *Their* bedroom. Where had she gone?

He elbowed up, sniffed the air.

No smells from the kitchen.

Sweeping back the covers, he set his bare feet on the floor and craned his neck. No sign of life from the attached bathroom, either. He dragged on some trousers, trod out into the hall and looked up then down and up again.

"Laura! Laura, where are you?"

A twinge knotted high in his gut.

But she couldn't have vanished. Most likely she was on one of the verandas or lounging around the setting on the eastern porch. It was her favorite place, particularly in the mornings. His, too.

He moved past the empty kitchen; no breakfast preparation in sight. Past the offices, the library and other rooms. His heartbeat picking up, he strode out onto the porch and flung a glance around. The mountains murmured with the usual soothing noises of the Australian bush—a kookaburra laughing, insects clicking. Everything was eerily calm.

That twinge grew into an ache and he turned back to the house. Perhaps she'd taken the car and gone into town. She was a stickler for having her pantry well stocked.

At a jog, his soles slapped on the timber hall floor all the way to the other end of the house. He flung back the adjoining door.

Both cars were parked in the garage, engines cold. Bishop rotated in a slow, tight circle. The walls started to close in and the edges of his world began to darken. He couldn't shake the thought that had scratched at the back of his mind since he'd opened his eyes and found her gone. A horrible, this-can't-be-happening-again feeling.

His heart in his throat, he sprinted out the door.

Flying down the front steps, he spotted her in that long red negligee she'd slipped into late last night. She was exactly where he'd worried she would be—standing on that footbridge, right on the edge, peering out as if in a trance.

"Laura!"

Panic rocketing through him, he shot off. He didn't stop

until, out of breath, he reached her and snatched her away from any possibility of another fall. His grip hard on her arms, he willed her to meet his eyes. But her gaze—her mind—was a thousand miles away.

He held her face, tilted up her chin. Gradually her gaze tracked back from some faraway spot. But she looked at him as if he were a stranger. Or as if she couldn't see him at all.

"Are you all right? Laura, answer me."

Her brow creased and she shut her eyes tight. After a heart-stopping moment, she shook her head slowly.

"I…I'm not sure." Her eyes blinked open and she seemed to focus more. "I woke before you and decided to take a walk. I didn't mean to…I didn't mean to come this way…this far." The distant look in her eyes cleared more and then she shuddered enough for goose bumps to rise on her arms.

"Bishop, I had the weirdest… I think it was a dream."

"Come inside." He swallowed against the lump rising in his throat. "It's cold out."

But she wound away, edging two steps back toward the railing. As if dizzy, she touched her brow with one hand, gripped the wooden rail with the other, and peered over the edge at the bed of hedges below.

With measured steps, Bishop moved to join her. Her hands were shaking. So were his.

This was it—the moment when all the snippets that Laura had been too proud to mention these past days filtered together and gelled. He'd planned to tell her everything last night. No matter the outcome, he believed she needed to be brought back to the present. But he'd been weak. When she'd told him she wanted to make a baby, he'd remembered the thought he'd had earlier…about her falling pregnant and being able to keep the baby and their marriage this time. To his core he'd known it was wrong and yet he'd gone ahead and had sex with his ex without protection.

Last night at the party had affected him as much as it had her. He wanted a son. He wanted to be with his wife.

Had he fallen back in love with Laura?

He wanted to feel what she had felt this past week without reservation. But this moment, when she began to remember—remember it all—had constantly played on his mind, holding the possibility of total surrender to hope back.

"I remembered a miscarriage," Laura murmured, her gaze turning inward. "I remember pain. And blood. Lying in the hospital and..." She cocked her head as though she were trying to see the memory from a different angle. Then her face screwed up as if someone had pinched her. "I remember... *crying*. But that can't be. I've never been pregnant. I've never lost a child. If that ever happened..."

Stripped of defenses, she found his gaze and unshed tears filled her eyes.

Bishop leaned his hip against the rail. Now the process had begun, the memories would flow like water from a running tap. First the miscarriage, then the growing distance between them, the fall, the arguments, the total disintegration of trust. Of anything remotely resembling faith. He couldn't help but believe that last night, when they'd made love without contraception, had brought this about. What would she have to say when the final pieces settled into place? More importantly...

Last night had they created a baby?

"We'll go sit down." His hands on her waist, he encouraged her away.

"It doesn't make sense, does it?" Wincing again, she held her head. "It's all mixed-up."

He rubbed the back of his neck. He'd never felt more helpless in his life. "Come on, Laura. Come inside."

Finally, she agreed and carefully they made their way back to the house. He took her into his office and helped her as she lowered into the Chesterfield couch, confusion still stamped on her face.

Anxious, she rubbed her palms down the lap of her negligee and sent him a lame smile. "I suppose I do need to see that doctor later in the week."

He found a blanket. After wrapping it around her shoulders, he folded down close beside her. "You'll be okay."

She smiled, but then searched his eyes. "There's something that's been bugging me more than anything." Her lashes were wet and a pulse beat erratically at the side of her throat. "Last week, you said something," she started. "You said that you wished you'd told me more often how much I meant to you. I said it didn't quite make sense." She inhaled, then blew the breath out in a shaky stream. "Bishop, now I want to know. Tell me. *Please*."

His head began to tingle. Nausea burned up the back of his throat.

You knew this would happen. You thought you'd be prepared.

But he wasn't. He was seriously low on preparedness. All the things he'd rehearsed in his head didn't seem even half-adequate now.

She stiffened as her hands wound into that red silk. "Whatever it is, don't hold back. I trust you. I want to know. I want to know everything."

He took one of her hands in his and held it tight. His voice was deep, but remarkably calm.

"I wasn't sure what to do. But when the doctor said I could take you home…that you'd remember in time, I was cornered."

"Cornered in what way?"

"When we got home, things got more mixed-up for you. Certain things were making less and less sense, right?"

She examined their entwined hands and nodded. "I didn't want to worry you. I didn't think it was a big deal. I'd find clothes, shoes, dishes I couldn't remember buying. I thought the plants around the house had grown or perhaps I'd shrunk. Even looking at our wedding photo..." Her face blanched. "Something didn't sit right."

He siphoned in a breath. Where to begin? He wanted to save her as much pain as possible without coming across as the biggest jerk of all time. He'd slept with this woman when she'd been far worse than vulnerable. Could she even begin to understand?

She sat straighter. "I don't have some degenerative disease, do I? Is that why I fell? From losing my balance? My mind?"

"I don't know how you slipped on that footbridge. Either time."

She shook her head, trying to understand. "*Either* time?"

There was no easy way, so he'd simply say it. "When you fell last week and hit your head, you lost a portion of your memory. More than just the time directly before and after the accident."

Her eyes narrowed. "How much more?"

"This last week, you've been living in the past. Two years in the past."

Her hand slid away from his. Her smile looked slightly hysterical. "Okay. Sorry, but that doesn't make sense. Am I hearing you right? You're saying we've been married over two years?"

"It's more complicated than that. This time two years ago..." He let out a long breath. "You fell pregnant."

Laura felt as if a bowling ball had smacked her in the stomach, leaving her winded and seeing stars.

What Bishop had suggested was ludicrous. *Absurd*. So crazy she wanted to laugh in his face. She could swallow that she'd lost part of her memory. If she'd been pregnant, however, she sure as hell would've known.

Inside her head a squeaky cog turned and, taken aback, she blinked several times.

Hadn't he implied the same thing a few days ago? She'd laughed at him then. Had been more than a touch offended, in fact. And yet now...the way he was looking at her, as if nothing more serious had ever been said, some part of her was inclined to believe him, except for one rather obvious point.

"If we were pregnant, Bishop, where's the child? And if you say we gave her away, that I *won't* believe." His face remained grave and Laura's heart contracted then sank. "She didn't... die?"

His nostrils flared and his gaze dropped away.

An unbelievable anger jetted up inside of her, heating her face and making her want to slap his. Did he truly expect her to believe that she'd carried a baby for nine months, given birth and didn't remember? She couldn't bear to even *think* such an impossibility was true.

Her throat convulsed and the anger turned dangerously close to rage. As well as an unexpected urge to cry.

"You're lying."

He held her arms and his voice deepened. "Listen to me. You had a miscarriage in your second trimester. You were devastated. I couldn't get through to you. Nobody could."

That flash came again—pain, mess, anguish, so powerful and real, it threatened to tear her apart. She searched the eyes of the man she loved...*had* loved?...and like a ball circling then rolling into a shallow hole, the memory fell into place. She and Bishop were no longer married. They were divorced, and had been for an entire year! Much more than that—

All the breath left her lungs. A feeling crept over her, heavy and black, like a tainted, rough knit shroud. She remembered Grace being there to console her. The doctor explaining there was no reason not to try again. And Bishop...

She saw Bishop sitting in his home office, staring at his

computer screen, that Rubik's Cube rolling around in one hand, no emotion on his face.

"I'd been afraid of what might happen if we conceived," he was saying. "With my history, I worried about losing the child after it was born. I never considered a miscarriage. It left me numb, Laura. I tried to tell myself it could be worse even though I knew that sounded heartless. And I wasn't there for you. I tried to be, but I didn't know what you needed, what to say, and whenever I tried to get close—"

"I pushed you away." She looked at him, her eyes stinging. "I was so angry with you. Angry because you were right. Us falling pregnant was a bad idea. I thought I was strong but afterward..." Fresh hot tears sprang to her eyes. "I wasn't. But you were." Her slim nostrils flared. "And, God, how I hated you for it."

More memories fell, raining down now, pummeling her brain, weighing on her heart. She pushed to her feet. "We had arguments." Looking inward, she blindly crossed the room. "We spent more and more time apart."

"You didn't want to try to fall pregnant again, and I didn't want to push."

Then another memory landed and she held her stomach. "I fell." She spun on her heel and hunted down his gaze.

He was nodding. "Off that footbridge. That was the first time, eighteen months ago."

The room began to swirl and close in.

Yes. She remembered. Remembered it all. She'd been walking across the bridge very early. The planks were wet with dew and there was gravel in a patch to one side. She'd slipped—she remembered the sound—and fell straight under the rail and onto the river stones below. But now hedges grew where the stones had once been. Because Bishop had planted them after her fall, she recalled. Just in case...in case she "fell" again.

She studied Bishop, every mesmerizing, anguished inch. A

moment ago she'd been in *love* with this man. Now, not only did she recall the disappointment, she *felt* it. The sensation made her physically ill. Her heart had been shredded and the scars were as fresh as if the wounds had been inflicted only yesterday.

A tear slipped from the outside corner of her eye.

"How *could* you, Bishop? I was hurting so badly, I needed you to prop me up, support me, and when I fell..."

"I didn't know what to think. You'd been so—"

"Unstable?" Fisting her hands, she cursed at the ceiling. "I'd lost a baby. But no matter how down I felt, I would *never* try to hurt myself. I slipped—it was an accident—and at the hospital..." Her voice dropped to a hoarse, pained whisper. "You wouldn't even look at me."

He found his feet. "I was wrong."

Holding her stomach, she asked in a soft injured voice, "Why didn't you say that back then?"

"I *tried.*"

She sent him a withering look. "Don't lie to me, Bishop. Don't you dare lie to me now."

He took two steps forward. "I'm trying to talk to you, for God's sake."

"Don't you think it's too late for that?"

Throwing up his hands, exasperated, he spun to face the wall. "This is why I left—"

"Why I *asked* you to leave."

"—because no matter how long we hammer it out, we'll never get past this."

A realization struck, so strong, so shocking, Laura's knees turned to water and every scrap of strength disappeared out her toes. She thought this situation was bad, but it could get a hundred times worse.

She balanced her sagging weight against the edge of his desk.

"Oh, God, Bishop. Oh, God. Last night."

His back to her, he scrubbed a hand over his face. "I know, I know."

She held her stomach again, lightly this time.

"What if I'm pregnant?"

Bishop turned back as Laura's expression changed from one of shock to outright alarm. He stood tall, ready to take whatever came. Shouts, tears, accusations that he probably deserved.

Her beautiful green eyes rimmed with red, she dragged herself away from the desk and toward him. "You knew… this entire week, you knew. And you had *sex* with me—"

"Made love."

"—knowing how I really felt? You took advantage of me."

"Did I? I've wondered whether some part of you was purposely holding back. You wanted to be with me, didn't you?"

Her face screwed up as if she'd tasted something sour. "What kind of question is that?"

Damn it. "It's a question a husband asks his wife."

"Divorce, Bishop. Remember that word? We're not married anymore."

"We have been this past week." Growling, she pivoted away. But he grabbed her arm and swung her back. "Tell me you weren't in love with me last night, the night before and the night before that."

As if he'd slapped her, her head drew back. "That's not fair."

"I don't care about being fair. I care about you. Laura, I care about *us*."

Glaring at him, she sucked down a shuddering breath as a tear sped down her cheek. More calmly she said, "You have a strange way of showing it."

He released her arm, then set his hands on his hips. "You're taking this badly enough when you're ready to hear it. What would've happened if I'd sat you down that first night and laid out the facts, cold and hard? Should I have done that? Would that have made me less of a jerk?"

She lifted her chin. "Yes."

"Yes?"

The spark of malice in her eyes faded the barest amount. She moved to the windows, set her hand on the jamb and stared out for a long considering moment.

"No." She admitted, "I suppose you could've done that... been brutally honest. Or you could've just walked out of the hospital when you found out I'd lost my memory."

"Or, when your sister phoned, I could have flat-out refused to come at all."

She curled some hair behind her ear. "And you did make that appointment with Dr. Chatwin. Took that time off work. That was amazing, even before I knew you loathed the sight of me."

What did he have to do to prove it to her? "I never hated you."

"Is *couldn't stand the sight of me* better?"

He growled. "Laura, I wanted to work it out."

"I'm sorry, but you didn't do a very good job."

He locked his shoulders and coughed out a mirthless laugh. "Know what? If you want to blame me, go ahead. I'm used to it."

"It's way too late for that."

"No kidding."

She searched his eyes with a laser beam and he wondered what she'd come up with next.

"Why did you do it?" she finally asked. "Why did you have sex with me...make love to me," she conceded, "without protection, when we'd lived apart for over a year? When it was all finally finished?"

"This last week proved we weren't finished. Over these

past days, I came to hope, to believe, that you and I might be able to work things out this time."

Laura pressed her lips together then, as if she were afraid he'd see tears fall, abruptly peered back out the window. When she only continued to stand there, one hand on the jamb the other bunched by her side, he moved closer.

"Tell me what you're thinking," he said. *For God's sake, don't close up again.*

Her throat bobbed on a deep swallow. "I'm afraid to."

"Do it anyway."

She blinked her tear-rimmed eyes before she spoke. "There's some totally crazy, masochistic side of me that wants to be…"

He said it for her.

"Pregnant?"

Looking bereft, she nodded at the view.

He cut the remaining distance between them and threaded his hands around her waist. He waited and gradually she let her gaze edge up. When her eyes met his, he smiled, warm and reassuring.

"We'll work it out."

She didn't look convinced. "You said that once before."

He brought her mercilessly close. "Did you know that when you were in that hospital room, your sister said this might be another chance for us?"

"Grace said that?"

"I know. Hard to believe. I thought she was talking out her ear." His grin faded. "But then I took you home and little by little, day by day, my perception changed."

Her head tipped to one side and he felt her slide a notch nearer to surrender. But then her hands found his at her back and tried to pry them away. "You're doing this on purpose."

"Doing what?"

"Trying to confuse me."

"I'm trying to *un*confuse." She stilled and, despite everything, gave in to a smile. He grinned, too. "And, yes, that's not a word."

With his fingers threaded through hers, he shepherded her back toward the couch. After an eternity, she sat, then he folded down, too, and waited for her to speak…to say what she'd wanted to say for two long years.

Her gaze wandered around the room and he knew she was taking herself back. Remembering.

"You agreed we could try to fall pregnant," she began in a faraway voice. "And it happened straightaway. I was so excited. You seemed happy, too, but you were busy at work, expanding something or other, and you spent more and more time away, staying in the city apartment." Her fingers dug into the couch. "But when you were home, I saw the look growing in your eyes. You like to be in charge of the next move. *Every* move. When we conceived, what you wanted to control most was taken out of your hands." She blew out a stream of air to compose herself before going on.

"I said we should buy some furniture and linen for a nursery. One day in Sydney I saw those symbols I liked in a jewelry store window. I wanted to buy them—the heart, cross and anchor—but you said *next time*. Then, after the miscarriage—" her eyes filled again "—I felt as if some part of you was relieved. That you were proven right in some way and the risk was gone. You had the reins back and you weren't about to let them go again. Then I had that accident," she went on. "Fell off the footbridge. You thought I'd been so upset that I'd tried to hurt myself." Her head lowered. "We didn't make love again after that."

She squeezed her eyes shut and her shoulders winged in, as if something sharp had pierced her chest. Bishop felt the ache in her throat as deeply as he felt his own. He remembered her wanting to buy those little gold symbols. She'd been so animated and committed. Although it wouldn't have made a difference to how things had worked out in the end, he'd been wrong not to get those trinkets. Truth was that he didn't have faith that her falling pregnant would turn out well. He would have tried to deny his pessimism back then, but he'd proved as much by not going into the jewelry store that day.

"When I lost my memory," she said, "you were happy for me to forget about that time in my life, weren't you?"

"It only made you sad."

"But it was a *part* of me. I want to remember, no matter how much it hurts."

"So you held on to the grief and the hopelessness to the bitter end," he concluded, unable to keep the frustration from his voice, "even if it meant killing what we had."

"I needed your support, Bishop," she said, almost pleading now. "Not your cold shoulder. You left..." She shifted in her seat, glanced dejectedly around the room and grudgingly conceded, "But you left because I told you to go." She blew out a long, resigned breath. "Let's face it. I drove you away."

His mouth swung to one side. He'd been disappointed with himself when he'd finally accepted defeat and had walked out. He'd failed and that had been a blow not only to his ego, but to his sense of self; Samuel Bishop always came out on top. Still, he'd maintained that a man would need to be made of high tensile steel to have withstood the ice storm he'd endured all those cold, bitter months after the miscarriage. Now Laura was telling him she'd felt the same way. Isolated. Lonely. Wanting to reach out. Or be reached.

He shrugged a shoulder. "Guess we can share the blame."

She turned a little toward him, hesitated, but then sought out his gaze. "I'm sorry, Bishop. It's too late, but I am. I'm sorry it all turned out so badly."

He ground his back teeth together to stop his mouth from bowing. "Yeah. Me, too."

"Hard part is—" she sat back "—where do we go from here?"

Where, indeed?

After all the direction he'd handed out this week, and her accusation of needing to hold the reins, he offered, "Must be your call."

Her eyes widened. "My head is still spinning. I'm not sure I'm ready to decide on breakfast cereal let alone how I feel about what happened last week."

He thought it through.

Okay. "I think we need sit back and let our emotions settle. See where we are in a few days' time."

"You mean see if I'm pregnant?"

He remained poker-faced to mask the fact that his heart was beating so hard, he thought his ribs might crack.

"If you're pregnant," he paused and amended, "if we're pregnant, then we both have some serious decisions to make."

Laura didn't know if she was more sad or relieved to see Bishop leave a little later that day.

After their revealing talk, they'd agreed they had a lot to think over, and staying under the same roof would only confuse already high emotions. Despite all she'd learned today, at her deepest level Laura was critically aware that she still longed for Bishop's affection. She longed to have his arms gather her in and his innate strength keep her warm. She ached to absorb the comfort and intensity only the man she'd married could bring. Had married…and divorced.

With dawn breaking, Bishop had passed on eggs Benedict. He said he'd best get a head start on the road, although on Sunday, Laura suspected, the traffic would be less than frantic.

As her ex-husband's Land Rover edged down the long drive, she stood on the front veranda, leaning against a column, trying to shake the hollow feeling of being left in limbo. With regard to their relationship. With regard to her life. But she didn't have time for reflection or self-pity. She wanted to know as soon as possible whether she was or whether she wasn't pregnant, and she knew from previous enquiries that some tests could be performed as soon as six days after the event.

Would she be able to get on with her life, rather empty though it now seemed, or was the dream she'd nurtured for so long about to come true? Although, falling pregnant was only part of the equation, as she well knew. She had to carry to term.

She recalled doing lots of research on miscarriages after her loss and being surprised by the number of women who'd suffered the same pain and grief she had. That knowledge had given her comfort—she wasn't alone—but the information had also left her more than a little anxious. Two years ago she'd been so certain she wanted to conceive, and she'd wanted Bishop to be positive, too. And yet after she'd miscarried, it seemed all her courage had deserted her. She'd withdrawn. She'd been unwilling to talk about her crippling sense of failure much less consider trying again.

And now?

Well, now she was almost frightened to hope.

Seeing Bishop's Land Rover about to disappear around that last bend, she pushed off the column, ready to go back inside, but then another car—silver and stately—wound up the path. Grace's Lexus.

The two vehicles stopped side by side; Bishop was no doubt cluing Grace in on the latest. Laura eased out a breath. At least she wouldn't need to explain to her sister. Or not everything. And while she didn't feel much like talking, she did want to hear Grace's rationale in letting Bishop take her home that day over a week ago. Grace had never approved of her ex and yet Bishop had said that he and Grace had spoken about second chances.

A few minutes later, Bishop's car disappeared and Grace's car pulled up. The moment the door flung open, she flew up the steps and wrapped her arms around her baby sister. Laura felt Grace trembling and realized she was shaking a little, too. One minute she was married, the next she wasn't. She'd had unprotected sex with her ex. She could possibly be pregnant. It was a lot to take in all in one morning.

Inside, with that wedding portrait peering over them and dominating the room, she and Grace folded down together on a couch. Laura got straight to the point.

"Bishop told you?"

Grace's pearl drop earrings swung as she nodded. "Briefly."

"Did he tell you...that we slept together?"

"He didn't need to. I can tell by both your faces."

"We didn't use protection."

Grace's eyes widened. "He agreed to that?"

With her heart beating high in her throat, Laura tried to explain how it'd come about.

"I was living in the past. I was the same person I was just after we'd married." She focused inward, to the happiest times they'd recently spent together, and recalled the almost surreal feeling. "Now I realize when I told him I wanted to conceive our own child, I was pressing a replay button."

"You remember the miscarriage?" Grace asked gently.

Laura shut her eyes to try to block out the pain. It didn't work. The memories were raw and vivid.

"Grace, why did you let Bishop take me home from the hospital? You knew how we'd parted. If I'd had any inkling, I would never have gone."

"We could've made up some story, I suppose, that Bishop had to go out of town and you should come stay with Harry, me and the kids for a while. But my children are two years older than you remembered, and I thought you had more chance of regaining your memories here. Besides, you were in love with Bishop." Grace smoothed her sister's hair. "I don't think you ever stopped loving him."

"Bishop said you thought this might be a second chance for us."

"You were never so happy as when you were with Bishop. At least at first." Before Laura could ask the next obvious question, Grace answered it for her. "It wasn't that I didn't approve of the man, Laura. With mum and dad gone, I saw it as my place to let you both know that I thought you ought to sit down and properly sort out how you were going to achieve your life's goals—and face any consequences—before you exchanged rings."

Laura's gaze dropped to her left hand. Through misty eyes the diamonds shot off hazy prisms of light and color. She felt so hollow inside, so different from the sense of contentment she'd enjoyed only yesterday.

"We were both so in love," she croaked, barely able to speak over the rising emotion.

"And now there's a chance you might be pregnant?"

"A slim chance."

"Still… It's a chance for you to take the best care of yourself and for things to work out the way we would've liked the first time."

Laura leaned her head into her sister's shoulder and they sat together in the quiet for the longest time like they used to when they'd been young and Grace would read to her at night. Laura hoped she wasn't pregnant; what if she miscarried again? If she went to term, could she and Bishop ever forget how they'd treated each other in the past or the pain of having pushed the other away? On the other hand she prayed that she was. More than anything she wanted to be a mother.

Laying a light palm on her belly, she thought over Grace's words.

This time everything could go pear-shaped again or maybe, just maybe with some hope, faith and love, things would turn out right.

Twelve

As Bishop braked in front of the Blue Mountains house a week later, he guessed Laura must have heard his vehicle revving up the long drive. Looking remarkably fresh, and more beautiful than he remembered, she appeared at the door then moved gradually out onto the porch.

This morning he'd rung to say that after seven days and nights apart they should touch base. See where they each stood. He hadn't told her about the guest he'd brought along. And he hadn't asked if she'd taken a test.

The test.

While he slid out of the car, Laura remained at the top of the landing. Her lips weren't curved into a smile. Nor was her brow lined with a frown. The knots that had amassed in his stomach during the trip jerked and snagged all the more. But he wasn't unhappy that he'd come. The whole time he'd been gone, he couldn't focus on work. He particularly hadn't been able bring himself to make a decision over the sale of Bishop Scaffolds. He'd thought only of her, wanting to feel her lips beneath his again, needing to hear and feel her warm, seductive whisper at his ear. Not that he expected her to throw herself at him when they said hello now. But later…

Who knew what lay ahead?

She smiled softly down while the light blue dress she wore swirled around her knees in the breeze. "Hello, Bishop."

He had no time to reply before the guest in his Land Rover tipped his hand. Following a single bark, a playful growl then three or four sharp yaps sounded in a row. Laura's expression opened up. After two halting steps forward, her hands lifted to her mouth and her gaze flew from the rear of the car back to him. Her eyes wide, she gave a little squeak.

Feeling as if he wore a big-bellied red suit and long snowy beard, Bishop unlatched the tailgate and edged out the pet carrier. The puppy's brown eyes were full of life and her tail was beating furiously. She was soft and cuddly and, no matter what happened between Laura and him, this dog would make his ex-wife a fine companion.

He scooped the puppy—Laura had called her Queen—out of the container.

As she flew down the steps, Laura's smile split her face. "You didn't tell me."

"Wouldn't have been a surprise if I had."

Meeting at the bottom of the steps, he offered over the wriggling pup. She held out her arms then, sighing, brought the bundle close. Queen immediately set about licking her mistress's cheek, her nose, her ear. Laura laughed like he'd never heard her laugh before, except for that brief time when she'd been pregnant and beyond happy.

"She's just so beautiful."

"And probably hungry." He headed back to the car. "Take her in and I'll bring up her gear."

Five minutes later, Queen's paws were scratching over the timber floor as she scuttled around, sniffing and wagging, while Bishop set up the food bowl, litter tray and bedding. Crouching, Laura ruffled her pup's ears every time she skittered close.

"You like your new home, little one?" she asked.

Queen yapped once then padded off, her nose zigzagging

over the ground. Laura stood and straightened her dress before she sent a coy smile his way.

"Thank you. It feels like Christmas."

He returned her smile. Then he wasn't the only one.

Queen was running around his feet. "She was supposed to be the quiet one but looks like she's got lots of energy. I think puppy school's a must."

"I'll book her in." Smoothing down her dress again, she inhaled deeply as if to steady herself. "I have a surprise, too."

Moving to the fireplace, she found a pharmacy bag on the mantel. While his pulse began to hammer, she revealed a slim box.

"I've had it sitting there for days," she admitted. "The results are supposed to be extremely accurate."

"This soon?"

She nodded. "It checks hormone levels."

"Ah. I see."

With an awkward but glowing smile, she glanced down and rolled the packet over and over. Her gaze crept up and she blew out a long, shaky breath. "Guess you can tell I'm nervous."

Join the club.

He ironed his damp palms down the sides of his trousers. "So you can do it now?"

"It'll show a result in a couple of minutes." Her gaze flicked away. Came back. "I'm *really* nervous."

As the puppy scampered down the hall, he came forward and folded his hands over hers. He eyed the box that held the instrument that would predict the course of the rest of their lives, one way or the other. Scary. And exciting. As long as nothing went wrong.

He squeezed her hands. "I'll wait here."

As she moved off down the hall, Bishop drove two sets of fingers through his hair and paced the room a few times. He dug out a tug toy from Queen's bag and they played around. When five minutes dragged on to feel more like thirty, he buckled and headed for the liquor cabinet. If ever a man deserved a drink, God save him, it must be now.

The test sticks sat on the end of the double vanity while Laura sat on the top step of the spa bath, her hands holding her burning face. The pack had contained two tests. She'd known the results of both for at least ten minutes, but the news was still sinking in. The shock was still wearing off.

When the numbness tingling across her brain subsided and she knew she couldn't delay any longer, she pushed on her thighs and found, to her amazement, that her legs were steady enough to hold her weight. She wasn't crying. She was totally okay with this. *Way* okay. Bishop would be, too. She simply had to find the wherewithal to go out and tell him.

When she reentered the living room, Bishop was standing by a back window, gazing out over the eucalypt-covered hills, swirling a short glass of amber liquid. Hearing her footfalls, his gaze snapped over and those masculine shoulders, cloaked in that heavenly chambray shirt, straightened.

His delayed smile was supportive, but the emotion didn't quite reach his eyes. He was waiting for her to tell him the news, show him the proof. And while she'd never felt more wound up in her life than she did at this moment, now a certain, almost eerie calm settled upon her, like a mist curling over a long, slow day.

He'd stand by her. This time they'd make it work. Because they needed to for the baby's sake. And they'd be happy. She knew they would.

If only she were pregnant.

Sprawled out under the piano, Queen must have worn herself out. Laura padded past, careful not to disturb her. Quivering inside, she tacked on an ambivalent smile and made herself shrug.

"Guess you're a free man."

His smile dropped. He took one measured step forward, blinked several times and then rasped, "No?"

"I didn't think you'd want to see the sticks. No point really."

The breath seemed to leave his body and he visibly slumped. She'd never seen anyone look so dazed.

"It's probably best," she went on, needing to fill the silence. She needed him to speak. To say *something*. Because, in truth, she'd wanted this…to have been a victim of fate and have the choice made for her, and she'd thought he'd wanted that, too.

He ran a hand down the side of his clean shaven jaw and she noticed he still wore the ring. "Are you sure?"

"As sure as I need to be. Both results were clear. I could go to a doctor, but I don't think there's any need." She'd probably get her period in a day or two.

His gaze distant, he lowered to sit on the edge of the piano stool, his foot inches from Queen's sleeping head, while Laura held the breath fluttering in her chest, waiting. But of course it took a while to sink in, thinking you might be headed in one direction then being shunted off in another. Hoping you were going to be a parent, then not. They'd both been through the ups and downs before.

Then he inhaled sharply. The surprise his next words delivered almost knocked her over.

"We could try again."

She gaped at him, wanting to tug her ears. Had she heard right? She said the first thing that came to mind.

"We're not married anymore."

Was he asking her to marry him again?

His brows drawn together, he pushed to his feet. "The other week it felt like we were."

"That's only because I couldn't remember that you'd signed divorce papers."

His brows knitted more. "I wasn't the one to instigate proceedings. You sent the papers, Laura, not me."

"You didn't have to send them back."

He held her gaze for a torturously long moment before he succumbed to a tight smile. "No. You're right. I didn't." But then the sharp glint in his eyes softened and he took another step closer. "I'm sorry the test wasn't positive."

"Are you?"

She'd sounded indignant, but she truly wanted to know, and know the truth. Had he honestly wanted a positive result or was the greater part of him relieved—again—that the risk and possible danger had passed?

His jaw visibly tightened. "I wanted this...wanted *us* to work, but I knew we didn't have a hope unless you were pregnant. That week we spent together..." His chin tipped up as his gaze penetrated hers. "I think we can have that again."

In that instant, her doubts seemed to evaporate and her heart began to melt. She didn't know if she could speak over the emotion swelling in her throat. But the obvious question swooped down.

"How?"

"We can go from here. Work out each move, step-by-step, together."

"But we'd come up against that same roadblock straight out of the grid."

He gripped her left hand and his heat, as well as his will, consumed her. "We can work it out."

She felt herself teetering as her surroundings drifted in then out. She wanted to agree, so much it hurt. But she simply couldn't go the way of denial. Now that she remembered it all, she couldn't put on her rose-colored glasses even if her heart broke admitting what they both knew to be true.

Her voice was hushed and scored with regret. "Bishop, you said we'd work it out the first time."

His eyes grew dark. "You fell pregnant. What happened after that wasn't my fault. Laura, it wasn't *anyone's* fault."

"I know that."

And she did. But that unhappy fact didn't help them now. Or take away her continuing sense of loss. Or her fear it would happen again.

His voice deepened. "Do you still want a family?"

"Yes…but…"

She tried to battle the doubt, but now, more than ever, the memories seemed so frighteningly clear. The threat of it happening again—of losing a baby well into a pregnancy—left her skin clammy and her throat dry.

"Without being pregnant already, I don't know that I can risk that kind of loss again," she confessed.

She'd named that baby. Imagined how she'd look. Miscarriage might seem like a by-the-by word and occurrence to some, but that day she'd lost a child she already loved.

His shoulders rolled back as he measured her with his eyes. "And you won't consider adoption?"

"No." She slid her hand from his. "Or not yet." Drained, she leaned against the piano and admitted, "I'm not sure. I don't know that I ever will be."

A resigned look dulled his eyes. She'd seen that shadow before in the months leading up to the day he left a little over a year ago. She had no illusions as to what that expression meant now.

"There's no point me asking again, is there?" he asked in a flat tone.

Laura held herself firm. She felt as if she were trying to walk a swaying tightrope. She wanted to reach out and draw him near, feel the comfort of his body against hers and give him some comfort too. But what would that achieve? The chiseled planes of his face had never looked sharper. His eyes, seemingly piercing her soul, had never looked more detached.

They'd been through this before, over and over. There was no solution. And like never before she suspected they both knew it.

He'd wanted to know if it would make a difference if he asked again.

Slowly she shook her head. "No, Bishop. It wouldn't."

After a drawn out moment, he glanced down at his drink as if he'd forgotten he'd poured it then he shot the Scotch down his throat. Mentally exhausted—at a loss to know what more to do—she tried to go off topic. Maybe if they talked about something else for a while...

"Would you like another one? Or maybe some coffee."

He crossed to the mantel and rested the empty glass below their photograph. The barbed wire ball rotating at her center scratched and grew. Next week, would she be taking that picture down again?

On leaden feet, she edged close. "I made some scones fresh this morning—"

"They wouldn't go down so well with Scotch."

His voice was graveled and low. When he turned away from the fireplace—from the picture—his gaze landed on the door and a fist rammed through Laura's chest.

He was leaving?

She studied the drawn line of his jaw, imagined his mind turning over. Neither one of them could ignore the truth. No matter how much they seemed suited, how well they seemed to fit, the past would always cast a long, sour shadow over their present and, subsequently, their future, as well.

Garnering her strength, she clasped her hands, lifted one shoulder and let it fall. She hoped her voice didn't come across as shattered as she felt.

"Seems neither of us has anything much else to say."

His jaw shifted and he probed her eyes. When she waited him out, gave him the chance to communicate, his hard gaze fell away and he admitted, "Seems not." Then he jerked a thumb toward the door. "I should probably start back." His gaze found the puppy. "Glad you like the dog."

Her throat closed off as a colossal weight anchored down upon her shoulders.

That was it. He was going. This time for good.

It took all her willpower to pin that smile back in place when it would've been far easier to crumple up and cry. But she wouldn't let him see how crushed she was. Neither one of them wanted a replay of this time last year and they both knew that if he stayed that's exactly what would transpire.

A few minutes later, as he slid into his vehicle and buckled up, she stood alone on the porch. He hadn't kissed her goodbye. Hadn't touched her, not even a token reassuring brush of his hand against her arm. He certainly hadn't told her that he loved her.

He stared down at the wheel, then his stormy gaze dragged over to hers and her heartbeat began to thunder. Would he swing open the door, take the steps two at a time and enfold her in his arms? Tell her that he was staying, no matter what?

But he didn't move. And when he only continued to sit there, staring, the tears, crouched at the back of her throat, squeezed higher. If he was leaving, why the hell didn't he hurry up and go!

Rather than sounding like a shrew and shouting for him to quit the dramatics and end the torment, she tossed out a blithe, "Traffic will be building. Say hi to your folks when you call."

The hard line of his mouth curved with a whisper of a smile and then he nodded. "Too easy."

A moment later, as the vehicle ambled down the drive and Bishop drove out of her life for good, Laura withered onto the top step.

Now she knew why two simple words had set off alarm bells that morning when she'd asked if he could take another day off, and again when she'd assured him her heart condition was under control.

One year ago, when she'd asked to him leave, after he'd thrown his wedding ring into the fireplace then had slammed the door a final time closed, he'd said precisely those words.

Easy, he'd jeered.

Too easy.

Thirteen

Sitting behind the desk in his Sydney penthouse office, Bishop gazed blindly out the window, absently tapping his pen on the blotter. He wasn't interested in the impressive view of the young cityscape, or the fact that it had been teeming with rain for a week. A stack of emails from Willis filled his in-box, telling him to snap out of it. He wasn't interested in that, either.

Samuel Bishop was well-known for his sometimes agonizingly thorough approach to any important problem. Once he made a decision, however, it was the right one and he stood by it. But for the life of him he couldn't find the wherewithal to give a devil's damn about making a decision on anything right now. His old friend logic said it was a temporary malady. The cogs would start turning again soon enough, even if he barely recognized the lifeless face that gazed back from the bathroom mirror. This morning, he'd fleetingly thought staying in bed might be easier.

The knock on his partly opened door pulled him from his thoughts. His secretary knew he wasn't to be disturbed. Clearly Willis wasn't buying. He strode in, the knot of his tie loose, his expression beyond exasperated.

"Sam, I get that you're the boss—"

"Yes, I am," Bishop confirmed, flicking his pen aside.

"—but I need an answer. *Now.* Clancy Enterprises have given us until midday or they're walking away and, believe me, they won't be back."

Bishop swung in his chair, one way then the other. He wanted to say he'd decided to go ahead with the sale. That he wanted a clean start. A new challenge. He couldn't sit around like an ambivalent lump for the rest of his life. Fact was that he'd wanted to sell the company before Laura had taken her tumble. Now that all the twists and turns of their roller-coaster couple of weeks were done, all indicators pointed to going with his previous decision. So why was he torturing himself, sitting here day after day, wishing that this second time around things had turned out differently?

Closing his eyes, Bishop pinched the ache simmering beneath his brow.

Dammit, why hadn't he dug his heels in, kissed Laura senseless then announced that this time he was staying? Because he didn't love her? Or didn't love her enough?

Exhaling, he opened his eyes and swung to face the desk. He leaned forward, forearms on the blotter, fingers tightly clasped.

"Give Clancy the green light," he finally said. "I want this done."

Willis's jaw unhinged. Then he shook his head as if to clear it. "Are you sure?"

Bishop's temper flared. "You said you needed an answer."

Willis's shocked expression faded into one of understanding as he slung a hip over the corner of the desk. "Want to talk about it?"

Was he referring to Laura?

"Thanks, but I'd be happy never to talk about it again." Bishop tipped out of his chair and headed for his chessboard on the other side of the mile-long room.

"Did it ever occur to you that you're still in love with her?"

"You saw me with her exactly twice."

"At the party she was upset. Hayley saw you leaving, too. Later she commented on how wonderful it was that you'd found each other again. That you were both so obviously in love."

Bishop's smile and voice were tight. "Let me tell you something."

Willis folded his arms. "I'm listening."

"I've thought about this. Thought about it in great depth. Just say, for argument's sake, I *did* love her. It wouldn't make a difference to where we stand now. It wouldn't be enough." Wasn't then. Wasn't now.

"So you're going to close down shop and walk away. Again."

Bishop's jaw hardened. "Be careful, Willis."

"Why? Because you might have to admit that you're wrong?"

"I thought you'd be pleased about selling."

He'd told Willis he'd take him along on whatever venture he started next. They'd even talked partnership. Willis had guts as well as business acumen. He talked straight. Bishop could trust him.

Should he trust him now?

Having crossed the room, too, Willis collected a chess piece off the board and inspected its lines. "She gave you that chess set, didn't she?"

Bishop narrowed his eyes. Where was Willis going with this? "It was a wedding gift."

"And you kept it."

"It's a valuable set."

"And it always reminded you of her, right across from where you sit every day."

Bishop opened his mouth to refute it. But the truth was glaringly clear. He'd wanted to keep something of Laura close.

Could he get rid of this chessboard now as Laura would, once again no doubt, shut away their wedding portrait?

Bishop sank in the tub chair while the yellow gold and platinum pieces shone up at him. Elbow on the armrest, he braced his brow on the slope of his index finger and thumb and massaged the ache that had grown exponentially. He had to get it off his chest.

"Last week," he admitted, "Laura thought she might be pregnant."

"Holy…" Willis dropped into the chair opposite. "She wasn't?"

Staring at the board, Bishop shook his head. "She said she wanted to try for a baby. I agreed, even though she was living in the past—we both were—back when we were newly married."

"And she hit the roof when she finally got her amnesia files open?" Willis said without a hint of *I told you so,* for which Bishop was grateful.

"At first, she was angry. But eventually we agreed, if she was carrying our child, we'd work things out."

"And when it turned out she wasn't, you left?"

"She wouldn't listen. Nothing got through to her, just like last time."

Willis grunted. "Right."

Bishop's voice lowered. "She was thinking exactly the same thing I was. Without a baby cementing us together, the past would always be there, cleaving us apart. There's too much history. Too many bad memories." His gaze slid from the board. "Too much to forgive."

"And what kind of memories will you have when you hit sixty-five? That's roughly another half of a lifetime of sitting around feeling like crap."

Bishop's hackles went up. "What do you expect me to do?"

"Win, for God's sake! Win for you both."

Bishop's grin was sardonic. "Great speech. But this isn't a game."

Willis shook his head slowly. "I don't get it. With everything else you're like a tiger on its prey. You lock down and don't let go. But when the prize concerns something as inconsequential as your happiness from this point until the end of your days, you can't tell right from left."

Done listening, Bishop went to stand and walk away, but Willis reached over and gripped his arm.

"Listen to me. I know what I'm talking about. Hayley and I broke up for a time. Swallowing my pride and asking her to take me back was the best thing I ever did."

His head thumping now, Bishop gazed down at the chessboard. The pieces seemed to look up at him, so still and cool, as if they were prepared for any contest, the more demanding and extended the better. Bishop digested what Willis had said, then shut his eyes and kicked open the stiff lock at the end of the mental chain that was keeping him back. Then, for the first time since he was a youth, he changed his mind.

"Let Clancy know we're not selling." With a determined gait and a suddenly focused mind, he set off for his desk.

He heard the frown in Willis's voice. "We were talking about Laura."

"And send Meryl in on your way out." Bishop pulled in his chair. "We have a mountain of catching up to do."

"And Laura?" Willis persisted, following.

Bishop reached for a document that had been sitting in his in-box far too long. Seizing that pen, he began to make notes on a site drawing and muttered, "I'll call."

"When?"

"When I do."

Willis huffed. "You know you're a fool if you don't."

Bishop's steely gaze tipped up. "And everyone knows I'm not that." Not a third time anyway. Willis was about to push more, but Bishop held up a hand. "Discussion closed."

As Willis left, Bishop reaffirmed the choices he'd made. He'd decided to keep his company. He'd thought he'd needed a new challenge, but this one was far from over. There was more work to do, more victories to be won, before he could ever consider walking away. Same went for his situation with Laura. As he'd told Willis, he would call…

But not yet.

Where his ex was concerned, he'd seemed compelled to act on impulse. But this time when he made his move, his strike would be well planned. He simply had to find the right time, the right place. Then he wouldn't back down until he'd claimed his mate.

Fourteen

New Year's Eve had always been such a special night. When they were young, Laura and Grace had stayed up with their parents, growing increasingly excited the closer midnight had come. When the hands of the grandfather clock in the dining room finally hit twelve, they'd join in the celebrations happening all over the east coast—blowing paper whistles, lighting sparklers, hugging and kissing, as well as making wishes that hopefully the new year would bring.

Sipping on a glass of fruity white wine now, Laura scanned the busy room, studying the glitter and hype through the slots of her masquerade mask, a band of green and gold sequins covering only her eyes. This New Year's she was at a charity function in Sydney, a celebration she'd helped organize on a professional basis.

The fifteen-thousand-square-foot room boasted a double-tiered layout with the mezzanine level reserved for the crème de la crème. Pink, pearl and iridescent yellow helium balloons hung suspended in the air, their multicolored tails swaying high above the heads of several hundred affluent guests. Magnificent Corinthian columns supported soaring sixty-foot ceilings while the center Wedgwood dome crowned an atmosphere that celebrated an ultra-stylish event sponsored by the socially elite.

Unfortunately, Laura wasn't able to absorb much of the bubbling atmosphere. In fact, she was counting the seconds until she could leave. She hadn't felt much like partying of late.

She and Bishop had said goodbye a final time eight weeks ago. Her ex had acted improperly when he'd agreed they should try for a baby. He shouldn't have taken advantage of her amnesiac state. No matter how difficult, no matter how much he'd thought she hadn't wanted to hear the truth, he should have told her…about the miscarriage…about their divorce.

But she wasn't angry over that. How could she be when she'd wanted to be with him as much as he'd obviously wanted to be with her? The simple truth was that she still wanted him now.

But from the beginning the odds had been stacked against them. They both wanted a family, but in trying to achieve that, they'd only succeeded in carving out a rift that now was impossible to bridge. Their differences would never be solved or puttied up by anything as simple as talking it out; they'd tried that both times around.

Still she couldn't help but wonder…

If they'd fallen pregnant that night two months ago, would she and Bishop be together now, anticipating the birth of a healthy child, discussing getting married again? Or would she have miscarried a second time?

With her memory restored, Laura found it difficult to imagine ever taking the risk and trying to conceive again, and she hated herself for losing the faith she'd reclaimed briefly during that week with her ex. She'd become what she'd once accused Bishop of being—a person who preferred to live life without risk…but also without the danger of adding any new pain to the old.

She only wished she didn't love Bishop so much, but the

truth was she'd loved him the whole time, even when she thought she'd had enough and wanted him gone for good. Sometimes, especially when she lay awake alone at night, she couldn't accept that they were truly finished. It was like trying to believe that summer wouldn't follow spring.

But now, studying the animated effervescent scene buzzing all around, Laura reaffirmed the promise she'd made to herself after Bishop had left a second time. She was done living in the past. She had to build on her strengths and move on with her life. She and Bishop were history and it was best she swallow that pill, no matter how bitter. No matter how painful.

She was gazing absently at revelers on the dance floor, gyrating to a disco tune from the seventies, when someone bumped into her back. As cool wine splashed her hand, she wheeled around. Louis XVI and Marie-Antoinette tipped their powdered wigs in apology then blended back into the thick of the partying crowd. To her right, a butler topped off Casper's and Wendy's champagne. Laura recognized one of Australia's wealthiest media magnates decked out like a spaghetti Western star from the sixties, checking the time on his Rolex.

Tonight Laura was Tinker Bell, complete with pom-pom slippers and gossamer thin wings, although she didn't feel the least bit mischievous or daring. When Captain Hook had asked her to dance a moment ago, she politely declined as she'd done to others many times tonight. Watching the captain from a distance now, she wondered if she might recognize the face should he remove the mask.

Tickets had asked that guests keep their masks in place until twelve. Not until you'd given or had received a kiss were you permitted to reveal your true self. Not everyone had gone along with the adventurous spirit of the request, however. That man standing next to one of the bars, for instance. Indiana Jones. His hat was worn at a forward slope, all but covering his eyes. The adventure-scarred thirties flight jacket suited his masculine physique…tall, broad, a posture that said *commanding, aloof*. Even *arrogant*. Everyone attending tonight was wealthy or here courtesy of someone who was. If it was good enough for the majority—top models, champion race car drivers, *Forbes* businessmen—to abide by the keep-your-mask-in-place edict, why should Jones think he was exempt?

Indiana drank from his heavy-based glass then tipped his hat back. When a pair of bright blue eyes indolently swept the room, Laura's blood froze in her veins. Then she broke out in a sweat. Pressing her hand against the nerves jumping rope in her stomach, she set her glass down on a passing waiter's tray before it could slide through her tingling fingertips and smash on the floor.

Bishop?

It couldn't be.

Desperate to see more clearly, she removed her mask, blinked several times then focused again. At the same time, the man in the hat flicked a glance her way. Their gazes hooked. Stuck.

Fused.

She'd given the attendance list a good going over. Or she thought she had. Had they come close to bumping into each other tonight? Had they brushed, touched, unbeknownst to either one of them?

Shaking inside, Laura gulped down a breath and straightened her spine.

Forget all that. What did she do now?

He made the decision for them both.

Removing his hat, holding it at his chest, he crossed to her. Somewhere in the recesses of her mind, Laura heard someone call out, "Five minutes to midnight!" And then he was standing before her, so tall and more darkly handsome than any man had a right to be. On his hip he wore a coiled whip. Beneath his eyes lay shadows she didn't remember seeing before. Had he slept as little as she had these past months?

Beyond nervous, she pasted a smile on her quivering lips.

"Bishop...this is a surprise."

"A pleasant one."

That husky comment would've been enough to unbalance her, but the slant of his kissable mouth, the sparkle in his eyes, left her dizzy.

Sucking in a breath, she shored herself up.

Cool. Collected. Don't let him know how affected you are. You don't want his pity. Let him see you don't need anything from him, particularly the pain of hope.

She adjusted her fairy wing shoulder strap. "I didn't see your name on the attendance list."

His gaze had dropped to her mouth and was now licking a deliberate line over her lips. Her heart raced faster. She thought she'd remembered how deeply he affected her. Now, with no more than a lidded look, she was dissolving into a warm puddle.

"I decided to attend at the last moment," he told her. "I believe you're a functions coordinator now."

It was on the tip of her tongue to ask how he knew. But she deliberately smoothed the questions from her expression and, as calmly as she could, explained.

"I was always into food. Catering. Making things nice. I wrote up a few proposals, did some promotion and got a few gigs, including this one."

Approval shone in his eyes, transforming them into glittering blue mirrors beneath the lights. "Congratulations. I'll have to put our promotions department onto your website."

"So you kept the company?" He nodded and a sense of right filtered over her. "I'm glad. That place was so much a part of you. You always wanted to build it up into all it could be. I can see you taking Bishop Scaffolds all over the world."

"My suit with its giant S printed on the chest is on order."

He chuckled and for the first time in months, she wanted to laugh, too. How wonderful to feel something other than listlessness.

A call from the center microphone went up. "Three minutes. Get your lips ready, folks."

Laura had unconsciously been checking out the beautiful bow of Bishop's mouth. Now the reference to kissing jolted her back. Her cheeks hot, she redirected her attention to a dazzling nighttime view of the harbor and bridge visible beyond the multistory glass wall. Below, a glittering sea of sparklers lit the boardwalks and streets.

"The fireworks should be spectacular tonight," she said, her gaze on the view while she felt his own gaze sizzling over her.

"Spectacular. Yes," he replied. "Not long to wait now."

While the crowd stirred and the excitement around them grew, her gaze joined with his again and they simply looked at each other, soaking each other up, one drinking the other deeply in. She felt herself being drawn up, like early morning dew to the sun, but then nearby someone blew a party whistle, reality intruded again and she dropped her gaze to her pom-pom slipper feet.

Time to move on before she did something foolish like throw herself at him and beg him to take her home.

She rubbed the back of her neck above her fairy wings. "Guess I'd better let you get back to the party." Her expression suitably poised, she nodded a farewell. "Happy New Year, Bishop."

"Take care, Laura."

He touched her arm and the skin-on-skin contact shot a hot flash straight to her belly before it spread drugging warmth down her suddenly unsteady legs.

She cleared her throat and mumbled, "You, too," before, more than a little shaky, she walked away.

Bishop watched Laura, in that sexy-as-sin pixie outfit, as she vanished back into the crowd. Her legs were just as delectable and her smile still melted his heart. If anything she'd grown more beautiful. More desirable.

Over these past two months, whenever his mind hadn't been otherwise completely occupied, his thoughts had tracked back to his ex and the incredible time they'd spent together when fate could have taken them one way but had pitched them in the other instead. But after his talk with Willis, he'd seen things more clearly...well enough to push himself to climb back on top. He'd made the firm decision to keep his company and had dived back into work with fresh gusto.

And then there was Laura.

That day, when he'd decided he would win back Laura's love, he'd also decided to act only when all the pieces were lined up to give him the best chance of success. His nature was to be cautious; every step needed to be the right one. And yet in the past he'd acted impulsively where Laura was concerned. She fired up emotions that flicked a switch in him that demanded immediate action. He'd asked her to marry him too soon, had left when he should have held on and seen the rough times through. Hanging off from approaching her these past weeks had been agony. But the wait would be worthwhile. Tonight he felt the time was right. Soon he would make his move.

As the "one minute to midnight" warning echoed through the vast room, Bishop knocked back the rest of his drink. Then, setting down his glass, he shouldered a path through the elaborate costumes and masks and found a relatively quiet spot against a column near the main entrance. Crossing his arms, he leaned back and absently watched an assortment of guests prepare themselves for twelve.

Soon the countdown cry went up.

"Ten, nine, eight, seven..."

He'd caught up with a few friends tonight and had made a

few new contacts. But he hadn't come here to socialize. Not in that sense anyway. He was here because of Laura.

When they'd touched a moment ago, the sensation had been the same. Almost too hot. Too good. If they met and touched in ten years' time, it wouldn't be any different. He'd still nurse the same maddening urge to carry her away despite any protests. Tonight, if he had to, that's precisely what he intended to do.

The countdown ended. Cheers and cries of *"Happy New Year!"* exploded through the ballroom. Beyond the windows, Sydney ignited in a limitless show of sky-high flares, sparks and luminous color. Crowds clapped and hugged. Inside, streamers flew, whistles blew and everyone seemed to be kissing and embracing.

Bishop waited, anticipating his next move and how the scene he'd envisaged a thousand times would ultimately play out. His gaze landed on a nearby couple. They were young, clearly in love. She was heavily pregnant.

The anticipation in his gut spiked and looped, and rather than that couple, Bishop imagined he and Laura standing there looking that happy. That pregnant.

That in love.

As the couple broke apart and gazed tenderly into each other's eyes, Bishop set his hat aside and moved out. The cacophony of noise expanded to a deafening pitch, but now Bishop blocked it out. On a mission, his heart pounding louder than the fireworks hitting the stars outside, he drove through the tightly-packed crowd until he reached the center of the room. He angled around, focused as his gaze whipped over countless heads and a pulse beat furiously in his throat.

He'd purposely let Laura walk away five minutes earlier. He'd wanted the realization that they were indeed in the same room to sink in. He wasn't concerned he wouldn't find her again, and for one simple reason.

He had faith. At this moment, whether she wanted to admit

it or not, she would be searching for him as earnestly as he was now searching for her.

From the first time they'd spoken, the first time they'd kissed, he'd made up his mind to have her, and marry before anything got in their way. When she'd told him about her heart condition, it made no difference to how he'd felt. He'd work it out. That's what he did. Logically. Methodically.

One maddening step at a time.

He'd married Laura on impulse and despite all they'd been through, it was the best decision he'd ever made. Tonight he intended to tell her just that.

Still searching, he rotated slowly back around and a path seemed to open up through the center of the crowd. At the far end of the room, with her silver wings and fluff ball slippers, stood Laura. Even with a sparkling mask covering half her face, he could see that their eyes had locked. She angled more toward him and he strode up until he stood, determined, before her.

"Time is nothing but a great empty void without you," he said, as cheers and whistles continued to wail all around. But he didn't worry she couldn't hear him. Behind her mask, her emerald eyes were swimming. She'd heard every word.

But when his hands searched out hers, to hold and urge them close, her shoulders thrust back and she wound away.

"We don't need to do this again. Especially not here. We said all we needed to two months ago. There's no point rehashing it."

"You're right. No rehashing. There's been enough of going over old ground. We need to push forward. Get over the past once and for all."

"The only way to get over it, Bishop, is to leave it behind. Leave *us* behind."

"You know neither of us can do that."

"We *have* to. Don't you see? There's no answer."

"I won't accept that."

The breath seemed to leave her and her lower lip trembled the barest amount. "Please, Bishop, don't. I can't do this again."

Blocking out the commotion, he found her hands and held them tight.

"When I left over a year ago, I was angry. Not with you. At how things between us had turned out. You've heard the saying, what you fear most you create. What we were both so scared would happen, did." He stepped nearer and the distance separating them closed more. "We lost a child."

Her shoulders hitched as she swallowed back what he suspected to be a quiet sob. Her heart was there in her eyes as the tips of her fingers reflexively curled over his. "I...I never thought you understood how I felt."

"I thought you'd get over it," he admitted, "and when you did, I wanted to try again. But when you didn't want to—" He corrected himself. "When you *couldn't*, it suited me because at the edges of my mind I kept thinking...what if it happens a second time, a third? What if we go to term and it's my twin brother all over again or there's problems with his heart?" A rock pressed on his chest. "How could I do that to a child?"

She was biting her lip, clearly holding back tears.

"I should have been there for you," he went on, "even when you didn't want me to be." He rotated her hands until their backs rested against the buttons on his chest. "I love you, Laura. Till the end of time I'll love you."

A tear slid past the ridge of her mask, down her cheek, around her chin.

"You love me? Still?"

He nodded, smiled and cupped her cheek. "I want you to give what you always asked of me. Have faith in me, Laura. We were in love again two months ago. I know we can have that again." He brought his cheek to hers. "I'll never stop holding you," he murmured against the shell of her ear as he stroked her back below its wings and willed all the forces of heaven and hell to this time have it turn out right. "I'll never stop loving you, no matter if we live out one lifetime together or ten."

Slowly, he released her. As fireworks ignited the night sky and the party continued to explode, Laura's throat bobbed up and down. Needing to see her face, he found the sequined edge of the mask and slid it off. What he saw left him short of breath. It was there in her eyes, so clear and bright, and he knew what she was going to say before she said it.

"I can't help loving you," she got out. "Even when I didn't want to. I was the one who wanted to take a risk, but when the worst happened, you were the one who stayed strong while I—" Her cheeks wet, she leaned into him. "I gave up. I gave up on us." Her hands knotted in his shirt. "I don't want to give up again." Then she blinked and concern flared in her eyes. "But Bishop, even if we walk out of here together tonight, we still won't have solved our problem."

The dilemma of when and how or *if* they should have a family.

He reached into his top shirt pocket. When his hand withdrew and he opened his palm, Laura's eyes went wide and her hands lifted to cover a disbelieving smile. Gingerly she scooped up the delicate gold pieces. She held them high and the gold symbols caught and reflected a hundred lights. Bishop could see her heart caving, and his did too, as she twirled the pieces so that prisms planed out from a cross, an anchor and a heart.

"We'll try again," he said. "We'll fall pregnant. But only when and if you're ready. And no matter what comes, good or bad, I'll always, always be there right beside you."

That sob escaped and, looking as if she couldn't find her voice beneath a world of emotion, she pressed her lips together and nodded. At that moment, all the commotion in the room seemed to fade. He lifted her chin higher so he could see her eyes…and the open gift of her love.

"Guess that means I have an answer to my question," he said, smiling, too.

"Which question is that?" she choked out.

He cupped her face and searched her eyes until he felt his soul touch hers.

"Will you marry me?"

More tears pooled in her eyes—happy, grateful, as-soon-as-we-can tears. But then she asked, or was it teased? "You don't think we need more time?"

"I only know I can't wait for you to be Mrs. Samuel Bishop again." His lips brushed hers. "I can't wait for the rest of our lives to begin."

While the other revelers were finishing their embracing, Bishop gathered his only love adoringly near. He cherished her...loved her...and with all his heart, he kissed her. A kiss to seal their future and a promise neither one would ever forget.

Epilogue

Sitting in the living room of their Blue Mountains home, Laura and Bishop huddled together on the couch, watching their favorite DVD. With her head on her husband's shoulder, Laura sighed as the camera's eye panned the interior of the quiet church while a hundred guests smiled and gazed on.

On the screen, proud father Bishop carefully handed over his baby daughter for the minister to perform the long-anticipated ceremony. Laura stood beside them, her hands clasped under her chin as her eyes shimmered with more love than many hearts could ever hope to contain. Their baby, Abigail Lynn, had her father's thick dark hair and her mother's striking green eyes. She was dressed in the christening gown her grandmother had sewn and trimmed with white ribbon over twenty-five years earlier.

The minister held Abbey's tiny head over the font and carefully anointed her crown. Cameras clicked and at least one camcorder caught all the action, including the godparents' smiles (Willis and Grace had been honored), and the approval radiating from both sides of the aisle. Bishop's parents had flown in from Western Australia the day before and planned to stay a few weeks. But by far the strongest, sweetest emotion captured that day was the expression on Bishop's face. Gratitude. Pride.

Unbridled love.

The ceremony wound up. She and Bishop, with their baby girl, made their way down the crimson-carpeted aisle, soaking up the best wishes of the people with whom they'd chosen to share this special day. On a close-up, Mum and Dad kissed their baby on each cheek. A moment later the images on the plasma screen flickered to black.

Misty-eyed, Laura reluctantly let Bishop leave her side to remove the DVD from the player. Her gaze wandered to their darling eight-month-old, sitting up by herself on her pink blanket. While Abbey played with her animal friends phone, Queen dozed directly behind, a living, breathing, soft place to land should the baby happen to topple. Bishop ejected the disc while Laura leaned forward to scoop the baby up.

"I'll never get tired of remembering that day." Laura popped her daughter onto her lap and, humming a nursery rhyme, gave her a bounce. Laughing, Abbey raised her arms and squealed, begging for more. "I could play that DVD over and over." Laura rubbed her nose with the baby's. "What about you, sweet pea?"

"Abbey's not old enough to talk." Bishop slid the christening DVD into its labeled jacket. "If she's anything like her mother, God help our phone bill when she is."

"That's what women do," Laura pointed out. "They talk." She spoke to the baby. "And boys flex their muscles and play with balls, both skills, of course, being vital to the happiness and survival of our species."

"I know something else that's vital to our survival." DVD in hand, he made his way back over. "To mine anyway."

Bishop joined them on the couch. Cupping his wife's nape, he brought her lips to his. They kissed, tenderly and with a sincerity that softened Laura's heart and refreshed her belief in all that was pure and good.

Slowly, he released her, but she wasn't ready to let go just yet. Arching a brow, she filed her fingers suggestively through his dark hair. "Tell me more."

"As soon as the baby's down," he murmured, in that deep, seductive voice that made her quiver, "I intend to do just that."

But then he came close again. His mouth was about to capture hers once more when Laura pulled back and looked down. The baby had gripped the edge of the DVD jacket and was giving her first teeth a serious work out.

Gently, Laura pried the jacket away. "No, no, baby. We need to take good care of this."

"That's right, kitten." Bishop stroked his daughter's head. "We have to play it at your twenty-first."

"Twenty-one." Laura held Abbey's little fingers and inspected the tiny dimpled hand. "It'll be here before we know it. Then she'll be moving out, getting married." She studied her baby's soft pink skin, those bright green eyes, and her heartstrings tugged. "I think I'm suffering empty nest syndrome already."

"I know a way to delay it."

"Spoil her rotten so she never wants to leave?"

A fingertip trailed her jaw as his lips whispered over hers. "Have another one."

Laura's breath caught. She never thought she'd hear him say the words. Agreeing to try again to have their first child had been a big enough step, and for them both. But she'd adored being pregnant this time and hadn't suffered one hiccup, not even a single day of morning sickness. More importantly, their child was not only beautiful, she was also brimming with good health. There was no sign of a heart problem, thank heaven, and there was no reason to believe there would be in the future.

So did he really mean…?

"Have another *baby?*"

His smile warmed every inch of her. "Would you like that?"

Laura could barely speak over the emotion—the sheer happiness—clogging her throat. "I would like that very much. *Infinitely* much."

His chuckle faded as an earnest gleam surfaced in his eyes. "Have I told you today how in love with you I am?"

Tipping forward, she nuzzled his bristled cheek. God, how she loved him, too. "Remind me again."

His breath warmed her ear. Warmed her heart.

"You give me direction, give me meaning."

Her eyes stung with another rush of emotion. She pinched the bridge of her nose, uncertain why she wanted to stem tears that came from a place of such perfect bliss. "You're making me all foggy."

"In a good way, I hope."

"The very best way."

So in tune, they looked down at their child at the same time. Just like that, Abbey had fallen asleep on her mother's lap.

"You put down the baby," he said and held up the disc. "I'll put this away. Then I'll light a fire."

"And we'll meet back here."

If they were as lucky as she now believed them to be, history would repeat itself. This time next year they'd have another perfect little addition in their lives.

But as Bishop carried away that disc that held such sweet memories, and she carried their precious bundle to the nursery, Laura caught sight of those two portraits hanging above the fireplace and knew there was no need to guess at the future. They would always be a family who loved and supported each other, no matter what.

No matter what.

* * * * *

ONE NIGHT WITH PRINCE CHARMING

ANNA DePALO

A former intellectual-property attorney, **Anna DePalo** lives with her husband, son and daughter in New York City. Her books have consistently hit the Borders bestseller list and Nielsen BookScan's list of top one hundred bestselling romances.

Her books have won the *RT Book Reviews* Reviewers' Choice Award, the Golden Leaf and the Book Buyer's Best and have been published in more than a dozen countries. Readers are invited to surf to www.annadepalo.com, where they can join Anna's mailing list.

One

She'd just witnessed a train wreck.

Oh, no, not a literal one, Pia shook her head now at the wedding reception. But a figurative one was just as bad.

It was funny what a train wreck looked like from one end of a church aisle, with yards of ivory satin on display and the mingled scents of lilies and roses in the June air. As a wedding planner, she'd dealt with plenty of disasters. Grooms with cold feet. Brides who'd outsized their wedding dress. Even, once, a ringbearer who'd swallowed one of the rings. But surely Pia's always-practical close friend would have no such problems at her wedding. Or so Pia had thought up until about two hours ago.

Of course, the passengers in their pews had all been agape as the Marquess of Easterbridge had stridden purposely up the aisle and announced that, in fact, there *was* an objection to Belinda Wentworth marrying Tod Dillingham. That, in fact, Belinda's hasty and secret marriage to Colin Granville, current Marquess of Easterbridge, had never been annulled.

Collectively, the cream of New York City society had blinked. Eyes had widened and eyebrows had shot up in the pews of St. Bart's, but no one had been so gauche as to actually faint—or pretend to.

And for that, Pia was grateful. There was only so much a wedding planner could do once the dog ate the cake, or the cab splattered mud on the bride's dress, or, as in this case, *the legal husband,* for God's sake, decided to show up at the wedding!

Pia had sat frozen in her position off the center aisle. Angels, she'd thought absently, were in short supply today.

And on the heels of *that* thought had come another. *Oh, Belinda, why, oh, why didn't you ever tell me about your Las Vegas wedding to, of all people, your family's sworn enemy?*

But in her gut, Pia had already known why. It was an act Belinda regretted. Pia's brow puckered, thinking of what Belinda was dealing with right now. Belinda was one of her two closest friends in New York—along with Tamara Kincaid, one of Belinda's bridesmaids.

And then, Pia heaped some of the blame on herself. Why hadn't she spotted and intercepted Colin, like a good little wedding planner? Why hadn't she stayed at the entrance to the church?

People would wonder why she, the bridal consultant, hadn't known enough to keep the Marquess of Easterbridge away, or why she hadn't been able to stop him before a very public debacle ruined her friend's wedding and Pia's own professional reputation.

Pia felt the urge to cry as she thought of the hit that her young business, Pia Lumley Wedding Productions, would take. The Wentworth-Dillingham nuptials—or more accurately now, *almost*-nuptials—were to have been her most high-profile affair to date. She'd only struck out on her own a little over two years ago, after a few years as an assistant in a large event planning company.

Oh, this was horrendous. A nightmare, really. For Belinda *and* herself.

She'd come to New York City from a small town in Pennsylvania five years ago, right after college. This wasn't the way her dream to make it in New York was supposed to end.

As if in confirmation of her worst fears, right after the bride and both her groom *and* her husband had disappeared at the church, presumably to resolve the irresolvable, Pia had been standing in the aisle when a formidable society matron had steamed toward her.

Mrs. Knox had leaned close and said in a stage whisper, "Pia, dear, didn't you see the marquess approaching?"

Pia had smiled tightly. She'd wanted to say she'd had no idea that the marquess had been married to Belinda, and that, in any case, it wouldn't have done any good to intercept His Lordship if, in fact, he'd still been married to Belinda. But loyalty to her friend had kept her silent.

Mrs. Knox's eyes had gleamed. "You might have avoided a public spectacle."

True. But, Pia thought, even if she had known enough to try to stop him, the marquess had been a man on a mission, and one who had at least sixty pounds and more than six inches on her.

So Pia had done what she *could do* after the fact in order to try to save the day. After a quick consultation with assorted Wentworth family members, she'd encouraged everyone to repair to a show-must-go-on reception at The Plaza.

Now, as Pia looked around at the guests and at the waiters passing to and fro with platters of hors d'oeuvres, the low and steady murmur of conversation allowed her to relax her shoulders even as her mind continued to buzz.

She concentrated on her breathing, a relaxation technique

she'd learned long ago in order to help her deal with stressed-out brides and even more stressful wedding days.

Surely, Belinda and Colin would resolve this issue. *Somehow.* A statement could be issued to the press. With any luck something that began with *Due to an unfortunate misunderstanding...*

Yes, that's right. Everything would be okay.

She shifted her focus outward again and, right then, she spotted a tall, sandy-haired man across the room.

Even though he was turned away from her, the hair at the back of her neck prickled as a sense of familiarity and foreboding hit her. When he turned to speak to a man who'd approached him, she saw his face and sucked in a breath.

And that's when her world *really* came to a screeching halt. In her head, engines collided, the sound of crunching metal mixing with the smell of smoke. Or was the smoke coming out of her ears?

Could this day get any worse?

Him. James Fielding...aka Mr. Wrong.

What was James doing here?

It had been three long years since she'd last seen him, when he'd abruptly entered—and then promptly exited—her life, but there was no mistaking those seduce-you, golden Adonis looks.

He was nearly a decade older than her twenty-seven, but he hardly looked it, damn him. The sandy hair was clipped shorter than she remembered, but he was just as broad, just as muscular and just as impressive at over six feet tall.

His expression was studied rather than the fun-loving and carefree one she'd memorized. Still, a woman never forgot her first lover—especially when he'd vanished without explanation.

Unknowingly, Pia started toward him.

She didn't know what she would say, but her feet impelled her forward, as anger sang in her veins.

Her hands clenched at her sides.

As she approached, she noted that James was speaking with a well-known Wall Street hedge fund manager—Oliver Smithson.

"...Your Grace," the older and graying man said.

Pia's stride faltered. *Your Grace?*

Why would James be addressed as *Your Grace?* The reception room held its share of British aristocrats, but even marquesses were addressed as *My Lord*. As far as she knew, *Your Grace* was a form of address reserved for...dukes.

Unless Oliver Smithson was joking?

Unlikely.

The thought flashed through her mind, and then it was too late.

She was upon them, and James spotted her.

Pia noted with satisfaction the flicker of recognition in his hazel eyes.

He looked debonair in a tuxedo that showcased a fit physique. His facial features were even, though his nose wasn't perfectly sloped, and his jaw was square and firm. Eyebrows that were just a shade darker than his hair winged over eyes that had fascinated her in their changeable hue during their one night together.

If she wasn't so fired up, the impact of all that masculine perfection might have knocked the air from her lungs. As it was, she felt a sizzle skate along her nerve endings.

She could be excused for being a fool three years ago, she told herself. James Fielding was sex poured into civilized attire.

Though his rakish air, so undeniable when she'd first met him, had been tamed, both by his clothes and his demeanor, she sensed that it was still there. She was *intimately* acquainted with it.

"Ah, our lovely wedding planner," Oliver Smithson said, seemingly oblivious to the tension in the air, and then laughed heartily. "Couldn't have predicted this turn of events, could we?"

Pia knew the comment was a reference to the drama at the church, but she couldn't help thinking grimly that it applied just as well to the current situation. She would *never* have expected to run into James here.

As if following her line of thought, James raised an eyebrow.

Before either of them could say anything, however, Smithson went on, addressing her, "Have you made the acquaintance of His Grace, the Duke of Hawkshire?"

The Duke of...?

Pia's eyes went wide, and she stared in mute fury. *So he really was a duke?* Was his name even James?

No, wait—she knew the answer to that question. She had, of course, reviewed the guest list for the wedding. She'd had no idea, however, that her Mr. Wrong and James Carsdale, Ninth Duke of Hawkshire, were one and the same.

She felt suddenly light-headed.

James glanced at Oliver Smithson. "Thank you for attempting to affect an introduction, but Ms. Lumley and I have met before," he said before turning back to her. "And please address me as Hawk. Most people do these days."

Yes, they were more acquainted than anyone could guess, Pia thought acerbically. And how dare Hawk stand there so haughty and self-possessed?

Her gaze clashed with that of the man who was an intimate stranger to her. Angling her chin up, she said, "Y-yes, I-I've had the pleasure."

Immediately, her cheeks flamed. She'd meant to make a sophisticated double entendre, but she'd undermined herself by sounding unsure and naive.

Damn her stutter for making an appearance now. It just showed how flustered she was. She'd worked a long time with a therapist to suppress her childhood speech impediment.

Still, Hawk's eyes narrowed. Without a doubt, he'd understood her intended dig, and he didn't like it. But then his expression turned intense and sensual, before changing again to a perplexing flash of tenderness.

Beneath her sleeveless brown sheath, Pia felt a frisson of awareness, her breasts and abdomen tightening. Surely she was mistaken about that fleeting look that appeared almost tender?

Was he feeling sorry for her? Was he looking down at her, the naive virgin whom he'd left after one night? The thought made her spine stiffen.

"Pia."

As her name fell from his chiseled lips—the first time she'd heard it from him in three years—she was swamped by thoughts of a night of blistering sex between her white embroidered sheets.

Damn him. She rallied her resolve.

"What an unexpected...pleasure," Hawk said, his lips quirking, as if he, too, knew how to play at a game of hidden meaning.

Before she could reply, a waiter stopped beside them and presented them with a platter of canapés with baba ghanoush purée.

Staring down at the appetizers, Pia's first thought was that she and Belinda had spent an entire afternoon choosing the hors d'oeuvres for today.

Then, as another thought quickly followed, she decided to go for broke.

"Thank you," she acknowledged the waiter.

Turning back to the duke, she smiled sweetly. "It's a pleasure to savor. Bon appétit."

Without pausing a beat, she plastered his face with a fistful of eggplant.

Then she turned on her heel and stalked toward the hotel kitchen.

Dimly, she recorded the astonished gazes of the hedge fund manager and a few nearby guests before she slapped open the kitchen's swinging doors. If her professional reputation hadn't already been ruined, it was surely going down in flames now. *But it was worth it.*

Hawk accepted the cloth napkin from the waiter who came scurrying over.

"Thank you," he said with appropriate aristocratic sang-froid.

He carefully wiped baba ghanoush from his face.

Oliver Smithson eyed him. "Well…"

Hawk wiped his lips against each other. "Delicious, though a bit on the tart side."

Both the appetizer and the petite bombshell who'd delivered it.

The hedge fund manager laughed uneasily and cast a look around them. "If I'd known the Wentworth wedding would be this exciting, I'd have shorted it."

"Really?" Hawk drawled. "This is one stock that I'm betting won't fall in price. In fact, isn't notoriety the route to fame and fortune these days? Perhaps the bride will have the last laugh yet."

Hawk knew he had to do what he could to dampen today's firestorm. Despite the affront to his person, he thought of the pixie wedding planner who moments ago had stormed away.

He also wondered where his friend Sawyer Langsford, Earl of Melton, had gone, because right now he could use some help in putting out the blazes that were burning. He was sure Melton could be recruited despite being one of Dillingham's groomsmen. Sawyer was a distant relative and acquaintance of the groom's, but he was an even better friend of Easterbridge's.

Hawk realized that Smithson was looking at him curiously,

obviously debating what, if anything, to say at an awkward moment.

"Excuse me, won't you?" he asked, and then without waiting for an answer, stepped in the direction in which Pia had gone.

He supposed he shouldn't be so dismissive of a valuable business contact, but he had a more pressing matter to attend to.

He flattened his hand against the swinging kitchen door and pushed his way inside.

As he strode in, Pia swung around to face him.

She was unintentionally sexy, just like the first—and last—time they had met. A compact but curvy body was bound in a satin dress that hugged everywhere. Her smooth dark blond hair was caught up in a practical, working-glam chignon. And then there was the smooth-as-satin skin, as well as the bow lips and the eyes that still reminded him of clear amber.

Her eyes flashed at him now, just as Hawk was doing a quick recovery from being hit with all that stop-and-go sexy at once.

"C-come to find me?" Pia demanded. "Well, you're three years too late!"

Hawk had to admire her feistiness, much as it came at his expense at the moment. "I came to check on how you're doing. I assure you that if I'd known you'd be here—"

Her eyes widened dangerously. "You would have what? Run in the opposite direction? Never have accepted the wedding invitation?"

"This meeting comes as much of a surprise to me as it does to you."

A little surprisingly, he hadn't caught a glimpse of her until she'd come upon him at the reception. Of course, he'd been among the throng of four hundred invited guests—and one decidedly *uninvited* one—at the church. And then everyone, including him, had been transfixed by the appearance of

Easterbridge. Who the hell would have known the bride had a husband stashed away—who was none other than London's most famous landowning marquess? But that shock had been nothing compared to the surprise of seeing Pia again...and seeing the mingled astonishment and hurt on her face.

"An unfortunate surprise, I'm sure, *Your Grace*," Pia retorted. "I don't recall you mentioning your title the last time we met."

A direct hit, but he tried to deflect it. "I hadn't succeeded to the dukedom at the time."

"But you weren't simple Mr. James Fielding, either, were you?" she countered.

He couldn't argue with her point there, so he judiciously chose to remain silent.

"I thought so!" she snapped.

Hell. "My full name is James Fielding Carsdale. I am now the Ninth Duke of Hawkshire. I was formerly entitled to be addressed as Lord James Fielding Carsdale or simply—" his lips twisted in a self-deprecating smile "—Your Lordship, though I usually preferred to dispense with the title and the formality that came with it."

The truth was that, back in his playboy days, he had grown used to moving around incognito simply as Mr. James Fielding—thereby avoiding tiresome gold diggers and shaking off the trappings of his position in life—until someone, Pia, had gotten hurt by his charade and his dropping out of sight without a word.

He hadn't even been the heir apparent to his father's ducal title until William, his older brother, had died in a tragic accident, Hawk thought with a twist of the gut. Instead, he'd been Lord James Carsdale, the devil-may-care gadabout younger son who'd dodged the bullet that was the responsibilities of the dukedom—or so he'd thought.

It had taken three years of shouldering those very responsibilities to understand just how thoughtless, how careless, he had been before, and how much damage he might have done. Especially to Pia. But she was wrong if she thought he'd avoid her. He was glad to see her again—glad to have a chance to make amends.

Pia's face drew into a frown. "Are you suggesting that your behavior can somehow be excused because the name you gave me wasn't a total lie?"

Hawk gave an inward sigh. "No, but I am trying, belatedly, to come clean, for what it's worth."

"Well, it's worth nothing," she informed him. "I'd actually forgotten all about you until this opportunity presented itself to confront you about your disappearing act."

They were drawing curious stares from the kitchen staff and even some of the waiters, who were, however, too busy to linger and ogle the latest wedding spectacle.

"Pia, can we take this conversation elsewhere?" Hawk pointedly glanced around them. "We're adding to the events of a day that only needs a little push to tip it over into melodrama."

"Believe me," she retorted, "I've been to enough weddings to know we're nowhere near melodrama. Melodrama is the bride fainting at the altar. Melodrama is the groom flying to the honeymoon by himself. Melodrama is not the bridal consultant confronting her loutish one-night stand!"

Hawk said nothing. He was more concerned for her sake than his, anyway. And she was probably right. What was another scene in a day full of them? Besides, it was clear that Pia was very upset. The wedding disruption had to be troubling her more than she cared to admit, and then there was *his* presence.

Pia folded her arms and tapped her foot. "Do you run out on every woman the morning after?"

No, only on the one and only woman who'd turned out to be a virgin—her. He'd been attracted to her heart-shaped face and compact but shapely body, and the next morning, he'd known he was in too deep.

Hawk wasn't proud of his behavior. But his former self seemed aeons removed from his present situation.

Though even now, he itched to get close to her...to touch her...

He pushed the thought aside. He reminded himself sternly of his course in life ever since he'd become the duke, and that destiny didn't involve messing up Pia's life again. This time, he wanted to make up for what he'd done, for the gift he'd taken from her without realizing...the one she hadn't bothered to warn him about in advance.

Hawk bent toward Pia. "You want to talk about secrets?" he said in a low voice. "When had you been planning to tell me you were a virgin?"

Pia's chest rose and fell with outrage. Under other circumstances, Hawk thought with the back of his mind, he might have been able to enjoy the show.

"So I'm somehow responsible for your vanishing act?" Pia demanded.

He quirked a brow. "No, but let's agree that we were both putting on an act that night, shall we?"

Heat stained Pia's cheeks. "I turned out to be exactly who I said I was!"

"Hmm," he said, studying her upturned face. "As I recall, you disclosed that you'd never had unprotected sex—now who was shading the truth?"

After he'd accompanied her back to her apartment—a little studio on Manhattan's Upper East Side—they'd done the responsible thing before being intimate. He'd wanted to assure her that he was clean and, in return, she'd...lulled him into unintentionally taking her virginity.

Damn it. Even in his irresponsible younger days, he'd vowed never to be a woman's first lover. *He didn't want to be remembered. He didn't want to remember.* It didn't mesh with his carefree lifestyle.

But she'd claimed to have forgotten him. Was it pride alone

that had made her toss out that put down—or was it true? Because he hadn't succeeded in getting her out of his mind, much as he'd tried.

As if in answer to his question, Pia stared at him in mute fury, and then turned on her heel. "Th-this time, I'm the one walking away. Goodbye, Your Grace."

She strode away from him and deeper into the recesses of the kitchen, leaving Hawk to brood alone about their chance encounter—the perfect cap to a perfectly awful day. Pia had been nonplussed, to say the least, by his unexpected appearance and her discovery of who he really was.

But it was also clear that Pia was worried—Belinda's almost-wedding couldn't have good consequences for Pia's wedding planning business. And the fact that Pia herself had given him an unexpected taste of baba ghanoush before some stupefied guests couldn't have helped matters, either.

Pia obviously needed help. For, despite tasting eggplant and their angry confrontation, he still felt an overriding and overdue obligation to make amends.

And with that thought, Hawk contemplated a burgeoning idea.

Two

When Pia got home from the reception at The Plaza, she did *not* conduct an exorcism to banish Hawk from her life again. She did not create a likeness of him with ice cream sticks to ceremonially take apart.

Instead, after picking up and removing Mr. Darcy from her computer chair, she went straight to Google and typed in Hawk's name and title. She told herself it was so she could find a photo to make an Old West sheriff's poster: WANTED: RENEGADE DUKE MASQUERADING AS MR. RIGHT. In reality, she was thirsty for information now that she had Mr. Wrong's real name.

James Fielding Carsdale, Ninth Duke of Hawkshire.

The internet did not disappoint her. It offered up a bounty of hits in a few seconds.

Hawk had started Sunhill Investments, a hedge fund, three years ago, shortly after he'd—she let herself think it—taken her virginity and run. The company had done very well, making Hawk and his partners multimillionaires many times over.

Drat. It was hard to accept that after his dumping of her, he'd been visited with good fortune rather than feeling the wrath of cosmic justice.

Sunhill Investments was based in London, but had recently opened an office in New York—so Hawk's presence on this side of the Atlantic might be for more than the Wentworth-Dillingham wedding that wasn't.

As Pia delved beyond the first few hits, she absently scratched Mr. Darcy's ears as he stroked by her legs. She'd adopted the cat from a shelter close to three years ago and taken him back to the two-bedroom apartment that she'd just moved into—still, however, on the less fashionable edge of Manhattan's Upper East Side.

The fact that the apartment was rent-stabilized and also served as a tax-deductible office permitted her to afford a place that was on the outer fringes of the world that she wanted to tap into—that of Upper East Side prep school girls and future debutantes with well-heeled parents and with living quarters in cloistered prewar buildings guarded by uniformed and capped doormen standing under ubiquitous green awnings.

She'd decorated the apartment as a showcase for her creativity and style because she had the occasional visit from a potential client. Mostly, however, she traveled to see brides in their well-appointed and luxurious homes.

Now, she clicked on her computer mouse. After a few minutes, she brought up a link with an old article about Hawk from the *New York Social Diary.* He was pictured standing between two blond models, a drink in hand and a devilish glint in his eye. The article made it clear that Hawk had been a regular on the social circuit, mostly in London and somewhat in New York.

Pia's lips tightened. Well, at least the article served as some confirmation that she was his physical type—he appeared to have an affinity for blondes. However, at five-foot-four, she was a few inches shorter—not to mention a bit fleshier—than the leggy, skinny catwalkers he'd been photographed with.

The only saving grace in the whole situation was that Hawk's detestable behavior three years ago had given her the courage to embark on her own and start her namesake wedding planning business. She'd realized it was time to stop waiting for Prince Charming and take charge of her life. How pathetic would it have been if he'd been scaling the heights of the financial world while she'd been pining away for him, cocooned to this day in the studio apartment where she'd lived three years ago?

She'd moved on and up, just as he had. And Hawk—the duke or His Grace or however he liked to be referred to—could take a flying leap with his millions.

Still, she couldn't help digging for further information online. It was an exercise in self-flagellation to understand the extent to which she'd been a naive virgin who'd given away the goods to a smooth-talking playboy.

After a half hour of searching, she discovered that Hawk's reputation didn't disappoint. He'd dated models, actresses and even a chanteuse or two. He'd been part of the social whirl of people with money to spare even before his recent incarnation as a top financier.

How unworldly she'd been to expect more than one night with him. How stupidly trusting.

And yet, she reminded herself, it hadn't only been naiveté. She'd been tricked—duped—and used by a practiced player.

She pushed away from the computer screen and padded into her bedroom. Her mind on autopilot, she removed her brown satin dress and slipped into cotton striped pajama bottoms and a peach-colored sleeveless top. In the bathroom, she removed her makeup, moisturized her face and brushed her teeth.

Walking back into the bedroom again, she began to take the pins from her hair as she moved to her dressing table—bought used at a flea market—and sat down. When her hair was loose, she ran a brush through it and stared at herself in the mirror.

She'd never been glamorously beautiful, but she'd been able to lay some claim—if the occasional comments she'd received since high school were to be believed—to being a sort of *cute pretty*. Now, though, she forced herself to be more critical.

Was there something about her that screamed *Take advantage of me?* Did her face sing *I'm a pushover?*

She sighed as she stood, switched off the bedside lamp and slid into bed. She felt Mr. Darcy spring onto the bed and curl his warm weight next to her leg.

Pia turned her face to the window, where rain had begun to pelt the glass, blurring the illumination cast by the city lights outside.

It had been a long, too eventful day, and she was bone-tired. But instead of weariness overtaking her, she found herself awake.

In the privacy of her bedroom, in her own bed and covered by the shadows of the night, she was surprised by the sudden moisture of tears on her face—a reflection of the rain outside. She hadn't cried over Hawk in a long time.

Since she'd switched apartments, Hawk had never invaded this sanctum. But he'd slept in this bed.

Drat Hawk.

With any luck, she'd never have to see him again. She was over him, and this would be the absolute last time that she'd shed tears about him.

Déjà vu. Hawk looked around him at Melton's picturesque Gloucestershire estate, which wasn't so different from his own family seat in Oxford. The centuries-old limestone estate was surrounded by acres of pastoral countryside, which was in full greenery in the August warmth. They could and did set period movies in places like this.

Except his friend Sawyer Langsford, Earl of Melton, was going to have a very real wedding to The Honorable Tamara Kincaid, a woman who could barely be persuaded to dance with him at the Wentworth-Dillingham near-miss of a wedding two months ago.

At the thought of weddings, Hawk admitted to himself that he'd reached a point in his life when his professional life had quieted down a bit, and at age thirty-six, the responsibility to beget an heir for the dukedom had begun to weigh on him.

In his younger, more carefree days, he'd dated a lot of women. In fact, he'd reveled in distinguishing himself as the bon vivant younger son—in spite of his steady job in finance—in contrast to his more responsible older brother, the heir.

And now one of his closest friends was getting married. Hawk had come at Sawyer's request for what was to be a small wedding in the presence of family and close friends. Easterbridge would also be present, and heaven help them, at the bride's invitation, so would his wife, Belinda Wentworth—without, however, her almost-husband, Tod Dillingham.

And Hawk had it on good authority that none other than Pia Lumley would be the wedding planner today. He'd been forewarned by Sawyer. For, as circumstances would have it, Tamara Kincaid was another good friend of Pia's.

As if conjured by his thoughts, Pia walked out from the French doors leading to the stone terrace at the back of the house, and then down to the grassy lawn where Hawk stood.

She looked young, fresh and innocent, and Hawk felt a sudden pang. She'd been all those things three years ago when he'd first met her—and left her.

She was wearing a white shirt with cuffs rolled back beyond her elbows and lime-green cotton pants paired with pink ballet flats. The pants hugged her curves, and just a hint of cleavage was visible at the open collar of her shirt. Her smooth blond hair was caught in a ponytail, and her lips looked shiny and full.

Hawk felt a tightening in his gut.

Despite having been plastered with eggplant at their last meeting, he felt drawn to her. She had sex appeal without being contrived—so different from many of the women in his social circle.

She was everything he wanted, and everything he couldn't have. It would throw him off track from the life that he was supposed to be living now if he got involved with her again. He had put his playboy days behind him.

He was thirty-six, and he'd never been more aware of his responsibilities than since he'd succeeded to the dukedom. Among other things, he had a duty to produce an heir to secure a centuries-old title. And in the normal course of events, he would be expected to marry someone of his class and social station—certainly his mother expected that of him.

In the past year, his mother had taken it upon herself to bring him into contact with eligible women, including, particularly, Michelene Ward-Fombley—a woman whom some had speculated would have made a wonderful duchess for his older brother, before William's untimely death.

He pushed aside thoughts about his most recent transatlantic phone conversation with his mother, and the unspoken expectations that had been alluded to...

Instead, Hawk couldn't help noting now that Pia resembled an enticing wood sprite. She was clearly unafraid to wear flats with her petite frame for a working casual look on a tepidly warm August day typical for this part of England. In his own nod to the weather, he had dispensed with anything but a white shirt and tan pants.

Pia looked up and spotted him as she walked across the lawn.

He watched as she hesitated.

After a moment, she continued to move toward him, but

with obvious reluctance. He was clearly standing in the direct path of her intended destination—very likely, the pavilion on the property that would serve as one of the backdrops for the wedding.

He tried to break the ice. "I know what you're thinking."

She gave him a haughty, disbelieving look.

"We don't see each other for three years," he pressed on, "and now we somehow run into each other for the second time in two months."

"Believe me, it's no more pleasant for me than it is for you," she responded, coming to a stop before him.

He scanned her face, angling his head to the side.

He pretended to make his perusal casual, joking even. Still, he caught the way a stray strand of sun-kissed honey-blond hair caressed her cheek gently. He stopped himself from reaching out to touch her soft skin and run his thumb over the outline of her jaw.

Then he made the mistake of picking up the light scent of lavender that he'd associated with her ever since their first night together. He couldn't help being attracted to her—he just couldn't act on that attraction.

"Wh-what are you doing?" she demanded.

"I'm checking to see if you're hiding hors d'oeuvres or canapés somewhere. I wanted to be prepared for another missile attack."

His attempt at a jest was met with a frosty look.

Pia raised her chin. "I'm here to make sure this wedding proceeds without a hitch."

"Ah, trying to rehabilitate your image?"

He'd meant to tease and test, and at her momentarily arrested look, he realized he'd guessed correctly.

Pia was still worried about her business. Belinda Wentworth's almost-wedding had likely blemished Pia's professional reputation.

In a moment, however, Pia recovered herself, and her

eyes sparked. "My only concern is that you and your two compatriots, Easterbridge and Melton, are in attendance. I have no idea why another friend of mine would get mixed up with a friend of yours. Look at what Easterbridge did to Belinda!"

"What Colin did to Belinda?" Hawk asked rhetorically. "You mean speaking up as *her husband?*"

Pia narrowed her eyes and pressed her lips together.

Hawk had started out this conversation trying to put Pia at ease, but ruffling her feathers was proving to be irresistible. "I defer to your superior experience with wedding etiquette. Are husbands even allowed to speak?"

"The marquess needn't have done so at the wedding. A nice, private communication from his attorney to hers would have sufficed."

"Perhaps Easterbridge had little notice of Belinda's impending wedding to Dillingham. Perhaps he did what he could to prevent a crime from occurring." Hawk arched a brow. "Bigamy is a crime in many places, including New York, you know."

"I'm well aware of that!"

"I'm relieved to hear it."

Pia gave him a repressive look, and then eyed him suspiciously. "How much notice did you have of Easterbridge's actions?"

"I wasn't even aware that Easterbridge was married to Belinda."

Hawk was glad he could set the record straight because Pia obviously suspected him of double-dealing as a wedding guest of Dillingham's but a friend of Easterbridge's. Not only hadn't he known about Easterbridge's past marriage, but he suspected that the only reason he'd been invited to the wedding in June was because Dillingham wanted to cement important social ties, however tenuous up to that point.

"And *I* have no idea what would have made Belinda wed

a friend of yours two years ago, in Las Vegas, of all places," Pia countered.

"Perhaps my friends and I are irresistible," he replied mockingly.

"Oh, I'm well aware that you're irresistible to women."

Hawk raised his brows and wondered whether Pia was admitting to her own past susceptibility to him. Had *she* found him not merely attractive but irresistible? Had she fallen into bed with him because she'd been swept up in the moment and carried away by passion?

"Once I had your real name, a little internet search revealed a good deal of information," Pia elaborated, dashing his hopes that she'd been referring to herself when she'd called him irresistible.

Hawk had no doubt as to what an internet search had revealed. He mentally winced at the thought of the news reports and gossip that must have come up about his younger, more spirited days. The women...the carousing...

"You know, I suppose I should have been wary three years ago when my Google search on James Fielding turned up nothing in particular, but then I supposed *Fielding* was such a common name..."

He quirked his lips. "My ancestors are no doubt rolling in their graves at being labeled *common*."

"Oh, yes, pardon me, *Your Grace*," Pia returned bitingly. "You can rest assured that I'm no longer ignorant of the protocol due to your rank."

Damn protocol to hell, he wanted to respond. It was one of the reasons he'd preferred flying under the radar as plain James Fielding. Except these days, of course, having succeeded to the ducal title, he could no longer afford such a luxury. Then, too, he was all too cognizant of his responsibilities.

The irony wasn't lost on him that having succeeded to the title of Duke of Hawkshire, he'd gained all manner of wealth—and responsibilities—that most men coveted, but had lost the things he craved most: anonymity, a certain freedom and being valued for himself.

"Tell me about your wedding business," he said abruptly, turning the conversation back in the direction he wanted. "Three years ago, I recall you were still working at a large event planning firm and had big dreams of setting out on your own."

Pia looked guarded and then defiant. "I did manage to start my own business, as you can tell. It was shortly after your abrupt disappearance, in fact."

"Are you saying you have me to thank?" Hawk asked with exaggerated aristocratic hauteur and faint mockery.

Pia's hand curled at her side. "*Thanks,* I think, would be going too far. But I believe it was your abrupt exit that provided me with the impetus to strike out on my own. After all, there's nothing like a momentary disappointment to fuel the drive to succeed in another area of life."

Hawk gave a weak imitation of a smile. He very much regretted his actions in the past, but he wondered what she'd say if she knew the extent of his responsibilities, ducal and otherwise, these days.

"You were very creative with the décor at Belinda's wedding," he said, ignoring her jab in an effort to be more conciliatory. "The gold and lime-green color scheme was certainly unusual."

At Pia's look of momentary surprise, he added, "You needn't look so taken aback that I noticed the detail. After savoring baba ghanoush, I believe contemplating the scenery became a much more engaging pastime."

He had let himself study the décor because he had been curious about any detail that would reveal anything about *her*—and it had beat deflecting curious looks and probing questions from the other wedding guests.

"I'm glad my excellent aim had at least one beneficial consequence," Pia responded dryly.

"Ah, I assume the consequences to your wedding business weren't so satisfactory?" he probed, taking advantage of his opening.

Pia's expression turned defensive, but not before Hawk saw the fleeting distress there.

"What sort of wedding would you have for yourself, Pia?" Hawk asked, his voice suddenly low and inviting. "Surely you must have envisioned it many times."

He knew he was playing with fire, but he didn't care.

"I'm in the wedding business," Pia responded frostily. "Not the romance business."

Their eyes held for moments...until a voice called out Pia's name.

He and Pia turned at the same time to look back in the direction of the house, where Tamara was descending the terrace steps.

"Pia," Tamara announced, coming toward them across the lawn. "I've been looking for you everywhere."

"I was just walking over to the pavilion," Pia responded. "I wanted to see what can be done with it."

Hawk watched as Tamara glanced curiously from Pia to him and back.

"Well, I'm glad I found you," Tamara said, and then hooked her arm through Pia's.

Tamara spared Hawk a cursory look. "You don't mind if I commandeer Pia, do you, Hawk...I mean, Your Grace?" And then not waiting for an answer, she turned Pia toward the pavilion. "I thought not."

Hawk's lips quirked. Tamara wasn't one to stand on ceremony. Though she was the daughter of a British viscount, she'd been raised mostly in the United States and had the decidedly democratic tendencies of the bohemian jewelry designer she was.

She'd also obviously sailed in like a mother hen to rescue Pia.

"Not at all," Hawk murmured to Tamara's retreating back.

He watched the two women cross the lawn.

When Pia turned back briefly to glance at him, he returned her gaze solemnly.

He'd gleaned a lot from their conversation. He'd guessed correctly—as evidenced by her momentary distress just now—that Pia's wedding business needed help in the wake of Belinda's wedding. The fact that Pia's firm had managed to survive for more than two years said something, however.

Pia obviously had talent, and she'd nurtured it since their one night together.

With that thought, as he turned back to the house, Hawk realized that a conversation with his sister, a prospective bride, was in order.

Three

As she and Tamara walked toward the pavilion, Pia noticed her friend glance at her.

"I hope I wasn't interrupting anything," Tamara remarked, and then paused at Pia's continued silence. "On second thought, perhaps I hope I did."

As Tamara suddenly stopped to speak with one of the staff who hailed her, Pia stood nearby and soon found herself lost in thought about the night that she and Hawk had first met.

The beat of the music could be felt in the bar stools, on the tables and along the walls. In fact, everything vibrated. It was loud and packed, bodies brushing past each other in the confines of the tavern.

A bar wasn't her preferred scene, Pia thought, but she'd come here with a coworker from the event-planning business she worked for in order to rub shoulders with bright young things and their beaus.

People who liked a party—and needed event organizers—

usually attended parties prodigiously. And it had almost been a job directive from her boss to be social after work hours, making connections and trying to bring in business.

Except Pia's interest wasn't in anniversary parties or coming-of-age celebrations.

Instead, she liked weddings.

Someday, she promised herself, her dream of having her own wedding planning business would become a reality.

In the meantime, she shouldered her way past other patrons and reached the bar. But at her height, she could barely see above those sitting at the bar stools, let alone signal the bartender.

A man next to her gestured to the bartender and called out an order for a martini.

She glanced up at him and, a second later, sucked in a breath as he looked down at her with an easygoing grin.

"Drink?" he offered.

He was one of the most attractive men she'd ever seen. He was tall, certainly over six feet, his sandy hair slightly tousled, and his hazel eyes, flecked with interesting bits of gold and green, dancing. His nose was less than perfect—had it been broken once?—but that added to his magnetism. His grin revealed a dimple to the right of his mouth.

Most importantly, he was looking at *her* with warm, lazy interest.

He was the closest thing to her fantasy man as she'd ever seen—not that she'd ever admit to anyone that, at twenty-four, she'd had a fantasy lover and no other kind.

Pia parted her lips—*please, please let me sound sophisticated.* "Cosmopolitan, thank you."

He gave the briefest nod of acknowledgment, and then looked away to signal the bartender and order her drink. Within seconds, he effortlessly accomplished what to her had been blocked by multiple obstacles.

When he looked back at her, he was smiling again.

"Are you?" he asked, his low and smooth voice inviting intimacy.

She stalled. "Am I...?"

His eyes crinkled. "Are you a Cosmo girl?"

She pretended to consider the question for a moment. "It depends. Are you a pickup artist?"

He laughed, his expression saying he was respectful of her parry even as his interest sharpened. "I don't suppose you'd give a hint as to what the right answer is supposed to be?"

Pia played along. "Do you need a hint? Doesn't charm get you the answer you want?"

His accent wasn't easy to pinpoint—he appeared to be from here, there and anywhere—but she thought she detected a faint British enunciation.

"Hmm, it depends," he mused, rubbing his chin and showing his dimple again. "Are you here with anyone?"

She knew he meant a man—a date. "I'm here with a coworker, but I seem to have lost track of Cornelia in the crowd."

He looked momentarily intent and seductive beneath his easygoing veneer, but then his casual appeal took over again. "Great, then I can be as charming as I'm able. Let's start with names. No woman as lovely and enchanting as you can be called anything but—?"

He quirked a brow.

She couldn't help smiling. "Pia Lumley."

"Pia," he repeated.

The sound of her name falling from his chiseled lips sent shivers chasing over her skin. He'd called her *lovely* and *enchanting*. Her fantasy man had a voice, and it was dreamy.

"James Fielding," he volunteered.

Just then, the bartender leaned in their direction and slid two drinks across the bar between seated patrons.

James handed the cosmopolitan to her, and then picked up his martini.

"Cheers," he said, clinking his glass against hers.

She took a small sip of her drink. It was stronger than her usual party libation—a light beer or a fruity beach drink was more her style—but then again, she'd wanted to appear sophisticated.

She suspected that James was used to chic women. And she'd grown used to projecting a polished and stylish image when trying to drum up business for work. Potential clients expected it—people didn't want an inexperienced girl from small-town Pennsylvania running their six-figure party.

After sipping from his drink, James nodded at a couple departing from a corner table near them. "Would you like to sit?"

"Thank you," she said, and then turned and slid into a padded booth seat.

As she watched James sit down to her left, a little thrill went through her. So he meant to continue their conversation and further their acquaintance? She was happy she'd held his interest.

She hadn't had many men hit on her. She didn't think she was bad-looking, but she was short and more understated than bold, and therefore easily overlooked. She was cute, rather than one to inspire lust or overwhelming passion.

He looked at her with a smile hovering at his lips. "Are you new to New York?"

"It depends on what you mean by new," she replied. "I've been here a couple of years."

"And you were transported here from a fairy tale called—?"

She laughed. "Cinderella, of course. I'm a blonde."

His smile widened. "Of course."

He rested an arm along the back of the booth seat and reached out to finger a tendril of her hair.

She drew in a breath—hard.

"And a beautiful shade of blond, it is," he murmured. "It's gold spun with wheat and sunshine."

She looked into his eyes. She could, she thought, spend hours studying the fascinating mix of hues there.

James cocked his head, his eyes crinkling. "Okay, Pia," he continued in his smooth, deep voice, "Broadway, Wall Street, fashion, advertising or *The Devil Wears Prada?*"

"None of the above?"

His eyebrows rose. "I've never struck out before."

"Never?" she asked with feigned astonishment. "I'm sorry I ruined your track record."

"Never mind. I trust your discretion will spare my reputation."

They were flirting—or rather *he* was flirting with *her*—and she was, amazingly, holding her own.

It was all exhilarating. She'd never had a man flirt with her this way, and certainly no one of James's caliber.

In fact, though, she wasn't an actress, a banker, a model, or in advertising or publishing. "I'm an event planner," she said. "I organize parties."

"Ah." His eyes gleamed. "A party girl. Splendid."

There were party girls and then there were *party girls,* she wanted to say, but she didn't correct him.

"What about you?" she asked instead. "What are you doing here in New York?"

He straightened, dropping his arm from the back of the seat. "I'm just an ordinary Joe with a boring finance job, I'm afraid."

"There's nothing ordinary about you," she blurted, and then clamped her mouth shut.

He smiled again, his dimple appearing. "I'm flattered you think so."

She lifted her drink for another sip because he and his

smile—and, yes, that dimple—were doing funny things to her insides.

He was studying her, and she tried to remain casual, though he sat mere inches away.

She was very aware of his muscular thigh encased in beige pants on the seat beside her. He wore no tie, and the strong, corded lines of his neck stood in relief against the open collar of his light blue shirt.

He nodded, his eyes fixed at a spot near her collarbone. "That's an interesting necklace you're wearing."

She glanced down, though she knew what he'd be seeing. She wore a sterling silver necklace with a flying fish pendant. In deference to the July heat, she'd worn a sleeveless turquoise blue sheath dress. The pendant was one of her usual accessories.

She'd come directly to the bar from work, and she figured he'd done the same from the way he was dressed. Though he wasn't wearing a suit, his attire qualified as business casual. Work dress code was more relaxed in the summer in the city, especially on a dress-down Friday.

She flushed now, however, at the thought that between the color of her dress and the symbol on her pendant, she resembled nothing so much as a pond with a solitary fish swimming in it.

Drat. Why hadn't she thought of that when she'd dressed this morning?

But James's face held no hint of amusement at her expense—just simple curiosity.

She fingered her pendant. "The necklace was a gift from my friend Tamara, who is a wonderful jewelry designer here in the city. I like to fish."

"A woman after my own heart then."

Pia checked her surprise. Of course, he would be interested in fishing. He was her fantasy man—how could he not be?

"Do you fish?" she asked unnecessarily.

"Since I was three or four," he said solemnly. "What kind of fishing do you do?"

She laughed with a tinge of self-consciousness. "Oh, anything. Bass, trout… There are plenty of lakes where I grew up in western Pennsylvania. My father and grandfather taught me how to bait and cast a line—as well as ride a horse and, uh, m-milk a cow."

She couldn't believe she'd admitted to milking cows. How would he ever think of her as an urban sophisticate now? She ought to have quit while she was ahead.

James looked nothing but fascinated, however. "Horseback riding—even better. I've been riding since I could walk." His eyes glinted. "I can't say the same about milking cows, on the other hand."

She flushed.

"But I sheered a few sheep during a stay at an Australian sheep station."

Pia felt her lips twitch. "Well, then, you've bested me. I concede."

"Good of you," he deadpanned. "I knew sheep would win out."

"I've done some fly-fishing," she asserted.

He smiled. "Point to you. There are not many women who are willing to stand around in muck all day, wearing waders and waiting to get a bite." His smile broadened into a grin. "As petite as you are, I imagine you couldn't wade in very far."

She struck a look of mock offense. "I'll have you know I stood as still as a chameleon on a branch."

"Then I'd have been tempted to drop a frog down the back of your waders," he teased.

"Oh, you would! Don't tell me you have sisters whom you tormented."

"No such luck," he mourned. "I have one sister, but she's

several years younger than I am, and my mother wouldn't have looked well on any pranks."

"I wouldn't have expected she would," she said with mock indignation. "And if you'd attempted to foist a frog on me, I'd have—"

"Yes?"

He was enjoying this.

"I'd have thrown you for a loop!"

"Don't fairy-tale heroines need to get to know a few frogs?" he asked innocently.

"I believe the expression is *kiss a few frogs,*" she replied. "And, no, the requirements have been updated for the twenty-first century. And anyway, I'd know when I kissed a frog."

"Mmm…do you want to put it to the test?"

"I—I—"

What a time for her stammer to make another appearance.

Not waiting for a clearer sign of encouragement, he leaned in, and as her eyelids lowered, gently pressed his lips to her. She felt the momentary zing of electricity, and her lips parted on an indrawn breath. And then his mouth moved over hers, tasting and sampling, giving and receiving.

His lips were soft, and she tasted the faint lingering flavor of his drink as they kissed. The crowd around them receded as she focused on every warm stroke of his mouth against hers.

Just as their kiss threatened to become more heated, he drew back, his expression thoughtful and bemused. "There, how was that?"

She searched his eyes. "Y-you are in no way related to Kermit the Frog."

He grinned. "How about my fishing? Am I reeling you in?"

"A-am I on the hook or are you?"

"James."

The moment was interrupted as he was hailed by someone and turned in the direction of a man coming toward them.

Pia straightened and sat back in her seat, belatedly realizing with some embarrassment that she was still leaning forward.

"The CEO of MetaSky Investments is here, James," the man announced, sparing her a cursory look. "I'll introduce you."

Pia judged the man to be a contemporary of James's. Perhaps he was a friend or a business colleague.

At the same time, she sensed James hesitate beside her. She could tell that whoever this CEO was, it would be valuable for James to meet him. After all, he was important enough for a friend to have sought James out in the crowded bar.

James turned toward her. "Will you—"

"There you are, Pia! I've been searching for you."

Cornelia materialized out of the crowd.

Pia pasted a bright smile on her face as she glanced at James. "As you can see, you no longer need to worry about leaving me alone."

James nodded. "Will you excuse me?"

"Of course."

Pia tamed her disappointment as James rose to depart. She noticed that he didn't say he'd be back. And she knew better than to expect that he would return. She understood—sort of—that these flirtations in bars were fleeting and transient.

On the other hand, the romantic in her believed in kismet. He was the most magnificent man she'd ever met.

And if that had been the last she'd seen of him, she probably would have remembered him as nothing more than a handsome, charming fantasy—a brief glimpse of a fairytale prince to brighten her disappointing night. Certainly, the evening began to show few signs of success once they went their separate ways.

Two hours afterward, however, it was hard to keep

disappointment at bay. She hadn't glimpsed James since he'd departed, nor had she had any luck in making potential contacts, aside from handing her business card out to a couple of women who'd expressed a casual interest in retaining an event planner.

Pia sighed as she slid off a bar stool, having settled her tab. Cornelia had departed twenty minutes ago while Pia had still been conversing with a potential client. The woman who'd just vacated the bar stool next to Pia was an office manager at a small real estate firm, and though she'd had someone whom she used to help plan the firm's annual holiday party, she'd been willing to listen to Pia's pitch.

Business development was the part of her job that Pia found most challenging. Coming from Pennsylvania, she didn't have an extensive social network in the city. And it was so disheartening to get the brush-off from strangers. She supposed that telemarketing could be worse, but then again, at least telemarketers only had to deal with rejection by phone rather than face-to-face.

There was no doubt about the high point of the evening. James had shown real interest in *her*—however briefly.

Pia felt her heart squeeze. *Definitely time to leave.*

She'd head home to a rent-stabilized apartment on the unfashionable edge of the Upper East Side. She decided she'd pop in a DVD and lose herself in one of her favorite Jane Austen flicks, spending the rest of the evening forgetting what would never be.

It was a decent feel-good plan. Except as soon as she stepped out of the bar, she realized that it was pouring rain.

Oh, great.

She huddled under the bar's awning and looked down at herself. Even with the platform heels on her beige sandals, she knew her feet—and likely more—were going to get soaked. She'd tucked a small umbrella into her handbag this morning, just in case, but she'd been betting it wouldn't rain when she'd chosen what to wear. The weather report had said showers weren't in the forecast until the wee hours of the morning.

Her one hope was hailing a cab, but she knew one would be scarce in this kind of weather, and in any case, on her salary, taxis were a luxury she tried to avoid. The only alternative was walking to the subway and then making the long hike from the train station to her apartment.

As she stood there, hugging herself for warmth and debating her options, the tavern door behind her opened.

"Need a ride?"

She turned and glanced up. *James*.

Paradoxically, she felt embarrassed—as if she were the one running out on *him*, when in reality he hadn't sought her out again.

"I thought you'd already left," she blurted.

A slow smile spread across his face. "I did, but I came back in. I was conversing with the CEO of MetaSky outside, where we could hear each other and speak with more privacy." He looked around them. "It wasn't raining then."

She blinked. "Oh."

"Do you need a ride?" he asked again, glancing down at her.

She tried for some belated dignity, even as a gust of wind pelted her with raindrops. "I'm f-fine. I'm just debating whether to walk, row or swim home."

His smile spread. "What about a car instead?"

She raised her eyebrows. "How are we ever going to catch an empty cab in this weather?"

She knew that rain made New York City taxis disappear.

"Leave it to me."

She watched as James scanned the street. Two cabs passed them but their lit signs indicated that they were occupied. As the two of them waited, they made idle chitchat.

Close to fifteen minutes later, by a stroke of luck, James spotted a cab letting out a passenger beyond the nearest intersection. He moved swiftly from the shelter of the awning and into the street when the empty cab started to make its way down their block. He raised his arm, a commanding presence, and hailed the cab.

As the rain continued to assault him, he opened the taxi's door and motioned for her to step in.

"What's your address?" he called as she hurried toward him. "I'll tell the driver."

She called it out to him, realizing that he had an excuse to find out where she lived. He made everything appear smooth, charming and effortless.

"Are you leaving? Do you want to share a cab?" she asked as she reached him. "You're getting drenched! I should have offered you the umbrella in my bag but you stepped out so suddenly."

She couldn't stop the flow of words, though she knew she was nearly babbling. She had no idea what direction was home for him, but it seemed churlish not to offer to share the cab that he'd hailed for her. Yet again, he'd handily managed to accomplish something she herself often found difficult, being petite and certainly less imposing.

James looked at her and his lips quirked. Even with his hair getting matted by the rain and his face wet, he looked unbelievably handsome.

"Thanks for the offer," he said.

She wasn't sure if he meant to accept her offer, but once she entered the confines of the cab, she slid across the seat so he would have room to join her.

A moment later, he slid in beside her, folding his tall frame onto the bench seat and answering her unvoiced question.

She felt relief and a happy flutter, even as she also experienced a sense of nervous awareness. She had never left a bar with a man before—she was cautious. But then again, no man had attempted to pick her up in a bar before.

"I live on First Avenue in the high Eighties," she cautioned

James belatedly as he closed the car door. "I don't want to put you out. I don't know in what direction you need to head."

"It's no problem," he said easily. "I'll see you home first."

She noticed that he didn't divulge whether she was taking him out of his way or not.

He leaned forward to the partition separating the front from the backseat and told the cab driver her address. And in no time at all, they were speeding through Manhattan's wet and half-empty streets.

They were content to make some more desultory chitchat as the car ate up the distance to her apartment. She discovered that he was thirty-three to her twenty-four—not ancient by any means, but older and more worldly than the boys she'd dated back in high school and college in Pennsylvania.

Perhaps in order to make the gulf between them seem less so, she shared her dream of opening her own wedding planning business. Surely, he wouldn't think of her as so young and inexperienced if he knew she had plans to be a business owner.

He showed enthusiasm for her plans and encouraged her to proceed with them.

All the while, as thoughts raced through her mind, she wondered if he felt the sexual tension, too. Would she ever see him again?

In no time at all, however, they arrived outside her building.

James turned toward her, searching her eyes in the silence drawing out between them. "Here we are."

"W-would you like to come up?" she asked, surprising herself.

It was a daring move. But she felt as if their evening had been cut short when he'd had to meet with the CEO of MetaSky.

He paused and looked at her meaningfully for a moment. "Sure...I'd love to."

He settled the cab fare, and then they raced up the front stoop of her building, sharing her small umbrella.

She managed to fish out her keys in record time and let them inside. They stumbled into the vestibule and out of the cold and wet.

She lived in a studio on the top floor of a four-story brownstone. At least, however, the rental was hers alone. On a night like tonight, she didn't have to worry about the awkwardly timed arrival of a roommate or two. She'd made the best of her situation by putting up a partition wall to create a separate bedroom, though she couldn't do anything to alter the fact that her windows were the small ones beneath the roof.

As she heard and felt the tread of James's feet behind her on the stairs, she couldn't help feeling nervous about having him step into her little world.

Fortunately, she didn't have much time to dwell on the matter. Within a few minutes, they reached the uppermost floor, and she inserted her key in her door and let them inside.

She dropped her handbag on a chair and turned around in time to see him scanning her apartment.

He dominated the small space even more than she'd anticipated. Here there were no fellow bar patrons to defuse the full force of the magnetism that he exuded. There was no crowd to mitigate the sexual attraction between them.

James's eyes came back to hers. "It's cute."

She'd tried to make the apartment cheerful, as much to lift her own mood as anything else. A tiny table flanked by two chairs and sporting a vase of pink peonies and tulips sat near the door. The kitchen lined one wall, and a love seat guarded the space on the opposite side. Facing the entry, a small entertainment center stood in front of the partition that separated her bedroom from the rest of the space.

Pia knew what lay beyond the partition that shielded what remained of her apartment from James's gaze. A white croquet coverlet covered the full-size bed that occupied most of her sleeping area.

Nervously, she wet her lips. She couldn't keep her eyes from straying to the rain-soaked spots of his shirt. Some of those wet areas clung to the muscles of his arms and shoulders.

She'd never done this before.

"Pia."

Pia found herself jerked from her memories as Tamara closed the space on the lawn between them. Over Tamara's shoulder, she noticed the member of the household staff with whom Tamara had been speaking was heading back toward the stone terrace and French doors at the back of the house.

Hawk was nowhere to be seen. He, too, must have gone indoors.

"I'm sorry to have left you stranded here."

Pia pasted a bright smile on her face. "Not at all. It's all part of the prerogatives of the bride."

And one of her prerogatives, Pia thought, was to stay away from Hawk for the rest of this wedding...

Four

Pia walked along East 79th Street on Manhattan's Upper East Side looking for the correct house number. She'd received a call from Lucy Montgomery yesterday about being hired as a bridal consultant. She hadn't paid much attention to the particulars, but had jumped at the chance for new business because it had been a slow summer.

She hadn't liked to dwell on how much her silent phone was due to the Wentworth-Dillingham wedding being, well, both *more* and *less* than expected. She hadn't been directly to blame for the first part of the debacle. But the hard truth was that if the wedding had been a resounding success, her phone might have been ringing with more interested brides.

True, she'd been called on to help with Tamara's wedding last month. But that had been a small wedding—mainly family—and had transpired in England, so her involvement hadn't counted for much in the eyes of New York society. And while she'd also worked on a wedding in Atlanta over the summer, she'd been retained for that function *before* Belinda's nuptial debacle.

Now, though, on a breezy day in late September, with clouds overhead and the threat of rain in the air, she walked along one of Manhattan's tonier side streets, glad she'd worn her belted trench to ward off the threatening elements and even happier for the possibility of a new client.

Finding the house number she was looking for, she stopped and surveyed the impressive double-width, four-story limestone town house. A tall, black, wrought-iron fence guarded the façade, and flower boxes and black shutters framed tall, plate-glass windows. In the center of the building, stone steps ascended to the double-door front entrance at the parlor level. But instead of windows, the parlor floor boasted French doors embraced by tiny balconies.

There was no doubt that Lucy Montgomery came from money. This house was a well-preserved example of Manhattan's Gilded Age.

Pia ascended the steps and knocked before ringing the doorbell.

Within moments, an older gentleman, dressed in somber black and white rather than a clear uniform, responded. After Pia introduced herself, the butler took her coat and directed her to the parlor.

Pia soon discovered that the parlor was a spectacular room with a high, molded ceiling and a marble mantel. It was decorated in gold and rose and outfitted with antique furniture upholstered in stripes and prints.

She knew she should recognize the furniture style, but for the life of her, she could never remember how to separate Louis XIV style from its successors, Louis XV and Louis XVI. In any case, expensive was expensive.

She sat on one of the couches flanking the fireplace and contemplated her surroundings, taking several deep breaths to calm her nerves. *She'd never needed an account more.*

She hoped she would sufficiently impress Lucy Montgomery. She'd dressed with care, donning a chic and timeless short-sleeved peach dress and beige pumps, and keeping her jewelry to a minimum. She'd chosen wedding colors, even on an overcast day, because they were cheery and they resonated with brides.

At that moment, the parlor door opened, and with surprising promptness, Lucy appeared, a smile on her face.

Her hostess was a slim, attractive blonde of medium height with hazel eyes. She looked crisp in a salmon-colored shirt and knee-length tan skirt cinched by a wide black belt. Her legs stretched down to strappy sandals and showed off a tan that was courtesy, no doubt, of time spent at one of the sand-dusted retreats favored by the rich or famous or both.

Pia guessed that Lucy was around her own age or younger.

She rose from her seat in time to shake her hostess's outstretched hand.

"Thank you for scheduling this appointment on such short notice," Lucy exclaimed, her inflection British. "I was just about to come down the stairs when Ned told me you were here."

"It was no inconvenience, Ms. Montgomery," Pia responded with a smile of her own. "Client service is what my business is all about."

"It's Lucy, please."

"Pia, then."

"Good," Lucy responded happily, and then glanced at the clock. "I'll have tea brought in, if that meets with your approval." She smiled. "We British consider late afternoon to be teatime, I'm afraid."

"Yes, please. Tea would be wonderful."

After Lucy had gone to the door and spoken in low tones with a member of the household staff, she returned to sit on the sofa with Pia.

"Now then," she said. "I'm rather in desperate need of help, I'm afraid."

Pia tilted her head and smiled. "Many brides come to that conclusion at some point during their engagements. May I offer my congratulations, by the way?"

Lucy lit up. "Thank you, yes. My fiancé is American. I met him while working on an off-Broadway play."

Pia's eyebrows rose. "You're an actress?"

"Shakespearean trained, yes," Lucy replied without a hint of boast, and then leaned forward conspiratorially and winked. "He was one of the producers."

Money married money, Pia thought, if only because the people involved tended to move in the same social circles. She'd seen it many times before. And yet, it was clear from the way Lucy lit up that she was in love with her fiancé.

"You see," Lucy explained, "Derek and I were planning to marry next summer, but I've just landed a new role and we need to move up the wedding. Suddenly, everything seems upon us at once. Since I'm currently working in another production—" Lucy spread out her hands helplessly "—I have no time to organize things myself."

"How quickly would you like to wed?"

Lucy gave her an apologetic smile. "I'm hoping for a New Year's Eve wedding."

Pia kept her expression steady. "Three months. Perfect."

"I should say that the church has been booked and that, quite astonishingly, the Puck Building is available for a reception."

Pia's shoulders relaxed. The most important details had been taken care of. Since the church and the reception hall were set for the new date, she wouldn't have to scout locations.

She and Lucy discussed some other details for a few minutes, until Lucy glanced at the door.

"Ah, tea. Perfect," Lucy said as a middle-aged woman,

obviously one of the household help, appeared with a tray of tea.

Pia felt she was going to like Lucy. Her hostess had a sunny disposition, and there was already a lot to suggest that she would be easy to work with.

Lucy leaned forward as the tray was set down on a table in front of them. "Thank you, Celia."

"How do you take your tea?" Lucy inquired as Celia departed, and then shot Pia a teasing, self-deprecating look. "No matter how long I've been in New York, this is teatime for me. You can imagine the problems it causes when I'm giving a matinee performance!"

Before Pia could respond, Lucy glanced toward the door again. "Hawk," Lucy acknowledged with a smile. "How nice of you to join us."

Pia followed the direction that Lucy was looking, and froze.

Hawk. Him.

It wasn't possible.

What was he doing here?

Pia felt a sensation like emotional vertigo.

Hawk looked relaxed and at home in a green T-shirt and khakis, as casual as she'd ever seen him. He looked, in fact, as if he might have sauntered in after watching some television or grabbing a bite to eat in another part of the house.

Pia glanced at Lucy, bewildered.

"Have you met my brother, James Carsdale?" Lucy said with an inviting smile, seemingly unaware of anything untoward happening.

Lucy cast her brother an impish grin. "Do I need to recite all your titles, or will it suffice to enlighten Pia that you're also known as His Grace, the Duke of Hawkshire?"

"Carsdale?" Pia repeated, still forcing herself to focus on Lucy. "I thought your surname was Montgomery."

"Pia knows I have a title," Hawk said at the same time.

It was Lucy's turn to look perplexed. She glanced between her brother and Pia. "I feel as if I've walked in during the middle of the second act. Is there something I should know?"

Pia swung to look at Lucy. "Your brother and I are—" she spared Hawk a withering look "—acquainted."

Hawk arched a brow. "Well-acquainted."

"Past tense," Pia retorted.

"Obviously—on all counts," Lucy put in before turning to look at her brother. "You didn't tell me that you knew Pia. You suggested only that, on good authority, you had the name of an excellent wedding planner whom you wanted to recommend to me."

"The truth," Hawk responded.

Lucy arched a brow. "I take it *the good authority* was none other than yourself?"

Hawk inclined his head in silent acknowledgment, a mocking look in his eyes as they met Pia's.

"Yes," Pia put in acidly, "your brother is practiced in making the artful omission."

Lucy looked with interest from her brother to Pia and back. "On the stage, this would be called a moment of high drama," she quipped. "And here I thought, Hawk, that I had a lock on the thespian skills in the family."

Pia stood and reached for her handbag. "Thank you for the offer of tea, Lucy, but I won't be staying."

As Pia tried to step by Hawk on the way to the door, he took hold of her elbow, and she froze.

It was the first time he had touched her in three years—since the night they had first met. And despite herself, she couldn't help feeling Hawk's casual touch on her elbow to the tips of her toes. Her skin prickled at his nearness.

Why, oh why, did she have to remain so responsive to him?

Pia forced herself to look up. It was at a moment such as

this that she rued her lack of stature. And Hawk bested her on all counts...physical height, bearing and consequence in the world.

"I see you have the knack of anticipating requests," he said smoothly. "It's a useful skill in a wedding planner. And, as it happens, I was going to ask for a private word."

Fortunately, she regained some of her combativeness at his words, and she fumed silently even as she let Hawk guide her out the door to the parlor without protest. She was headed in that direction anyway and there was no use making a scene in front of his sister.

Once in the hall, however, she pulled away from Hawk's loose hold. "If you would summon your butler or majordomo, or whatever you call him, for my coat, I'll be on my way and we'll put an end to this charade of an interview."

"No," Hawk responded, pulling shut the parlor door.

"No?" *The gall...the utter nerve.*

Hawk smiled grimly. "Why pass up the chance to tell me, again, what you think of me? Or better yet, say it with finger food?" He nodded toward the room they'd just exited. "I noticed at least a few good scones in there."

"I'll permit Lucy to enjoy them."

"What a relief."

Her gaze clashed with his.

"It seems we're at an impasse," Hawk said dryly. "I refuse to let you leave with your coat until we've spoken, and you're—" he looked at a nearby window and the steady drizzle coming down "—determined to get wet."

"You're all wet," she retorted. "And for your information, I have a compact umbrella with me in my handbag."

Hawk sighed. "We can do this the hard way, and perhaps make a scene that Lucy will overhear, or we can retire to somewhere with a bit more privacy."

"You leave me little choice," Pia tossed back, her chin set at a mutinous angle.

Without waiting for a further invitation, Hawk steered her into a room across the hall.

As Hawk shut the door behind them, Pia noted that this room was unmistakably a library or study. It had built-in bookshelves, a marble mantel as impressive as the one in the parlor, and a large desk set in front of high windows. With plenty of dark, leather-upholstered furniture, the room was clearly Hawk's domain.

Pia turned back to confront Hawk. "I had no idea Lucy was related to you. She gave her name as Lucy Montgomery. Otherwise—"

"—you'd never have come?" he finished for her, his tone sardonic.

"Naturally."

"Montgomery is the stage name that Lucy adopted. It is, however, also a surname that appears in our family tree."

Pia raised her eyebrows. "Do all you Carsdales operate under a variety of names?"

"When it suits."

"And I suppose it suits when you're intent on seduction?"

She'd intended the comment as a sharp riposte, but he had the audacity to give her a slow, sensuous smile.

"Is that what it was—seduction?" he murmured. "To which you fell victim?"

"Through foul means."

"But still you were seduced by the man…not the title."

Pia detected a note of naked honesty in Hawk's banter, but she didn't let herself dwell on it. She didn't let herself dwell on anything—including the fact that they were in his library alone together—except holding on to her outrage.

"You masterminded this," she accused, looking around them. "You arranged to have me come here when you knew I was not suspecting…not ex-expecting…"

Words deserted her.

"It's not a charade, however," Hawk countered. "How could

it be? My sister needs to move up her wedding date, and you're a wedding consultant, last I heard."

"You know what I mean!"

"Does it matter if you can use the business?" Hawk replied.

Pia's eyes widened. "I don't know what you mean. In any case, I'm not that desperate."

"Aren't you?" Hawk said. "You've dropped hints that you've been less than busy lately."

Pia's eyes widened further.

"Never play poker."

"Seeking to make amends?"

"In a sense."

Pia placed her hands on her hips, contemplating him and his vague response. It *couldn't be* that he was feeling guilty about his behavior toward her in the past. He was a seasoned player who had forgotten her easily. That much was clear from the *three years* it had taken for their paths to cross again.

There was only one other possibility, then, for his motivation in linking her to Lucy.

"I suppose you feel some sense of responsibility since it was your friend who torpedoed my professional standing by ruining Belinda's wedding?" she asked.

Hawk hesitated, and then inclined his head. "I suppose *responsibility* is as good a term as any."

Pia eyed him. He was holding out a lifeline to her business, and it was hard not to grasp hold of the opportunity that he was offering. What better way to signal to society that all was well than to be hired to organize the wedding of the sister of the man whom she'd bearded with baba ghanoush?

She was being foolhardy.

"Lucy isn't part of New York society, but her future husband's family is," Hawk cajoled, as if sensing her weakness. "This wedding could help establish you. And Lucy has many ties to the theater world. I'm betting you've never planned a wedding for an actress before?"

Pia shook her head.

"Then Lucy's wedding will let you tap into a whole new market for your services."

"Wh-who would be employing me?"

She hated herself for asking—and hated herself more for stammering—but the question came out of its own volition. Rather than appear satisfied, however, Hawk's expression turned into a study of harmlessness.

"I'd be employing you, but only as a minor, technical detail."

"Minor to you."

"I'm the head of the family, and Lucy is young—only twenty-four." Hawk's lips twitched. "It seems only fair that I support her bid to remove herself from under the imposing family umbrella. Lucy was an unexpected bonus for my parents more than a decade after my mother delivered the heir and the spare."

Pia noted that Hawk had deftly turned an act that might be viewed as generous and loving on his part into a statement of sardonic self-deprecation.

She started to waver. She *had* liked Hawk's sister even on the basis of a very brief acquaintance. She felt a natural affinity for Lucy. It had deepened on learning that Hawk's sister was only three years younger than she was. Lucy was, in fact, the same age that Pia had been when she'd first met Hawk.

If her own tale with Hawk wasn't destined to have a happy ending, then at least she could see to it that one Carsdale...

No, she wouldn't let herself think of matters in that vein.

"You'll be dealing with Lucy mostly, obviously," Hawk continued, his expression open and unmasked. "I'll try to make myself as unobtrusive as possible."

"H-how?" Pia asked. "Are you planning to sequester yourself at your country estate in England?"

"Nothing so drastic," Hawk replied with amusement, "but, rest assured, I have no interest in weddings."

"Obviously—judging from your past behavior."

"Ouch." He had the grace to look abashed. "I stepped right into that comment, and I suppose I deserved it."

She raised her eyebrows and said nothing.

"The town house belongs to me," Hawk went on unperturbed, "but Lucy has had the run of it since I haven't been in regular residence until recently. And though I'm based in New York, rather than London, for business at the moment, I expect that my corporate dealings will still mean I'm not much at home."

Pia knew all about Hawk's hedge fund, of course. She'd read about it online. The success of his company over the past three years had raised his reputation to that of a first-class financier.

Darn. He must have women throwing themselves at him.

Not that she was interested, of course.

Pia wondered why Hawk was at home now, actually. The thought had occurred to her earlier, too—the minute he'd walked into the parlor. It could only be that he'd chosen to come into her meeting with Lucy, possibly betting that once she said yes to his sister, it would be best to reveal his connection to Lucy sooner rather than later.

Hawk arched an eyebrow. "And so…?"

Pia regarded him.

"I make you nervous, don't I?"

"N-naturally. I have a fear of snakes."

He grinned, unabashed.

"The endearing hiccup in your speech tells me everything I need to know about how much I affect you," he said, his voice smooth as silk and doubly seductive.

Pia felt a shiver of awareness chase down her spine for a

moment, but then Hawk's face changed to one as innocuous as a Boy Scout's.

"Of course," he went on solemnly, "we'll say no more on that topic. I plan to be on my best behavior from now on."

"Promise? Really?" she parried.

Before Hawk could reply, the library door opened. Lucy stuck her head inside, and then walked in when it was clear that she'd found them.

"Ah, there you are," Lucy said. "I was wondering if you'd run off, Pia."

"Nothing so drastic," Hawk responded mildly. "Pia and I were just discussing the terms of her employment."

Lucy looked at Pia with some surprise, and then clasped her hands together in delight. "You've agreed? Splendid!"

"I—"

"The hot water has gotten cold, but I'll order another pot for tea," Lucy said. "Shall we all return to the parlor?"

"Yes, let's," Hawk responded, his lips twitching.

As Pia followed Lucy from the room, and Hawk fell into step behind her, she was left to wonder if all the Carsdales had the gift of polite and subtle railroading.

For despite everything, she was finding herself agreeing to be Lucy's bridal consultant.

When Hawk emerged from the elevator, he had no trouble locating Pia's place. She'd opened her front door and was standing in the entrance to her apartment.

She looked fresh as a daisy in a yellow-print knit dress that displayed her lithe, compact body to perfection. The cleavage visible at the V-neck was just enough to give a man interesting thoughts.

He wondered whether he would always experience a quick jolt of sexual awareness when he saw her.

"How did you find me?" she asked without preamble.

He gave a careless shrug. "A little digging on Pia Lumley Wedding Productions. It wasn't hard."

Pia, he'd discovered, now lived on the fifth floor of a modest white-brick doorman building. The older man downstairs—more guard than doorman—had glanced up from his small television set long enough to ring Pia and announce Hawk's arrival. Even though Hawk had been privy only to a brief one-sided conversation—and from the guard's end at that—he'd sensed Pia's hesitancy when she'd been informed of his unexpected arrival. Still, moments later, he'd been directed to the elevator, and then the guard had gone back to viewing his talk show.

"Naturally," Pia responded now with a touch of sarcasm. "I should have expected you'd do some digging of your own. With a business, I'm easy to find, whether I like it or not."

Despite her words, she stepped aside to let him into the apartment, and then shut the door once he'd entered.

"In a way, I'm glad you're here," she said as he turned back to face her. "It makes matters easier."

He quirked a brow. "Only *in a way?*" he queried with dry amusement. "I suppose I should be happy there is at least one way."

"I've been having second thoughts."

"Of course you have." He let his mouth tilt upward. "And that's why *I'm* glad I'm here."

Hawk watched as Pia sucked in a deep breath and squared her shoulders.

"I'm afraid it wouldn't be wise for me to accept the job as Lucy's wedding planner."

"She'll be devastated."

"I'll find a suitable replacement."

"A rival?" he questioned sardonically. "Are you sure you want to?"

"I have contacts—friends."

"And I'm not one of them, presumably."

Hawk glanced around. The apartment wasn't big, but nevertheless bigger than he expected.

The living room was dressed in a pastel theme, from the peach-colored couch to the rose-print armchair. *Wedding colors.*

Binders of various wedding vendors—for invitations, decorations, flowers and more—stood out on the cream-colored bookshelves.

He glanced down as a cat sauntered in from an adjoining room.

The animal stopped, returned his stare, still as a statue, and then blinked.

"Mr. Darcy," Pia announced.

But of course, Hawk thought. A wedding planner with a cat named after Jane Austen's most renowned hero.

Hawk's lips twisted. Pia had wound up with Mr. Darcy, so all should be right with the world. Except Mr. Darcy was a damn cat, and Hawk surmised that *he'd* been cast as the villainous Mr. Wickham in this drama.

Still, he bent and rubbed the cat behind the ears. The feline allowed the contact and then moved to rub himself against Hawk's leg, leaving behind a trail of stray animal hairs on Hawk's pants.

When Hawk straightened, he caught Pia's look of surprise.

"What?" he asked. "You look astonished that I'd cozy up to your cat."

"I thought you would be a dog person," Pia responded. "Aren't all of you aristocrats fond of canines? Fox hunting and such?"

Hawk smiled. "Afraid I'd feed Puss 'n Boots here to the dogs?"

"The possibility wouldn't bear thinking about except that you've already proven yourself to be a wolf in sheep's clothing," Pia retorted.

He gave a feral grin and then, just to annoy her, allowed his gaze to travel over her. "And are you Little Red Riding Hood? Is that the fairy tale you prefer these days?"

"I don't prefer any fairy tales," she shot back. "N-not anymore."

Hawk's smile faded. She didn't believe in fairy tales anymore, and he felt responsible for robbing her of her innocence in more ways than one.

Of course, all that made it even more imperative that he change her mind and get her to accept his help. He intended to make restitution of sorts.

He pulled some papers from the inside pocket of his blazer. "I suspected that you might have a change of heart once you had a chance to think about what you were getting into with Lucy."

"You were the one who wanted time to review the contract!" she accused. "I'm within my rights to change my mind, and if you don't have any recourse, you have only yourself to blame."

It was true that when Pia had handed Lucy her standard written wedding services contract on Monday, before she'd left Hawk's house, he'd taken the contract in hand and had asked to review it. But only because he'd thought it would give him another opportunity to interact with her when he brought it back to her.

He'd come here this afternoon directly from work, and was still wearing a navy business suit.

The discussion of the contract, he told himself, would afford him a chance to change her low opinion of him. Maybe he could begin to demonstrate that he wasn't quite the reprobate she thought he was. Not anymore.

"I did do as I said," he acknowledged, unfolding the paper in his hand. "I did review it."

Pia arched a brow. "One wonders why you don't bring

the same thoroughness and discrimination to your choice of dates."

Hawk stifled the dry chuckle that rose unbidden. "You've done some research on me, I take it."

Pia nodded. "The internet is a wonderful thing. I believe you were referred to on at least one occasion as Jolly Lord James, his Rollicking Rowdy Ruffianness?"

"Ruffian?" Hawk rubbed the bridge of his nose with his finger. "Ah, yes, I believe I had my nose broken at least once in a brawl. A useful thing once I became Hawkshire, as I was able to live up to the profile implied."

"Charming."

"And did your research also reveal how I succeeded to the title of Duke of Hawkshire?" he asked with deceptive casualness.

Pia shook her head. "I believe the tabloids were already fully occupied with your ne'er-do-well travails."

"So I've heard," he deadpanned. "Much to my regret, however, my sojourn as the rollicking younger son of the previous Duke of Hawkshire was cut short when my older brother died from injuries sustained in a boating accident."

He saw Pia hesitate.

"An early morning phone call awakened me from a pleasant slumber, as I recall," he went on, searching her gaze. "I still remember the view from your apartment window as the news reached me."

Pia looked momentarily bewildered. He knew he'd flummoxed her.

"So you departed without a word?"

He nodded. "On the first flight back to London."

The unexpected news about his brother had changed the trajectory of his life. He'd left Pia's apartment quietly, while she'd still slept. Then he'd rushed back to London for a bedside vigil that had ended days later when William had taken his last breath.

With the tumult in his life that had followed the tragedy, he'd been able to push Pia to the back of his mind. Then with the space of days and miles, and the weight of his newfound responsibilities as a ducal heir, he convinced himself that it would be better if he didn't get in touch with her again—if he let matters end as they were.

It had all been convenient, too, he admitted to himself now. Because the truth was that after sleeping with Pia and discovering that she'd been a virgin, he'd had the feeling of being in too deep. It had been a novel and uncomfortable sensation for him. His younger, inconsiderate self had simply been looking for a steamy fling. But he'd been spared the need to figure out how to handle it all by the news of his brother's tragic accident.

"I'm sorry, however belatedly, for your loss," Pia said, a look of openhearted feeling transforming her face.

"I'm not asking for your sympathy," he responded.

He didn't deserve it. As much as Pia had claimed to have developed a more cynical shell since they'd been lovers, she still, he could tell, possessed a soft-hearted fragility about her that showed how easily she could be hurt.

He was thankful for that sign that he hadn't changed her too deeply, even though it made her all that more dangerous. *To him.*

He was here to help, he reminded himself. He was going to make amends for past wrongs, however inadequately, and that's all.

"My father died months later," he elaborated, forcing himself to stay on topic. "Some would say brokenhearted, though he'd already been in poor health. So by two quirks of fate within a year, I became the duke."

"And then you started Sunhill Investments," Pia observed without inflection. "You've had a busy few years."

He inclined his head. "Again, some would say so. And yet it was all born of necessity, and nothing more so than the need to find a new cash flow for the maintenance of the ducal estates."

When his father had died, the full weight of the dukedom had been thrust upon his shoulders. He'd stepped up to take care of the family...become responsible...

He'd already started exploring his options for starting a hedge fund, but the costs associated with the ducal estates had added new urgency to matters.

And in the shuffle—in the crazy upheaval and burdensome work schedule that had been his life for the past three years—it had been easy to shut the door on his discomfort as far as Pia was concerned. He had, at many moments, been too busy to think about their one stupendous night, when he'd broken his vow and done what he said he'd never do, even in his careless playboy days—be remembered as a woman's first lover. And even in his younger days, he hadn't been the type to leave without a word—instead, he stuck around and made sure there were no hard feelings.

"You never got back in touch," Pia stated, though without rancor.

He searched her eyes—so unusual in their warm amber tone that he'd been arrested by them on their first meeting.

Now, he sensed in them that her adamancy from when he'd walked in the door was weakening, exactly as he'd wanted. Still, what he said next was the truth. "None of this explanation was intended as an excuse."

"Why go out of your way to arrange for me to be Lucy's wedding planner?" Pia asked. "To make amends?"

Hawk couldn't help but smile at her astute query. Pia might still be rather sweet and naive, despite her posturing to the contrary, but she was intelligent. He'd been drawn to her wit on the night they'd first met.

"If I said yes, would you let me?" he parried.

"I've found from past experience that letting you do anything is dangerous."

He gave a low laugh. "Even if it's a favor?"

"With no strings attached?"

He could sense her weakening toward him, so he gave her his most innocent look. "Would you let me wipe some of the dirt off my conscience?"

"So this is an act of mercy on my part?"

"Of sorts."

"So you're acting not only to make up for your friend Easterbridge's actions at Belinda's wedding but for yours in the past as well?"

"I don't believe I was ever motivated by Easterbridge's actions."

Then, not giving her a chance to backtrack, he withdrew a pen from his inner jacket pocket and using the nearby wall as support, he inked her contract with his signature.

"There, it's signed," he said, handing out the contract to her.

She looked at him with some wariness, but nevertheless took the contract from him and glanced at it.

"Hawkshire," she read, and then looked up, a sudden glimmer in her eyes. "How grand. Sh-should I receive it as a benediction of sorts?"

He shrugged, willing for her to be amused at his expense. "Am I being permitted to try to make restitution, however inadequately? Then please view this contract as a grant of clemency from you to me."

Deliberately, he held the pen out to her.

Pia seemed to understand his gesture for the meaning-laden act it was, and hesitated.

Hawk glanced down at Mr. Darcy for a moment, and then arched a brow. "Our one witness wants you to sign."

And indeed, Mr. Darcy was looking up at them, unmoving and unblinking. Hawk was starting to realize that it was a customary pose for the cat, and he got the uncomfortable feeling that Mr. Darcy understood too much for a feline.

"I'm not in the business of reforming rakes," Pia said as she reached for the pen.

Their fingers brushed, causing a sizzle of awareness to shoot through him.

Hawk schooled his expression. "Of course you are," he contradicted her. "I assume you adopted Mr. Darcy from a shelter?"

"That was saving a soul, not reforming a rake."

"Is there much difference?" he asked. "And anyway, who knows what dastardly deeds and reprobate behavior Mr. Darcy engaged in before you met him?"

"Better the devil you don't know," she responded, turning a well-known saying on its head.

He placed his hand over his heart. "And yet one could say we encountered each other under blind circumstances not so different from your first meeting with Mr. Darcy. Surely, if you can find it in your heart to take him…?"

"I am not taking you in like…a-a stray," she responded reprovingly.

"Much to my regret," he murmured.

Giving him a lingering cautionary look, she turned her back and, using the wall for support in imitation of his earlier action, signed the contract.

She turned back to him and handed him a copy of the contract.

"Splendid," he said with a grin. "I'd kiss you to seal the deal, but I'll venture to guess you wouldn't find it appropriate under the circumstances."

"Certainly not!"

"A handshake then?"

Pia eyed him, and he returned her regard with a bland look of his own.

Slowly, she extended her hand, and he grasped it in his.

He let himself feel the vibrant current coursing between

them. It was the same as when they'd met three years ago. It was the same as it always was.

Her hand was small and fine-boned. The fingers, he'd noticed, tapered to well-manicured nails that nevertheless showed not a hint of polish—so like her, delicate but practical.

When she tried to pull away, he tightened his hold, drawing out the contact for reasons he didn't bother to examine.

She looked up at him questioningly, and he read the turbulent sexual awareness in her amber eyes.

In a courtly gesture, he bent and gave her a very proper kiss on the hand.

He heard Pia suck in a breath, and as he straightened, he released her hand.

She swallowed. "Why did you do that?"

"I'm a duke," he said, the excuse falling easily from his lips. "It's a done thing."

In fact, Hawk admitted to himself, the context wasn't fitting even if the gesture might have been. He wasn't greeting a woman—one of higher social status—who'd offered him her hand. But he brushed aside those niceties, not least because it had been tempting to touch her.

"Of course," Pia acknowledged lightly, though a shadow crossed her face. "I know all about your world, even if I'm not part of it."

"You've agreed to be part of it now," he countered. "Attend the theater with me tomorrow night."

"Wh-what?" she asked, looking startled. "Why?"

He smiled. "It's Lucy's off-Broadway show. Seeing my sister on the stage, in her element, might give you useful insight into her personality."

Pia relaxed her shoulders.

He could tell she'd been wondering whether he was reneging on his promise even before the ink had dried on their contract. Was he trying to entice her back into his bed?

Yes—*no. No.* He corrected the response that had jumped unbidden into his head. Fortunately, he hadn't spoken aloud.

Nevertheless, Pia seemed ready to argue. "I don't think a show would be—"

"—the ticket?" he finished. "Don't worry about it. I've got two seats in the front orchestra." He winked. "I worked the family connection."

"You know what I mean!"

"Hardly. And that seems to be a recurring problem of mine."

Pia looked as if she wanted to continue to protest.

"I'll see you tomorrow night. I'll come by at seven." He glanced down at the cat. "I hope Mr. Darcy won't mind spending the evening at home alone."

"Why?" she jabbed, but lightly. "Is he an uncomfortable reminder that the role left to you might be that of villain?"

He felt the side of his mouth tease upward. "How did you guess?"

Pia raised her eyebrows, but the look she gave him was open and unguarded.

"I'm not too concerned."

"Oh?"

He glanced down at Mr. Darcy again. "I feel confident that only one of us can waltz."

"Oh."

Pia looked startled and then, for a moment, dreamy—as if the idea of a waltz had called to the romantic in her.

Mr. Darcy just continued to stare at them unblinkingly, and Hawk realized that now was as good a time as any for him to leave, before he gave in to too much temptation.

He let the side of his mouth quirk up again. "Since I appear to have exhausted my options for acceptable salutations and social niceties, I'm afraid my goodbye will have to be rather dull."

"How reassuring," Pia answered, recovering.

He touched his finger to the tip of her pert nose in humorous salute of her impertinence.

And then, unable to stop himself, he let his finger wander down and smooth over her pink and inviting lips.

They both quieted.

"Tomorrow night," he repeated.

He turned away before he was tempted to touch her lips with his, and then let himself out the way he'd come in.

As he pulled shut the apartment door behind him, Hawk refused to let himself think about why he found it hard to leave Pia.

It was a vexing situation that could only mean no good for his best of intentions.

Five

Pia found herself staring at her apartment door after Hawk had left. Flooded with conflicting emotions, she hugged herself and sat down on her couch.

She touched her fingers to her lips, in imitation of Hawk's action moments ago. She could swear he'd wanted to kiss her. The last time he'd kissed her had been on the night that they'd first met....

Pia turned away and picked up the remote to her MP3 player because music relaxed her. Within a few moments, the dulcet tones of an orchestral ensemble drifted through the apartment from her small speakers.

"W-would you like a drink?" she asked.

James laughed close behind her. "What a question to ask, considering we've just been to a bar."

In truth, she felt light-headed herself. It must have been that last cocktail she'd had at the bar while trying to converse with the real estate office manager.

"Pia," James said quietly, laying his hands on her shoulders. She froze at the contact, her nipples tightening.

"Relax," he murmured close to her ear.

Oh.

He removed his hands...but moments later, she felt his fingertips trail up her arms as he nuzzled the hair near her ear.

She shivered. "Really, I—"

He nipped her earlobe.

She gulped, and then forced herself to say, "D-don't you want to get to know each other better?"

"Much better," he agreed on a soft laugh.

His body brushed hers from behind, sending delicious shivers through her.

Slowly, he turned her to face him, and then searched her eyes. "I've been wanting to do this—" he bent and tasted her lips "—ever since we left the bar."

"Oh," she breathed.

This was her fantasy. *He was here now.*

He cupped her shoulders, his thumbs tracing a soothing circular pattern. "We won't do anything you don't want to do."

"Th-that's what I'm afraid of."

He smiled. "Ah, Pia. You really are special." Then his expression turned more intent and amorous. "Let me show you how much."

He cupped her cheek, laid his lips against hers and tasted her.

She sighed and gripped his shirt, fisting her hand into the material, as little shock waves of pleasure jolted her.

She felt his arousal grow between them as his mouth stroked hers. Within moments, they had fitted their bodies together, giving in to the desire that had been kindled in the bar and stoked on the cab ride to her apartment.

He cupped her face with both hands, his fingers delving into her hair as he sipped from her mouth.

She relaxed her grip on his shirt and flattened her hands against his chest, where she could feel the steady beat of his heart.

Around them, the sweet notes of string instruments sounded, the tune low and soulful.

Pia felt herself relax even as every inch of her skin tingled with awareness. She sighed against James's mouth, wanting the kiss to go on and on as his hunger matched her own.

Giving in to the urge to shed attire, she kicked off her sandals. In the next moment, she lowered a couple of inches, enough to break the contact of her lips with James's.

"My bed isn't very big." They were the first words to pop out of her mouth, her tone apologetic, and she flushed.

James looked indulgent, and then dimpled as he nodded beside them. "You've never made love on a love seat before?"

She'd never made love *period*. But she was afraid if she told him, he'd flee out the door. She knew he must be used to more experienced women.

She shrugged one shoulder. "Why bother when a bed is available?"

"Mmm," he said, and then bent and nuzzled her ear.

Oh. She gripped his upper arms for support, her fingers digging into his biceps, as his action did funny things to her insides.

She felt his hand go to the zipper at the back of her dress.

"Would it be okay if I did this?" he murmured.

"Yes, please," she breathed.

She heard the rasp of the zipper and felt her dress slither downward, exposing to his gaze that she wasn't wearing a bra.

James stepped back and looked at her with a hooded, rapt expression.

"Ah, Pia, you're so beautiful." He raised his hands to cup

and caress her. "You're just as pretty as I thought when my imagination was running rampant in the bar."

"Kiss me," she whispered.

He sat on the arm of the love seat beside them and, pulling her toward him, fastened his mouth over one pert breast.

Pia was lost. Her heart beat wildly, and she tangled her fingers in his hair.

He pushed the rest of the dress off her, and then peeled her panties away without lifting his mouth from her.

Pia moaned.

He shifted his focus to her other breast, but then paused, his lips hovering over her taut flesh, his breath fanning her erect nipple.

"And would it be okay if I kissed you here?" he said hoarsely.

Pia had never been so close to begging and pleading.

But instead of answering, she guided his head to her breast, her eyes fluttering shut on a sigh as his lips closed over her.

He soothed and aroused her with his tongue, fanning the fire of their desire.

Before she knew it, she was on his lap on the love seat, and they were kissing passionately but yet like longtime lovers who had all the time in the world. His arousal pressed against her flesh, and his hand caressed up and down her thigh.

When they finally broke away, he groaned softly. "Have mercy, Pia."

In response, she snuggled closer. He nuzzled her temple and his breath rasped in her ear. She shivered and rubbed against him.

She let her hand go to the buttons of his shirt, undoing one and then another. The strong, corded line of his neck came into view.

"Pia," he said from somewhere above her head, "please say you don't want to stop."

"Who said anything about stopping?" This was her

fantasy, and she found that she wanted to see it through to its conclusion. Her last drink at the bar had given her a delicious, unbound feeling, and James's seduction had lowered her inhibitions even more.

"Ah, Pia." He slipped his hand between her thighs and pressed, giving her a heady sensation. "I just want to assure you that I'm clean."

"I am, too," she answered, understanding what he was alluding to. "I've never had unprotected sex."

It was literally true, though it hid the truth—that she'd never had sex at all.

He kissed her neck. "Are you…? If not, I have something with me. Not that I walked in here with any expectations, of course, but I'd be lying if I said I wasn't attracted to you from the first moment I spotted you."

"Mmm…when did you first notice me? Are you saying our encounter in the bar wasn't by chance?"

"I saw you minutes before you tried to order a drink," he admitted. "When I spotted a damsel in distress, though, I saw my opening. I took a chance that Cinderella was looking for a Prince Charming to come rescue her, and that she'd mistake me for him if I tried to do her a favor."

Pia's heart gave a little squeeze. It was as if he knew her well already. Did he suspect that she was a romantic at heart? Did he know that she'd thrilled to stories of true love, though a part of her knew better?

She pulled his head down for a kiss as the music reached a low crescendo around them.

They kissed deeply, their mouths clinging, unable to get enough of each other.

When he finally broke their kiss, he stood up with her in his arms. "What's your preference, Cinderella?"

She glanced down at the love seat—next time.

"Bed," she said.

"My sentiments exactly," he said, and then strode with her

around the partition to where the bed was. "See, we have a lot in common."

"Besides riding and fishing?"

He paused in the act of placing her on the bed. "Oh, Pia, sweetheart," he said huskily, a wicked glimmer in his eye, "isn't that what tonight is all about—fishing and riding?"

Pia felt a full-body flush sweep over her. As she came down on the mattress, she propped herself up on her elbows to stop from lying completely on her back.

She swallowed, unable to say anything.

Holding her eyes, James undid the remaining buttons on his shirt and cuffs, and then pulled fabric from his waistband, stripping off his shirt and undershirt.

Pia soaked up the sight of him. Taut muscle rippled underneath the planes of smooth and lightly tanned skin.

She hadn't been mistaken. He was fit and in top shape.

He made short work of the rest of his clothes, working methodically until he was naked.

His arousal stood in imposing relief against his toned frame.

Pia sucked in a breath. "You're very beautiful."

James gave her a lopsided smile. "Isn't that my line?"

It occurred to her that while she'd viewed pictures of naked men, this was the first time she'd seen one in the flesh. And again, James was beyond her expectations. He was impressive—tall and built as well as fit. The flat planes of his abdomen tapered down to...a definite sign that he wanted to couple with her. *Right now.*

A tingle went through her, a tightening of anticipation.

As if in response, he pulled her toward him on the bed and began kissing his way down her body.

Pia looked up at the white plaster ceiling, her hands tangling in his hair, and thought she'd die of pleasure.

James kissed the jut of her hip and then worked his way down the soft skin of her inner thigh to the sensitive spot behind her knee. He lifted her other leg and turned his head to nip and brush the pliant flesh of her other thigh.

With one finger, he traced down the cleft at the juncture of her thighs, and she moaned, her head twisting until she pressed her face into the coverlet beside her.

James muttered sweet encouragement as he lowered her leg and caressed his hand down her thigh.

Then he bent, picked up his pants from the floor and fished out a packet of protection. He donned the sheath with economical moves. Stretching out beside her on the bed, he gathered her to him and soothed her with his lips and hands as he muttered soft endearments under his breath.

Pia was lost to the sensation and emotion sweeping her. She was petite and felt surrounded by him.

When James shifted over her, parting her thighs and settling against her, she worried about being able to accept him. But within seconds she was again consumed by the desire flaring between them.

"Touch me, Pia," he said hoarsely.

He sipped and feasted on her lips, his hands readying her with a gentle kneading. Pia responded in kind, meeting his mouth and trailing her fingertips over the corded muscles of his back.

This was the moment she'd waited a lifetime for. *He* was the man she'd waited for.

James nudged her, and Pia concentrated on relaxing as he sucked on her lower lip.

Lifting his head, he muttered, "Wrap your legs around me."

Oh, sweet heaven. She'd never been plastered, open and exposed, to an aroused male before.

She concentrated on what she'd imagined countless times in her fantasies, where her partner's features had always been indistinct but he'd carried an aura so very much like James's.

She did as he instructed, and James grasped her hips in his hands.

He looked deeply into her eyes and then gave her a quick, gentle kiss.

"Let me take you, Pia," he said throatily. "Let me bring you pleasure."

She arched toward him, and in response, he buried his head in her neck and penetrated her.

Pia gasped, and then bit down hard on her lip.

James froze.

Moments passed and they held still. The thumping of his heart sounded against hers.

He lifted his head, his expression puzzled, and also shocked and doubtful.

"You're a virgin."

He stated it with surprise.

She wet her lips. "W-was. I think past tense is appropriate."

She felt full and stretched, almost to the point of the unbearable, where pleasure met pain. It was a strange sensation that she tried to get used to.

"Why?"

She swallowed, and then whispered, "I wanted you. Is that so bad?"

James closed his eyes, his muscles remaining full of tension as he rested his forehead against hers and then muttered a self-deprecation. "You're so unbelievably tight and hot. Sweet like I've never experienced… Pia, I can't—"

Afraid he'd pull out, she clamped her legs around him. "D-don't."

After a moment, some of the tension eased out of him—almost as if he was reluctantly admitting defeat.

"I'll try to make it good for you from now on," he muttered, as if the words were torn from him.

"Yes."

He moved slowly then, his hands pressing the right spots and easing the tension in her body.

Pia focused on relaxing and concentrated on the sensation of his movements.

Slowly, slowly, she felt a small spark, and then a faint tingle. She was awakening, her body coming to life under his sure ministrations.

Eventually, as she relaxed further, tension built. She felt herself reaching for a release that she'd never experienced with a man before.

James stroked between their bodies, his fingers pressing on her most sensitive spot.

Within moments, she cried out with pleasure and then crested before she knew it. She was carried on a wave of sensation as feeling after feeling swamped her.

Her body undulated around James of its own accord, massaging him into his own frenzy of need.

"Have mercy, Pia," he groaned.

It was too late, however. With a hoarse oath, he grasped her hips and pumped into her.

She came for him again. And then with a final thrust, he took his own release.

As James slumped against her, Pia hugged him and suddenly became aware of tears in her eyes.

He'd taken her across the final barrier to realizing herself sexually as a woman. Their joining and her first time couldn't have been more wonderful.

Pia closed her eyes, and of their own accord, exhaustion and sleep claimed her.

The next time she blinked up at her ceiling, he was gone.

In a moment, Pia was brought back to the present. She realized she wasn't staring at her ceiling, but at her apartment wall.

Different apartments, three years apart.

Same man, though.
Hawk.

His presence was palpable still, and her body was awakened and aware as if they'd made love moments, not years, ago.

Pia shook her head. *No.*

She'd let him into her sanctuary—her apartment—again, but she resolved not to let him into her life one more time.

The night after Hawk signed the contract at her apartment, Pia discovered they had a couple of the best theater seats in the house—no doubt thanks to Hawk's personal connection.

Hawk had appeared at her apartment at seven and driven them so they could make the eight o'clock curtain call for Lucy's show, an off-Broadway production of the musical *Oklahoma,* in which Lucy had a supporting role.

Pia made a show of studying her program as they waited for the lights to dim. Tonight, she reminded herself, was all about business. She'd dressed in a short-sleeved, apricot-colored dress that she'd worn to work-related parties before and that she hoped sent the appropriate message. She'd avoided those items in her wardrobe that she considered purely off-hours attire.

She stole a quick sidelong glance at Hawk, who was looking at the stage. Even dressed casually in black pants and a light blue shirt, he managed to project an air of ducal self-possession.

She just wished she wasn't so aware of his thigh inches away from her own, and of his shoulder and arm within dangerously close brushing distance. If there was a petition right now for having individual armrests in places of public accommodations, she'd sign on the spot.

Determinedly, she pulled herself in, making it clear that she'd cede the shared armrest to him.

In the process, she absently tugged down the hem of her dress, and Hawk's gaze was drawn to her actions.

As Hawk surveyed her exposed thighs, his expression changing to one of alert but lazy amusement, Pia rued her involuntary action.

Hawk's eyes moved up to meet hers. "I have a proposition for you."

"I-I'm not surprised," she shot back, rallying and cursing her telltale stammer. "They do appear to be your forte."

He had the indecency to grin. "You bring out the best—" he waited a beat as her eyes widened "—urges in me."

She hated that he could bait her so successfully. "You give me too much credit. As far as I can tell, your urges don't need any help in being called forth. They appear of their own volition."

Hawk chuckled. "Aren't you at least curious about what I have to offer?"

She frowned, but forced herself to adopt a saccharine-sweet voice. "You forget that I already know. Unless your offer involves business, I'm not interested."

Was his facility with sexual innuendo boundless?

He shifted toward her, his leg brushing her own, and Pia tried to stifle her response of frozen awareness before he could discern it.

Hawk looked too knowing. "As it happens, it does. Involve business, that is."

This time, Pia didn't try to hide her reaction. "It does?"

Hawk nodded. "A friend of mine, Victoria, needs help with a wedding."

"A female friend? Ready to give up on you, is she, and move on?"

She couldn't stop herself from needling him, it seemed.

He flashed a grin. "We never dated. Her fiancé is an old classmate of mine. I introduced them to each other at a party last year."

"You do seem to know quite a few people who are getting

married." She raised her eyebrows. "Always the matchmaker, never the groom?"

"Not yet," he replied cryptically.

She fell silent at his vague response.

Once upon a time, *he* might have featured in *her* wedding fantasies, but they were well past that point, weren't they? Instead of the well-trod path, they'd veered down a detour from which there was no turning back.

"When is the wedding?" she heard herself ask.

"Next week. Saturday."

"Next week?"

She wasn't sure she'd heard correctly.

Hawk nodded. "The wedding planner is quarantined abroad."

Pia raised her eyebrows.

Hawk quirked his lips. "I'm not joking. She went on safari with her boyfriend, and they were both exposed to tuberculosis. She can't get back to New York until after the wedding date."

Pia shook her head in bemusement. "I suppose I should thank you…?"

"If you want to," he teased. "It might be appropriate under the circumstances."

Pia bit her lip, but Hawk looked down and pulled out a piece of paper from his pocket.

"Here's the bride's contact information," he said. "Will you do it? Will you call her?"

Pia took the paper from him, her fingers brushing his in a contact that was anything but casual for the two of them.

She noted the name and phone number that he'd written. *Victoria Elgemere.*

Just then the lights overhead blinked a few times, indicating that people should take their seats because the show was about to begin.

"I'll call her," she said quickly.

"Good girl," Hawk responded, and then mischievously patted her knee, his hand lingering. "I'll be a wedding guest, by the way."

"Then it'll be déjà vu."

He grinned. "I've developed a taste for baba ghanoush."

She threw him a stern look, and then picked up and returned his hand to him. Her actions belied the emotional tumult that he so effortlessly engendered in her.

Facing forward as the lights dimmed, she was left to reflect that her company had again received a desperate transfusion of new business thanks to Hawk.

She'd acted quickly in accepting the job—or, at least, agreeing to call—forced into an impulsive decision by the imminent start of the show, but she didn't want her feelings toward him to get murky.

She could start feeling gratitude or worse.

Six

Hawk emerged from an Aston Martin at the New York Botanical Garden—where Victoria's wedding would shortly be held at four o'clock on a Saturday afternoon—and looked up.

He saw nothing but clear blue skies. There was just the faint hint of a warm breeze. *Perfect.*

As the valet approached for his car keys, Hawk heard his cell phone ring and smiled as the notes of "Unforgettable" by Nat King Cole sounded. He'd assigned the ringtone to Pia's cell, whose number he'd acquired ostensibly for business reasons.

He'd thought of using the theme music from *Jaws* for her ringtone, but then he figured that while it might be appropriate, given the sparring nature of his relationship with her, she didn't need further encouragement, if she ever found out, to attempt to annihilate him.

With a grin, he took the call.

"Hawk, where are you?" Pia demanded without preamble.

"I'm about to hand my cars keys to the valet," he responded. "Should I be anywhere else?"

"I'll be right there! The bride left her veil in the back of a Lincoln Town Car that departed minutes ago. I need your help."

"What...?"

"You heard me." Pia's voice held an edge of crisis. "Oh, I can't be associated with another wedding disaster!"

"You won't." *Not if he could help it.* "What's the name of the car service?"

As Pia gave it to him, Hawk shook his head at the valet and jumped back into his car to start the ignition.

"Call the car company," he told Pia, "and tell them to contact the driver."

"I already have. They're trying to get in touch with him. He can't go too far. Otherwise, we'll never get the veil back in time for the ceremony."

"Don't worry, I'm on it." He started to steer back down the drive with one hand. "Do you think he's heading back to Manhattan?"

If he had some idea in which direction the car was heading, he'd know which way to go once he got out of the Botanical Garden. Then when contact was made with the driver, at least he'd be nearby and they could meet at a convenient exit or intersection.

"I think he is heading south, and I'm coming with you," Pia replied.

"No, you're needed here."

"Look to your left. I'm heading toward you. Stop and I'll hop in."

Hawk turned to look out the driver's-side window. Sure enough, there was Pia, hurrying toward him across the grass, a phone pressed to her ear.

"Good grief, Pia." He disconnected the call and stopped the car.

Moments later, she pulled open the passenger-side door and slid inside.

As he pulled away again, he observed with amusement, "I don't think I've ever seen a woman so anxious to get into a car with me."

"It's an Aston Martin," she said, breathing heavily from her jog. "You can really accelerate, and I'm desperate."

"The first time I think I've been praised for my ability to go fast."

"J-just drive." She breathed in deep, then, pressing a button, put her phone to her ear once more.

Hawk assumed she was calling the car service again.

He glanced at her. She was wearing a short-sleeved caramel-color satin dress with a gently-flared skirt and matching tan kitten heels. He'd already identified the outfit as she was racing toward him as another of what he'd come to think of as her working-party dresses—festive but not so eye-catching that they'd detract attention from where it was meant to be.

Now he listened to her half of the conversation with the car service. It seemed as if she was getting good news.

In fact, when the call was over, Pia slumped with relief.

"They got through to the driver," she said. "He's getting off the highway and meeting us three exits away at a gas station rest stop."

"Great." *On to more enchanting matters.* He nodded to her dress. "You look nice."

She threw him a startled look, as if not expecting the compliment. "Thanks."

He felt a smile pull at his lips as he tossed her a sidelong look. "Do you pick your wedding clothes with an eye toward being able to make a quick sprint? You made good time across the grass. Rather impressive in those shoes."

"Weddings can be full of the unexpected," she replied. "You should know that as well as anyone."

He arched a brow. "Still, I'm curious. You phoned me to come to your rescue. Am I your modern-day knight riding to the rescue in a black sports car?"

"Hardly," she replied tartly. "There are very few people I know at this wedding, and you got me into this mess—"

He laughed.

"—so the least you could do when you arrived at just the right moment was to lend a set of wheels."

"Ah, of course."

He let the discussion go at that, though he was tempted to tease her some more.

Moments later, he took the highway exit that she indicated and found the gas station.

The driver of the car service was waiting for them, a shopping bag in hand.

After Pia took the errant veil from the driver and thanked him quickly, she and Hawk hopped back into his car.

"The day has been saved," Hawk remarked as he put the key back in the ignition.

"Not yet," Pia responded. "The wedding isn't over. Trust me on this one. I've been to more weddings than there are lights in Times Square."

"Yes, but isn't this the moment when you thank your hero with a kiss?"

She jerked to look at him, her eyes widening.

Not giving her a chance to think it over, he leaned forward and touched his lips to hers.

Lord, he thought, her lips were as pillowy soft as they looked. *Just as he remembered.*

Even though he knew he should stop, when he heard and felt Pia's breath hitch, he deepened the kiss, settling his lips more firmly on hers.

She didn't pull away, and he drew out the kiss, molding her lips with his. With his hand, he stroked the soft skin of her jaw and throat.

She relaxed and sighed, and leaned toward him. And it was all he could do not to draw her into an embrace and feed the desire between them.

He finally forced himself to pull back and look at her. "There...recompense received."

"I—I—" Pia cleared her throat and frowned. "You're quite the expert at stealing kisses, aren't you?"

Solemnly, he placed his hand over his heart. "It's a rare occasion that I have the opportunity to act so gallantly."

She hesitated, and then gave him a stern look and faced forward. "We need to get back."

They made it back to the New York Botanical Garden in record time while Pia filled him in with desultory wedding details.

When he pulled up in front of the valet again, Pia rushed away to help the bride. As Hawk dealt with the car and the valet again, he reflected that he'd heard nothing but good things from Victoria and Timothy about Pia's eleventh-hour help with their wedding. He was impressed by how professionally Pia had handled herself with little time to prepare.

After leaving the valet, Hawk sauntered alone toward the other guests mingling on the grassy outdoor space where the ceremony was to take place, surrounded by the Botanical Garden's rich greenery. The bridal arch and bedecked chairs, arranged by the florist, stood at the ready.

He made idle chitchat with some fellow guests, but within twenty minutes, everyone was seated and the ceremony started.

The bride looked pretty and the groom beamed, but Hawk only had eyes for Pia, standing discreetly to one side, within a few feet of the seat he'd chosen for himself in one of the back rows.

Suddenly catching Pia's eye, he motioned for her to take the empty seat next to him.

She hesitated for a moment, but then slipped into the white folding chair next to him.

Hawk smiled to himself. But as he stared ahead, watching the bride and groom, more weighty thoughts eventually intruded.

He'd chosen long ago to attend this wedding alone. Victoria and her groom, Timothy, were longtime friends of his, and he'd found that for this occasion at least, he wanted to be free of expectations. At his age, society and the press were apt to view any date of his as a potential duchess.

Hawk reflected that Victoria and Timothy were going through a rite of passage that would soon be expected of him. Tim was an Old Etonian, like him, and Victoria was a baron's daughter who had attended all the right schools and now had a socially acceptable job as the assistant to an up-and-coming British designer.

Victoria, in fact, had precisely the pedigree and background that would be expected for the bride of a duke. She was the sort of woman of whom his mother would approve.

Hawk's mind went to his mother's attempt at matchmaking with Michelene Ward-Fombley in particular, but he pushed the thought aside.

He stole a look at Pia next to him. Her business had trained her in the etiquette of the elite, but that couldn't change her background or give her connections that she didn't possess. With the crowd here today, she'd always be the bridal consultant, never the bride.

At that moment, Pia's lips parted as she looked to the front, and her expression became rather emotional.

Pia cried at weddings.

The thought flashed through Hawk's mind like a news bulletin and was closely followed by the realization that Pia was doing what she loved to do. Weddings, he realized, were more than a job to her.

He'd meant to make things up to her, in a way, by arranging for her to coordinate this wedding and Lucy's. But he'd also, in the process, tested the limits of their relationship because he enjoyed teasing her.

It had been too tempting to spar with her and watch her eyes flash. He admitted to himself that any reaction from Pia was better than having her treat him with indifference. And her kiss…it was hard to imagine a better reaction than that.

But the last thing he wanted to do was to hurt Pia again, he reminded himself. A relationship wouldn't be possible for them, and he shouldn't tease either of them with kisses that couldn't lead to anything more. She deserved to be able to get on with her life, and so did he.

A dog started barking, recalling him from his thoughts.

Beside him, Pia sat up straighter.

Hawk had noted before that the only surprising touch to the ceremony was the bride's King Charles Spaniel, who'd been dressed with an ivory collar and bow and had been led down the aisle by an attendant.

Now, he spotted the dog up front near the bridal arch, playing with—or rather, tearing at—a flower arrangement on the ground.

"Not the dog, please," Pia said under her breath. "We haven't even taken photos with the bridal bouquet yet."

Hawk glanced at her. At the beginning of the ceremony, he'd seen the bride place her flowers on a small pedestal. The pooch-cum-bridal attendant had somehow gotten hold of them.

Hawk couldn't remember the name of Victoria's canine. Finola? Feefee? In any case, *Trouble* seemed appropriate at the moment.

He watched as the bride knelt down, and then her dog sprinted away, bouquet in mouth.

So much for asking if anyone had any objections to this marriage...

"I have to do something," Pia muttered as she started to rise.

Hawk wasn't sure if Pia was talking to herself or to him, and if it mattered. He rose, too, and laid a staying hand on Pia's wrist. "Forget it. In those heels, you'll never catch—"

"Finola."

"Full of trouble."

Hawk moved forward as the dog eluded a well-intentioned guest.

The wedding had truly been disrupted now. Everyone had turned to watch the wily four-legged perpetrator of chaos.

The dog headed toward the back of the gathering, as if sensing that with another few passes, she'd be home free, dashing away from the assembled guests.

Hawk shoved back his chair as he moved into the aisle. He knew he had one shot at catching Victoria's renegade pooch.

He tensed and then dove forward as the furry and furious fuzzball tried to whiz by.

In mid-lunge, he heard gasps, and someone called out a bit of encouragement. And in the next moment, he'd caught the excited Finola with his outstretched arms before landing hard on the ground.

The dog relinquished the bouquet as she was tackled and started yapping again.

A few guests began clapping, and a man called out, "Well done."

Hawk held on firmly to the squirming animal as he straightened and then stood upright. He held Finola away from him.

Victoria rushed forward. "Here, Finola."

Pia snatched the battered bouquet, her expression one of disbelief mixed with dismay.

Hawk watched her, and then murmured, "Just remember, bad luck comes in threes."

She looked up at him, eyes wide. "Please tell me this is number three."

Before he could reassure Pia, Victoria reached to take Finola from him and then snuggled the dog close.

The bride started to laugh and some of the guests joined in. Others broke out into smiles.

Hawk watched Pia relax and smile herself. He could practically read her mind. *If the bride and everyone else could see the humor in the situation, then everything was going to be okay.*

"Who's been the naughty pooch, hmm?" Victoria said.

Hawk resisted rolling his eyes. *Perhaps he did have a preference for women who owned cats rather than dogs.*

With a wave of the arm, he acknowledged the scattered praise from the wedding guests and righted his fallen chair.

Victoria looked at him. "Thank you so much, Hawk. You saved the day."

Hawk glanced at Pia, a smile pulling at his lips. "Not at all. I'm glad I was able to be of service."

Pia lifted her eyebrows.

Victoria walked back up the aisle so the ceremony could resume, and Pia returned the bouquet to its position on the pedestal. Someone kept a firm hold on Finola.

Everything proceeded without a hitch after that. Much to Hawk's regret, though, Pia did not retake her seat next to him but chose to remain positioned near the front of the assembled guests. He couldn't blame her, though, in light of all the recent excitement.

Once the ceremony was over, however, he was able to approach her at the indoor reception, where he spotted her standing with her back to him near the open bar.

"Drink?" he said as he came up behind her.

She turned around at his query, looking as if she was

amused in spite of herself. "For some reason, I'm experiencing a sensation of déjà vu."

Hawk grinned. "I thought so." He chucked her under the chin. "You acquitted yourself splendidly today."

"With your help. Victoria seems to think you went above and beyond the call of duty."

"It was the least I could do," he demurred with a touch of self-mockery. "I was the one who got you involved with the crazy bride."

She smiled. "Only with the best of intentions."

Hawk felt momentarily dazzled by Pia's smile. She could light up a room with it, he thought. Give her a wand and she could sprinkle some glittering fairy dust, no problem.

He pushed aside the whimsical thought, and for Pia's benefit, he shook his head in resigned amusement. "A doggy attendant dressed up to match the bride? Who'd ever have thought it?"

"You'd be surprised," Pia returned. "I've even seen a pet pig march up the aisle."

"Well, Finola is no match for Mr. Darcy."

Pia laughed. "Mr. Darcy would agree with you, I'm sure."

They discussed the wedding at that point, with Pia remarking on how beautiful Victoria had looked, and Hawk commenting on some of the faces he recognized among the guests.

"This is a working party for me," Pia said eventually, as if to remind herself as much as him.

"I suppose you'll have to stay until the very end then?" he remarked.

She nodded. "I'll have to make sure everything is wrapped up."

Hawk looked through the reception room's paned windows and noted it was already dark.

"How are you getting back home?" he asked, guessing that she hadn't come in her own car because she'd had to borrow the services of his earlier.

She lifted a shoulder, and said simply, "I'll order a car service."

His eyes met hers. "I'll stick around then."

"I...i-it's not necessary."

"I know." He smiled. "Nevertheless, I'm at your disposal."

It wasn't until a few hours later that he was able to make good on his offer. He noted that Pia still managed to look as edible as dessert by the end of the evening, even though she also seemed drained.

They drove back to Manhattan mostly in silence, content to observe the darkened world whizzing by after a long day—and comfortable enough in each other's company not to make forced conversation.

When Hawk pulled up in front of Pia's building, however, he glanced over, only to notice that she had fallen asleep.

Her head was leaning back against the headrest, her lips parted.

He turned off the ignition and then stopped, taking a moment to study her face. For once, she looked unguarded.

Her blond hair had a fine, wispy quality, and he knew from experience that it was as soft as a baby's. Her eyebrows were delicately arched over eyes that he knew were large and expressive and a fascinating, changeable mix of amber hues.

Hawk let his gaze roam down to her lips. They held the sheen of a shimmery pink lipstick, but they needed no embellishment for their natural charm as far as he was concerned. He'd tasted them earlier in the day, because the temptation had been too great.

He debated for a moment, and then, unable to help himself,

leaned over, tilted her chin toward him with a light touch and pressed his lips to hers.

He rubbed his lips against hers, feeling the tingle of sensation, and then gently worked her lower lip with a small suck.

Dessert hadn't been nearly as good.

Pia's eyelashes fluttered. She opened her eyes and lifted her head.

Hawk pulled back, and then gave her a lopsided smile.

"Wh-what?"

"I was awakening Sleeping Beauty with a kiss," he responded in a low voice. "Isn't that the fairy-tale heroine that you are today?"

She blinked, coming further awake. "Unintentionally. This isn't a good idea."

He glanced past her and then back down again, keeping his expression innocent. "Did you prefer not to be awakened when we arrived at your apartment? Should I have driven straight on to my place instead?"

"Absolutely not," she said, though in a halfhearted tone.

He smiled for a moment before turning to open the driver-side door.

He reached her side of the car in time to help her alight, though she hesitated for a second before placing her hand in his.

By now, he was used to the sizzle of any physical contact between them.

"Good night, Your Grace," she said when she'd gotten out of his car, her eyes meeting his.

He let his lips drift upward. "Good night, Pia."

He watched as she made her way into her building, the doorman looking up from his television set to acknowledge her.

Only after she'd disappeared from view did he get back into his car.

As he pulled into traffic, Hawk acknowledged that he was pushing the boundaries with Pia. But, he told himself, he knew what the limits were.

Or so he hoped.

Seven

"*Ducal Gofer*. Gazillionaire bridal assistant, the Duke of Hawkshire…"

Pia gritted her teeth as she read Mrs. Jane Hollings's gossip column in *The New York Intelligencer*.

"What's wrong?" Belinda asked.

Pia had just sat down at a table in Contadini, where she, Belinda Wentworth and Tamara Langsford—née Kincaid—were having one of their Sunday brunch dates.

"Mrs. Hollings has written about me and Hawk in her gossip column," Pia said as she scrolled down the article on her smartphone. "Apparently she received notice that Hawk helped me handle some wedding escapades last night."

"That was fast," Belinda commented.

"Well, it's in her online column," Pia responded, looking up. "Her regular print one will appear in Monday's paper, where no doubt I will be able to savor the joy of having my name appear in print with—" her lips pulled down "—the Duke of Hawkshire's."

Belinda looked at Tamara. "Doesn't your husband own this paper? Can't you do something about this awful woman?"

Tamara cleared her throat. "I have news."

"You already told us, remember?" Belinda quipped. "We know you're knocked up, and Sawyer is the daddy."

"Old news." Tamara looked from Pia to Belinda. "The new news is that Sawyer and I plan to stay together."

"For the sake of the baby?" Belinda shook her head. "Honey…"

Tamara shook her head. "No, because we love each other."

Belinda stared at her blankly for a moment. Then she waved to a passing waiter. "Another Bloody Mary, please."

Pia knew this was a sore point for Belinda, since her friend still needed to get an annulment from the Marquess of Easterbridge.

"I suppose I should be addressing you both as *My Lady*," Pia mused. "Sawyer is an earl, making Tamara a countess, and since Colin is a marquess, you're entitled to be called—"

"Don't you dare," Belinda retorted. "I'm planning to shed the title as soon as possible."

Pia sighed. "Oh, well."

Belinda turned to Tamara. "I can't believe you're abandoning our trio of girlfriends for the aristocratic cadre."

"I'm not. It's just…"

"What?" Belinda asked, her expression sardonic. "You moved in with Sawyer and made a marriage of convenience. And then—" she snapped her fingers "—next thing you know, you're pregnant with his child and declaring yourself in love."

Tamara smiled and shrugged. "It's the most exciting thing that's ever happened to me," she admitted. "I wasn't looking to fall in love, and if you'd asked me months ago, I'd have said Sawyer was the last man…"

Tamara got a faraway look as her words drifted off. "I realized Sawyer was the one I wanted all along," she eventually continued. "And the best part is he feels the same way about me."

Belinda accepted the Bloody Mary that the waiter was about to set down in front of her, and took a healthy swig. "Well, I'm happy for you, Tam. One of us deserves to find happiness."

Tamara gave a faint smile. "Thanks. I know you and Pia don't like Sawyer's friends—"

"You mean my husband?" Belinda asked archly.

"You mean Hawk?" Pia said at the same time.

"—but Sawyer and I are hoping you all will make nice enough to be in the same room together. In fact, we're hoping to have all of you over next Saturday night for a small postwedding celebration."

"A we're-staying-married party?" Belinda queried.

"Sort of," Tamara acknowledged before looking across at Pia, who'd taken the seat to Belinda's right. "Please come. You love anything having to do with weddings."

Pia sighed again. She did. And she hated to disappoint Tamara, though it wasn't wise for her to spend too much time in Hawk's company.

"How are you getting along with Hawk these days, Pia?" Tamara asked suddenly, as if reading her mind. "I know you're planning his sister's wedding. And you just noted that Mrs. Hollings is gossiping about how he helped you last night."

Pia hesitated. How much should she reveal? Certainly not the stolen kisses—and the fact that she'd enjoyed them.

He'd said he was trying to make amends. And so far, she'd let him. *More than let him.*

The kisses came back to her. The tingle of excitement, the remembered feeling of delicious passion—just like the first time, and just like in her dreams—and the sensation of melding with a kindred spirit.

Pia shook her head slightly as if to clear it. *No.*

She was playing with fire, and she'd be foolhardy to go down that road again.

And yet...

She'd felt an acute sadness for Hawk when she'd discovered what had precipitated his abrupt departure from her apartment after they'd slept together. Her parents were alive and well back in Pennsylvania, and while she didn't have any siblings, she imagined that Hawk had been understandably devastated by the unexpected loss of his brother.

None of this is intended as an excuse.

Hawk had still acted toward her as if he felt he was at fault and was feeling guilty. Of course, his brother's untimely death didn't explain why he hadn't sought her out after their night together. Had the abrupt severing of ties made it easy for him to forget her? The thought hurt. And yet what other explanation could there be? She hadn't meant enough to him.

And yet...

She knew even if she softened toward him, let their explosive chemistry play out to its natural conclusion, this time she would no longer be the naive virgin who was new in town. She could show Hawk that she could play in more sophisticated circles, too, these days.

He was flirting with her, and she could enjoy it and not become besotted.

Why couldn't she be one of those women who enjoyed a fling or a casual hookup? She'd already had a one-night stand. *With him.*

These thoughts and more flitted through her mind.

Pia became aware of Belinda and Tamara staring at her.

She cleared her throat. "Hawk has been...helpful," she hedged, and then shrugged. "I—I suppose I'm feeling ambivalent at best."

"Ambivalent?" Belinda questioned, and then rolled her eyes. "Isn't that one step away from infatuated these days? Pia, please tell me you're not falling for the guy again."

"Of course not!"

"Because you have a soft heart, and I'd hate to—"

"D-don't worry. Once burned, twice shy." She shrugged. "But I am planning his sister's wedding, and I do need to be on cordial terms with him."

"Great," Tamara commented. "I'm so glad you won't have any trouble being in Hawk's company next weekend."

Belinda frowned. "It's not Hawk I'm worried about."

Pia refused to admit that Hawk *was* the one *she* was worried about.

Hawk took another sip of his wine and his senses came fully alert.

Pia.

He spotted her immediately when she came into the parlor of the Earl and Countess of Melton's Upper East Side town house. But it was as if he'd been able to sense her presence even before seeing her.

She looked spectacular. Her high-waist sheath dress with its black bodice and white skirt flattered her curves, making her seem taller than she was and showing off her great legs in black patent peep-toe pumps.

He glimpsed the deep pink color of the nail polish on her toes, and his gut tightened.

Heaven help him, but she packed a wallop in a small package. It was almost as if she'd been sent to entice him—to test his best resolutions.

He started toward her, but was suddenly stopped by a staying hand on his arm.

He turned his head to look inquiringly at Colin, Marquess of Easterbridge.

Colin gave him a careless smile. "Careful there. Your lady-killer ways are showing."

Hawk let the side of his mouth quirk up. "The opposite is more likely the case. She looks harmless but—"

Colin laughed shortly. "They all do."

Hawk had no doubt the marquess was also referencing his own wife, Belinda Wentworth, who legally remained the Marchioness of Easterbridge. Hawk was curious about the exact state of affairs between Colin and Belinda these days, but he didn't want to pry. Colin was an enigma even to his friends at times.

"I have it covered," Hawk responded. "I'm proceeding only with the best reconnaissance."

Colin gave another knowing laugh. "I'll wager you are."

Hawk shrugged, and then started toward Pia again, leaving Colin standing where he was.

So what if the look he'd given Pia made it clear that he found her desirable, and everyone knew it?

Pia was looking at *him* expectantly right now, though there was also puzzlement in her eyes—as if she wondered about his brief exchange with Colin.

"I won't offer you a drink," he quipped as he reached her. "You look fabulous, by the way."

There was no *by the way* about it, he thought. Everything else was tangential.

Pia flushed. "Th-thank you. I wouldn't mind a glass of wine."

He snagged a couple from a waiter who happened by, and handed one to her.

"Cheers," he said as he clinked his glass to hers. "How is the wedding planning going? I understand from my sister that she's been to your apartment twice this week."

Pia took a sip of her drink. "Yes, we were discussing invitations and décor. Fortunately, she already had a dress picked out." She smiled as if sharing a joke. "Everything with this wedding is going smoothly, so far."

"I've only been to your apartment once. Can I express envy?"

Pia raised her eyebrows for a moment, and then laughed. She tapped him on the wrist. "Only if you play your cards right."

Hawk hesitated. If he'd heard her correctly, she'd just met his flirtation with a bit of her own. He was used to banter between them, but it wasn't usually so…receptive.

"How is Mr. Darcy?" he tried, testing. "Perhaps he's in need of a male role model?"

"If he is, would you be one?"

Ah. "I am more than willing to try."

Pia gave an exaggerated sigh. "Are you ever serious?"

In response, he banked his amusement.

"Would it matter if I said yes?"

Though he could lapse into well-practiced flirtation—he remembered his old self well—he felt the weight of his responsibilities too much these days to be anything other than what was expected of him. A duke.

Pia searched his eyes, and he held her amber ones solemnly.

"That comment was rather unfair of me," she said. "I've seen how you feel a responsibility to your sister as the head of the family. A-and you've certainly helped me."

"Lucy has been talking?" he queried, not answering her directly.

She nodded.

"Burnishing my image, that's my girl."

Over Pia's shoulder, Hawk glimpsed Colin approach Belinda before Pia's friend turned on her heel and stalked toward the door. Colin followed at a more leisurely pace, drink in hand.

Realizing that she no longer held his attention, Pia turned

in the direction of his gaze. "Oh, dear," she said in a low voice as she swung back to face him. "Was that a confrontation I just missed?"

Hawk looked down at her. "A near-miss. Belinda walked away before Easterbridge could approach her."

"In contrast to you and me."

He shot her a surprised look, and then gave her a game smile. "Some of us are lucky."

Pia sighed. "Easterbridge should give Belinda the annulment that she's looking for, and let her move on with her life. Instead, he seems to enjoy tormenting her."

"My friends are not unlikable, despite what you may believe."

"In a way, it's hard to believe that you and Easterbridge are friends. He can't get unmarried, while you—"

Hawk quirked a brow. "Yes?"

"—have never been married," she finished lamely.

He could tell from the look in Pia's eyes, however, that she had intended to label him a commitment-shy player. The fact that she hadn't said something, at least.

Had Lucy's words had a salutary effect on Pia's opinion of him? There was only one way to find out.

Hawk took a sip of his wine. "Let's turn back to a more soothing subject for my ego. Lucy has been singing my praises."

A small smile rose to Pia's lips, and she nodded. "Lucy mentioned that you've been working nonstop these past three years as you've moved into your role as duke, learned the running of the estates and started Sunhill Investments."

"Are you surprised?"

Pia hesitated, and then shook her head. "No. You've acted... differently than you did three years ago." She paused. "It must have been very hard for you after your father and brother died."

He didn't recollect stories about his father and his brother every day anymore—not like three years ago—but their joint passing had set his life on a new trajectory. "William and I were two years apart. We grew up as friends and playmates as well as brothers, though I always knew I got a free pass as the younger son while William had his life and responsibilities mapped out for him."

It was more personal information than he was accustomed to divulging.

Pia didn't look as if she was sitting in judgment, however. "And then one day the free pass disappeared…"

He nodded. "As fate would have it."

"You had a reputation as a player," she stated without inflection. "The stories—"

"Old news, but reports will hang around the internet forever." His mouth twisted. "I do have two jobs that often take up more time than one person can handle, believe it or not. I do need to be serious for those."

"I've hardly had an opportunity to see it," she protested.

He'd meant to tweak her nose about her earlier query about his lack of seriousness, and he could tell she understood it.

"Maybe you just bring out the devilish side of me." He tilted his head. "Perhaps with you, I can relax and tease."

She flushed. "I'm such an easy target."

"You hold your own," he offered, taken in by her blush.

She moistened her lips, and he watched longingly.

"Would you like to see a more intense and focused side of me?" he asked, suddenly going with an idea. "I'm going rock climbing at a gym in Brooklyn tomorrow. The gym keeps me in shape for the real thing."

Pia's eyes glinted. "Who ever heard of a duke rock climbing?"

He assumed a suitable hauteur. "I'm a modern-day duke. This is an outlet for all those go-forth-and-conquer genes that my ancestors bequeathed to me."

"All right."

Accepting her response, he didn't add that rock climbing was also a good pressure-release valve.

Because right now, he was feeling an ungodly urge to conquer and possess *her*.

Eight

He had his hands all over her.

At least that's how it felt to Pia.

Between teaching her how to use the equipment and instructing her on how to place her feet on the climbing wall, it felt as if Hawk had covered her body even more thoroughly this morning at the gym than he might have in bed.

Downing a flavored-water drink, her heart thumping with spent energy, and sweat soaking her sports bra and biker shorts, she eyed Hawk and tried not to think of jumping him.

She was petite and a featherweight, so she doubted that even if she launched herself at him, he'd do more than stagger a step—if that.

He looked all primal male standing in the middle of the cavernous gym in his own sweat-dampened shirt and shorts, his lean, muscular frame exposed to her avid gaze. It was a sign of how physically fit he was, however, that *he'd* only perspired a little.

Still, she could smell the sweat—and, yes, she could swear, even the male hormones on him—and her body reacted in response. She willed her nipples not to become more pronounced. With any luck, he'd think it was all due to a blast of cool air hitting her damp skin, anyway.

Finishing off a swallow of water, Hawk eyed her speculatively as he capped his bottle. "You're the first woman who has indulged my rock-climbing hobby. You're the only one who, astonishingly, agreed to come along for the ride."

"So I was hoodwinked by you?" she teased, though inside she felt a thrill at his admission.

"You did well," he said, sidestepping the question. "You made it to the top of the wall and down." His eyes gleamed with respect and admiration. "More than once, in fact. Congratulations."

"Thank you."

She didn't know why it should matter that she'd proven herself at one of Hawk's pastimes—aside from fishing and horseback riding—but it did.

Even though it was a Sunday morning, several other patrons moved around them in the open gym.

Pia realized that she was tagging along on one of Hawk's regular workouts, except it hadn't been the typical gym that they'd gone to when he'd picked her up at her apartment in his car this morning. She did not have a wedding to attend to this weekend, so she'd easily been able to rise early herself.

She capped her drink bottle. She realized that she'd slaked her thirst—for water, anyway.

"Have you ever encountered one of your namesakes on any of your rock-climbing adventures?" she asked to make conversation.

She tried to distract herself from what he looked like in his clingy gym clothes.

He looked amused. "Have I met a hawk?" He shook his head. "Only once. I don't think the bird was impressed."

She wet her lips. "Did you become known as Hawk upon assuming the title?"

He nodded. "My father was known as Hawkshire, in the customary way of addressing peers by their titles rather than their given names. It felt right to distinguish myself in some way when I assumed the title. But in the end, I didn't have a say in the matter. Easterbridge and Melton began calling me Hawk, and it caught on."

She contemplated him. "It suits you."

He rubbed the bridge of his nose, looking further amused. "You mean this?"

"How did you break your nose?" she asked, glad that he didn't look insulted.

"Ah…" He smiled, but then hesitated. "At the risk of highlighting my former raffish ways, I'll admit to getting into a barroom brawl during my university days."

"Through no fault of your own, of course."

"Naturally," he deadpanned, dimpling. "And all participants have been barred from speaking further about the matter."

"I'll bet Easterbridge or Melton would know."

Hawk laughed. "You're at liberty to attempt to unearth the information."

"Maybe I'll try," she responded lightly.

He glanced down at himself and then at her, his gaze seeming to linger on all her softest places. "In the meantime, why don't we get ourselves ready and get out of here?"

She nodded. "Okay."

"Don't you have an appointment to meet with Lucy this afternoon at the house?"

She nodded again. "Lucy's understudy is filling in for her for today's performances."

"Then why don't you come straight back with me?" he offered. "The house will be a more comfortable place for you to shower and change than the gym. We could have something to eat and kill some time before you need to take your meeting with Lucy."

Pia hesitated. Shower and change at his residence? *Nò, no, no.* She thought of her gym bag in her locker. In the ladies' room, she'd be safe and surrounded by other members of the female tribe—not by a descendant of conquerors.

Hawk smiled. "I promise I won't bite. There are a couple of guest bedrooms with en suite bathrooms where you'll feel comfortable. You choose."

Pia blushed because it seemed he'd read her mind.

But, then again, what could it hurt to accede to his suggestion? Lucy would most likely be at home or there soon, and then there would be the presence of the household help.

Except when they got back to Hawk's house, Pia discovered that Lucy was not home and not expected back until shortly before her afternoon appointment with Pia. The staff, typically discreet, was nowhere to be seen.

Nevertheless, she chose a guest bedroom with cheery yellow-and-blue-chintz upholstery and a white canopy bed. She showered in the adjoining marble bath, and then wrapped herself in a plush blue towel.

The house was clearly appointed with luxury throughout, she realized. Before now, she'd only been in Hawk's home to talk with Lucy, and she'd never been on the upper levels.

As she came out of the bathroom, Pia eyed the bed. It was tempting to allow herself to sink onto it and revel in its comfort. The mattress and the counterpane seemed soft and thick. In fact, the whole bedroom was decorated in a way she'd have aspired to in her apartment if she'd had the money. Instead, she'd contented herself with the budget version of many items.

Turning away from temptation, she dressed, pulling on an emerald top with a square neckline edged with red ribbon. She paired it with a full taupe skirt, wide black patent belt, black leggings and gold ballerina flats.

Today, the weather was a little cooler, the breeze having a little nip, so she'd pulled some of her fall attire from her wardrobe while packing her gym bag.

When she was done getting ready, she wandered out of the bedroom and down the hall. Stopping before the door of the bedroom that Hawk had pointed out to her as his, she hesitated just a moment before knocking.

When Hawk opened his door, however, she found herself swallowing and wetting her lips.

He wore a crisp white shirt and black pants, and his hair was still damp from his shower. He exuded a virile magnetism.

Why must he look so effortlessly but devastatingly attractive?

And then he looked at *her*, his eyes making a quick but thorough perusal.

He smiled, slow and sexy, and Pia felt her heart thump.

"A gorgeous woman knocking on my door. Under other circumstances, my next move would have been to invite you in and—" he winked "—allow my licentious nature free rein."

She heated. "I—I didn't want to wander around your house by myself, and I didn't know where we'd be having lunch." She decided to try to lighten the moment. "Heaven forbid someone spotted me and thought I was snooping."

His smile widened. "Which fairy-tale heroine goes around snooping? I can't recall."

"No one," she protested. "A-and I—I don't believe in fairy tales."

He took her hand. "Great, then we'll just have to make up our own story."

He stepped aside and tugged her into his room.

As Pia glanced around, Hawk made a sweeping motion with his arm.

"This is my bedroom." He shot her a devilish smile. "In case you were wondering what it looked like. Or should I say, in this tale, the heroine *wants to know* what it looks like."

And she wanted him to want her.

The thought flashed through her mind, and she couldn't deny its truth.

She made a visual sweep of the room. "V-very nice."

Dark, rich furniture contrasted with stripe and damask upholstery in varying shades of cream and green.

A four-poster bed was dominated by a scrolled wooden headboard.

She parted and then wet her lips.

Her eyes connected with Hawk's, and she realized that he'd caught every reaction.

She wanted to say something, and then stopped.

"I hate my speech impediment," she blurted inanely.

He gave a lopsided smile. "I love your verbal quirk." He leaned close, a twinkle in his eye. "It tells me just how much I'm affecting you."

She felt flustered because he was affecting her right now. "Mmm…y-you p-promised you wouldn't bite."

"Little Red Riding Hood and the Big, Bad Wolf?" he queried as he moved closer. "Okay, I can work with that story line."

Despite herself, she laughed. "You're incorrigible."

He reached out and caressed her arm. "I promised I wouldn't bite, but that leaves much unbargained territory."

"I am not Little Red Riding Hood."

"Of course," he agreed soothingly. "Not into role-play?"

She gave a helpless laugh.

He ducked his head and brushed his lips across hers.

He made to pull back almost immediately, but then his lips lowered to hers again—as if Hawk couldn't help himself—and this time the kiss lingered.

Hawk's arms came around her, and she slid her own up to his neck. They pressed close, hard planes meeting soft curves and fitting together without gap, despite their difference in height.

He tasted minty and fresh, and as his tongue invaded her mouth, she made a sound deep in her throat and met him eagerly.

The kiss was intense, but finally slowed.

"Pia," Hawk muttered against her mouth. "It's been too long. How could I ever forget?"

She didn't want him ever to forget. She wanted him to remember her in the way he'd similarly always be with her.

She'd always remember him. *Her first lover.*

Suddenly Hawk bent and hooked his arm under her knees, and laid her on the bed. He came down beside her and took her in his arms again.

"Pia." He brushed the hair away from her face. "You remind me of a nymph or a fairy."

"I suppose it doesn't help that I'm wearing ballerina flats today."

He gave a short laugh. "Even when you're not in flats, you're petite." He brushed her hair so that it fanned out over the coverlet. "I've never seen a wood nymph climb a rock wall before."

She wrinkled her nose at his words as his delicious weight pressed her into the mattress. "I can just imagine what I looked like from the ground."

"I had trouble stopping myself from reaching out and doing this," he said, caressing her leg.

"Oh."

Hawk shifted, his knee wedging between her legs as he leaned over her. He kissed her then, sipping at her lips and lazily tracing their outline with his tongue.

"L-lucy will come home," Pia breathed against his mouth.

"Not for a long time," he whispered back.

Pia felt his arousal press against her, evidence of his growing need. Mirroring his response, her nipples felt tight, and a moist heat had gathered between her thighs.

She shifted. "Why did I bother getting dressed?"

Her remark elicited a low chuckle from him, and she felt it reverberate through his chest.

He placed a moist kiss near her ear. "Don't worry. We can remedy the situation."

True to his word, he made quick work of her shoes and leggings, and then settled himself between her legs.

She felt his warm breath on her thigh, and her delicate skin was stroked by the slight abrasiveness of his jaw.

He squeezed her calf as his lips grazed her thigh. He let his lips trail down first one leg and then the other.

Pia quivered in response.

In the next moment, she moaned as he sucked on her tender flesh. She couldn't help herself, but it seemed to excite him to hear how he was making her feel.

Her hands tangled in his hair, and she urged him upward for an urgent kiss. She met him halfway, sitting up, and they kissed, his hands wandering her back urgently.

She was crazy to think she could be unforgettable to a man of his experience. She was loony to think she could match his level of sophistication in seduction.

But then he obliged her with a groan deep in his throat. "Ah, Pia...what you do to me."

She rubbed his arousal. "I can tell."

He grew in a sharp breath. "You're not as shy as I remembered."

She hoped not.

Since he'd left her, she'd made a point of studying romantic movies, reading a book or two and renting some videos—all in an attempt to overcome some of her naiveté and inexperience. She'd thought she'd never have fallen for Hawk's practiced skills if she'd been more knowledgeable. And at the same time, irrationally, she'd started to believe that Hawk wouldn't have left her if she'd been more of a seductress.

Still, she didn't think now was the time to mention to him that she'd been educating herself.

Instead, she tilted her head, and asked innocently, "You don't want me to be...uninhibited?"

"Of course I'd love it."

She gave him a smile.

"How am I going to get you out of these clothes?" he mused, his eyes sweeping over her.

She straightened, and then slid off the bed and turned to face him. "You won't have to. I-I'm going to strip for you."

He smiled, slow and sexy, doing funny things to her insides.

The room was cool and shadowed, the shades apparently still drawn from when he was dressing and undressing.

Pia pulled her top over her head and tossed it on a dresser.

Catching Hawk's hot gaze, she teased him by tracing the edges of her lacy pink bra with her fingertips.

Hawk continued avidly watching her with hooded eyes.

Pia wet her lips, running the tip of her tongue over the plump and swollen formation of her mouth.

She still felt the imprint of Hawk's kisses there. And judging from the look of him, Hawk was on a tight leash, stopping himself from giving her more and then some.

"This is going to be the shortest strip on record," he murmured thickly. "Need some help there?"

She knew her nipples were outlined against the nylon fabric of her bra, the coolness of the room adding to her arousal. Her breasts were a bit oversized for her frame, giving her the appearance of a busty fairy. However, since high school, she hadn't caught a guy eyeing them as lustily as Hawk was.

She shivered, and Hawk crooked his finger at her.

Her stomach did a somersault.

She came to him, and he caught her, leaning back to lie down on the bed as she straddled him.

Mouth met mouth in a voracious kiss. Then he was feasting

on her breasts, and she threw back her head and luxuriated in the sensation.

"Hawk."

He unclasped her bra and peeled away the offending barrier, his mouth barely leaving her in the process. He suckled her, his hands bunching her breasts together for his greedy lips.

Pia felt sweet and piercing-hot sensations shoot through her. In response, she rubbed against him.

Hawk lifted his mouth from her breast and sat up so they were face-to-face. "If we don't slow down," he muttered thickly, his mouth close to hers, "this is going to be over in two minutes."

"Th-three y-years is a long time to wait."

"Too long."

With one hand, she opened the first button of his shirt, and then the next and the next. All the while, she was aware of the rasp of his breath as her gaze focused on the strong column of his throat.

She finally undid his cuffs and tugged at his shirt.

He obliged her by sitting up and shrugging out of his white shirt and the undershirt below.

He quirked his lips. "Now what?"

"D-do you have a blindfold for yourself?"

He laughed helplessly.

"You're only half-naked," she protested.

"It's a situation I'm more than happy to rectify."

She moved aside, and he got off the bed.

But before he could make a further move, she stopped him, laying a hand on his arm.

"Let me."

Getting up herself, she worked slowly but surely, her hands brushing his arousal and causing his breathing to deepen.

She slid his belt free of its loops and then lowered his zipper.

He helped her then, and the room sounded with the thud of his shoes and the slither of his pants and boxers.

Pia caressed his arousal freely before bending and kneeling before him.

Hawk groaned. "Pia, Pia…ah, sweet."

Pia was lost in the experience of making love in a way she never had before. She felt the tension in Hawk's muscles and the throbbing heat of his flesh. And when she gave him the most intimate kiss she could imagine, he stiffened and groaned again, gripping the bedside table.

"Pia," Hawk said, his voice heavy and thick with arousal. "You've definitely…changed."

She'd had time over the past three years to replay the night she'd lost her innocence to Hawk. She'd had time to imagine different scenarios. She'd had time to see herself as the seductress instead of the one being seduced.

And now, unexpectedly, she had a chance to realize some of those fantasies. *With him.* Because he'd always been the lover whom she'd imagined.

She focused on giving pleasure and soaking in the sounds of how much Hawk was enjoying her ministrations.

She wanted to make him lose control.

Moments ticked by, and then, on an oath, Hawk disengaged her, pulling her up for a rough kiss.

"I'm not going to ask where you learned that," he said darkly.

If only he knew, Pia thought.

She thrilled at the tacit admission that she'd given him unexpected pleasure. She warmed to the tinge of jealousy in his voice.

"T-take me," she said, her request a plea and a demand. "H-Hawk, p-please."

He swept her up into his arms and laid her on the bed again. He rid her of her belted skirt, her last piece of clothing and of protection from his avid gaze.

He leaned over her and caressed her body. "You're so beautiful, you make me ache."

Pia felt her heart squeeze.

"Are you using any protection?" he asked.

She shook her head. "No."

He opened a nearby nightstand drawer and removed a packet.

"I don't think I can be near you without being prepared," he said with self-deprecation.

She gave a small smile. "S-sort of like leaving the house without your BlackBerry?"

He chuckled. "Sort of. But you make me lose my mind, whether I like it or not."

He sheathed himself, and Pia reached her arms up to him.

She wanted him to lose control right now. The need to be joined to him was overwhelming. She wanted to experience falling over the edge again with him into paradise. It had been so long…

Hawk settled his weight on her. "Ah, Pia, let me in…"

He entered her, and they both closed their eyes, savoring the sweet sensation of their joining.

Hawk started to move, and a delicious friction began to build in Pia.

They kissed and moaned, and he bit down gently on the tender skin at the side of her throat, while she let her hands roam over his hard muscles, urging him onward.

Pia convulsed gently, once and then twice.

"That's right," Hawk muttered. "Come for me, Pia. Come again."

He whispered sweet encouragement.

Pia felt herself tremble, her body on the cusp of deliverance. She tightened around Hawk, and her hands fell from his back to grasp the coverlet.

He was relentless in pursuit of her pleasure. "Pia," he breathed in her ear. "Sweetheart, tell me."

"H-Hawk, p-please, y-yes."

The sound of how much he affected her was his undoing.

Hawk groaned and stilled just as her body began to shake. He spilled himself inside her, wondrously joining her powerful climax with one of his own.

Pia cried out with her release, and Hawk clasped her to him, his skin hot and damp.

Their hearts racing, they came back down to earth—or some version of it.

This, she thought, was what dreams were made of.

Nine

In the normal course of things, lunch with Colin, Marquess of Easterbridge, and Sawyer Langsford, Earl of Melton, in the dining room of the historic Sherry-Netherland Hotel should have been a tame and relaxing affair.

Hawk knew better.

Lately, notoriety had come nipping at the heels of his trio of friends.

Colin looked up quizzically from his BlackBerry. "Well, Melton, it seems Mrs. Hollings has done it again."

Sawyer nodded at a waiter who then proceeded to fill his wineglass, and took his time addressing Colin. "What, pray tell, has she deemed worthy of acid ink this time?"

"The topic is us...again," Colin said, his tone bland. "Or, more exactly, the subject is Hawkshire."

"How very fair of you, Melton," Hawk commented dryly, "to include us in the *Intelligencer's* gossip column."

Sawyer's lips quirked. "So what does our Mrs. Hollings have to say today?"

"Apparently Hawkshire has a second career as a wedding planner's apprentice."

Sawyer raised his eyebrows and swiveled his head to look at Hawk, his expression droll. "And you kept this tidbit from us? How could you?"

Damnation. Hawk knew he was in for a ribbing from his two friends. Still, it was worth mounting a defense, however feeble. "My sister is getting married."

"'We've heard,'" Colin said, quoting the text from his BlackBerry, "'that a certain very wealthy duke has been keeping company with a lovely wedding planner. Could it be that wedding bells are in the air?'"

"Charming, our Mrs. Hollings," Sawyer said.

"A veritable fount of useful information."

Hawk remained steadfastly mum, refusing to add his two cents to his friends' comments.

Sawyer frowned. "How is your mother these days, Hawk? The last time I had the opportunity to be in her charming company, she talked of finding you a bride. In fact, I believe one name in particular crossed her lips."

"Michelene Ward-Fombley," Hawk said succinctly.

Sawyer nodded. "Ah, yes, that sounds—" he paused to give Hawk a shrewd look "—exactly right... A suitable choice."

Of course, Sawyer and Colin would have a passing acquaintance with Michelene, Hawk thought. She was from their aristocratic social circle. Her grandfather was a viscount, not someone from a small town in Pennsylvania...

He and Michelene had dated a few times, back when he was still trying to sort out what his role as the new duke should be. He'd gingerly tested the waters by stepping into William's shoes with one of the leading candidates to be a future duchess. But then his work with Sunhill Investments had consumed him, and still grieving, he'd allowed himself to stop calling Michelene. It had been easy to do, since she hadn't awakened any strong emotion in him. But then, in the past year, the idea of Michelene as the Duchess of Hawkshire had gained renewed life, thanks to his mother's prodding.

"What game are you playing, Hawk?" Sawyer asked, going straight to the point.

Hawk kept his expression steady. Ever since Sawyer's marriage of convenience to Tamara had turned into a real one, he'd been protective of her and her girlfriends, Pia and Belinda.

Pia.

Damn it, he was not going to discuss Pia with Melton or Easterbridge.

Yesterday had been the most passionate experience of his life—for the second time. Inexplicably, he felt a visceral connection to Pia. Maybe that explained why he'd never forgotten her…

She'd been a virgin, but if last night was anything to judge by, she'd learned a lot in the past three years.

He acknowledged as much with a punch to the gut. He'd been unprepared for the Pia of yesterday afternoon. She'd caught him by surprise—again. He'd intended to be the seducer, and instead had been seduced.

Yet…had he really intended to seduce her again? Despite all his noble intentions?

Certainly, by the time she'd entered his bedroom, his mind had turned toward kissing her and more. But the idea had been gaining steam well before then. Without a doubt, while she'd been giving him a tantalizing view of her luscious posterior all morning. And maybe even before then…when she'd been running across the grass toward him at the New York Botanical Garden, or when…

He wanted her. All he'd been able to think about for the past twenty-four hours was getting Pia in bed again. And now that they'd crossed the threshold to being lovers again, he admitted he also didn't want to turn back. He wanted to remain lovers—unlike the first time three years ago—even if his relatively newfound principles were in jeopardy as a result!

They'd been forced to end their afternoon tryst yesterday when Lucy had arrived home. Otherwise, Hawk was sure that he and Pia would have spent all day in bed.

Instead, Pia had descended the stairs as if nothing untoward had happened—such as Lucy's wedding planner having completely undone her brother—and had met with Lucy as if she'd arrived at the house only a little early and had been awaiting her.

Why was it so upsetting that their lovemaking left her so unaffected? He couldn't fall into a too serious entanglement with her—not with all his responsibilities to his title.

Hawk noted belatedly that Sawyer was waiting for an answer, and even Colin looked intent.

"There's no game," he said, choosing his words with care.

Blast it, even *he* didn't know what to make of his relationship with Pia. Not anymore. He had no compass.

Sawyer looked dubious. "Then you're not practically eng—"

"There is no game," he repeated.

Sawyer eyed him, his expression thoughtful. "You might want to make sure Pia doesn't get hurt, either."

Right. If anything, Hawk thought, *he* was the one in danger here.

Pia felt a quiver of anticipation when her doorman rang and announced that Hawk was downstairs.

"Tell him to come up," she said before replacing her receiver and turning away from the phone.

She hugged herself and glanced at Mr. Darcy, who was eyeing her like a friend resigned to watching her make the same mistake twice.

She could sense the feline's disapproval—almost read his thoughts, if that were possible.

Wickham. Him again. Have we learned nothing?

"Oh, don't look at me that way," Pia said. "His name is not Wickham, as you well know. And I'm sure he has a very good reason for being here."

Right. And a cat has nine lives. I wish.

"You're way too cynical for a feline. Why did I adopt you from the shelter?"

You know why. I'm the antidote to your trusting romantic nature.

I'm not as naive as I once was, Pia responded in her head.

Mr. Darcy turned and padded toward his basket, set against one wall of her living room space. He stepped in, made himself comfortable and closed his eyes.

Pia stood there and then blushed as she remembered her afternoon idyll with Hawk on Sunday.

It was shocking how easily she lost her inhibitions with him. She'd forgotten herself in the moment. But he'd seemed equally affected.

At least she hoped so.

She still couldn't quite believe her daring—or foolhardiness—in trying to play in Hawk's league of seduction. She'd met him and upped the ante. And though she hadn't been able to admit it to herself, perhaps she'd set out to prove that she could bind him, unlike their first time.

Careful, careful. She couldn't and wouldn't risk her heart again. She was beyond being the naive virgin who believed in fairy tales. Instead, she'd take what she wanted from Hawk for her pleasure and be prepared to say goodbye with no regrets when the time came.

She looked at the clock. It was just after five. He must have come directly uptown to see her after the close of the New York financial markets.

She hadn't seen him since they'd wound up in bed together, but that was about to change.

Hawk stepped out of the elevator and immediately spotted Pia at her door—waiting for him.

"H-Hawk," Pia said, her voice a touch breathless.

She was dressed in a casual, cinched blue dress, her hair loose and with just a touch of shine to her lips.

She looked good enough to eat.

Without hesitation, he strode to her, wrapped his arms around her and gave her a bone-melting kiss.

When he finally lifted his head, he searched her gaze. "Blast it, I get so aroused when I hear you stutter."

She blushed. "I don't know why. Th-that has to be one of the most unusual compliments a woman has ever received."

He kissed her nose. "Do you know it's the most erotic thing in bed when your adorable speech tick is on full display?"

"How embarrassing."

"How perfect."

"Oh."

Over Pia's shoulder, Hawk noticed Mr. Darcy lift his head from his cushioned basket and eye him.

Hawk got the sense that the pet's opinion of him had soured since the first time he'd been in Pia's apartment. Perhaps the cat had figured out who he was: The Duke Formerly Known as Mr. Wickham. Or rather, Mr. Fielding—wicked and wrong—as the case might be.

He held the feline's stare, giving the cat a stern but reassuring look, until Mr. Darcy lowered his head, closed his eyes and went back to his nap.

"Is something wrong?" Pia asked, stepping back and letting him into the apartment.

He followed her in and waited while she shut the door behind him.

Then he slid an arm around her waist and pulled her close. "Nothing is wrong except that since Sunday I've been desperate to see you."

He'd left work early to come here, hoping his appearance would be a welcome surprise. And judging from Pia's reaction, he'd bet right.

Pia slid her arms around his neck. "Oh?"

"I had a storm of work this week, and by the time I flew back from Chicago last night, I knew phone calls were no longer enough to sustain me."

"Mmm—really?"

He nuzzled her ear. "Nothing but your presence would do."

"You know, Your Grace," she responded playfully, "this is rather irregular. A client could arrive at any moment, or the phone could ring. We're on work hours."

He lifted his head to look into her eyes. "Are you expecting anyone this late in the day?"

"No," she admitted.

"Then there's no problem, as far as I see."

"There *is* a problem," she teased. "This has all the trappings of the lord of the manor cornering the backstairs maid."

"Because you're on my payroll?" he murmured, grazing her temple with his lips.

She nodded. "Exactly right. W-we had sexual relations in your bedroom right before I was to meet with your sister about wedding plans."

He almost laughed at her mock prudish tone even as *every* part of him was coming to stimulating arousal. He was finding this interchange with Pia more erotic than any of the more blatant attempts at seduction he'd been the recipient of in the past. It appeared that, after all, Pia might be skilled at role-play...

"Perhaps I should ask directly," he said, playing along. "Will you nevertheless oblige me?"

Pia tilted her head, pretending to consider. "Mmm..."

Not waiting for a response, he stroked her leg, and then let his hand wander under the hem of her dress until it connected with her hip. Sliding her panties to one side, he caressed her intimately.

He watched as her eyes clouded with desire.

"I want to know every inch of you," he murmured. "I want to taste your flavor and learn your scent."

Pia's eyelids drooped, and she gripped his arm hard.

"Pia?" he murmured when she still hadn't said anything.

He scanned her face and watched her eyelashes flutter against her pale skin.

She wet her lips. "Oh, y-yes. I-I'll oblige you."

They were both so turned on, they could hardly speak.

"This is the most erotic exchange I've ever had," she said as if she'd read his mind.

He had to have her. He kissed her, and then, removing his hand from under her dress, he wrapped his arms around her and lifted her off her feet.

He headed with her toward the bedroom.

"Are we destined to make love in the afternoon?" she asked.

He glanced down at her, a smile hovering at his lips. "Anytime becomes you, princess."

He stepped into her bedroom and deposited her on the bed, on top of her feminine white coverlet.

Straightening, he took a moment to let his eyes travel over her.

She looked up at him with desire. Her golden hair was spread out over the cover, and her lips were pink and wet from his kisses.

She was beautiful.

Pia parted her lips. "Oh, H-Hawk."

He closed his eyes and drew in a deep breath.

When he opened them again, he said with helpless amusement, "Don't say another word. I may go up in flames."

He pulled off her shoes, raised the skirt of her dress and pulled down her panties.

Bending toward her again, he slid his hands up under her thighs to cup her buttocks and pull her toward him.

She was open for him as he leaned in and kissed first one inner thigh and then the other.

Pia quivered and then tensed as he finally laid his mouth against her. Moving at a leisurely pace, he darted and licked with his tongue, and in no time, the room was filled with the sounds of Pia's gasps and moans.

"H-H-Hawk…o-oh!"

Pia tensed and let out a long moan, coming for him.

Only then did Hawk raise his head. She was so unbelievably responsive, he was fighting for control.

Holding her gaze, he undid his shirt and opened his pants, bothering to take off only his shoes. He removed protection from his pocket, sheathed himself and then leaned over her.

It didn't get any more passionate than this, Hawk thought. Lovemaking immediately after work, and they were so randy, they couldn't be bothered to eliminate more than the minimum of clothing.

He couldn't remember being this turned on since he'd been a teenager just discovering sex.

For her part, it was clear that Pia could hardly wait. She slid her hands up his arms in a light caress and arched her body toward him.

They both sighed as he slid inside her.

Hawk fought for control as he felt it slipping. Pia was still as tight as the time he'd taken her virginity.

He could, Hawk thought, lose himself in her again and again.

And in the next moment, he did.

He slid in and out of her, bringing them both mindless pleasure. Coherent thought shut down, and his focus narrowed down to one goal.

He felt Pia gasp and spasm around him with a small climax.

"That's right," he urged hoarsely.

"Hawk, oh, p-please…"

She didn't have to beg. The moment she spoke, a mighty climax shook him. And, dimly but with satisfaction, he was aware of Pia claiming her own peak once again.

With a hoarse groan, he thrust into her one final time, and then slumped against her.

Afterward, they lay on her bed, spent and relaxed. As Pia lay tucked against his side, he caressed her arm.

Since she appeared completely content, he decided to press his advantage.

"Come fishing and riding with me," he said without preamble.

Pia stilled and then stifled a sudden laugh. "You do know how to approach a woman at the right moment." She paused. "Isn't that what we just did?"

He shook his head and responded drolly, "Not that kind."

"Oh?"

"Come fishing and riding with me at Silderly Park in Oxford," he said, naming his ancestral estate in England.

Pia tilted her head to glance up at him.

He knew what he was asking. This had nothing to do with Lucy's wedding anymore. By visiting Silderly Park, Pia would be coming into the heart of who he was as a duke.

He'd made the request unexpectedly, and only belatedly realized how much her answer mattered.

"Yes."

Her answer came out as a breathy whisper before she lowered her head back down to his shoulder.

He smiled slowly, relaxing. "Good."

Pia was his, and he was going to make sure things remained so.

Ten

"The wedding invitations will go out next week," Pia remarked, her comment meant to reassure in case it was necessary.

It was Monday afternoon, and she and Lucy were sitting in the parlor of Hawk's Upper East Side town house. They were meeting over afternoon tea to discuss wedding details.

Most professional shows did not have performances on Monday nights, explaining why it was possible for Lucy to meet with Pia over tea today. Any other day of the week, Lucy might already have been preparing to head to work at this hour.

"Splendid," Lucy said, smoothing her blond hair. "Derek will be happy to know that detail has been taken care of."

It had been a pleasure to work with Hawk's sister, Pia reflected, trying not to dwell on when Hawk might be arriving home.

Lucy and Derek had wanted a relatively simple wedding

ceremony and reception, but one that nevertheless incorporated some nods to Lucy's English ancestry and theater work.

Everything so far had gone smoothly. During previous consultations, the couple had settled on a photographer, band and florist with a minimum of fuss. And today she and Lucy had already discussed wedding music, readings and various ceremony logistics.

"Now the florist has a website," Pia continued, "which you should consult, but in order to give you more ideas, I have my own book of photos from weddings that I've been involved with."

She slid a scrapbook across the coffee table toward Lucy, and Hawk's sister leaned forward and reached for it.

"I'll leave it with you so you can take your time going through it," she added as Lucy opened the book. "You'll see that some brides like more elaborate floral arrangements, and others prefer a simpler concept. Next time we talk, let's discuss what you're looking for before we meet with the florist."

Lucy nodded as she flipped through the scrapbook. "This is helpful." She looked up. "You're so organized, Pia."

"Thank you."

Pia smiled to herself because wedding planners received few acknowledgments of their work. Many brides were too consumed by preparations for their big event to thank the paid help, at least until the wedding was over.

"The other item on our agenda that you should be thinking about now," Pia went on crisply, "is the music that you'd like to be played at the reception."

"Definitely Broadway show tunes," Lucy said with a laugh. "Can I enter on the theme song from *Phantom of the Opera?*"

"You can do whatever you like," Pia responded before a thought intruded that she decided to query about delicately. "Has your mother voiced any opinions?"

In her experience, weddings were fraught with family

negotiations, and often no one had more of an opinion than the mother of the bride. Pia had been called on to referee in more than one instance.

Lucy sighed at Pia's words and sat back, letting the book of photographs fall closed. "Mother means well, but she can be a bit of a dragon, unfortunately."

Pia raised her eyebrows.

"But Hawk doesn't let her have complete free rein." Lucy grinned suddenly. "Of course, it helps that the wedding is happening in New York, thousands of miles from Silderly Park and Mother's back lawn."

In the past, Pia had studiously avoided probing Lucy for more information than she volunteered about her brother. But Lucy had just reminded her of who Pia's de facto employer was, and, as the current duke and head of the family, Hawk undoubtedly had some say in keeping his mother from overriding Lucy's wishes.

In any case, it was a revealing remark on Lucy's part about Carsdale family dynamics.

"Well, it was a deft maneuver to have the wedding here," Pia conceded, "if your intention was to keep interference at a minimum."

Lucy looked sly. "Thank you. It was Derek's idea."

"Ah, right." Pia's lips curved. "He also had the idea of a New Year's wedding, didn't he?"

"Brilliant, isn't it?"

"It's certainly an unorthodox choice."

"I know." Lucy laughed. "I'm sure Mother went absolutely wild. I can picture her pruning her garden with a vengeance after she found out."

A picture popped into Pia's head from Lucy's description, though she'd never met Hawk's mother. She fought an involuntary smile.

"You do have a flair for the dramatic visual, Lucy," she teased. "Anyone would think you should be on the stage."

Lucy gave another laugh. "My first act of rebellion."

"Your family objected?" Pia asked, curiosity getting the better of her.

Lucy's eyes twinkled. "Of course! Mother is well aware that the only actresses in the family tree were all born on the wrong side of the blanket."

Pia was tempted to ask flippantly whether any Carsdale ancestor had kept a wedding planner as a mistress, but she clamped her mouth shut. She wondered, though, how much Lucy knew or suspected about her relationship with Hawk, and what the other woman would say if she knew she was talking to a current lover of the present Duke of Hawkshire.

"Hawk was supportive of me, however," Lucy went on, seemingly oblivious to Pia's reticence. "He's the reason I'm in New York, frankly."

Pia gave a small smile. Lucy clearly thought the world of her brother.

"Speaking of Hawk," Lucy said, "he mentioned you'll be in Oxford and visiting Silderly Park."

Pia hesitated. Just what had Hawk said to Lucy? Did Lucy believe she simply had an incidental interest in touring Silderly Park while she was visiting England, if only because she was planning the wedding of the Duke of Hawkshire's sister?

She had been careful not to discuss Hawk with Lucy because, at first, she hadn't trusted herself to be less than withering in her opinion. And afterward, well, it had become problematic to speak about Hawk...

And, of course, now... Pia heated to think of all the things she *couldn't* bring up with Lucy about how she and Hawk passed the time.

She bit her lip. "Yes, I'm, um, planning to stay at Silderly Park for a few days to fish and ride."

As the words left her mouth, Pia felt a flush crawl up her neck. Drat—would she ever be able to talk about fishing or riding again without blushing?

"Please say you'll stay in Oxford until the first of December then," Lucy pleaded. "It would be so wonderful if you could attend the small engagement party that my mother insisted on hosting at Silderly Park."

"I—"

Pia had never been invited as a guest to a client's wedding function.

"In fact, it would be so nice to have you there."

Pia searched the younger woman's expression, but all she saw there was pure, unguarded appeal.

"I—" Pia cleared her throat and gave a helpless smile. "Okay."

Lucy returned her smile with a grateful one of her own.

Pia wondered whether all the Carsdales were so adamantly persuasive.

Lucy either had no clue about the current state of affairs between her brother and her wedding planner, or, well, she was a very good actress.

In her gossip column, Mrs. Hollings had twice referenced her and Hawk—once right after Belinda's almost-wedding, and more recently, when she'd hinted at a warming of their relationship after Hawk had unexpectedly played her assistant. But Mrs. Hollings had stopped short of naming them as lovers.

And, what's more, Pia wasn't sure if Lucy even paid attention to Mrs. Hollings's column. True, the column included a fair amount of society gossip, but Lucy was immersed in the theater world rather than in the social whirl, and Mrs. Hollings's column focused on New York rather than Britain.

Pia pushed those thoughts aside. "Thank you for the invitation."

Lucy laughed. "Don't be silly. I should be thanking you because you'll be putting up with my mother and my brother."

Ah, yes. *Hawk*.

If Lucy only knew, Pia thought.

Even though her acquaintance with Hawk three years ago had been fleeting—a one-night stand, if she looked at the matter unflinchingly—Pia recognized that he'd changed a lot. He was shouldering a lot more responsibility, and could claim a lot of success through his own hard work. He was also considerate. Look at how he'd tried to help her with her business—insisting on making amends. And she had intimate knowledge that he was a terrific lover.

Still, she couldn't help wondering how Hawk viewed their current sexual interlude. They'd never attempted to attach labels to it. Whatever was the case, though, she insisted to herself, this time she would no longer be the naive and vulnerable young thing.

Lucy regarded her closely. "If you don't mind my saying so, I couldn't help noticing that you and my brother had a testy interaction when you arrived here for our first meeting."

Pia schooled her surprise—Hawk's sister had never brought up that first meeting in prior conversations.

Still, she couldn't deny the truth.

"We did," Pia confessed. "I...didn't form a good opinion of him when I first met him a few years ago."

Now that was a lie. She'd been so taken with him, she'd fallen into bed. It was after their romantic interlude had ended that her opinion of him had soured.

Lucy gave her a small smile. "I can understand why you might not have. I know my brother had his party years, though he never shared the details with me because I was so much younger." She paused, looking at Pia more closely. "But that phase of his life all came to end three years ago."

"Hawk told me," Pia said with sympathy.

Still, Pia got the distinct impression that Lucy meant more than she was saying. Was she trying to persuade Pia that Hawk wasn't so terrible anymore? And if so, why? Because she cared what her wedding planner thought of her brother?

Again, Pia wondered how much Lucy suspected, and what she would say if she knew Pia and Hawk knew each other intimately these days.

Lucy sighed. "I guess there's no going back, is there?" she asked rhetorically. "In any case, Hawk has taken over as head of the family remarkably well. And Sunhill Investments has reversed the state of the ducal finances in just a couple of years—it's remarkable."

Pia fixed a smile. She was reminded of how Hawk had spent his time while he was apparently forgetting her, and an element of doubt intruded again. She was crazy to think she could somehow become remarkable herself—let alone unforgettable—to a man like him. He was a duke and a multimultimillionaire. She was a wedding planner from Pennsylvania.

She pushed back the heart-in-the-throat feeling and convinced herself again that she was prepared for the eventual end of their fling.

Lucy reached out a hand and touched her on the arm. "All I'm saying, Pia, is that Hawk isn't the person that he was even three years ago. You should give him a chance."

Pia wondered what kind of chance Lucy thought she should be giving Hawk. Was she suggesting that Pia should like him enough to interact nicely with him…or more?

Pia opened and closed her mouth.

"All is forgiven," she said finally for Lucy's benefit. "You needn't worry that Hawk and I are unable to get along."

In fact, lately, they'd gotten along so well, they'd gotten into bed together.

"Good," Lucy said with a smile, seemingly accepting her vague answer. "Because I know he likes you. He sang your praises when he suggested you to me as a wedding coordinator."

Pia smiled uncertainly.

She wasn't sure upon what basis Hawk's sister was resting the observation that Hawk *liked* her, but she felt a flutter of happiness at the thought.

Her reaction was both wonderful *and* a cause for concern…

Pia walked beside Hawk in his impressive landscaped gardens.

Since arriving at Hawk's family estate near Oxford two days ago, she and Hawk had gone fishing and riding on his estate, as promised. She'd also been busy working long distance and taking in the many, many rooms that comprised Silderly Park.

She'd tried not to be overwhelmed by the medieval manor house itself. On a previous trip to Britain, she had toured nearby Blenheim Palace, the Duke of Marlborough's family seat. And she could say without a doubt that though Silderly Park didn't carry the identifier in its name, it was no less a palace.

Pia glanced momentarily at the windowed stories of Silderly Park as she and Hawk strolled along and he pointed out various plantings to her. They were both dressed in jackets for the nippy but nevertheless unseasonably warm November weather.

Hawk's principal residence had two wings, and its medieval core had been updated and added to over the centuries. The manor house boasted beautiful painted plaster ceilings, two rooms with magnificent oak paneling and a great hall that could seat 200 or 300 guests. The reception rooms displayed an impressive collection of eighteenth- and nineteenth-century artwork, from various artists, including Gainsborough and Sir Joshua Reynolds.

Even though the income was no longer necessary to him, Hawk had kept Silderly Park open to the public, so that the formal reception rooms could be visited by tourists.

Still, Pia couldn't help feeling as if *she* didn't belong here. Unlike Belinda and Tamara, she hadn't been born to wealth and social position. Maybe if she had, she would have recognized Hawk as more than a plain Mr. James Fielding on the first occasion she'd met him.

"The gardens were created in the late eighteenth century," Hawk said, calling her back from her thoughts. "We use at least five or six different types of rose plantings in the section we're in now."

Pia clasped her hands together in front of her. "This would be a wonderful place to consult for roses to use in weddings. Every bride is looking for something different and unique."

"If you're interested, the gardener could tell you more," Hawk said, sending her a sidelong look. "Or you could come back in the Spring."

Pia felt a shiver of awareness chase down her spine. Was Hawk thinking their relationship would continue at least until Spring—well past Lucy's wedding?

"Perhaps," she forced herself to equivocate, careful not to look at him. "Spring is my busy season for weddings, as you can well imagine."

"Of course, only if you can fit me into your schedule," Hawk teased.

She chanced a glance at him. He looked every inch the lord of the manor in a tweed jacket and wool trousers.

"I'm becoming quite busy these days thanks to you, as you well know," she returned lightly. "I received a call just before we left New York from another friend of yours seeking a wedding coordinator."

Hawk smiled. "I'm hurrying them all to the altar for your sake."

"I'm surprised that you didn't spring for the ring and stage the proposal in this case."

"If I could have, I would have," he said with mock solemnity, "but my expertise lies in locating wedding veils and saving flower bouquets from canine bridal attendants."

Pia laughed, even as she silently acknowledged all of Hawk's help.

With the exception of Tamara's, the weddings that she'd coordinated this past summer had been ones that she'd been contracted for before the Marquess of Easterbridge had crashed Belinda's ill-fated ceremony. Since then, new business had come to her thanks mainly to Hawk.

She had a lot to thank him for, including arranging and paying for both their first-class tickets on a commercial flight from New York to London—though she knew in reality *that* had nothing to do with Lucy's wedding.

She and Hawk came to a stop near some elaborately shaped hedges, and he turned to face her.

He reached out and caressed the line of her jaw, a smile touching his lips.

Pia's senses awakened at his touch, even as time slowed and space narrowed, and her brain turned sluggish.

"D-don't tell me," Pia said, her voice slightly breathless, "that romantic assignations in the gardens are de rigueur."

"If only it wasn't November," he murmured, his eyes crinkling. "Fortunately, there's a bed nearby."

Pia heated as Hawk ducked his head and touched his lips to hers.

She knew the bed to which he was referring. She'd slept in it last night.

Hawk's bedchamber at Silderly Park was in an enormous suite, bigger than her apartment in New York. The suite was fronted by a sitting room, and the bedroom itself boasted a large four-poster bed, red-and-white wallpaper, and gold leaf detail on the molded ceiling.

Everything was fit for a duke.

Everything in Hawk's house, in fact, was out of a fairy tale. Including its owner, Pia thought whimsically.

It was easy to be enthralled, especially for a romantic such as herself...and Pia reminded herself again to keep her feet planted on the ground.

Hawk linked his hand with hers, and Pia allowed him to turn them back in the direction of the house.

Though it was a good fifteen minutes before they arrived at his suite, they snuggled and exchanged the occasional kiss along the way, heedless of whom they might encounter.

In his bedroom, Hawk looked into her eyes as he undressed her, slowly and tenderly, bringing tears to Pia's eyes.

They made love languorously, as if they had not a care in the world, but all the time.

Afterward, Pia lay in Hawk's arms, and sighed with contentment.

"We really have to stop doing this," she remarked.

"What?" Hawk glanced down at her. "Making love in the afternoon?"

"Yes, it's decadent."

"It's the only indulgence I'm allowed these days," Hawk protested. "And my BlackBerry is beeping nearby."

Pia lifted her head and smiled at him. "I'm not used to it."

He raised an eyebrow. "This is beyond your realm of expertise?"

"Oh, Hawk, haven't you guessed?" she asked tentatively.

He stilled, searching her gaze.

"You're my first and only lover." She paused, and then added, "Th-there hasn't been anyone else in the past three years."

Hawk's brows drew together in puzzlement. "You're a desirable woman—"

Pia gave a small, self-conscious laugh, her heart bursting. "I-it wasn't for lack of opportunity, b-but by choice."

Hawk shifted so he was looking down at her as she lay

back. "I don't understand. You've taken the initiative...unlike what I remembered."

"Books and videos," she answered succinctly. "I wanted to educate myself."

So I'd never run the risk of losing you again to lack of experience.

Hawk said nothing for a moment, and Pia gave him a tentative smile.

Hawk's expression softened. "Ah, Pia." He gave her a gentle kiss. "I'm honored."

She arched into him, responding intuitively to his advance.

"So that's why you weren't on any protection when we were first intimate again that day after rock climbing," he murmured.

Pia nodded. "There hadn't been any need."

"That day, you said three years was a long time," Hawk mused. "I thought you were referring to how long it had been since we'd last been together. But you meant since the last time you'd had sex, too, didn't you?"

Pia nodded again, and then her eyes crinkled. "Care to shorten the time between sex?"

Hawk gave a half groan, half laugh. "Ah, Pia. It's going to be difficult to keep up with you."

She gave him a quick kiss, her look mischievous. "Your performance has been off the charts so far. I thought—"

"Minx." He silenced her with a kiss.

And after that, neither of them got out of bed for a long while.

Hawk knew he was in too deep.

It was déjà vu. Except the first time he hadn't suspected that Pia was a virgin, and this time, he hadn't divined that she'd only ever had one lover. *Him.*

He felt a rush of possessiveness. He hadn't liked thinking

of Pia with other men—learning things…things that *he* could teach her.

Blast it.

"What do you think, Hawk?"

Hawk met three pairs of expectant female eyes. His mother, his sister and Pia were sitting in the Green Room at Silderly Park discussing assorted wedding details. He'd assumed a position by the mantel, at a safe remove.

"What do you think about seating Baron Worling next to Princess Adelaide of Meznia at dinner?" his mother asked, repeating and elaborating her question.

Hawk knew there was some nuance that he should understand, otherwise his mother wouldn't have bothered asking. But for the life of him, he couldn't think what it was.

Was Baron Worling a poor conversationalist? Did Princess Adelaide believe the baron was beneath her notice? Or perhaps one of the baron's poor ancestors had dueled to the death with a member of Princess Adelaide's royal family?

Hawk shrugged and punted. "I'm sure whatever you decide will be fine."

His mother looked nonplussed.

"What about placing the Crown Prince of Belagia on Princess Adelaide's left?" Pia suggested.

His mother brightened. "Splendid idea."

Hawk shot Pia a grateful look.

She looked superb in a navy polka-dot dress and heels. The dress accentuated her bust without being over the top, so that she looked demure but professional.

Whether Pia knew it or not, Hawk reflected, she'd chosen exactly an outfit of which his mother, the Dowager Duchess of Hawkshire, would approve.

As the wedding conversation resumed, Hawk started idly plotting ways to be alone again with Pia.

Could he invent a phone call that required her immediate

attention and called her away? Or perhaps he could feign a pressing need for her to consult on his attire for the wedding day? He stifled a grin.

Yesterday they had gone horseback riding and he'd shown her the various natural and architectural wonders on his estate. He couldn't remember when he'd enjoyed playing tour guide more, though he had an understandable bit of pride in his ancestral estate and childhood home.

His mother glanced up and caught his eye, and Hawk returned her look blandly.

He wondered whether his mother suspected that there was more than a business relationship between him and Lucy's wedding planner, and decided to leave her to speculate. He and Pia had separate bedrooms, and they'd been discreet about their late-night rendezvous, even though Silderly Park was so large that it was unlikely they'd have attracted the attention of anyone while slipping in and out of each other's rooms.

The truth was, he was still trying to sort out his feelings and next steps as far as Pia was concerned. How could he articulate them for someone else when he himself didn't understand them?

He'd started out trying to make amends, true, but matters had gotten more complicated from there. He bore a large share of the responsibility for his current circumstances—mostly because he couldn't seem to help himself as far as Pia was concerned. He must have been absent that day in grade school when they taught everyone about keeping their hands to themselves.

He was Pia's first and *only* lover.

It was astounding. It was wonderful.

It also made him freeze, not knowing what to do.

For years, his code of conduct with respect to women was never to get too involved. It was the reason why he'd never been or wanted to be a woman's first lover—until Pia.

And while he still wasn't sure about many things, he did know that he didn't want to see Pia hurt again.

The butler entered, followed by a familiar-looking brunette.

Hawk watched as his mother brightened, and as recognition set in, he was struck with an impending sense of doom, even before the butler spoke.

"Miss Michelene Ward-Fombley has arrived."

Eleven

Pia looked up as an attractive brunette walked into the room, and immediately and inexplicably sensed that something was wrong.

The Dowager Duchess of Hawkshire, however, rose gracefully from her seat on the settee, a smile wreathing her face. "Michelene, darling, how lovely of you to join us here."

Michelene stepped forward, and the two women exchanged air kisses.

Pia glanced around the room, noticing that Lucy had a worried expression while Hawk was still as a rock by the mantel.

Following Lucy's lead, Pia rose from her seat as introductions were made.

"...and this is Miss Pia Lumley, who has been ever so helpful as Lucy's wedding coordinator," the duchess said with a smile.

Pia shook hands with Michelene, whom she pegged as a

cool self-possessed blueblood. Though the other woman had said only a few words, Pia could tell that Michelene spoke Queen's English with a distinctive upper-class inflection.

Michelene looked over at the mantel.

"Hawk," Michelene murmured, her voice low and sultry.

Hawk? *Not Your Grace?* Pia frowned. Exactly what was the status of the relationship between Michelene and Hawk?

Pia knew that never in a million years—not even in the shower—could she imitate Michelene's smoky tone. She even stuttered during sex—for which she was self-conscious, though Hawk claimed to like it.

"Michelene," Hawk acknowledged, remaining at his spot by the mantel. "How nice to see you. I wasn't made aware that you were coming today."

Pia watched as Hawk threw his mother a meaningful look, which the dowager duchess returned with one—Pia could swear—of the cat who ate the canary. Score one for the dowager, it seemed.

"Did I not mention that Michelene was arriving early for Lucy's engagement party tomorrow?" the duchess said, raising her brows. "Oh, dear."

Michelene gave a little laugh. "I hope it's no inconvenience."

"Not at all. You are more than welcome here," Hawk said smoothly, his eyes traveling from Michelene to his mother. "Silderly Park is large enough, of course, to accommodate the occasional unexpected guest."

Whoever Michelene was, Pia thought, it was clear that she was close to the Carsdales.

Was she, in fact, a former lover of Hawk's? Pia tamped down the well of jealousy.

"We were just finishing up our discussion of the wedding," the duchess said as she sat back down. "Won't you join us, Michelene?"

Pia and Lucy followed the duchess's lead in retaking their seats.

"Thank you," Michelene said as she sat down as well. "I believe I would find listening to be vastly informative." She smiled toward the side of the room where Hawk was standing. "There was a time when I imagined I'd enjoy becoming a wedding planner myself. Unfortunately, life had other plans, and I remained in the fashion business."

Pia shifted uncomfortably. She wondered whether Hawk and Michelene had not only been lovers, but had come close to a walk down the aisle. Or perhaps Michelene had hoped for a marriage proposal that had never materialized, and Hawk had ended the relationship instead?

Pia mentally braked. She knew she was letting her imagination run away with her. She had no proof that Hawk and Michelene had even dated, let alone come close to marriage. And she was making an assumption that Hawk had ended any relationship between the two.

"Wh-what type of fashion?" Pia blurted, disconcerted by her thoughts.

A second later, she clamped her mouth shut. She was embarrassed by the sudden and unexpected appearance of her stutter. She must be more rattled than she realized.

Michelene looked at her keenly. "I'm a buyer for Harvey Nichols."

Pia was familiar with the upmarket department store. She just wished she could afford more of their goods.

"It must be so interesting to be a wedding planner," Michelene continued, hitting the ball back into Pia's court. "You must have some entertaining stories."

This year more than others, Pia thought.

"I do enjoy the job very much," she nevertheless responded honestly. "I love being part of one of the most significant days in a couple's life."

Pia could feel Hawk's gaze on her, his expression thoughtful.

"Pia has been a great help," Lucy put in with an encouraging smile.

"I see," Michelene said. "I'll have to get your business card, Ms. Lumley—"

"It's Pia, please."

"—just in case anyone I know is in need of the services of a wedding coordinator."

Pia again got the sense there was a subtext to this conversation that she wasn't privy to.

Before she could say anything else, however, the butler appeared again to announce that Lucy's dressmaker—the one Pia knew had been commissioned to make a suitable confection for the engagement party—had arrived.

As the dressmaker was shown in, Pia cast a speculative look at Hawk's enigmatic expression.

She wondered if she'd be able to learn the subtext of today's conversation sooner rather than later. Because she *and* Hawk would no doubt be seeing Michelene again tomorrow at Lucy's engagement party.

Pia surveyed the glittering crowd from her position near one end of the long dining table, one of two that had been set up parallel to each other in the Great Hall.

There would be dinner and dancing for the engagement party tonight, as befitted a formal reception given by a dowager duchess, since Hawk's mother was playing hostess. The men wore tuxes, and the women gowns.

Lucy had dismissed all of tonight's pomp and circumstance as more of a to-do than the wedding itself would be. But she had conceded that her mother should have a free hand tonight if the dowager duchess was to have very little say over the wedding itself.

Pia had donned one of the two floor-length gowns that she

owned. The nature of her line of work required her to dress very formally on occasion.

She wore a lavender, one-shoulder, Grecian-style dress whose artfully draped fabric accentuated her bust and gave her the illusion of additional height. She'd bought the designer Marchesa gown at an Upper East Side consignment shop that was a favorite with the rich and fashionable who looked to retire their clothes at the end of the season.

As she cut into her remaining filet mignon—during a momentary lull in conversation with the guests seated to her right and left—she shot a surreptitious look down the middle of the table at Hawk.

He looked handsome and debonair as he chatted with the graying man to his left—a prince of some long-defunct kingdom, if she recalled correctly, who also happened to be distantly related to Derek, Lucy's fiancé.

She herself sat far away from Hawk, near one end of the table, as befitted her position as a less notable guest—an employee, really, and no more, in the dowager duchess's eyes.

She couldn't help but note that Michelene, on the other hand, had been seated diagonally across from Hawk—within speaking distance.

She wished she'd questioned Hawk about the other woman, but, truth be told, she'd been afraid of the answers. She hadn't wanted her suspicions confirmed that Michelene and Hawk had been more than friends at one point. And Hawk hadn't volunteered any information.

Pia patted her mouth with her napkin and took a sip of her wine.

As waiters began clearing plates from the table, Hawk rose and a hush fell over the room.

Pia kept her gaze on him, even though his own eyes traveled over the room, surveying the assembled guests.

Hawk said a few short words, thanking all the guests for

joining his family in tonight's celebration and regaling the crowd with a couple of amusing anecdotes about his sister and future brother-in-law. Then he toasted the happy couple and all the assembled guests joined in.

When he took his seat again, the dowager duchess rose from hers. She gave the engaged couple seated near her an indulgent smile. "I'm so very happy for Lucy and Derek."

Hawk's mother cleared her throat. "As many of you know, Lucy hasn't always followed my advice—" there was a scattering of laughter among the guests "—but in this case she has my unqualified approval." She raised her glass. "Well done, Lucy, and it is with great pleasure that I welcome you to the family, Derek."

"Hear, hear," chorused some of the guests.

The duchess lifted her glass higher. "I hope I shall have the opportunity to make another toast on a similarly happy occasion in the not-too-distant future." Her gaze shifted for a moment to Hawk before returning to her daughter and future son-in-law. "To Lucy and Derek."

As everyone raised their glasses in toast and sipped their champagne, Pia watched as the dowager duchess's gaze came to rest on Michelene. In turn, the younger woman glanced at Hawk, who was gazing at his mother, his expression inscrutable.

Pia felt her stomach plummet.

Sightlessly, she placed her glass back on the table without taking a sip.

Feeling suddenly ill, she experienced an overwhelming need to get away—to get some air.

Pia murmured an excuse in the general direction of her nearest dinner companions and rose from her seat.

Trying not to catch anyone's eye, she hurried from the room as fast as decorum would allow.

In the hall, she ran up the stairs. She was roiled by emotion that threatened to spill over into tears.

She'd been so naive yesterday. It was something that she'd

vowed to herself she'd never be again. And yet, she'd mistaken the situation entirely.

It wasn't that Michelene and Hawk had a *past* relationship that had been broken off. It was that they had a *current* tie that had an expectation of marriage.

Pia had gathered as much from the interchange that had just occurred during the dowager duchess's speech, and from the significant looks that had been exchanged.

She'd finally pieced together yesterday's puzzle, but in the process, she'd nearly humiliated herself in front of dozens of people.

At the top of the stairs, she turned left. Her bedroom was down the hallway.

"Pia, wait."

Hawk's voice came from behind her, more command than plea. He sounded as if he was taking the stairs two at a time.

She picked up her pace. She hoped to reach the sanctuary of her room and throw the lock before he caught up with her. It was her only hope. She didn't want to risk having him see her break down.

She could hear Hawk's rapid steps behind her. In her gown, she couldn't move as fast as he could, though she had the hem raised with one hand.

And in the next moment, it was too late.

Hawk caught up with her, grasping her arm and turning her to face him.

"Wh-what?" she demanded, her throat clogged. "It's not midnight yet and C-Cinderella isn't allowed to disappear, is that it?"

"Are you leaving behind a glass slipper?" he countered, dropping his staying hand.

She gave an emotional laugh. "No, and you're not Prince Charming."

His lips firmed into a thin line. "Let's go somewhere and discuss this."

At least he understood why she was upset, and he wasn't going to pretend otherwise.

Still. "I'm not going anywhere with you!"

Hawk sighed. "Will you let me explain?"

"D-damn you, Hawk," she said, her voice wobbly. "I—I was just starting to trust you again! Now I discover that all along you've more or less had a fiancée waiting in the wings."

Pia's jaw clenched. Did he know how fragile trust was? How could she ever trust him again?

He looked her in the eye. "That's what my mother would like to believe."

"Oh? And you were unaware of this expectation?"

He remained silent.

Obviously, he was refusing to incriminate himself, Pia thought acerbically. He knew anything he said could and would be used against him.

"It appears that your mother had more than an expectation."

Michelene herself obviously did, too. And Pia recalled Lucy's troubled expression yesterday in the Green Room. Had Hawk's sister realized that Michelene's unexpected appearance would present an awkward situation for her brother?

Hawk muttered something under his breath.

"You and Michelene seemed quite familiar yesterday!"

"You're mistaking matters or else deliberately mischaracterizing them," he responded in a clipped tone. "I recall remaining by the fireplace when Michelene appeared."

"You know what I mean," Pia said, feeling like stamping her foot—as childish as that might be. "And why should I believe anything that you tell me? You failed to mention Michelene's existence to begin with."

"I was involved with Michelene briefly after my brother's death. Michelene had been considered an eligible candidate to be my brother's future duchess." Hawk shrugged. "I was stepping into my brother's shoes, and Michelene was part of the package."

And Pia wasn't. She could hear the words as clearly as if they'd been spoken aloud.

As Hawk trailed off, Pia acknowledged the situation that he'd been in. He'd fallen into doing what had been expected of him. She could almost understand that.

And yet. "Your mother acts as if an engagement announcement is imminent. If I hadn't stayed for the party at Lucy's request, is that how I would have heard about Michelene? An engagement notice in the paper?"

Hawk's engagement to another woman. She couldn't help feeling hurt as well as betrayed. She'd told herself she'd be prepared for the end of their affair, but she hadn't foreseen *this.*

"I am not engaged, I assure you," Hawk shot back, looking frustrated. "I hadn't planned a proposal or bought a ring."

"Well, then, you're running late," she replied. "Michelene is waiting."

She glanced down the hall. Someone could come at any time, interrupting and witnessing their argument. And he had to get back downstairs to the party. His absence would be noticed soon.

"Pia, you are the damnedest fe—"

"That's right I—I am," she responded. "I happen to be cursed with rotten luck as far as men are concerned. So much for fairy tales!"

"If you'll just give me a chance—"

"That's the problem," Pia tossed back. "I have."

She turned and started down the hall. "I can't believe I was charmed a-and tricked by you again. How could I have let myself be such a fool?"

Hawk caught up with her and took hold of her arm again, forcing her to look up at him.

His face was set and implacable, and Pia got a glimpse of the part of him that had made a fortune in the span of a few short years.

"I did not trick you," he grated.

A moment later, his lips came down on hers. The kiss packed all the potency of their past ones and then some.

She tasted the champagne on his lips, and inhaled the male scent of him. It was a combination heady enough to make her head swim, despite her anger.

Still, summoning an effort of will, she pulled away as soon as the kiss tapered off.

"You didn't trick me?" she inquired, repeating his words as he raised his head. "Perhaps not. I suppose I tricked myself. All you did was let me."

Hawk looked at her, eyes glittering.

She read her own meaning in his silence.

"I didn't think you approached me again with the idea of a marriage proposal," she scoffed, though she was willing the tears away with all her might.

Hawk searched her eyes. "You know why I approached you..."

Yes, to make amends.

"Pia—"

"I-it's t-too late, Hawk," she said, her voice agonized. "The cat's out of the bag, and we're finished. Our affair was going to have to end sometime, so why not now? Except this time, I'm the one walking away."

Before Hawk could respond, someone called his name, and she and Hawk turned as one to glance down the hall.

Michelene was standing at the top of the stairs.

Not waiting for more, Pia turned and hurried down the hall in the opposite direction, leaving Hawk standing where he was.

Pia slipped inside her bedroom and closed and locked the

door behind her. Then she leaned back against the wall of the darkened room, grateful for reaching sanctuary.

When all of this had started, Hawk's motivation was to make amends. His motivation had never been, she reminded herself, swallowing hard, to love her or promise forever more.

She bit her lip to stop it from trembling, even as the tears welled.

The only question was how was she going to mend her heart when this was over and she'd truly gotten away—if she ever could?

Twelve

As it turned out, Pia managed to make her escape more expeditiously than she'd imagined possible. After collecting herself and drying her tears, she packed her few bags in a hurry and summoned one of Hawk's chauffeurs to drive her to nearby Oxford.

She knew Hawk would remain occupied tonight with the engagement party, whether he liked it or not. She also knew Oxford would afford her a host of inns and hotels in which to stay for the night while she booked a flight back to New York—and planned her next move.

During the night at a small inn, however she remembered that the Earl and Countess of Melton were staying at their home, Gantswood Hall, in nearby Gloucestershire. So the morning, after a quick ring to Tamara, Pia used a rental car to drive to Gantswood Hall.

When Pia arrived after midday, Tamara greeted her inside the front door with a quick hug.

Before she'd left New York, Pia had mentioned to Tamara

that she planned to be in England for Lucy Carsdale's engagement party, so her friend was aware that she would be in the country.

But Pia had said nothing on the phone about the reason for her sudden trip to Gantswood Hall. And if Tamara had been surprised at Pia's impromptu plan to visit, she hadn't given any indication.

Now, as she and Tamara drew apart from their hug, Pia couldn't help experiencing a pang. She'd noticed that her friend's pregnancy had started to show. And Tamara looked happy and relaxed, dressed in a cowl-neck cashmere sweater and black tights, her red hair pulled back in a knot.

Pia knew her own situation was in startling contrast. She couldn't be further away from Tamara's happily-ever-after. She was sad and depressed, and she hadn't slept well last night. No amount of makeup this morning had been able to disguise her pallor and the peaked look around her eyes.

Tamara searched her face, her brow puckering. "What's wrong? You gave no indication on the phone. But I can see from the look of you that something is amiss."

Pia parted her lips. *What was the use in hiding the truth?*

"L-last night was Lucy Carsdale's engagement party," she said without preamble.

Tamara's eyes widened. "Did something go wrong? Oh, Pia!"

Much to her horror, Pia felt her eyes well with tears.

Tamara looked at her with concern for a moment, and then wrapped her in a hug again.

"It's okay," Tamara said soothingly, patting her on the back. "I've been prone to tears myself, what with raging hormones during this pregnancy. I'm sure whatever happened is not as bad as it seems right now."

Pia hiccuped and straightened, taking a step back. "No, it's worse."

Tamara had obviously concluded that Pia was upset because something had gone wrong with Lucy's engagement party, Pia realized. Tamara had no idea about Hawk's role.

When she'd told Tamara and Belinda that she'd be traveling to England in order to help with Lucy's engagement party, she'd left out that Hawk himself had extended an invitation to visit Silderly Park.

Tamara put an arm around her shoulders. "Come into the drawing room with me. We can be cozy there, and you can tell me all about it. I was about to have a light snack brought in."

As a member of the household staff appeared from the back of the house, Tamara added, "Haines, could you please arrange to have Pia's bags moved from her car to the Green and Gold Bedroom? Thank you."

"Of course," Haines acknowledged with an inclination of the head as they passed him.

Pia let Tamara guide her through the palatial house, Sawyer's ancestral family seat, until they reached a large room with French doors overlooking the back lawn and gardens. Despite the masterpieces framed on the walls, the room was warm and inviting.

Pia sat with Tamara on a brocade settee in front of a large fireplace.

Tamara handed her a tissue, and Pia made use of it to compose herself.

"Now," Tamara said encouragingly, "I'm sure this is nothing that you can't put behind you."

Pia bit her lip. *If only Tamara knew.*

"I don't know," she said. "I've been trying to put Hawk behind me for three years."

Tamara's eyebrows lifted. "Then all this emotion isn't because something went wrong with Lucy's engagement party?"

"Oh, something went wrong, all right. I found out Hawk had a fiancée waiting in the wings."

"Oh, Pia."

With some effort, Pia outlined what had happened at Silderly Park—from Michelene's unexpected arrival to what had transpired the night before at Lucy's party.

When she finished, she looked at Tamara beseechingly.

"How could I have been so stupid again?" she asked in an agonized voice. "How could I let myself become vulnerable to him once more?"

"You let yourself become susceptible to Hawk's charms…"

Tamara trailed off, and though she'd spoken without inflection, she seemed to be trying to guess at what Pia was really saying.

Pia sighed. Why not come out with the whole bald-faced truth?

She hadn't divulged details to Tamara and Belinda of her recent and evolving relationship with Hawk. She knew they would have tried to dissuade her from any deeper involvement—and certainly from trying to turn the tables in a high-stakes game with a seasoned player like Hawk.

"It's worse," Pia said succinctly. "I slept with him."

Tamara looked surprised, though not as caught unawares as Pia would have expected. Still, her friend didn't say anything.

"After the first time I slept with him, he disappeared for three years," Pia said, the words tumbling out of her. "This time, we sleep together, and then I discover he's nearly engaged to another woman!"

"Oh, Pia," Tamara said. "I had no idea, believe me. If I'd known, of course I would have said something."

Tamara frowned. "I wonder why Sawyer didn't say anything. He and Hawk are friends. He must have had at least some inkling about an engagement—"

Pia shrugged. "Perhaps Sawyer had no idea that a warning

was necessary. I mean, Hawk and I had a past but no present. And now, we definitely have no future..."

Pia felt a wave of pain wash over her. Had she started hoping for a future with Hawk? How much of her hurt was due to the fact that she really hadn't wanted the relationship to end, and how much due to the way she'd shockingly found out that it was over—because there was another woman?

It shouldn't hurt this bad.

If she was honest with herself, she'd say she'd never completely gotten over Hawk. And now...now she was in love with him while he was going to marry another woman.

The realization hit like a body blow.

"Pia?" Tamara said. "Are you okay?"

Pia could only nod, her throat too constricted for words.

Tamara stroked her arm soothingly. "I know it hurts. You'll need time."

Pia nodded, and then took a deep breath.

"I was so naive," she announced when she could speak again. "When Michelene arrived, I thought perhaps she and Hawk had dated in the past. It never occurred to me that I should be concerned about the future!"

"Well, don't worry. I'll have Sawyer call Hawk out," Tamara stated, trying to lighten the mood. "Sawyer must have some centuries-old ceremonial swords lying around somewhere that they can duel with..."

Pia gave a choked laugh. "I don't know. Hawk is in good shape. He's a rock climber."

Pia was thankful for Tamara's understanding. She wasn't sure if Belinda would have managed to be quite so deft at a time like this. But then Tamara was happily married, while Belinda was trying her utmost to be happily *unmarried*.

Pia tried to compose herself, and gave Tamara a watery smile. "Thanks for trying to cheer me up."

Tamara gave a rueful little smile of her own. "I know what

you're going through, Pia, believe me. It's where I was just a few months ago."

"But everything worked out for you. Sawyer adores you."

"I didn't think it was possible at the time. There'll come a day when you'll be happy again—I promise."

Pia sighed. "Not any time soon. I'm committed to seeing through Lucy's big event. How will it look if I end this horrible year by dropping Lucy's wedding at the last moment? It will truly be a fatal blow to Pia Lumley Wedding Productions!"

Tamara grimaced. "I wish I could question Sawyer right now, but he flew back to New York yesterday, and I know he's in a business meeting right now."

"It's okay. It won't change anything."

Nothing could make this right.

"What is Michelene's full name?" Tamara queried suddenly.

"It's Ward-Fombley. Michelene Ward-Fombley."

Tamara nodded. "I've heard of her, though I can't put a face to the name at the moment."

"She's genteel and attractive."

"So are you."

"You're loyal."

Tamara tilted her head. "I'm sure I've heard the name in connection with one social function or another here in England…"

"I'm not surprised," Pia admitted, though it hurt. "She's from Hawk's social circle. In fact, I believe she was a leading candidate to be Hawk's older brother's bride until William passed away."

Tamara grimaced again. "Oh, Pia, are you sure Hawk isn't just feeling some lingering halfhearted sense of obligation?"

"Even if he is, it doesn't change matters. He engaged in some artful omissions, and I can only assume that his sense of obligation remains."

Hawk had assumed responsibilities in the past three years, Pia reflected, and she was suffering the consequences.

She recalled the look on the dowager duchess's face last night. Yes, Pia thought with a stab, Hawk had his life mapped out for him, and their paths were apparently fated to cross only briefly and casually, with no serious feelings or commitment—at least not on his part.

"I need to book a flight," Pia told Tamara. "With any luck, I can catch a plane back to New York by tomorrow."

Her friend looked troubled. "Oh, Pia, please stay longer. You're upset."

Pia was glad for the offer, but still she shook her head. "Thank you, Tamara—for everything." She pasted on a brave smile. "But I have business that needs attending to back in New York."

At the moment, she added silently, she needed to put as much space as possible between her and Hawk.

She also worried that if Sawyer returned home, he'd inform Hawk of her whereabouts. Pia had come to like Tamara's husband, but she knew he was also Hawk's friend.

And she wasn't ready to face Hawk again quite so soon.

Once she was back in New York, she only had to figure out how to avoid Hawk until Lucy's wedding was over. Because one thing was certain—they were over as a couple.

Hawk sat in his office in New York in a rare quiet moment and reflected on the royal mess he'd made.

Pia had run from him, and he no doubt ranked even lower than the fictional wicked Mr. Wickham in her estimation at the moment.

Mrs. Hollings, no doubt using her crystal ball and her contacts across the Atlantic, had published more or less the heart of the matter in her column: "Could a certain rakish, hawkish duke have resurrected his randy dandy ways before heading to the altar with a suitable marriageable miss?"

His painstakingly built reputation as a serious financier with hardly a remarkable social life was threatening to collapse. He'd merited three thinly-veiled references in Mrs. Hollings's gossip column in the past months.

Pia had laid dust to his resolve to appear—and to *be*—strictly proper and responsible. He'd thought he was reformed. She'd proved him wrong.

She thought he'd played her false, and the truth was, he'd been less than aboveboard and forthright. As a result, Pia had been crushed by the unexpected events at Lucy's engagement party.

And Mrs. Hollings, blast it, knew it all.

It would be easy, of course, for him to track down Pia. He knew where she lived, and she was still working on Lucy's wedding—or rather, he thought she was.

Lucy had become rather tight-lipped on the subject of Pia. His sister had seemed to intuit what had transpired at Silderly Park, based on Michelene's unexpected arrival and Pia's abrupt departure. It was clear that Lucy disapproved of his treatment of Pia, though she'd refrained from outright verbal censuring.

And then again, what would he say to Pia if he tracked her down?

He should have told her about Michelene and *explained*—but what exactly? Until Pia had unexpectedly reappeared in his life on Belinda's wedding day in June, he and everyone else had thought he'd marry someone suitable. It had been, in so many ways, the path of least resistance. It was time to marry, and with his reputation as a top-flight financier in place, a predictable marriage had been the final step toward burying his playboy past for good.

Yet how serious could he ever have been about Michelene if she'd barely even crossed his mind the whole time he'd been with Pia? He asked himself that question now. The idea of proposing to Michelene had never assumed concrete terms…

When the phone rang, he leaned forward and picked up the receiver on his desk. "Yes?"

"Sawyer Langsford is here to see you."

"Tell him to come in."

After replacing the phone, he rose from his chair, just in time to see Sawyer walk into his office.

As Hawk came around his desk, he was glad to see his friend, even though he had some suspicion as to what had precipitated this visit.

"If you're here to castigate me," he said without preamble, "I can assure you that I'm already doing a fine job of it myself."

Sawyer smiled wryly. "Tamara suggested a duel at dawn, but I set her straight that it wasn't quite the thing anymore among us aristocrats."

"Good Lord, I should hope not," Hawk muttered as he shook hands with Sawyer. "I don't think my mother would take kindly to the dukedom passing into the hands of a distant cousin for lack of male heirs."

Sawyer's eyes crinkled.

Hawk nodded at one of the chairs set before his desk. "Have a seat."

Sawyer sat down, and Hawk went back around his desk and reclaimed his chair.

Sawyer's lips twisted into a sardonic smile. "My impression actually was that you were doing your utmost to sire an heir."

Hawk wasn't sure if Sawyer was referring to his liaison with Pia or rumors of his prospective proposal to Michelene. In any case, it hardly mattered.

"Ah, yes, the heart of the matter," Hawk said, steepling his fingers. "This is what has gotten me into hot water. Even your Mrs. Hollings is apparently on to the story."

Sawyer shrugged. "What can I say? Mrs. Hollings's realm extends even beyond my reach."

"Obviously."

"Much as I hate to point out the obvious," Sawyer said, "Mrs. Hollings was reporting a story of your own creation."

Hawk sighed, acknowledging the truth of Sawyer's statement. "Much to my regret."

Sawyer smiled. "In any case, my pretext for coming here was to extend an apology in person for your name's appearance in the wrong section of one of my newspapers."

Hawk inclined his head in mock solemnity. "Thank you. Far better than a duel at dawn."

"Quite." Sawyer arched a brow. "I did caution you about Pia."

"Yes, I recall," Hawk replied. "And I proceeded heedlessly. Obviously, I'm an inconsiderate libertine of the first order. A debaucher of innocence."

In fact, these days he found himself questioning what his intentions had been all along. Had he been disingenuous? And even if his intentions had been good, they now lay like flotsam on the shore.

Sawyer inclined his head. "You can always be reformed."

"I thought I was."

Sawyer gave a hint of a smile. "Again, then. You're the only one who can fix this situation."

Hawk twisted his lips. "How? I've been racking my brain and have yet to come up with a solution."

"You will," Sawyer replied. "I was sitting where you are only a few months ago, thinking similar thoughts about Tamara. Except that you came into your title unexpectedly as a younger son, unlike me and Easterbridge. You had less time to get accustomed to it. All I'll say is, yes, the title is a responsibility, but don't let yourself get overburdened by it. Think about what makes you happy rather than what's suitable."

Hawk nodded, surprised by Sawyer's insight, though maybe he shouldn't have been.

Sawyer's lips tilted upward. "And lastly, women appreciate grand gestures." He checked his watch. "Now, if you're free, let's have lunch."

Hawk shook his head in amused disbelief as he and Sawyer both rose from their seats. He'd had enough of grand gestures. Look where they'd landed him.

Still, he would venture to guess that Sawyer was correct.

Thirteen

Pia had decided to lie low.

She wasn't sure where and how Mrs. Hollings was getting her information, but the columnist seemed to have sources in the most unlikely of places.

In fact, Pia wondered fancifully for a moment if Mrs. Hollings had been able to bribe information out of Mr. Darcy. Mr. Darcy was known to be a pushover for having his tummy rubbed or for a handful of kitty treats.

As she moved along Broadway from the subway to her destination—jostled occasionally on the crowded street by a passerby or tourist—she noted that it was an unusually bright December day. *So unlike her mood.*

She'd suggested to Lucy that they meet in her dressing room before her performance tonight. She didn't want to run the risk of encountering Hawk at his house.

She didn't want to face him until she was ready, which might be never.

Still, though it was nonsensical, at the same time she missed Hawk terribly.

He appeared to be giving her a wide berth—it was the only way to explain why she hadn't heard from him. He could have tracked her down. He knew where she lived.

She was almost annoyed with him for *not* tracking her down. If he cared, wouldn't he beat a path to her door to mount a defense, however feeble?

Pia sighed. She ought to have hardened her heart against Hawk since their last confrontation. Instead, she was a mass of incredibly conflicted feelings.

Perhaps she was a pushover and always would be. She'd learned nothing, clearly, about eradicating her trusting nature and protecting her too-easily-bruised feelings.

Arriving at the Drury Theater, she went in the front entrance and was directed to Lucy's dressing room.

When she knocked on Lucy's partially-open dressing room door and then entered, Hawk's sister swiveled in her chair to face her.

"Pia!" Lucy rose and came over to give her a quick squeeze. "You're right on time."

She might have had a falling-out with Hawk, but Pia continued to like Lucy. The other woman's enthusiasm was almost contagious. And though this wasn't usually the case with her clients, she believed that she and Lucy had become friends of sorts over the past few months.

"Hardly anyone is here, since it's hours until curtain time," Lucy said as she stepped back. "Can I offer you something to drink? Tea—" Lucy's eyes sparkled with humor "—or maybe coffee or hot chocolate?"

"No, please," she declined. "I'm fine at the moment."

She removed her hat and coat, and Lucy took them and her purse from her to place on a nearby coatrack.

As they both sat down in vacant chairs, Pia looked around the smallish room. It boasted a mirrored dressing table lit by naked bulbs and strewn with an array of makeup and hair preparation items. There was also the coatrack, a few chairs and plenty of discarded wardrobe items.

Pia let her gaze come back to Lucy, and she smiled encouragingly. "You are one of the calmest brides whom I have ever worked with."

Lucy laughed. "I suppose I'd be more nervous if work wasn't keeping me so busy. But then I'm used to performing in front of people, and isn't a wedding a type of performance?"

"I suppose that explains it."

Lucy looked at her thoughtfully. "I want to thank you for attending the engagement party at Silderly Park. You left so soon, I didn't have time to say anything."

"Yes, well…" Pia found it hard to hold Lucy's gaze. "It was my pleasure."

Lucy tilted her head. "I don't suppose your abrupt departure had anything to do with Hawk and Michelene?"

Pia was startled by the direct question, and for a moment, she wasn't sure she'd heard correctly.

"Wh-what makes you ask that?" she said, eyes wide.

She flushed to think about how many of the other guests at the engagement party had surmised what happened.

Lucy smiled understandingly. "When it's your brother, and you're on the verge of getting married yourself, you notice things."

"You needn't worry," she tried gamely. "I'm well-prepared to deal with Michelene and H-Hawk's w-wedding plans."

"Pia…"

She fought to hold on to her composure. How humiliating would it be to break down in front of Hawk's sister, and to have Lucy tell Hawk about it?

Lucy's smile flickered, comprehension in her eyes. "If it helps, I'm convinced Hawk cares about you. Very much."

If he cared, Pia thought, he would have told her about Michelene instead of having her discover the other woman's position in his life in such a public way. If he cared, he would have called or contacted her.

If he cared, he wouldn't be so charming and easy to fall in love with.

Good grief, she thought, was there no end to Hawk's ability to toy with her life?

Lucy sighed. "I believe Michelene's arrival caught Hawk by surprise as much as it did you."

Pia thinned her lips. "I'm sure it did. I can just imagine what an uncomfortable position Michelene put him in. He suddenly had his current lover and his future wife under the same roof, and they weren't the same woman!"

Then she belatedly clamped her mouth shut, afraid she'd said too much.

Lucy grimaced. "Hawk has an amazing ability to muck things up, sometimes."

"Sometimes?" Pia queried, regaining some of her aplomb. "You know the first time I met him he presented himself as plain Mr. James Fielding?"

"So the rumors are true," Lucy murmured, as if speaking to herself.

Pia had wondered how much Lucy realized or suspected about her relationship with Hawk. Now she had her answer.

Lucy searched Pia's face, her own reflecting worry. "I've never seen Hawk as happy as he is with you. Please take that for what it's worth."

There was a part of her that yearned to believe Lucy's words. She was already a mix of conflicted feelings.

"Do you know he spoke glowingly of you when he suggested I use you as my wedding coordinator?" Lucy went on. "I could see from his face that you weren't a mere acquaintance. I could tell there was more he wasn't telling me."

Pia felt herself flush. "H-he told me he wanted to make amends for the past…"

"And he mucked up the setting-to-right part, too," Lucy guessed, finishing for her.

Pia nodded. "He didn't mention Michelene." She swallowed against the sudden lump in her throat. "But I should have known there'd be someone like her waiting in the wings. There's an expectation he'll marry someone suitable to his rank."

Lucy sighed again. "Well, there's no getting around the unfortunate fact that Hawk is a duke. However, I'm not sure what Hawk's feelings are, and it's possible not even he knows. He probably has never allowed himself to examine them. I sometimes think he's been on autopilot since William and Father died—on a one-man mission, if you will, to put the dukedom back on sound footing."

Pia felt her lips pull up in a reluctant smile. "You're a good advocate for him."

Lucy nodded. "I'm biased, of course, since Hawk is my brother. But I'd also like to think I'm just returning a favor." She smiled. "After all, Hawk found me a wonderful wedding coordinator—one I didn't even know I needed. And now I'm trying to persuade you to forgive him for his mistakes—just a little, and even if it is for the second time."

Pia chewed her lip.

Lucy gave her another understanding look. "All I'm saying is give him a chance."

One part of her, Pia knew, desperately wanted to grasp the shred of hope that Lucy was giving her. Lucy had said nothing about Hawk offering love, marriage or forever more, of course. But then again, if Hawk cared...

As her conflicted feelings assailed her, Pia let herself contemplate a heretofore unthinkable possibility.

She knew she loved Hawk.

Could she remain his lover, knowing their relationship could lead nowhere? Could she let go of the fairy-tale ending that she'd always wanted?

* * *

"I'm considering keeping my relationship with Hawk...a-at least until he really is engaged to Michelene," Pia said.

Her statement fell into the conversational void like a wrecking ball crashing through the restaurant's ceiling. It was why she'd waited awhile to make her statement.

Shocked stillness was followed by commotion inside Contadini, where she, Tamara and Belinda were having one of their Sunday brunches—indoors this time in a nod to the December weather.

"What?"

"What?"

Belinda and Tamara spoke practically in unison as they stared at her from the other side of the table.

Tamara sighed. "Oh, Pia."

"Have you lost your mind?" Belinda followed up.

Pia knew Belinda's harsh judgment was made simply in hopes of jolting her from a bad decision. "I know it may be hard for you to understand."

"Try impossible."

"Belinda means well," Tamara said, jumping in.

"On second thought," Belinda continued, "maybe you have the right idea, Pia. You can always walk away from an affair."

Pia understood what Belinda meant. Ironically, Belinda couldn't manage to get *unmarried,* while she herself, the romantic, couldn't find a ticket for a trip down the aisle...

"I knew it," Belinda mused, resting one silk-sweater-clad arm on the table as they waited for their meal to be cleared. "I knew the minute that you said you were wavering in your negative opinion of Hawk that there was reason to worry. What has he done to you?"

He's turned me inside out. He makes me want to be with him no matter what.

"It makes me happy to be with him," she said simply.

Belinda rolled her eyes, and Tamara touched her arm as if to restrain her.

"That's how it starts," Belinda argued, her brows drawing together. "One minute you're having a good time, the next you're in bed thinking you're ready to gift him your body forever more…"

"Are we talking about Pia here?" Tamara asked as she and Pia stared at Belinda.

Belinda pressed her lips together. "Sorry, yes."

Tamara pulled a worried frown of her own and searched Pia's face. "Have you really considered what this would mean?"

Pia hesitated, and then nodded. She could tell, however, that Tamara had picked up on her short pause before answering.

Tamara sighed. "I wish I'd been able to warn you about Michelene. After you left Gantswood Hall, I questioned Sawyer about what he knew. It seems he had his suspicions but felt he'd received enough assurance on the matter." She pursed her lips and shook her head. "I just wish Sawyer had bothered to tell me!"

"It's okay, Tamara," Pia responded. "It's not your fault."

Belinda shook her head, her expression perplexed and disbelieving. "Have you thought this through, Pia? Because, you know, he's a duke with an obligation to produce a legitimate heir sooner rather than later. This would give you only a little more time with him. And he's misled you now *twice*."

Pia had followed the same train of thought a dozen times already, tormenting herself. She was hoping it would be a long while before Hawk was officially engaged. He'd asserted during their argument that he hadn't planned a proposal or bought a ring. Did she dare believe him?

She'd managed to leave Silderly Park with a shred of dignity and self-respect, but only by the barest of margins. Was she willing to throw her self-respect out the window now by going back to Hawk's bed with no strings attached after all that had happened?

"Perhaps Tamara and I aren't the ones to be talking to you about this," Belinda joked with dark humor. "We're the first wives club, after all."

"The first and only," Tamara modified.

"For you, I hope," Belinda said. "For me, I wouldn't mind if Colin found another wife." A look of pain flashed across her friend's face in contradiction of her belligerent tone. "But even if Tamara and I can't fully relate to the situation, we still know *you*. Do you really think you could do this—hold on to Hawk for now and then let him go?"

"It's fine for you and Tamara to be married to aristocrats," Pia replied. "But unlike the both of you, I wasn't born into a world of titles and money. I don't know much about—"

"Oh, Pia, that's nonsense!" Tamara broke in. "If I had a dollar for every bonhomie aristocrat who married in questionable taste, I wouldn't have needed Sawyer to bail out Pink Teddy Designs."

Despite herself, Pia smiled.

"Not that a marriage to you would be in questionable taste, of course," Tamara hastened to add.

"Of course not," Belinda joined in.

"Look at me, for example," Tamara went on as a waiter cleared their plates. "I always considered myself poor countess material."

Pia smiled uncertainly. It was true that, until a few months ago, Tamara had been a bohemian New York jewelry designer. But she was also the daughter of a British viscount. And she was now, in the space of a few short months, adapting well to straddling the line of what was expected of her as the Earl of Melton's wife and as a New York-based designer.

On top of it all, Tamara glowed with happiness from an adoring husband and a pregnancy that was starting to show.

Pia wasn't sure if, given the chance, she'd fare so well.

Not that she'd have that chance. Hawk had protested that he wasn't ready to marry Michelene yet, but he'd said nothing about having any serious interest in Pia.

She'd longed for a happy ending for herself since she was a little girl. Could she settle for less? Perhaps she was deluding herself into thinking a dead-end affair with Hawk was for the best.

Tamara reached across the table and touched her hand. "I don't want to hear more talk about not being qualified to be a duchess. You're more qualified than I am to be a countess, frankly, if qualifications even enter into it. You know how to throw brilliant parties and entertain impeccably."

Pia swallowed hard.

"And you are a pro at two of the most important aristocratic pastimes—fishing and riding," Tamara continued. "I find fishing deadly dull, and as for riding, I only ever do it occasionally."

Pia gave a tremulous smile, even as she flushed with embarrassment. She didn't dare tell Tamara and Belinda that Hawk was interested in different types of fishing and riding with her—ones that had nothing to do with fishes and horses and everything to do with a bed and a lazy afternoon or evening, or morning, for that matter.

Belinda looked at her too knowingly. "My advice is not to be Hawk's plaything, even if I do think an arrangement without a legally binding contract is easier. I know you, Pia, and this isn't you."

Pia looked down and fiddled with her napkin. The rational part of her knew Belinda was right. The other part didn't want to think about tomorrow and consequences. She just wanted Hawk.

She'd been young, naive and romantic once, but perhaps she was always destined to act emotionally as far as Hawk was concerned.

Michelene. Oh, God.

Pia swallowed and looked up.

Belinda and Tamara were looking at her with worried but expectant expressions.

Pia bit her lip and punted. "Mr. Darcy is waiting for me at home."

Belinda relaxed a little, obviously taking her comment as a reassuring sign. "Good girl. Learn who the good guys are."

If only, Pia thought, she wasn't still so tempted by a certain wicked duke that her stubborn heart kept insisting was her Prince Charming.

Fourteen

Hawk looked up from his desk, and then automatically rose. "What a surprise to see you on this side of the Atlantic, Mother."

It seemed as if everyone was destined to pay a visit to his office these days. Everyone, that was, except Pia.

Undoubtedly, his mother must have told his secretary not to bother announcing her arrival after obviously having taken her coat and handbag.

The dowager duchess gave him a fixed look. "I thought it would be nice if we had lunch."

Hawk's lips twisted. His mother had shown up unannounced—a clear sign that something important was weighing on her.

"What is this I hear about you and Lucy's wedding planner, Pia Lumley?" his mother asked, not disappointing by going straight to the point. "Some dreadful woman has been writing—"

"Mrs. Hollings."

His mother stopped abruptly. "Pardon?"

"The Pink Pages of Mrs. Jane Hollings. It's a column that appears in the Earl of Melton's newspapers. Specifically, *The New York Intelligencer*."

"I don't know why Melton hasn't put a stop to it then," the dowager duchess huffed. "He's a friend of yours, isn't he?"

"Sawyer believes in freedom of the press," Hawk responded dryly, coming around his desk.

"Nonsense. This terrible woman is assailing your reputation. Something must be done."

"And what, precisely, is it you suggest I do, Mother?" Hawk queried.

The dowager duchess raised her brows and gathered herself into her full hauteur. "Quite obviously, it must be made apparent to all parties that you have no interest in Ms. Lumley."

"Don't I?"

"Certainly not. This Mrs. Hollings is suggesting that you are having the near equivalent of a liaison with the household help. The Duke of Hawkshire does not dally with those in his employ like...like—"

"Have a seat, Mother," Hawk said, pulling back a chair without breaking stride. "Would you like something to drink?"

He could use something strong and therapeutic himself.

"You are being rather obstinate, James. A simple denial will do."

"And what should I deny?"

The dowager duchess shot him a peremptory look as she sat down. "That you and Ms. Lumley are—"

"—liaising?"

His mother nodded.

"Ah, but you see, I cannot do that."

His mother stilled, and then closed her eyes briefly, as if in resignation. "Goodness. It's not just the resurrected image of you as a playboy that I need to contend with. It's the reality."

"Quite right."

He deserved every condemnation, Hawk thought. He'd dallied with Pia and hurt her. Again.

His mother fixed him with a stern look. "Well, you must put a stop to this at once. My grandfather was a renowned philanderer who left a mess in his wake—"

"You mean offspring born on the wrong side of the blanket?"

The dowager duchess straightened her spine. "We do not speak of it in this family. Kindly curb your blunt speaking. It isn't charming."

Hawk felt his lips quirk. "But, Mother, you like Great-Aunt Ethel."

"Precisely, and that is why we do not refer to the family peccadilloes. However, I still would not have the past repeat itself."

He arched a brow. "Then maybe it would be best if you did not press this matter of an engagement to Michelene. Perhaps the old earl's wandering eye could be traced to an unhappy arranged marriage."

"I had no idea I was pressing anything upon you, James," the dowager duchess huffed.

His mother had a disingenuous ability to parse the truth, but Hawk let the matter go. At the moment, there was a more important discussion to be had—perhaps one that was long overdue.

"Mother," he said with forced gentleness, "Michelene may be a lingering tie to William, but William is gone."

He'd done a lot of thinking since his return from Silderly Park, and especially after Sawyer's visit. One thing he'd realized was that he had to stop any expectations with respect to Michelene for good. He didn't love her—no matter how suitable she was—and he never would.

His mother looked at him for a moment—uncharacteristically without a ready response. And then, disconcertingly, her eyes became moist.

Hawk shifted. "I know this is difficult for you."

"William considered Michelene for his wife because she was a natural choice," the dowager duchess observed finally. "He was doing what was expected of him. He knew his responsibilities."

"Precisely, and I therefore wonder how enamored William really was of Michelene," Hawk replied. "There were times when I thought William enjoyed boating and flying so much because they were the rare moments when he could feel free. In any case, William was groomed for his responsibilities as duke from birth, and I wasn't."

His mother looked pained, but then gathered and composed herself. "Very well, but what do we know about this woman Pia Lumley?" she argued. "Where is she from? She will have no understanding of our ways and what will be expected of her as the Duchess of Hawkshire."

In the way that mattered most, Pia was well-equipped to fill the role of duchess, Hawk disagreed silently. She knew how to please him.

"She's from Pennsylvania," he said aloud. "She knows how to entertain because she's a well-regarded wedding coordinator to New York society—a respectable proving ground for women who marry well, you'll agree."

In Pia's defense, he cited the things that he knew would matter to his mother.

The dowager duchess said nothing, so Hawk pressed on.

"She knows how to ride and fish as well as any woman of my acquaintance," he said. "She is sweet and intelligent, and charmingly devoid of guile or pretense. A breath of fresh air."

"Well," his mother replied finally, "with all those sterling qualities, James, why ever would she have anything to do with you?"

Hawk laughed but it was filled with a note of self-derision. "I wonder that myself."

He was in love with Pia, and he was unworthy of her.

He'd been so intent on defending Pia to his mother that he'd stumbled upon an important realization.

He loved Pia.

Suddenly everything seemed so simple and clear.

"James?"

Hawk looked at his mother. "Yes?"

"You seem lost in thought."

"Or perhaps simply lost."

His mother stood. "Well, quite clearly I've misread matters."

"Never mind, Mother. It's nothing that can't be put to rights."

He hoped.

Hawk knew there were a few things he needed to clarify with Michelene.

And then he needed to find Pia.

If it wasn't too late, and he hadn't hopelessly botched things, this time for good…

Pia had every reason to believe that Lucy's wedding would be the worst day of her life—or near to it. In all likelihood, this day would be Michelene and Hawk's appearance as a couple, if not the announcement of their engagement.

Who else would Hawk take to his sister's wedding but his future bride? It made eminent sense.

One thing was certain: he would not be escorting her, Pia. She was working, and she supposed Hawk's days playing her gofer or man Friday were over.

Hawk's mother, the dowager duchess, would no doubt be eager to segue from seeing one of her children walk down the aisle to seeing the other married—especially when the *other* was the current Duke of Hawkshire.

But as the day progressed, it became clear that Michelene wouldn't materialize—Hawk had come alone to the wedding.

Still, Pia refused to read too much into that, and distracted herself with work.

Thankfully, Hawk didn't approach her. She wasn't sure what she would do if he did.

Instead, he remained busy at the reception, speaking with various guests and exchanging pleasantries with others.

Pia couldn't help wondering if he'd relegated her to being simply the hired help and no more these days. The thought hurt.

Nevertheless, she hungrily absorbed all her glimpses of him, storing them away for a time when she'd no longer see him.

He looked so handsome and attractive tonight that she ached.

Still, by the end of the evening, Pia was weary enough to want the night to end—if only so she wouldn't have to maintain appearances in front of Hawk and everyone else.

She had just walked out of the loftlike reception room when she heard her name called out behind her.

"Pia."

She turned around, but she already knew who it was.

Hawk.

He walked toward her, still looking impeccable in a navy suit and silver-gray tie as the evening was drawing to a close.

She looked at the clock. It was nearing midnight on New Year's Eve.

Too bad this Cinderella couldn't disappear quite yet. She'd worn a simple light blue strapless dress and matching heels.

But she didn't have a carriage, or even a car. And the wedding was slated to continue until one.

Still, she didn't think she could speak to Hawk right now.

She had to get away…get some air. *Anything.*

"I—I was just—"

He quirked a brow. "Leaving?"

Damn him. How dare he look so composed when he was the reason she was upset?

"I was taking a moment to compose myself," she replied with halfhearted honesty. "I was going to touch up my makeup."

Where was a ladies' room when one was needed? It was the only place where she knew Hawk *wouldn't* be following her.

"Why?" He surveyed her. "You look perfect."

Except for the fact that her heart was a wreck.

She sighed. "That's what women do, Hawk. They freshen up. Powder their nose…touch up their lipstick…"

"Why? Expecting someone to kiss you?"

She stared at him mutely. How could he be so heartless?

"Why disappear now?" he persisted. "It's almost midnight."

That was the point. She didn't want everyone to witness that she had no one to kiss—not even a frog. Okay, she had some excuse in that she was on the job, but still… With Hawk in the room—who knew the truth of her circumstances—that helped little.

"Isn't it customary for people to don boas and crowns and blow noisemakers? Why fix your hair when it'll get messed up anyway?" He moved a little, and Pia belatedly noticed that he was holding a small bag. "In fact, I brought some items for you."

"It was considerate of you to think of me," she said, wondering why they were having this inane conversation.

She had no plans to blow a horn or kiss anybody.

Hawk gave a little smile. "I thought it was considerate, too."

Pia thought it was too bad there wasn't another platter of hors d'oeuvres nearby.

How much would it cost her to precipitate another incident at a wedding?

Too much. She couldn't afford it.

Hawk reached into the bag he was holding and pulled out a jeweled headpiece.

It took Pia a moment to realize the tiara wasn't one of those plastic jewel concoctions that everyone wore on New Year's Eve, but the real thing.

Her brain slowed, her mind caught in a moment of disbelief.

The diamond tiara in Hawk's hand had a swirl pattern and was of equal thickness all around. Large diamonds also dangled within the swirls.

Hawk's smile was tender and thoughtful.

Her eyes, wide with shock, remained fastened on his as he moved to settle the tiara on her upswept hair.

It was the first time in Pia's life she'd ever worn a real tiara—though she'd donned plenty of make-believe ones, especially in her dreams.

"There," he murmured, easing back, his eyes meeting hers. "I have pins to anchor it in place. I've been told it's wise to do so, though I have no idea how to go about it."

Pia swallowed hard.

"I wasn't sure what color you'd be wearing," Hawk said, his voice low and deep. "So I decided to go with a sure bet. The Carsdale Diamond tiara."

She sucked in a breath, her brain refusing to function. "G-good choice."

Just inside the reception room, the guests continued their dancing and merriment, waiting for the countdown to the new year and heedless of the two people standing just outside one of the exits.

"It's the traditional tiara worn by Carsdale brides," Hawk said, his voice laden with meaning. "It was worn by my mother on her wedding day."

Pia felt her heart constrict. It pounded loudly.

She couldn't bear it if Hawk was toying with her. If this was a gambit to win her back into his bed even as he planned to marry Michelene or search for a properly-pedigreed duchess...

She bit her lip. "Why are you giving it to me to wear?"

"Why do you think?" he asked thickly, searching her face. "It's a new year and a new beginning...I hope."

"I—I don't need a tiara to ring in the n-new year."

Hawk touched her chin and rubbed his thumb over her lips.

"I know," he responded tenderly. "The question is do you need a duke who is very much in love? He comes with a big house that needs someone who can preside over large and boring parties."

Pia's eyes welled.

Hawk cleared his throat. "You once fell for plain Mr. James Fielding, and it was the greatest gift that anyone ever gave me."

Her shock turned into a crazy kind of hope as Hawk went down on bended knee. He fished a ring out of his pocket with one hand even as the other lifted one of hers.

Pia glanced down at Hawk and began to tremble with emotion. She reached up with her free hand to steady the tiara.

Hawk smiled up at her. "This is meant to match the tiara."

Pia could hardly breathe despite his attempt at levity.

Hawk's expression turned solemn, however. "Pia Lumley,

I love you with all my heart. Will you do me the very great honor of marrying me and becoming my wife? Please?"

Her first proposal. *Ever.*

She'd dreamt of receiving one—from him.

And yet...and yet...

"Wh-what about Michelene?" she couldn't resist asking.

Hawk's lips twitched. "Usually a man doesn't expect a marriage proposal to be met with a question of its own."

"Usually the woman concerned hasn't been expecting him to propose to someone else."

"Touché, but there isn't anyone else," he responded. "Michelene decided not to attend today after it became clear she could no longer have the expectation of becoming a Carsdale bride."

"Oh, Hawk." Pia's voice caught on a sob as she grasped the tiara and lowered it to her side. "I—I l-love you—" she watched as Hawk's face brightened "—and I want to marry you. B-but..."

"No buts." Hawk slid the ring on her finger, and then rose and, taking the tiara from her, placed it on a nearby table.

He took her in his arms and kissed her deeply, quieting her upset.

When he raised his head, Pia swallowed hard.

"I'm not fit to be a duchess."

"I disagree," he said tenderly. "Where else does the heroine of a fairy tale belong but in a palace?"

"Oh, Hawk," she said again. "I have lived a fairy tale. Not because you're proposing that I be your duchess, but because this was a test of character. After I found out about Michelene, I considered continuing an affair until you were officially engaged. But then I realized I couldn't do it. I loved you too much, and I wanted all of you."

His eyes sparked like brown and green flames. "You have all of me. My heart and soul."

"Your mother won't be pleased."

"My mother wants to see me happy," he contradicted. "She and my father had a happy marriage, unlike those of some of their ancestors."

"I'm not conventional duchess material."

He shook his head. "You are in character, if not background."

"But you're eminently responsible these days," she protested.

Hawk smiled. "Then I suppose it's time for me to follow Lucy in her rebellion. You know, as of today, my mother already has one American in-law."

"So far you've managed to shoot down every good reason I have for not getting married."

"That's because there are no good reasons." Hawk touched her cheek. "Pia, do you love me?"

She nodded. "I do."

"And I love you desperately. That's all that matters."

Their lips met, their bodies drawing together.

When they finally broke apart again, Hawk raised her hand. "This ring is one of the Carsdale family jewels. I didn't want to make a proposal empty-handed, but we can get you something you like better if you prefer."

Pia shook her head. "No, the ring's perfect."

"We got a second chance."

She smiled, though she remained misty-eyed. "I'm glad."

He grinned. "Your ringtone on my cell phone is the notes to the song 'Unforgettable.'"

"Really?" she inquired with a tremulous smile. "Then I succeeded. I never wanted you to forget me. It was one of the reasons—"

She stopped and blushed.

"Yes?"

"It's one of the reasons I went to bed with you again," she said in a rush. "I told myself that this time I'd leave you wanting more."

"You were unforgettable the first time."

"And yet you left."

He nodded. "Much to my regret."

"Because your brother died unexpectedly, and you needed to rush home."

"I left not because our night together meant too little," he said with a note of self-deprecation, "but because it meant too much."

"Why didn't you tell me you were Lord James Carsdale?"

"Because I'd grown used to moving around as James Fielding. It was liberating not to have to shake off women who were overly impressed by a title and money. And frankly, it was freeing for me to avoid some of the trappings of my life as a duke's younger son. Little did I know—"

"That one day you'd be the duke yourself?"

He nodded. "And that someone—someone I've come to care about very much—would be hurt by my charade."

"Oh, Hawk, we've lost so much time. I wanted to hate you—"

"But instead, deep down inside, you waited for me, didn't you, Pia?" he murmured, his voice low and intimate.

She nodded, caught by the sudden heat in his eyes.

"And I'll thank heaven every day for that," Hawk said as he lowered his head to hers again.

Pia opened her mouth under his, wanting more of him, wanting to feel their customary flare of desire.

"We can't do this here," she said eventually against his mouth between kisses. "We'll scandalize everyone."

"I hope so," he whispered back wickedly.

For he was her wicked duke.

Epilogue

"You look divine. I can't wait for the wedding night."

Pia turned from the mirror, her heart flipping over as she spotted Hawk in the doorway to the changing room.

He was dressed in a cutaway morning coat that displayed his masculine physique to perfection. She couldn't wait for the wedding night, either.

"You shouldn't be in here," she said, her words belying her feelings. "It's bad luck to see the bride…"

She'd chosen a wedding dress with an all-over lace overlay and a chapel-length train. The dress had a dreamy, fairy-talelike quality, with a straight neckline and fitted sleeves.

It was a dress fit for a princess—or a duchess.

Hawk smiled lazily. "You might feel differently about my appearance when you realize what I've come to deliver."

She surveyed him with mild suspicion. "I—I can't think what that would be," she responded, feeling the weight of the tiara that held her veil in place. "Isn't it customary to present the wedding ring during the ceremony?"

In over an hour, she and Hawk would be exchanging their vows in the chapel on Silderly Park.

"First, a kiss," Hawk said as he stopped in front of her and bent to press his lips to hers.

Pia swayed into him as she felt the warm and supple pressure of his mouth against hers.

When Hawk straightened, Pia wore a dreamy little smile. "I-if that's an indication of what you're here to deliver, then I feel compelled to warn you that we don't have the time or the appropriate easily-disposed-of attire."

Hawk chuckled, and then bent in close. "Later."

Pia felt a shiver chase down her spine at the promise in his voice. "Yes, well, first we have a major production to get through."

After the ceremony, there would be a wedding breakfast for several hundred, in a bow to the dowager duchess's wishes—and somewhat inevitable in light of Hawk's title and position. And in a few weeks' time, after a honeymoon around the Mediterranean, there would be an elegant reception in New York for those who had been unable to attend the wedding.

"After this," Hawk joked, as if reading her mind, "you'll have no end of prospective brides and hostesses seeking your event-planning services."

"I want to assure you that you'll always be at the head of the line," Pia teased back.

Hawk grinned. "How reassuring that I have first dibs on your talent as a party organizer in case I have any more friends who desire a wedding coordinator."

"I thought you exhausted all of those on your way to resurrecting Pia Lumley Wedding Productions!"

"I only called in a few favors," he disagreed modestly. "The lost veil and other capers were not my doing."

"I should hope not."

Hawk sobered a little. "This all brings me back to the reason for my sudden appearance here."

Pia arched a brow. "Yes?"

He reached over and opened a nearby dresser drawer. "I put them in here earlier," he said, withdrawing a velvet case. "I wanted to add the finishing touches to your ensemble."

"Oh, Hawk, no," Pia protested. "You've already given me enough."

"Well, that is true," Hawk conceded with a twinkle in his eyes. "The weight of my heart alone…"

She giggled.

"Nevertheless," he continued solemnly as he opened the jewelry case in his hands, "I hope you'll make an exception for heirloom earrings."

Pia gasped as she caught sight of a magnificent pair of diamond drop earrings.

"They were made for my paternal great-great-grandmother and presented to her on her wedding day," Hawk said as he gazed into her eyes. "Her marriage lasted sixty-one years."

Pia felt emotion clog her throat. "Oh, Hawk, what wonderful history and significance."

Of course, she'd replace the simple diamond studs that she wore—something borrowed from Tamara—with Hawk's gift to her.

Hawk quirked his lips. "Don't thank me just yet. My great-great-grandmother also had eight children."

"Oh!"

His smile widened as he leaned toward her. "Don't worry," he said in a low voice. "I'm already committed to raising the feline Mr. Darcy."

"Hawk?" Lucy's voice sounded from the corridor outside.

"If she finds you in here," Pia said, "she'll be sure to scold you."

Hawk stole a quick kiss. "I'll meet you at the altar."

Pia knew her heart was full to bursting. "And I'll write the fairy tale with you."

From the first day and for the rest of their lives.

* * * * *

MIDNIGHT KISS, NEW YEAR WISH

SHIRLEY JUMP

New York Times bestselling author **Shirley Jump** didn't have the willpower to diet, nor the talent to master under-eye concealer, so she bowed out of a career in television and opted instead for a career where she could be paid to eat at her desk—writing. At first, seeking revenge on her children for their grocery-store tantrums, she sold embarrassing essays about them to anthologies. However, it wasn't enough to feed her growing addiction to writing funny. So she turned to the world of romance novels, where messes are (usually) cleaned up before The End. In the worlds Shirley gets to create and control, the children listen to their parents, the husbands always remember holidays and the housework is magically done by elves. Though she's thrilled to see her books in stores around the world, Shirley mostly writes because it gives her an excuse to avoid cleaning the toilets and helps feed her shoe habit. To learn more, visit her website at www.shirleyjump.com.

To the Stone Soup Sisters. For all the advice, laughs and hugs over the years. I couldn't pick a better or more diverse group of friends.

CHAPTER ONE

THICK, WET, HEAVY SNOW tumbled onto Jenna Pearson's shoulders, blanketing her black hair, and seeping into her black leather high-heeled boots, as if Mother Nature wanted to test Jenna's resolve. To see whether a winter storm could derail her plans, and force her back to New York.

Jenna kept forging forward. Really, what other choice did she have right now? If Jenna had one quality, it was that ability to rush forward, to keep going when it seemed like all was lost.

And right now, just about all was lost. But she had a plan, and she'd get it all back. Definitely.

A two-inch carpet of flakes covered the sidewalk as Jenna walked, under the swags of Christmas pine, past the crimson bows dotting the wrought iron lamp poles. Downtown Riverbend had already buttoned down for the night, with most of the specialty shops lining the street shuttered and dark. Only the café's windows glowed, like a beacon waiting at the far end of the white storm.

Jenna drew her coat tighter and dipped her chin to bury her nose in her blue cashmere scarf. She'd forgotten how cold winters got here. Forgot how the snow carried a fresh, crisp scent. Forgot what it was like to be in the small Indiana town that most people called heaven.

And Jenna had called prison.

The streets were empty, quiet, people safe at home and in bed. She was in Riverbend, after all, the kind of town where nothing bad ever happened.

Well, not nothing bad, but not *that* kind of bad. She was safe. Perfectly safe.

She increased her stride. Goodness, the snow seemed to have doubled in strength and depth in the twenty minutes it had taken her to buy a dozen cookies at the Joyful Creations Bakery. Even though she'd come in at closing time, the owner, Samantha MacGregor, had insisted on staying to fill Jenna's order—and then spending a few minutes over a cup of coffee catching up with her high school friend. Jenna had heard just about everything about everyone in town, even about people she wasn't so sure she wanted to be reminded of.

People like Stockton Grisham. He was here in town, Samantha said. "Returned a few years ago, and opened up a restaurant."

Stockton had returned to Riverbend? The last she'd known, he'd intended to wander the world, plying his culinary talents in some far-off location. He'd told her he wanted to make his mark on the world, one bouillabaisse at a time.

What was it about Riverbend that kept people coming back, or worse, encouraged them to never leave? Most days, Jenna was definitely happy she had left.

Or thought she had been. For so many years, New York had been the only destination she wanted, the only address she imagined for herself. And now...

She increased her pace, shushing that persistent whisper of questions she didn't want to face. The snow blew and swirled around her but she kept going, her boots crunching on the icy crust forming over the snow. As she walked, sharp notes of ginger wafted up to tease at Jenna's senses, tempting her to eat one—just one—of the homemade windmill cookies.

She got into her car, laid the box of cookies on the passenger's seat and turned the key, waiting while the wipers brushed off the coating of snow building up on the windshield. When the windshield was clear, Jenna put the auto into gear. The Taurus fishtailed a bit, protesting how quickly Jenna had pulled away from the curb. She pressed on the brakes. Took in a deep breath. It had been a long time since she'd driven in snow. In New York, she walked almost everywhere, cabbed or subwayed it for longer distances. Riverbend was no New York. There wasn't any public transportation or yellow taxis. Just her and the mounting snow—

And the job ahead of her.

She thought of turning back, of heading for the airport and retreating to her third-floor walk-up apartment in New York. Anything other than return to the town that had whispered about her life like it was an ongoing soap opera. She supposed, in many ways, it had been. But that had been years ago, and surely things were different now.

Jenna's hand hovered over the turning signal. Take a left? Or go straight?

Really, what was waiting for her if she turned left, and got back on that plane? Her only opportunities lay straight ahead, in this town she had tried so hard to leave behind, and now had become her only salvation. Riverbend, of all places. Jenna sighed and started driving.

Swags of evergreen hung across Main Street, connecting to big red bows adorning the streetlights. The streetlights glowed a soft yellow against the white snow. Jenna didn't pause to admire the view. Didn't slow as she passed the town's Winterfest decorations glittering in the park and still blinking a rainbow of colors even now, two days after

Christmas. She drove two blocks, took a right, then pulled to a stop in front of a big yellow farmhouse-style home with white wagon wheel trim decorating the expansive front porch. Fat low shrubs ringed the house, all of them twinkling with tiny white bulbs that peeked out of the snow with a determined glow.

Before Jenna reached the top step, the front door was flung open and her aunt Mabel came hurrying out the door, her house slippers padding across the dusting of snow on the porch, her bright pink robe flying out behind her like a cape. "Jenna!" She crushed her niece into a hug scented with cinnamon and fresh-baked bread.

Jenna's arms wrapped around Aunt Mabel's ample frame. It had been two years since she last saw her aunt, but as they embraced, and she took in her aunt's short gray curls and light blue eyes, all those months disappeared and it felt as if she'd never left Riverbend. If there was one blessing she'd received from this town, it was her aunt Mabel, who had done the most unselfish thing anyone could ask for, and raised her sister's child as her own. "I've missed you so much, Aunt Mabel."

Her aunt drew back and smiled. "Oh, honey, I missed you, too." Then she patted Jenna's hand and waved toward the house. "Now let's get on inside and I'll put on a pot of coffee. I know you're hankering for one of those windmill cookies you've got in your hands as much as I am."

Jenna laughed. "Am I that predictable?"

Aunt Mabel nodded. "And I love that you are." They went inside the house, warm air hitting Jenna with a burst. As Jenna glanced around, she realized very little had changed in the house she'd lived in most of her life. The same overstuffed crimson sofa set sat in the living room, the same pink striped wallpaper lined the bathroom walls and the same family portraits hugged the hallway. When she'd been a teenager, the day-in, day-out sameness had drove her crazy, but now, as a returning adult, familiarity bred comfort, and the tension that had seemed to hang on Jenna like a heavy blanket eased a bit.

A few minutes later, they sat down at Aunt Mabel's scarred maple table in her sunflower bright kitchen, two steaming cups of coffee and a platter of windmill cookies before them. Jenna picked up a cookie, dunked it in her coffee, then took a bite before the softened treat fell apart.

Aunt Mabel laughed. "You still do that."

"What?"

"Dunk your cookies. When you were a little girl, it was in hot cocoa. Now, it's coffee." Aunt Mabel's soft hand covered hers. "You're still the same."

The words chafed at Jenna, and she pushed her coffee aside. "I've changed. More than you know."

Aunt Mabel tut-tutted. "People don't change, honey. Not that much. You might think you do, but you always come right back to your roots. Why, look at you, you're here now. And just before the new year, too. There's no better time for a new beginning." She put up a hand. "Oh, wait. I think I still have some mince pie. You know you should have some in the days after Christmas, to bring good fortune for the year ahead."

"I'm fine, Aunt Mabel, really." Her aunt saw signs in everything from birds flying south to overly puffy clouds. Jenna wasn't in the mood to go down that portent-laden path. "I'm only back in Riverbend to plan Eunice Dresden's birthday party." Her gaze met her aunt's. "Thanks for recommending me."

Aunt Mabel waved off the gratitude. "That's what family's for, to give you a boost when you need it most."

Her aunt had no idea how much Jenna needed this boost.

She had no doubt it had taken some doing on her aunt's part to get the Dresden family to agree to hire her. "I appreciate it, all the same."

Aunt Mabel wagged a cookie at Jenna. "You stay here long enough, you might find this town growing on you again."

She loved her aunt, even if they had the same argument every time she'd seen her. The only thing she'd ever really loved about this small, confining town had been the warm and gracious aunt who had raised her after her parents died. From the minute Jenna realized a big, bright, busy world existed away from insular Riverbend, she'd wanted to leave. "It never grew on me. And I'm not staying. I already have a flight back booked for the night of Eunice's party. The party should be done by six, which means I can be on the nine-o'clock flight back to New York."

A nagging doubt grew inside her. Would this break from the city, from her faltering business, be enough to restore her? To give her back what she had lost?

Aunt Mabel pursed her lips as if she might say something else, but instead she got to her feet and refreshed her coffee. "Well, you're here now. We'll see about the rest."

"It's clear where I get my stubbornness from."

"Me? I'm not stubborn. Just…focused on getting what I want."

Jenna laughed. "Aunt Mabel, you should have gone into politics. You have quite a way of dancing around words."

The older woman returned to the table, and wrapped her hands around her snowman-decorated mug. "Are you going to see anyone special while you're in town?"

"Sorry to disappoint you, Aunt Mabel, but I'm here to work. Not visit with anyone." She put her hand out and grasped the older woman's fingers. "Except for you."

"Jenna—"

"I know you mean well, but really, I'm not going to have time for anything more than planning the party." Jenna got to her feet, put her mug into the dishwasher and gave her aunt a quick hug. "I'm going to bed. It's been a long day and I have the meeting with Eunice's family first thing in the morning."

"Good luck, sweetheart."

Jenna waved a dismissive hand, one filled with more confidence than she'd been feeling over the past few months. "Aunt Mabel, party planning is what I do. The whole thing will be a piece of cake," she said, telling herself as much as she did her aunt. She could do this—and she would. It was a birthday party, not a presidential dinner. "You'll see."

Aunt Mabel laughed. "You don't know Eunice's sister like I know her, honey. And you ain't met stubborn like her."

Delicious.

Stockton Grisham put the teaspoon into the deep stainless steel sink, then made a note on his clipboard to add the tomato basil tortellini soup to tonight's menu. It would pair well with the Chicken Marsala, and make a nice light side to the house's namesake Insalata Rustica. His restaurant was celebrating its first anniversary this week, an occasion that surprised even him sometimes.

He'd done it. Taken what had always been a dream and turned it into a living, breathing, forty-table reality. And what's more, made it work in the little town of Riverbend. Everyone—including his own father—had told him he was crazy, that no one from Indianapolis would make the trek to the "boondocks" just to eat dinner, but they'd been wrong.

He wasn't sure if it was the outdoor seating under the

canopy of ivy, or the cozy booths and cushioned chairs, or, he hoped, the authentic Italian food he made, but something drew people out of the city and into Riverbend for a night at cozy, intimate Rustica, followed by an hour or two of wandering Riverbend's downtown, a boon to the other local shops. It had become the perfect relationship, and a measure of pride swelled in Stockton's chest.

He'd done it. When he'd been young, he had never imagined returning to this town and being a success, but as he'd traveled the globe, it became clear that the only place he wanted to build his culinary career was here.

In the very town his father had thought lacked the sophistication to house a restaurant. To Hank Grisham, true culinary enjoyment could only be found in places like Paris, or Manhattan. Small towns, to his French-born father, were the antithesis of fine cuisine. Stockton's mother had loved Riverbend, and she'd stayed here, putting down roots, raising her son, while Hank traveled and cooked, taking a job here for a few months, there for another few. Stockton saw more postcards with Hank's signature than he ever saw Hank.

At some point, it had become a quest to prove his father wrong. To show him Riverbend could, indeed, house a top-tier restaurant and that the residents would fill the tables. Stockton sighed, and thought of Hank, manning a stove somewhere in Venice right now. One of these days, his father would come home to Riverbend again and see the restaurant in action. Maybe then the biggest naysayer of Stockton's dream would admit that there were more places than Italy to find amazing food.

Stockton had everything he'd always wanted. And yet, an emptiness gnawed at him sometimes, long after the dishes were done and the food put away, he wondered if there was…

More.

Insane thoughts. He had the more, and then some. He just needed to remember to count those blessings instead of looking for others.

The back door opened, and a whoosh of cold air burst into the kitchen. "Goodness, when is winter going to end?" Samantha MacGregor stomped the snow off her boots, then whisked a few flakes from her blond hair. Even bundled in a winter coat, Samantha was still beautiful. Her cheeks held a soft pink flush, and a smile seemed permanently etched on her face. Clearly, marriage agreed with her. Ever since reporter Flynn MacGregor had come to town a little over a year ago, Samantha had laughed and smiled almost daily. She'd had a hard time of it the past few years between her grandmother's illness and the full-time job of running the Joyful Creations Bakery. Stockton was glad to see his longtime friend find happiness.

"Considering it's not even January yet, I'd say we have some time before spring returns," Stockton said. "You have my cookies?"

She grinned as she undid a few of her coat's buttons with one hand. The heat of the kitchen sometimes hit like a wave, nice in the winter, not so much in the summer, even with the A/C running. "Of course. Though I had to get up early to run this batch. Between the publicity from that article Flynn did on the shop, and your constant orders, I'm about ready to start a third shift."

He chuckled. "Glad to hear business is good."

"I could say the same to you." She laid the boxes of fresh cookies on the counter. "So...how are you?"

"Fine." He grinned. "I know you're asking for a reason."

"Am I that transparent?" Samantha laughed. "It's just... well, I worry about you."

"I'm fine," he reiterated.

Samantha made a face. "That's not what Rachel said when she called me from her mother's house today. She said you were working yourself into the ground. She also said, and I quote, 'I see my manicurist more often than I see that workaholic.'"

He sighed. He took a taste of the marinara sauce simmering on the stove, then reached for the salt and pepper, and added a dash of each to the stockpot. A stir with the ladle, then another taste with a fresh teaspoon. Perfect. Too bad life couldn't be fixed as easily as a sauce. "Rachel and I disagree about my work schedule."

"You know," Samantha said, running a hand over one of the counters and avoiding Stockton's gaze, "one would say that a man who doesn't make a lot of effort isn't very interested in a woman."

Stockton cursed under his breath. That was the problem with having personal conversations with people who had known him nearly all his life—they were far too observant and far too vocal with their opinions. "Rachel and I were never really serious. In fact, I wouldn't even say we were much more than friends."

Samantha sighed. "Too bad, Stockton. Because I think you'd make someone a fabulous husband if you just reshuffled your priorities a little."

"I'm fine," he said for the third time, avoiding Samantha's inquisitive gaze by doing the whole tasting-stirring routine again.

Samantha turned to some bundled foil dishes on the countertop. "Are these ready to go?"

"Yep. There's a lasagna, a salad and a whole lot of bread. Thanks for making the delivery for me today. I wasn't sure when I'd find time, what with Larry calling in sick again today. I hate to disappoint Father Michael."

Samantha laid a hand atop the three tiers of leftovers. "The shelter really appreciates these donations, Stockton. Great food, cooked by a great chef, makes everyone feel better."

He shrugged. "Just doing my part, Sam."

"You do your part and then some." She began buttoning her bright red coat, her gaze on the fasteners, not on Stockton. That, he knew, meant she was about to say something he didn't want to hear. He'd been friends with Samantha most of his life and could read her as easily as the front page. "You know, I saw Jenna Pearson last night."

Good thing Stockton had stepped away from the stove, or something would have ended up burned. Instead, he stood in the center of his kitchen, a gaping idiot completely unprepared for those words. And pretending they didn't affect him at all.

It had been eight years since he'd seen her. Eight years since he'd walked out of her life. Afterward, he'd spent two years wandering Italy, learning Italian methods of cooking, but more, finding out who he was and what he wanted out of life.

This, he told himself, glancing around the expansive, gleaming kitchen, this was what he wanted. What he should focus his energy on—not a past that had returned to town. "Jenna Pearson back in town. Why?"

"She's here to plan Eunice's birthday party. The family hired her."

Had Jenna come all the way from New York for that one job? Or for something else? He told himself he didn't care. That he wasn't going to see her either way. Their relationship had crashed and burned a long time ago, a disaster ending worse than anything he'd ever done in the kitchen. "Is she, uh, going to stay for a while? Or leaving right after the party?"

"She's going back to New York right after the event."

"Well, if you see her, tell her I said hello." He didn't really mean it, but it seemed the polite thing to say. And being polite was his best course of action when it came to his ex-girlfriend.

"You should tell her yourself," Samantha said softly. "You know, you have that one-year anniversary coming up in a few days. Sure would help to have a party planner around to fine-tune things for you. Especially one you know as well as Jenna Pearson."

"Don't you have baking to do?"

Samantha grinned and tied the belt on her coat, then flipped up the collar. "Okay, I get the hint. I'll go back to my work, and let you go back to avoiding the obvious."

"And what's the obvious?"

She opened the door, but didn't step outside yet. "You're wondering how long you can hold out before you go see Jenna."

Jenna sat across from Betsy Williams, Eunice's younger sister and owner of Betsy's Bed and Breakfast, a veritable Riverbend institution. Jenna had known Betsy most of her life, and when she'd been little, had been just a little afraid of the stern older lady. Betsy was the kind of woman who kept her house in order, and expected everyone else to fall in line, too, whether they were just stopping by for trick-or-treating (ask right or there'd be nothing put in your pillowcase but air) or riding bikes along the sidewalk (leave room for the pedestrians and cut out those crazy handlebar tricks).

With her customers, though, Betsy was another woman. Effusive and welcoming, she embodied the bed and breakfast she ran in her buxom frame, quirky shoes and hats, and endless supply of food. The entire Victorian house was decked out for Christmas, with little elves hanging from the crown molding, dozens of kitschy Santas in every nook, bright reindeer-decorated towels and even a reindeer-head umbrella holder. Jenna heard Betsy had started dating Earl Klein last year. Jenna wondered if finding love with the irascible garage mechanic had softened Betsy.

If it had, that softening was nowhere to be found today.

"You know I only called you because your aunt practically strong-armed me into it." Betsy frowned.

Well. Betsy knew how to get right to the heart of the matter. Jenna swallowed. "I appreciate the opportunity—"

Betsy waved off Jenna's words. "Mabel says you're good at your job. I don't know about that. I am not impressed so far."

Jenna thought of the hours she had put into the party proposal. The time she'd spent trying to think of a unique menu, memorable centerpieces, quirky favors. She'd spent a half a day alone tracking down a vendor who could make a cake that would include a mechanical calliope in the center, one of the things Jenna had heard Eunice really enjoyed in her childhood. "I have lots of ideas that I think—"

"I know what you think." Betsy eyed Jenna. "You come in here, in your fancy New York clothes—"

At that, Jenna regretted choosing the Chanel suit and Jimmy Choo stilettos for the meeting. She'd thought the outfit would spell *successful, competent*. If anything, from that first step up the walkway in the designer shoes, she had probably alienated Betsy.

"—and think people like us need someone like you to show us what a good party is."

"I never said—"

"You left this town, and I think you forgot what it's like here. People around these parts don't want something like this," Betsy said, waving at the thick blue presentation folder emblazoned with the logo for Jenna's company, Extravagant Events. "Folks here aren't that fancy. I've been in the business of serving meals and making people happy for more than two decades, and one thing I learned long ago is that people come here because they like plain, simple food. That's what Riverbend is all about. *Plain and simple.*"

Jenna shifted in her seat. Had she really thought this would be easy? That she could come in here, and Betsy would welcome her with open arms? "Miss Williams, roasted Cornish game hens are simple."

"Maybe where you are, but not here." She shook her head. "If folks can't walk into the local SuperSaver and buy it, they sure as tooting aren't going to know what to do with it if they see it on their plate. Why, they'll say you've got pigeons on a plate." She pushed the folder back toward Jenna, then crossed her arms over her chest. "You'll have to serve something else."

"If you don't want the Cornish game hens, perhaps we could have a veal piccata or—"

"Do you know the only reason why the family decided to hire you?" Betsy didn't wait for an answer. She leaned forward, her light blue eyes sharp and direct. "It wasn't just because your aunt was blowing your horn. It was because you're a local and locals know what Riverbend folks like."

Jenna didn't bother mentioning that she had left Riverbend years ago. That she'd never felt like a local, not in all the years she'd lived in town. Even after she had moved from the farm and into that yellow house with Aunt Mabel when she was seven, she'd always felt caught between two worlds—the one that had been taken from her in an instant and the new one she was expected to adjust to as easily as a duck slipping into a pond. A world filled with whispers and innuendos.

She kept mum about the truth—that she wouldn't return to living here if it was the last town on earth. And that she'd only taken this job because she hoped for a glowing recommendation she could use to rebuild her business in New York. "I appreciate that, Miss Williams."

The front door opened and Earl Klein stepped inside, ushering in a blast of winter's cold with him. He shook the snow off his ball cap, wiped it from his jacket. "You wait right there, Earl Klein, and wipe your feet," Betsy said. "I won't have you tracking the outside in with those monstrous clodhoppers of yours."

Earl scowled, but did as Betsy ordered, going so far as to take off his boots and set them by the umbrella rack. He hung up his coat, then crossed to Betsy's side and pressed a loud, smacking kiss on her cheek.

She gasped and slapped him on the arm. "Earl!"

"And hello to you, too." He grinned, then plopped onto the sofa beside her, his lanky frame dwarfing the rose patterned loveseat. He took off his grease-stained "Earl's Garage" ball cap, went to set it on the coffee table, then saw Betsy's horrified glare, and dropped it on his lap instead. He ran a hand through his gray hair, making what was already a mess into a disaster. "Why, if it isn't Jenna Pearson," he said with a friendly grin directed Jenna's way. "Been a long time since you been back to this town."

"It has," Jenna said. At least someone was happy to see her.

"Well, we're glad you're here. Riverbend could use a blow-out bash," Earl said. "And I reckon you're the right one to do it."

Betsy harrumphed.

"Now, Miss Williams, back to the menu," Jenna said, opening the folder and pointing to the list of entrée options. "We could also try—"

"A hog roast," Earl cut in. "Get a big fat porker from Chuck Miller's farm. Slap that baby on a spit, stick an apple in its mouth and wham-bam, dinner is done."

"A hog roast?" Jenna repeated. Surely she'd heard him wrong. They couldn't possibly think a hog roast would be appropriate for an event like this. For one, how on earth would she get a spit and a several-hundred-pound pig into the hall? And moreover, why would she want to? "Mr. Klein, this will be a slightly formal affair and—"

"First off," Earl said, leaning forward so far his knees bumped the coffee table, "don't call me Mr. Klein. I've known you practically since you were running down the sidewalk in a diaper, Jenna Pearson, and you've always called me Earl. I don't go for that fancy Mister thing. A man's name should be one word, not two."

The composure that had traveled with her from New York began to slip, not that she'd had such a firm hold on it lately. For years, Jenna had trained herself to be professional, calm, collected. To be a woman firmly in charge of her business and the situation. But in the past few months, that control had slipped out of her grasp, and now, with Betsy glaring at her and Earl throwing out crazy ideas, the last vestiges of control slipped away.

She bit her lip. Refused to cry. Refused to be anything but the can-do party planner she used to be. "Mr…uh, Earl, I really think we should consider something a little more… sit-down for Eunice's birthday party."

"Hell, you sit down to eat your roasted hog, don't you?"

"Yes, but—"

"And Eunice loves pork. Don't she, Betsy?"

Betsy nodded. With enthusiasm. "She does indeed. We all do."

Jenna had come to Riverbend with a nice, neat, typed and comb-bound idea of Eunice Dresden's birthday party. When she'd talked to Betsy on the phone two weeks ago, she'd thought they'd been on the same page. Granted, Betsy had been cantankerous and unsure she wanted Jenna in charge of Eunice's party, but Jenna had been sure once she presented the ideas, Betsy would come around. Somehow, she needed to get this derailed party back on track, without entrées that still had their heads and hooves attached. "I'm not sure a hog roast would work at the Riverbend Function Hall," Jenna said. "It's not quite the location for that kind of thing, and I'm not sure it fits the theme that we decided upon, the one that would celebrate the different decades of Eunice's life. However, we could have something simpler. Italian food, for instance. A nice lasagna—"

"Stockton Grisham!" The name exploded from Betsy's lips, echoed by a slap of her palm against her thigh.

"Stockton Grisham?" His name echoed in Jenna's mind, sent a tingle down her spine—one that she ignored. She'd intended to get through her entire trip without ever mentioning him, and here she'd been in Riverbend less than twenty-four hours and he'd already been the subject of conversation twice.

For a man she'd worked hard to forget, he seemed to be in her every thought. Or at least determined to be there.

"Good idea," Earl said, planting another noisy kiss on Betsy's cheek. She slapped his arm, then blushed. He crooked a grin at her, one that cemented a dimple in his left chin. He scooted his wiry frame a few inches closer to Betsy. "That boy can cook."

"Uh, I don't think—"

"Then it's settled," Betsy said, in that no-argument way she had. "Stockton will make the food. Oh, Eunice is going to be so pleased. She loves Stockton's cooking."

Earl nodded. "Stockton's the only one who can make food Eunice will eat, even when she forgets her teeth at home."

Jenna spent another ten minutes arguing against the use of Stockton as a caterer, but Betsy and Earl were adamant. They were sure no one could cook for the locals like one of their own. "I guess Stockton is our chef," she said finally, biting back a sigh.

A smile spread across Betsy's face, the kind of self-satisfied smile a cat might have once it had a mouse firmly under its paw. "Eunice is my sister, and she means everything to me. You *will* make sure she has the best birthday ever, or you'll never plan another party in this town again."

"It'll be fine," Jenna said. It would, wouldn't it? After all, she'd planned hundreds of parties. She had the experience. It was the confidence that had deserted her in recent months.

She *could* do this. She *would* do this. And in the process, show Betsy and the rest of Riverbend she was more than they'd ever expected her to be.

"Glad to hear it." Betsy patted Jenna's knee. "And I'm so glad Stockton will be a part of this. If anyone knows how to make a woman happy, it's him."

Jenna bit back her disagreement. She needed this job more than she needed to be right.

CHAPTER TWO

"We're closed," Stockton called out when he heard the front door of Rustica open. "Come back at eleven, when we start serving lunch."

"I'm not here to eat."

Even from all the way in the back of the restaurant, Stockton recognized the voice. Heard the familiar husky notes. Even now, even after everything, his pulse quickened. Damn.

Stockton took his time laying the ladle in his hands onto the stainless steel counter and removing the apron tied around his waist, before he pushed through the double doors of the kitchen and out into the dining room. And saw her.

Jenna.

His gaze started at the bottom and worked its way up, gliding over the knee-high black leather boots hugging her calves, past the dark green sweater dress clinging to her curves, lingering on the smooth length of her black hair—she'd let it grow out, and now the silky tendrils danced over her shoulders, begging to be touched—and then, finally coming to rest on her heart-shaped face. Big green eyes, the color of jade, and dark red lips that he knew from experience tasted like honey.

She was still beautiful. And undoubtedly still trouble.

The kind of woman who wanted more out of him than he could give.

"Jenna." Her name was almost a whisper, scraping past his throat with the rawness of a word that hadn't been spoken in years. He cleared his throat, tried that again. Why was he still so affected by her? It had to be the passage of time, the shock of seeing her. Nothing more. "How can I help you? Do you need a reservation?"

"I need a chef," she said. "And according to Betsy and Earl, you're the one I should be talking to."

The words were as devoid of emotion as a recipe book. He should have been glad. Their relationship had been over for years, and he wanted to keep it that way. He had his hands full with the restaurant. But for some reason, Jenna's business-like approach ticked him off. "I'm too busy right now to take on anything extra. Thanks for the offer, though." He turned and went back into his kitchen.

The warm, expansive space wrapped around him. The rich scent of fresh spaghetti sauce carried on the air, married by the warm, sweet notes of baking bread. He had chosen every countertop, every plate, every fork, himself. When he walked into Rustica every morning, he knew this place was his. Every inch of it.

The restaurant brought him a solace he hadn't found anywhere else, a peace he wasn't even aware he needed until he held it in his soul.

He'd loved food all his life, and on the rare occasions when his father was home, the two of them had bonded, not over a football in the backyard, but over a plate of lasagna in the kitchen. Stockton had begged his father to let him try his hand with some of the dishes, but Hank Grisham was firm about one thing—the kitchen was his domain, and no one was allowed to handle so much as a ladle but him.

Now Stockton had his own kitchen, and though he didn't ascribe to the same theories as his father, he understood the love Hank had had for his kitchen. Working at Rustica wasn't his job, it was his passion. His days here filled the holes in his nights, gave him something to look forward to, a vocation that completely suited him. He had a job he loved, a business that was doing well, and enough friends and family to fill a boat.

Now Jenna Pearson had walked into his restaurant and disrupted that quiet peace he'd spent years attaining.

The kitchen door swung open with a slight squeak. "You have to take this job, Stockton. I..." She hesitated.

He waited.

"I need you." The three words hung in the air. Her gaze darted away from his and lighted on the stainless steel countertops. "To work for me, I mean."

"Of course. What else could you mean?"

She jerked her attention back to him, a fiery flash in her green eyes. "This is business, pure and simple. I'm planning a party for Eunice Dresden's birthday, and I need a caterer."

He retied the apron around his waist, grabbed a kitchen towel and then crossed to one of the massive ovens to peek inside at the baking bread. Better that than to look at her and say what he really wanted to say—that she had never been about anything other than her career and her future when they'd been together. That her heart had been as remote as the other side of the world, and that distance had kept them from ever becoming truly close. He had no intentions of wrapping himself in that vicious, pointless circle again. "Since I own this place, I choose who I do business with." He withdrew the loaves, then set them on racks to cool. "Today, that's not you."

"Why are you being difficult?"

Because he hadn't been prepared for Jenna Pearson to walk through his front door. Because he knew if he took this job, he'd be spending hours with her. And most of all, because he knew where spending hours with her could lead—to rehashing a past he'd done a darn good job forgetting. He was his father's son in one way—he could whip up a killer coq au vin, but he couldn't make a mixture of business and relationships work.

"It's not a good idea for us to work together." He closed the oven door, then faced her. "Don't you remember how badly things ended between us?"

"That was different. We were young and foolish…and made rash decisions."

Rash decisions. His mind rocketed back to a heady weekend they'd spent in Chicago, a single night of insanity that had been the culmination of a long, hot summer. The last summer before the start of college, the summer he'd thought they were moving forward, when really, they'd been moving apart. An image of Jenna, nestled in the fluffy white comforter that had covered the hotel room bed, her dark hair spread out in an airy cloud around her head, intruded on his mind. He could still smell the vanilla notes of her perfume, a scent that had dusted every surface of the room. Could still feel the hope he'd felt that weekend, before everything had changed.

"I remember," he said, and pushed the memory aside. "I remember everything, Jenna. Do you?"

She ignored the question. "Working together would be different."

He closed the distance between them. "Would it? Really?"

Her chin jutted up. "Of course."

He told himself it would be, that he could provide the food for Eunice's party and not get wrapped up in Jenna again, and was about to say exactly that, when he drew in a breath, and with it, the scent of her perfume. Warm, spicy—

And exactly the same. Every inch of him wanted to trail a kiss along her throat, to taste her skin again. To feel her in his arms, to have Jenna against him. To make a mistake he knew would be monumental.

It had taken him a long time to get over her after they'd broken up. To give up the dream of a future that was never going to happen. To realize that being with her had nearly derailed him from his own plans. And most of all, to realize that if he had stayed with her, he would have ruined her life, as surely as his father had ruined his mother's.

"I don't have time," he said. It was a lie. He could easily make the time if he wanted to.

Operative words—*if* he wanted to.

"Because it's Rustica's first anniversary this month?" She gestured toward the dining room. "I saw the sign."

He'd hung a banner yesterday announcing the restaurant's birthday, and inviting the patrons to a celebration dinner on New Year's Eve. And while, yes, he'd be insanely busy with that, it wasn't the reason he was avoiding her job. Rather than tell Jenna the truth, he leapt on the handy excuse. "That party will consume a lot of my time. I'm sure you can find another caterer in Indianapolis."

Jenna pursed her lips, and crossed her arms over her chest. Avoiding her gaze, he turned out the bread loaves, then put another half dozen balls of dough into bread pans and slid those into the oven. The heat hit him in a thick wave, ebbing when he shut the heavy door again.

"What if I helped?" Jenna said.

Stockton chuckled. "You? Helping me? Cook?"

She shrugged. "I can cook."

"This isn't home ec, Jenna. It's real life." The words came out harsher than he'd intended.

Her gaze darted to the wall of spices, then returned to him. "What about planning your anniversary party? I'm sure you could use a hand with that."

Undoubtedly, Samantha had planted the same seed in Jenna's mind yesterday. "I'm fine. All under control. If I need help, I'll call—"

"This job is important to me, Stockton." She bit her lip, an action he knew meant she was worried. "I really want Eunice's party to go perfectly. It's going to be a huge event, for the whole town."

"Why do you care so much?" He pushed off from the counter and neared her, until he could see the gold flecks in her emerald eyes. Once, her gaze would have affected him. Made him find a way to compromise, to coax a smile from her lips. Those days were over. "Last I knew, you wanted to stay as far from this town as possible."

And me, but he didn't add that.

"Because..." She took in a breath, let it out, and he got the feeling whatever she was about to say was coming from some place deep inside her that she rarely visited, that side of herself that held the honest assessment of her life. He'd known Jenna Pearson since first grade, and knew she wasn't a woman who liked self-analysis. "Because I want to prove to this town that I made it, that my business is capable and successful."

Something in her words didn't ring true, but he couldn't figure out what. "And you had to leave New York to do that?"

A frown knitted her brows. "I'm here, and I need a caterer. That's really all you need to know."

"I hope you find someone," he said, returning to his sauces. "Whatever caterer you use, Eunice will undoubtedly be happy with the food. Because last I checked, it was the thought that counted when it came to parties, not the lasagna."

Jenna sat at one of the small rectangular tables in the dining room of Rustica, a hot cup of coffee she'd poured herself sitting on the white linen tablecloth. Delicate tendrils of steam filled the air. The steam only added to the tension still hanging in the air, a storm she'd stirred up from the minute she saw Stockton Grisham again.

Drat that man. Even after all these years apart, he could still push the wrong buttons.

She should have left. Should have gone down to Indianapolis and found another caterer, as Stockton had told her to. Hell, she shouldn't have come here in the first place, knowing she'd see him again.

She had to admit, Stockton had done an amazing job with the restaurant. It embodied his personality, yet maintained an authentic Italian feel. Rustica's décor was filled with rich russet hues, offset by the antique water jugs lining a shelf near the ceiling, and the multicolored hand-made round platters mounted above the booths. Stockton had created a warm, inviting atmosphere. Not too dark, not too light and definitely not too kitschy. No wonder he'd been such a success.

If she'd been another person, she would have been envious that he had made it—and she had lost what success she'd had. But she wasn't. She'd known Stockton forever, and his success was well-deserved. It was what he had wanted—what he had always wanted.

More than he'd wanted her.

She shrugged off the thoughts. She didn't have time to dwell on the past. She toyed with the hot mug, and considered her options. It didn't take long. She had none.

Her business in New York was nearly defunct. The last few jobs had been disasters, with one thing after another going wrong. Caterers who didn't show up, florists who delivered the wrong stems, bands whose music disappointed. The word hadn't taken long to spread, and before she knew it, her growing party planning business was almost dead.

Somewhere along the way, she'd lost her mojo. Every day, she woke up, faced the mirror and told herself that the pity party was over. That she would get this business, and by extension, her life, back on track.

But for some reason Jenna couldn't pinpoint, she kept derailing. Her passion for party planning had deflated, and every time she tried to go back to the way things had been before—before the day that turned her life upside down—she got even more lost.

She glanced at the closed kitchen door and decided no more. She would turn things around with this party. No matter what. Jenna got to her feet, crossed to the unattended bar and poured herself another cup of coffee.

"I thought you were leaving."

Stockton's voice drew her up. She took her time returning to the table. "You're the one Eunice wants. I'm not leaving until we've arrived at equitable terms."

Stockton laughed, the sound sharp and bitter. "Equitable terms? Is that we're doing now? Working out a contract?"

"I like to work with a contract. It's standard business practice."

He placed his hands on the table and leaned so close, she couldn't help but inhale the woodsy notes of his cologne. Not the same scent as before, and she had to wonder who had picked out the new cologne. A wife? No, his left hand was bare. A girlfriend? Or Stockton himself?

"Nothing between us has ever been standard. Or

business-like," Stockton said. Jenna started to speak and he stopped her by laying a piece of paper on the table. "I assume you aren't as familiar with this area as you used to be—" he paused a beat, long enough to make sure she got the hidden meaning, that she had been away too long to know much about anything or anyone here in Riverbend "—and so I took the liberty of writing down the names of a few chefs I would recommend. I suggest you call one of them." He picked up her still full coffee cup and left the room. The double doors of the kitchen swung into place with a deep thud-thud.

Jenna glanced at the list. She considered picking it up, and taking the easy way out by calling someone else. Her hand hovered over the white sheet, but in the end, she left it where it was. Eunice and Betsy wanted Stockton. If pleasing the client meant getting Stockton to agree, then that was what she'd have to do. Clearly, it was going to take more work than she'd expected.

Jenna grabbed her purse and walked out of Rustica. It wouldn't do any good to stay and keep arguing with him. She needed time to think, to figure out a way to bring Stockton around to her point of view.

Had she really thought it would be that easy? That she could just walk in there and convince Stockton to do what she wanted, as if they had never dated? Never had that turbulent breakup?

Jenna drove the few miles from Rustica to her aunt's house and worked on a plan. There had to be something she could leverage with Stockton. As she pulled into the driveway, she flipped out her cell, first dialing the number for her business voice mail. Maybe there'd be good news. A bunch of potential clients interested in booking parties through her, or a satisfied customer leaving a recommendation. But no...there were only two messages, one from a creditor and one from a client—canceling her upcoming anniversary event, the only other booking on Jenna's calendar for the next three months. Through the woman's sobs, Jenna gathered the marriage was over, and thus, the need for a tenth-anniversary party was, too.

Deep breath. This wasn't the end of the world. She had a booked event right here in Riverbend. One that would be a success, on every level.

With that newly cemented resolve in place, Jenna placed another call. A moment later, a cheery hello greeted her. "Livia. I'm so glad you're home." Of course, where else would Livia be? She used to work for Jenna, until business dried up, and she'd been forced to let her assistant go last week.

Olivia Perkins laughed, a light airy sound that seemed a million miles away from the worries crowding Jenna's shoulders. "Hey, Jenna! I've been wondering how you were faring in the backwoods of Indiana."

"Riverbend's not exactly the backwoods. We have a stoplight."

"A stoplight? As in one?" She could hear Livia shaking her head on the other end. "Tell me you at least have running water and electricity."

"Oh, no. It's all water pumps and gas lanterns here."

Livia laughed again. "Remind me never to vacation there."

"Actually..." Jenna let out a breath. "I was hoping you'd fly in and help me out."

"I thought you said this was a job you could handle with one hand tied behind your back."

She'd said that—before she'd encountered Betsy's resistance. Before she'd realized she'd be working with Stockton Grisham. And before her entire plan for the party had blown up before she got so much as one napkin in place.

A part of her worried that this simple birthday party would fall apart, just like the Martin wedding and the Turner Insurance Christmas party. And her plans for her great comeback would derail, as surely as her business had in the past few months. Her confidence, which used to be as solid as granite, had been shaken over the past few months, and she couldn't seem to get it back.

Damn it, she would. She refused to let this...this *funk*... last another minute.

"You're right," she told Livia. "This job's a piece of cake. I just had a crazy moment of doubt."

"Aw, Jenna, that's normal. You'll be fine, I'm sure."

"Thanks for the vote of confidence." Jenna ran a hand through her hair. Outside her car, a light snow began to fall. Snowflakes danced across the glass then slid onto the wipers. "Once I convince the caterer that working with us is in his best interests, it'll be downhill from there."

"Show him some of that Jenna Pearson determination. The same moxie you used to build your business. That man will be putty in your hands."

Jenna let out a laugh. "You haven't met Stockton Grisham. He's not so easily swayed." A tightness grew in her gut at the mention of his name. Why did she care? The last thing she'd come to Riverbend for was to reopen old wounds and past relationships. Work—that was her only focus.

On the other end of the phone, Jenna heard the click of keys on a keyboard, and Livia hmm-hmming for a moment. "It's probably not much help, but how about I come down on New Year's Eve?"

"Don't you have some hot date in the city?"

Livia sighed. "No. I broke up with Paul last week. I'm officially single again."

"Sorry, Liv."

"I'm not. Who needs a guy who looks in the mirror more than he does at his date?" Livia laughed. "Hey, you never know. I might just find Mr. Right in your one-stoplight town."

"If you do, let me know." Maybe Livia would have better odds than Jenna, who'd only found Mr. Definitely-not-Right here.

"No problem," Livia said. "I'll see you at the airport on New Year's Eve. Until then, chin up. You'll do fine."

The support rallied Jenna's flagging spirits. She could tackle this—and definitely tackle the Stockton Grisham... problem. "Thanks, Livia. You're the best."

"No," Livia said softly. "Just a good friend who knows when another friend is in trouble. Even if she doesn't want to admit it."

CHAPTER THREE

STOCKTON THOUGHT HE had seen the last of Jenna. Hell, he'd thought that eight years ago, and clearly he'd been wrong. Because she was back in his restaurant again. After yesterday, he was sure she'd abandon this insane plan of having him work with her.

Not that he wouldn't love to give Eunice, one of his favorite customers, a birthday to remember. And in the process, secure a little more business for Rustica, and spread the restaurant's name with the guests at the party, many of whom were undoubtedly coming in from out of town. Even though the restaurant had had a successful first year, it never hurt to keep growing the business. A party like Eunice's, filled with people who hadn't yet tried Rustica, could do that.

It wasn't the job itself, or the money he'd make, it was the price he'd have to pay—working side by side with Jenna for several days. Remembering how things used to be, how he'd once hoped for a future with her, and how badly things had soured. Surely she could find a caterer in Indiana she didn't share a history with. He'd go back to concentrating on his restaurant, and she'd eventually go back to New York—and he'd forget all about her again.

The plan sounded good in theory. But as his front door opened and Jenna walked into his restaurant for the second time in two days, he realized a plan was no good unless it was executed by both parties. Clearly, Jenna was reading from a different plan book than him.

She strode up to him, fire in her eyes, a set to her jaw that he knew as well as he knew his own name. He'd seen that same look back in high school when she'd had control of the ball on the soccer field, and blown past four opponents like she was brushing mosquitoes off her shoulder. The same look she used to get on her face when she'd been on the debate team and up against a particularly daunting opponent. The same look that had come over her face when she'd applied for a job at a banquet hall in a nearby town and the owner had told her she didn't have what it took to work in event planning. Stockton knew that look meant one thing—

She wasn't leaving here until she had what she wanted.

"I know what you said yesterday, but I'd like you to reconsider." She held up a hand to cut off his protests. "If you provide the food for this party, it would be great for your business."

"You said that yesterday. And I told you then that my business is doing just fine, thank you."

"Every business could stand to grow and expand its customer base."

He leaned back against the smooth oak surface of Rustica's bar and crossed his arms over his chest. He forced his gaze to her face, away from the enticing curves beneath her black V-neck blouse and dark skirt. Everything she was wearing was more suitable for a boardroom than a few days in Riverbend, where casual attire ruled the day, but he'd be lying if he said he wasn't intrigued by the understated sexiness in her clothing choices. She had on high-heeled black pumps that seemed to beg a man to keep his attention on her legs. Beg every man but him. "Even your business?"

"Well, of course." A flush filled her cheeks, then she shook her head and seemed to will the crimson from her face.

Stockton leaned forward, waiting until her gaze met his. In those deep green depths, he saw something he had missed the day before.

A lie.

"Why are you really doing this party?"

"Because Betsy wants her sister to have a happy birthday."

"You've never much cared for Betsy. Or she for you, if I remember my Halloweens correctly. And from the scuttlebutt I hear around town, she's not too keen on the idea of you running this shindig."

Jenna looked away. "The people in this town have always liked to talk."

Regret rocketed through him. His mouth had gotten away from his brain, and he needed to reel it back in. Jenna Pearson, of all people, wouldn't want to hear what the busybodies of this town had to say. Still, for her to battle such odds, there had to be something more than a party behind her return to Riverbend. "Tell me the real reason you're here."

That lower jaw set again, and a muscle ticked in her cheeks. She was fuming, but she wasn't going to show it to him. "Because I haven't seen my aunt in forever, and this seemed like a great opportunity to come back and visit with her."

"Half the truth," Stockton said, "is not the same as the full truth."

"I do have a job catering Eunice's birthday party. I did

think it would be nice to see my aunt again. It's a win-win. Nothing more."

He could see the lie in her eyes. Hear it in the strain in her voice. But why? And about what? He thought of pressing her on it, then decided to drop the subject. "Did you call any of the other caterers on the list I gave you?" He already knew that answer—after she left, he'd noticed the paper still sitting on the table.

She shook her head. "I don't want any of them. I want you."

The words slammed into him with a fierce electric rush. In Chicago all those years ago, he'd heard her whisper those same words in his ear, then she'd kissed a trail down his throat, over his chest, until he hauled her up into his arms and off to bed.

But the reasons why she'd said them then, and why she was now, were very, very different.

"I'm not available," he said.

Were they talking about business? Or something more?

"Stockton!"

He pivoted. Grace, the hostess, was standing in the kitchen, waving at him from across the room. "What's up?"

"Larry called in sick *again*." She made a little face, then ducked back into the kitchen to avoid the coming storm.

Stockton cursed. Three times in one week. "That man better have a fatal disease," he called to Grace, even though she was already gone. He turned back to Jenna. "I have to go."

"Wait!" Before he could walk away, Jenna lay a hand on his arm. The touch seared his skin, sent his hormones tumbling through his veins and rocketed his mind back again to the first and only time they'd made love.

Images of Jenna's naked body beneath his, her skin warm against his chest, his legs, flashed in his mind. He pushed the thoughts away. Thinking of the past would do him no good. Not now.

Not ever.

He glanced down at her delicate hand, firm on his arm. As if she realized what she'd done, Jenna jerked away. "I have to get into the kitchen," he said.

"What if...what if I helped?"

"Helped what?"

"Fill Larry's shoes. Just for tonight."

He smirked. "You. Do Larry's job."

"Sure. I mean, I waited tables in college for a couple months. It can't be that much different from—"

"Larry is my sous chef."

"Oh." Her eyes widened, and she took a half-step back. "Oh, well..."

"Exactly. Now, if you'll excuse me—"

Her hand latched on to his arm again. Why did something so simple still affect him? Half of him wanted to turn around and crush her to his chest, the other half wanted to fling off her hand and tell her not to open a Pandora's Box she didn't intend to shut again.

He did neither.

"I may not be the best sous chef in the world, but I'm sure I can be more of a help in the kitchen than not having a right hand man at all. And, I'll throw in free party-planning advice for your anniversary event. Surely, you can't turn down an offer like that." She shot him a tempting grin.

"And what, I'd owe you after that?" He shook his head, and tugged his arm out of her hand. "I don't think so. I know you, Jenna. You make it sound like you're here to help me out, but really, you're just running your own agenda."

She winced, and he wanted to take the words back, but

they were out there. The harsh truth, in broad daylight. "It's just one dinner service, Stockton. Nothing more."

He was about to say no, and in fact had the syllable formed on his tongue, when he thought of the night ahead. One that would surely be insanely fast-paced, as had the night before.

At least it was Thursday. It would undoubtedly be busy—the longer the week wore on, the busier the restaurant got, and with it being the holidays, people were in more often during the week. If Larry missed Friday, or Saturday, or worse, Sunday—New Year's Eve—well, Stockton wasn't going to think about that. Midweek was bad enough to be down an essential pair of hands.

Last night, Stockton had run the kitchen single-handedly, overworking the two prep chefs and himself trying to keep the orders moving in a timely manner, but they'd done it and managed not to screw up any orders. Stockton had gone home exhausted and cranky, as had the rest of the overworked staff. A second night of the same didn't sound appealing at all. Not to mention the reaction of the prep chefs when they found out they'd be doing double duty again. With the anniversary party so near, he couldn't afford to lose any of his help. Nor did he have time to interview and hire someone else.

"You can't cook," he said to Jenna.

"I'm not as bad as you remember," she said, and a part of him wondered again if they were talking about cooking or something else. "Let me help you, Stockton."

He could almost believe she was sincere, if he tried hard enough. But he knew Jenna Pearson—and knew she wasn't making the offer out of the goodness of her heart. She wanted to butter him up to convince him to say yes to catering Eunice's party. Or maybe something more.

The kitchen door banged open, and Denny, one of the

prep chefs, came storming into the front of the house. "Don't tell me we're shorthanded again tonight. I swear, I'm going to go to Larry's house and drag him—"

"We won't be shorthanded," Stockton said. The decision formed in his head. Whether he liked it or not, he had to take the deal on the table. He couldn't afford another night like last night.

"Larry showed up?"

"No," Stockton said, then turned to Jenna and gave her a short nod. "I hired some help. *Temporary* help."

Denny looked between Stockton and Jenna, taking in the ruffled blouse, the snug fit skirt, her high heels, none of which were appropriate for the hot, busy kitchen. He arched a brow in disbelief, then shrugged. "Whatever you say, boss." He hurried back into the kitchen, undoubtedly to tell the rest of the staff that the head chef had gone crazy.

"So we have a deal?" Jenna asked.

"First, you go home and change into something appropriate for the kitchen. Sneakers, a T-shirt. Put your hair back. Then come back here, ready to work."

"I didn't bring anything like that with me."

"You won't last five minutes in my kitchen in that," he said, waving at her skirt and heels. "And you should know by now that you won't last long in Riverbend looking like you walked off the pages of a fashion magazine."

She opened her mouth to argue. Shut it again. "I'll buy something else to wear."

"Good. Be here at four."

"Do you promise you'll let me talk to you about catering for Eunice's birthday party?"

"We'll see how you work out," he said, already wondering if he'd made the right decision. Jenna, in his kitchen, underfoot, all night? What had he been thinking? "I like my help to have staying power. And not run at the first sign of confrontation."

Her gaze narrowed, and he knew she realized he wasn't talking about cooking. "Unlike other people I know," she said, "you can depend on me, Stockton." She gathered up her coat and purse, and twisted her scarf around her neck. "More than you think."

Betsy was waiting in Aunt Mabel's kitchen. She looked like a Christmas tree gone awry, with her bright green sweater topped by embroidered silver snowflakes, and a matching pair of fleece pants. The only thing lacking from her festive attire was a smile. Dread filled Jenna's chest.

She took a deep breath. These were the people who had known her all her life, not ordinary clients. Whatever they had to say she could handle. For goodness' sake, it was a birthday party, not a wedding for five hundred.

"There's been a…development." Betsy took a sip from her mug and eyed Jenna over the porcelain rim. Outside, snow began to fall. Fluffy white flakes danced on the slight breeze, kissed the windows, then dropped away.

"A development?" Jenna forced a smile to her face, and took the seat opposite Betsy.

Aunt Mabel poured Jenna a cup of coffee and joined the other two. "Now, Betsy, don't exaggerate," she said. "This is hardly a problem."

Betsy pursed her lips. "I disagree. We need to rethink the entire event."

"Whatever the issue is, Miss Williams, I'm sure we can make the necessary changes and ensure the party goes off without a—"

"What happened with the Marshall wedding?"

Oh, God. Not that one, of all events. Jenna had thought coming back to Indiana meant she could leave her business past behind, that she could get a much-needed fresh start, one she could parlay into a comeback. How had Betsy found out about the Marshall wedding?

It didn't matter—she knew, as did most of New York. The debutante's wedding that had turned into a disaster of epic proportions, and ended up starring on all the gossip pages for several days afterward. Jenna should have known better than to think she could handle such a huge event after all the others that had gone wrong. If she'd been smart, she would have handed the reins over to Livia. Stepped aside.

"That event, uh, didn't go as well as I expected," Jenna said.

"I heard that the flowers didn't arrive, and the bride's brother ended up running out to the local supermarket to get some for the corsages and things. Now, here in Indiana, maybe something as simple as store flowers might be fine. But from what I read, that wasn't what the bride pictured for her wedding at that fancy-dancy hotel."

"There was an issue with the booking date for the florist. But I solved the problem." By scrambling to find another florist she'd worked with several times before, calling in a huge favor and paying a premium to have arrangements rushed over at the last possible second.

"Did the limo driver also get the date wrong? And the caterer?" Betsy asked. "The bride was quite upset about serving pizza to her guests. At least the pizza parlor threw in free soda so people had something to drink."

Jenna remembered the bride's screaming fit—a justified reaction—and all directed at the party planner who had ruined the wedding by scheduling all the vendors for the following weekend. Jenna remembered thinking she had it all under control, that she was doing great. And then the day of the wedding arrived and proved she was as wrong as she could be.

She'd thought the next job, and the one after that, and the one after that, would bring her back to her normal, organized, Type-A self. They hadn't. If anything, the mistakes had gotten bigger, the stress blossoming larger in her chest.

And now, all those mistakes had followed her to Riverbend. The one place she'd thought she could escape from everything.

Jenna sighed, and sat back in her seat. Aunt Mabel reached out, and placed a consoling hand on her niece's shoulder. "I made a few mistakes with that one," she said, "but everything was rectified in the end."

"Is that something you do often? Make mistakes?" Betsy leaned in, and Jenna got the feeling she was a bug under a microscope, about to get squashed by the scientist's lens. "Because I looked your business up on Google this morning," Betsy went on, "and I have to say I was shocked, Jenna Pearson. Quite shocked. Your aunt told me you were a great party planner. The best, in fact."

She had been a great party planner once. And she could be again, she told herself. One success—that was all she needed. "I've had some problems in the past few months, some…issues I've been dealing with. But things are on the upswing."

"Betsy, everyone has off days," Aunt Mabel said. "You need to be more understanding."

"We all have rough days, weeks, even months, Mabel," Betsy said. "I myself have had some days that were less than sunny, but I never served my guests pizza instead of a good home-cooked meal." She pursed her lips and looked ready to cancel the party at any second.

Silence blanketed the table. Betsy was right. Jenna had

let down her clients, the people who had trusted her. These were monumental events in their lives, and she had turned them into disasters.

Maybe she had lost her touch. Maybe she shouldn't be doing this job anymore. "You're right, Miss Williams. In the past, I made several mistakes. But I'm back on my feet now, and prepared to do the best job I can with Eunice's party." She could do this, she knew she could. Especially here, in Riverbend where the expectations were less demanding, the people happy with a "plain and simple" affair, as Betsy had said. She could handle plain and simple.

And then, after the party, be ready to return to New York, to the life she used to love, the job she used to be great at, and get back on top in no time.

"I'm not so sure about that," Betsy said. "In fact, perhaps I better make backup plans just in case."

"You don't need—"

"I think I do. People say the apples don't fall from the trees. I know the tree your family comes from, Jenna Pearson, and I think—"

"Betsy!" Aunt Mabel interrupted. "That's enough."

"Fine. But you have to know I love my sister," Betsy said. "More than all the tea in China. And if she ends up eating pizza instead of Stockton's lasagna, I'll put you on toilet-cleaning duty at the bed and breakfast for the next fifty years."

CHAPTER FOUR

THE FIRST HOUR WAS the hardest. Even though both the prep cooks were already there and busy in the kitchen, Stockton's radar attuned to one station. Jenna Pearson.

Every move she made, he noted. Every time she brushed past him to reach for a spice or a utensil, he caught a whiff of her perfume. The same scent she'd worn years ago, a warm, heady perfume with notes of vanilla, cinnamon. His gaze traveled her frame more than once, and he found himself wondering if she'd feel the same in his arms, if she'd taste the same under his lips.

Then he'd stop, get a grip and get back to work. There'd be no getting wrapped up with her, not again.

In the end, she wanted things he didn't. When they'd been younger, he'd been consumed by wanderlust. He'd thought only of leaving the small, confining boundaries of Riverbend and traveling the world, thinking— Well, hell, thinking he'd find more. Find the relationship with his father that he'd always craved. Find the secret to success. After two years of traveling, he'd realized one thing. That being home was the key to all of that. For him, Riverbend was home. For Jenna, it was anything but.

It wasn't about the town. He could understand why Jenna might not want to settle here, of all places. It was that they were two weathervanes, pointing in opposite directions.

What he craved now—community, purpose, home—had never interested her. At least he'd found that out years ago, before he could make a foolish mistake that would have hurt them both in the end.

He turned back to making soup, a far safer proposition—and with far more predictable results.

He rolled up several basil leaves and danced the knife down the green bundle, creating a quick chiffonade. Then he turned and dumped the freshly cut herb into a minestrone simmering on the stove. Across the kitchen, Jenna was peeling potatoes and dropping them into a pot of cold water. The prep chefs pretended not to eavesdrop, but Stockton was no fool. The kitchen was small, and nearly every conversation became a public event.

"So, what's your plan for the anniversary party?" Jenna asked.

"I've ordered some balloons. Put the customer favorites on the menu and I hired a DJ." He stirred and tasted the soup. He sprinkled in a little more salt, gave the pepper mill a few turns, then tasted again. Perfect. He moved on to starting the vinaigrette that dressed all the house salads at Rustica.

"That's it?"

"Sounds like enough to me. It's a party, not a White House dinner."

Jenna arched a brow, the kind that said the man didn't have a clue. "If you don't mind my saying so, I think you could take it up a notch…or ten."

He whisked oil into vinegar, his movements fast, creating a smooth emulsion of flavors. As he did, he couldn't help but think about the oil and vinegar of him and Jenna. "Do you like New York?" he asked.

The change of subject took her by surprise. She stopped

peeling for a moment and looked at him. "I like it well enough. Why?"

Because I want to know if it was worth it. Because I want to know if you found there what you could never seem to find here.

Even as the thoughts danced in his mind, a part of him questioned whether he had done the same. Had he found what he'd been looking for? What he'd wandered the world to find, and come back here, thinking everything he ever wanted was here.

"Just wondering." He sprinkled in some minced fresh herbs, and whisked some more. "Must be pretty different from Riverbend."

She laughed. "Most definitely." Then she paused, the peeler poised over a fat white potato. "But in some ways, it's very much like Riverbend."

"How's that?"

"New York isn't so much a city as a collection of little neighborhoods. It's like having dozens of small towns, all butted up against each other. When you move into an apartment in SoHo or Greenwich Village or the Lower East Side, that little pocket of the city has its own flavor."

"And its own quirky residents."

A smile danced across her features. "Oh, there are plenty of those."

"Just like here."

"Yeah." The word exhaled on a breath.

He knew what she was leaving unsaid. He let the subject alone. Jenna's years in Riverbend had been tough. First with the loss of her parents, then with the whispers that had followed her around for years, a persistent shadow to her personal tragedy.

"I'm surprised you had time to come down here and do

Eunice's party," he said, shifting the subject again. "Your company must be really busy in a city like New York."

Jenna flipped the half-peeled potato over and over in her palm. "My business has been struggling for a while."

He blinked, then took a moment to absorb what she'd said. "Your business is struggling? But I thought—"

"Well, you thought wrong. Things always look different from half a country away." She bent her head and went back to peeling potatoes. Long strips of dark skins flipped away from the furious movements of her hands.

In other words, he'd been too far away from her to have a clear picture of what was going on in her life. To be expected, considering how little contact they'd had after the breakup. A Christmas card or two, a mailed-back forgotten CD, a couple of phone calls. They'd dropped off the face of each other's worlds. And though it had been painful, because he couldn't remember a day when he hadn't had Jenna in his life, it had been the best decision all around.

Except now Stockton wondered what he had been missing. When he'd gotten on the plane to Italy, he'd had one last conversation with Jenna. She'd been breezy on the phone, her plate piled high with looking for new business, catering to the clients she'd just signed. She'd landed a couple of corporate accounts right off the bat, then her first wedding, pushing her up the hill of success quickly. He'd tried to call her twice more after that, but got only her answering machine. She'd been gone, lost to the consuming power of entrepreneurship. Gone to him, if she ever was his to begin with.

Now, after owning his own business, he could understand that single-minded focus, but at the time, he'd been seriously hurt. If anything had cemented their breakup, it had been that. Jenna off in New York, moved on to a new life.

One that no longer included him.

He'd gone to Italy, staying for a while with his father and Hank's second wife, then wandered the countryside, working for pay and sometimes for free for other chefs, honing his culinary skills. It had been an adventure unlike any other, one filled with tastes and smells and good Italian hospitality. By the time he'd returned to Riverbend, he'd found his center again, and decided leaving Jenna to her life was the best decision all around.

Except…occasionally those nagging doubts returned to whisper in his ear. He'd found the perfect place for his restaurant, yes. Found success. But there was something… something intangible…lacking still. The old itch to wander returned, but Stockton shrugged it off. Running would do him no good. Especially with his business about to celebrate its anniversary.

"Italy was like that, too," he said, changing gears once again, trying to avoid the tense bumps in the conversational road. "The towns are small and cozy, and every neighborhood had its own special touch. Even its own food. The lasagna I tasted in one part of Italy was just a tiny bit different in another place."

Jenna picked up her last potato and started peeling it. "Did you spend a lot of time with your father there?"

"No."

"I thought when you left—"

"You thought wrong." He scowled. He didn't like unrest in his kitchen, and now here he was, causing plenty of it. Regret flooded him. "I'm sorry. It's just my father has never been what I'd call supportive."

"I heard he owns a restaurant in Italy now."

Stockton nodded. "He thinks the only place you can have a truly successful restaurant is in either a big city or a country dedicated to culinary excellence. Indiana doesn't fit the bill in either of those categories."

"He's never been to Rustica?"

Stockton shook his head. "I suppose he doesn't want me to prove him wrong."

"If you ask me, he's the one who's missing out. It's a great restaurant, Stockton. The food is amazing. I want to eat everything that leaves this kitchen." She paused, and her gaze met his. "You've really done it."

"Thank you."

She fiddled with the potato peeler. Behind him, Stockton heard the bustle of the kitchen as the staff readied the restaurant for the night's onslaught. "Why did you choose Riverbend, though? You could have opened a restaurant anywhere. Even…New York."

Where she had been. He could hear the underlying question—why hadn't he followed her to the big city and embarked on his dream there? He, the one who had all that urge to travel, and had ultimately ended up back at where they'd both started? "Because I didn't have any ties to New York."

The truth sat there between them, cold and stark. He wanted to take it back, make up something else, but he didn't.

"Of course," Jenna said, and went back to the potatoes.

"It was more than that," Stockton went on, and wondered why it was suddenly so important to him that Jenna understood. "I love this town. I used to think my father was right, that the only place to have a truly successful restaurant was in the heart of a city or a renowned culinary country. But the more I traveled, the more I realized one thing."

She paused in her work. "What's that?"

"That what makes a restaurant successful isn't just the food or the location. It's the people who patronize it. A good chef learns to listen to his customers, and in turn, they shape the menu, the décor, but more, the mood. I always wanted a restaurant where everyone could feel at home."

"A neighborhood destination?"

He nodded. "Exactly." He thought of his father again and how Hank would never understand Stockton's approach to business. Hank was a man who couldn't even invite his own family into his kitchen. He'd never see the joy of letting the customers shape the restaurant.

"But there are a lot bigger markets out there than Riverbend, Indiana," Jenna said.

"There are. I've visited many of them, worked in a few. The more I did that, though, the more I realized this is exactly the size success I wanted, Jenna. Not everyone wants to be the biggest." He waved to indicate the restaurant beyond the double doors of the kitchen, with its intimate tables, soft lighting, amber tones. "This is exactly what I always dreamed of having. Not too big, and just busy enough to pay the bills but still let me have a life. Someday, I'll be able to settle down, have a family."

Then why had he avoided that so far? Why had he shied away from serious relationships?

Jenna fiddled with the peeler, spinning it round and round in her fingers. "So, you have everything you want now?"

"Pretty much." He dismissed the questions in his mind, then met her gaze. "The question is whether you do."

"Whether I what?"

"Have everything you want." A breath passed between them. "Do you, Jenna?"

She glanced away, quickly. "Uh, the last potato is done. I better get these on the stove for you." She dropped the peeler to the counter and went to lift the heavy pot onto the counter. Stockton crossed to her, his hands going to the handles. They touched, and he lifted his gaze to hers. Damn, she was still beautiful. Still had that way of looking at him that seemed to peer into his soul. Their fingers held the contact a moment longer, then Jenna broke away. "Thanks."

"It's nothing." Who was he trying to convince? Himself? Or her?

"Please cater Eunice's party," Jenna said. "I need you to do this for me, Stockton, regardless of everything between us."

Here they were, back to business again. In the comfort zone both of them liked to maintain.

He wanted to say no. He'd already spent an hour in the kitchen with her, and the whole time, a simmering tension had hung in the air. All those tangled threads that came with sharing a past with someone. If they spent enough time together, eventually one of them would be tempted to pick up a thread.

But as he looked at her, standing a few feet away, he noticed a tension in her shoulders, a worried line across her brow. He suspected she'd understated the trouble her business was in, especially if she'd taken a job here, of all places.

She needed him, she'd said. He'd never thought he'd hear those words from her again. And this week, he'd heard it twice.

The first time she'd said she needed him, he thought it had been a ploy. But now, reading Jenna's body language and the unspoken words in her tone, he realized she was telling the truth. It was more than to help out her struggling business, he suspected, but what more he couldn't discern.

The spurned lover in him could easily say no, just because. But he thought of how hard she had worked to convince him to say yes, and how much it must have taken to come to him, of all people, for help. Once, they had been friends, and that long-held urge to help her returned. Even as his better sense screamed out a warning, Stockton put down the pot and crossed to Jenna. Her green eyes met his, filled with hope, the kind he couldn't resist, no matter how hard he tried. "Seems you've just hired a caterer."

CHAPTER FIVE

THE DINNER RUSH WAS in full swing. Stockton allowed the work to become his sole focus. He bustled around the kitchen, calling out orders, sautéing steaks, grilling vegetables, boiling fresh pasta.

Avoiding Jenna.

For her part, she steered clear of him, too. They shared few words—only enough for him to give her direction and send her off to complete some small kitchen task. At some point, they would have to finish talking, not just about the plan for his anniversary party, but also the menu for Eunice's birthday, and work on bringing those plans together. Until then, there was work.

Work had been his salvation, his distraction, his life, for so long that Stockton had forgotten what normalcy was like. He ate, slept and breathed the restaurant. Spent more hours here than he probably had to, and spent his free time whipping up new recipes. In the early months of the restaurant, he'd had no social life. To be honest, he still had no social life.

Everything had been about building the business, growing the clientele and creating a stand-out environment. There would be time later to have the life he had put on hold. For a long time, he hadn't minded that delay. But lately—

He'd been wondering if maybe he was missing something. If maybe he should take more time off, consider making enough time to have a relationship with more than a knife and a cutting board.

For that reason alone, he'd decided having Jenna's help on planning the anniversary party was a smart idea. It would free up some of Stockton's time, and take a little of the pressure off his shoulders. After thinking about it, he'd realized his minimal plans could use a little wow factor, something Jenna specialized in creating. Surely, he could work on a couple of events with her and keep everything professional.

The acrid scent of something burning filled the air, and Stockton whirled toward the stove. He turned off the burner, removed the scorched pan, filled it with hot water and soap, and set it in the sink to soak, all in the fast, practiced moves of someone who had encountered that emergency a time or ten. "What happened?"

"Uh, a béchamel sauce gone awry?" Jenna offered him up an apologetic smile. "I said I could cook, not create a masterpiece. I guess I thought I had white sauces under control."

"Well, at least we know you can *burn*," he said, chuckling. "Maybe I should have you searing the steaks."

She laughed, then ran the back of her hand over her forehead. "This is a lot harder than I expected."

"You get used to it. Work here long enough and you develop a rhythm." Stockton retrieved another pot from the shelf and set it on the stove.

She gave the pan a dubious glance. "Does that mean you don't burn things anymore?"

He laughed. "I wish. Normally, when I do, it's because I'm trying to do too many things at one time."

"You always did," she said softly, and for a moment, he

could almost believe they were back to old times. To those high school days when his heart leapt at the sight of her, and his every thought centered around touching her.

For the first time, Stockton wondered if this older Jenna—a woman as dedicated to her own career and dreams as he was—would understand this older, more settled version of him.

Or maybe he and Jenna were too similar. Maybe there was something to that adage about opposites attracting. If that was so, then someone better tell his hormones because they weren't paying attention to anything other than her.

"Multitasking is a necessity in this field. You need to be able to talk, listen and manage two or three dishes, all at the same time." He gestured toward the pan. "Let's try the sauce again." Back to work. Always back to work.

"You are a harsh taskmaster." She gathered the butter and flour, then stepped back. When Stockton didn't move in to start the sauce, she gave him an uncertain glance. "You sure you want me to do this again? After I burned the last one? Isn't it better for me to watch you?"

"You can do this." He pushed the butter closer to her. "And when we get busy with customers in a little while, I won't have time to show you. You have to do it for yourself to truly learn."

And for him to be able to walk away, and bury himself in the kitchen instead of in whatever she was doing. Already, being this close to her had him distracted, and that was a bad sign.

She wrinkled her nose, but didn't protest further. Instead, she crossed to the pan, slid the stick of butter into it, then stepped back to wait for it to melt before adding the flour and seasoning.

"Now, whisk," he said.

She did as he said, picking up the stainless steel whisk,

and stirring the roux before Stockton moved in beside her and began adding milk. As soon as he did, he realized he should have had her make that liquid addition. Not just because she needed the experience, but because the sheer act of pouring the liquid put him within inches of her. All evening, he'd done a good job of maintaining distance between them—a few feet, a countertop, a stand mixer. Something that he could use as a wall to tamp down his awareness of her every move, every breath.

A lone tendril of her black hair had escaped the clip she'd used, and it curled along her neck, sweet and tantalizing. He wanted to capture that lock in his fingers, feel it slide silkily through his grasp. His gaze drifted over her neck, swooping down the hollows of her throat. Desire curled tight in his gut.

He swallowed hard and pushed the feeling away. Wanting Jenna had never been a problem. Making a relationship work between them had.

Right now, the last thing he had time for was a complicated involvement, particularly one he knew wasn't going to end happily. He'd learned his lesson long ago. A smart man didn't require multiple trips down Bad Experience Avenue to learn to make a detour.

"Uh, here," he said, nearly shoving the container of milk into her hands. "You should do this."

She glanced over at him, and a smile curved up her face. Damn. Why did she have to smile? "Don't tell me you're abandoning me. You saw what happened last time I tried this on my own."

"I'll be right here."

"Watching me screw up?"

"Something like that."

He'd wanted Jenna Pearson from the minute his hormones matured and he realized the girl he'd known since first grade wasn't a girl anymore, but someone on her way to being a *woman*. Worse now, he knew what it was like to have her, knew the intimate curves of her body, knew how she sounded when he entered her, when she was satisfied and happy, and curved into his arms.

He knew it all, and as much as he thought he had forgotten those details, it was clear they were very much alive in his memory.

He also remembered their breakup, the swift demise of a relationship that had once seemed golden. He'd taken her to Chicago, intending to propose. At the end of the weekend, just as he was about to pull the ring out of his pocket, Jenna had dropped a bombshell.

She wasn't going to college in Indiana. In fact, she wasn't staying in Riverbend one more day. She was moving to New York. She'd tried to talk him into going, too, into attending culinary school in the city. For a while, he'd considered it, then realized all those days of goofing off in high school had caught up with him and his grades weren't good enough for the prestigious culinary institutes. Nor did he have any desire to trade one permanent address for another. He wanted to see the world, and he'd thought Jenna would go with him, or worst case, wait for him to return.

But as he'd watched her pack, he'd realized something. They were headed in different directions. Stockton's dream had always been the same—wander the greatest cities in the world, learning the restaurant trade. Jenna had made it sound as if she wanted the same thing, but all the while, she didn't. She'd been making plans, applying to colleges, looking for apartments. The betrayal had stung.

After all this was over, she'd be leaving him behind again. If he was smart, he'd remember that.

The sauce came together, bubbling up and thickening

with each whisk. Stockton stepped back. "Now add a little nutmeg, taste it and see if it needs anything else."

She ran the nutmeg over a micrograter, watched the dark brown dots fall into the creamy sauce, then took a teaspoon and sampled the béchamel. She smiled. "Perfect." Then she held out the spoon to him. "Taste."

His lips closed over the spoon but he wasn't thinking about the taste of the sauce. He thought of how her lips had been here just a moment before, how if he kissed her, he would taste the béchamel, and so much more. And how incredibly foolish it would be to do that.

"Yeah, it's, uh, fine." He jerked away and got back to work mixing the cheese filling for his manicotti.

The waitstaff hurried in and out of the kitchen, shouting orders, asking questions. Conversing with them gave Stockton an excuse to stay away from Jenna. Across the room, Jenna listened to him talk to the staff, but kept quiet herself and focused on her work. With the sauce done, he had switched her back to basic prep work, which kept her busy chopping and dicing. Stockton stayed by the ovens, checking the roasted chickens and baking bread. Putting Jenna from his mind.

At least, that's what he told himself. But as the rush of orders continued to come in, he found himself right next to her over and over again. "Sorry," he said, as he bumped her hip for the third time that day, trying to reach for a spice on one of the upper shelves. It was as if his body was just looking for ways to contact hers, because he definitely didn't run into Larry, the regular sous chef, this often.

She gave him a quick smile. "No problem."

He plated the order of *bracchiole* and pasta, then slid it under the warming lamp until the waiter came to retrieve the plates. A quick glance at the clipboard running the length of the shelf showed no more pending orders. The dinner rush had passed. That meant it was after nine, and time to begin the clean up from today and some of the prep work for tomorrow.

"Why don't you go home?" he said to Jenna. "The dinner rush is over. There'll be a few more stragglers, but nothing me and the prep cooks can't handle."

She leaned against the counter, and let out a deep breath. The front of her apron was a rainbow of stains from the sauces she'd tended and the space under her eyes was shadowed. "Phew, thank goodness that's over. Is it always this busy?"

"Pretty much."

"I don't know how you keep up. I'm exhausted and all I've done is chop a bunch of vegetables and stir some sauces."

"You did more than that. You were a great help." His gaze skipped over the kitchen, past the mountain of dirty dishes that Paul was running through the automatic dishwasher, then over the stack of folded tablecloths, napkins and fresh silverware two of the waitresses were prepping to carry out to the tables. He turned back to Jenna. "I appreciate it a lot."

Jenna perched a fist on her hip. "Are you admitting I was right?"

"Right about what?"

"That you could use the help, and that having me here would be a good idea."

"Okay, yeah, you were right."

She grinned. "I usually am."

It was a moment of lightness, and one Stockton should take as such. But there was something in him—some masochistic urge to dredge up a past that he wanted only to forget—that had him opening his mouth. "Were you right about us?"

Her mouth opened, closed, opened again. "We were better off apart. We wanted two different things."

"We did. And we still do."

She looked as if she wanted to say something, but instead she nodded. "The proverbial fish and the bird."

"I'd say it was more like a shark and an eagle. One of us had to be in constant motion, hungry for the next challenge—"

"And the other flew away as far as possible."

"I remember that as a mutual decision." One of the waiters came in and tacked an order onto the shelf beside Stockton. He glanced at the slip of paper, then began readying a plate of lasagna. "Don't you?"

"You're right. I should go home. I have a lot to do tomorrow," Jenna said. Her voice held a cold, icy tone.

"Jenna," he said, before he could stop himself.

She turned toward him. "What?"

"Why didn't you wait for me?"

A long, sad smile crossed her face. "Because you were always traveling, Stockton. Not just with airplanes and cars, but with your heart. What's the point in waiting for something that was never going to be mine?" She brushed past him, then left the kitchen. Going, as always, in the opposite direction of him.

He reached for a ladle to add extra sauce to the lasagna. Steam wafted off the baked dish, and a melody of scents emanated from the layers of fluffy pasta, thick cheeses and spicy sausage. He'd always thought of lasagna as a marriage of tastes and flavors that pleased nearly every palate. Sweet, spicy, savory, all together. Stockton drizzled sauce over the dish, realizing as the first drops hit the pasta that he'd accidentally added Bolognese instead of the customer's order of classic red sauce.

He scraped the mistake into the trash, then plated

another slice of lasagna. That was where thinking about the impossible got him—making mistakes and trying to combine two things that would never, ever work.

Aunt Mabel had waited up, even though Jenna had told her twice that it would be a long, late evening. Jenna thought about begging off early, and heading to bed, but found herself craving the company. And maybe, over the mugs of tea Aunt Mabel had set out, Jenna could find some of the answers she needed.

"I talked to Betsy after you left for the restaurant today. I told her to go easy on you." It was as if Aunt Mabel had read her mind. Jenna had thought, spending all these years away from Riverbend, that the town gossip would die down. That people would stop judging her because of her mother's actions. But this afternoon with Betsy had proved differently. She was still Mary Pearson's daughter, and every mistake she made seemed to be compounded by that maternal legacy.

"You didn't have to do that."

Her aunt's wrinkled hand covered hers. "I most certainly did. My dear, you've been through enough. It's time that some people in this town learned to keep their noses on their own faces."

Jenna sighed. "That's never going to happen. You know how small towns are. Always dredging up the past, trying to make it fit with the present."

Aunt Mabel's lips thinned. "What my sister did shouldn't be any reflection on you. Why people insist on putting the two together, I'll never know."

Jenna remembered very little of her mother—she'd been seven when her parents died, and her memories were centered around Christmases and birthdays and long sunny days on the farm. But she remembered her mother's smile, and for Jenna, who'd been too young to understand what—or who—was making her mother smile, it had seemed like maybe things were improving, when really they were heading on a fast downward spiral. "Why did my mother do it?"

A long sigh whistled out of Aunt Mabel. "I knew you'd be asking these questions one day." She toyed with her mug. "She was unhappy. You knew that."

Jenna nodded.

"I don't know if it was really anyone's fault. I think she just got married too young and didn't really think it through. Your father was a good man, but they were more friends than anything else. And when life started throwing them lemons—"

"Those were grapefruits, Aunt Mabel." Jenna thought of all the years of poverty, the times when they had teetered on the edge of bankruptcy. Jenna had been too young to understand much more than the fact that every bill caused a fight among her parents.

"It was enough to test any marriage. For a while, your mother took a job at the library. The extra money was nice, I'm sure, but with it came…someone else." Aunt Mabel sighed. "I know she didn't go out looking for a relationship. It just…happened."

Happened. Jenna closed her eyes, and when she did, she was back at that day, sitting in this very kitchen, listening to her aunt Mabel tell her that she would be staying there from now on. "If she hadn't met that other man, maybe she never would have died in that car accident. And my father, rushing to see her, and going off the road, too. It was all because she met him, Aunt Mabel. And decided she loved him more than us."

"That's not the whole story, Jenna. Your mother—"

Jenna threw up her hands. "My mother ruined my life

by what she did, Aunt Mabel. I don't want to hear how I should be more understanding or how she loved her family deep down inside. Because in the end, she made the choices that destroyed everyone."

"Aw, Jenna—" Aunt Mabel's fingers closed over her niece's "—I wish you'd stop writing history in indelible ink. Sometimes there's a lot more gray than black to the stories we hear."

Jenna shook her head, refusing to have this conversation again. "Well, let's just hope that Eunice's birthday bash gives everyone something else to talk about."

Aunt Mabel took a sip of tea, then pursed her lips, as if she wasn't happy with the change in conversation, but would accept it. "I think the party will be fabulous. I'm not worried about that. What I am worried about is—" her gaze met her niece's "—you."

"Me? I'm fine." Jenna crossed to the refrigerator for a snack she didn't want or need. "I'm fine."

Aunt Mabel sighed. "I'd really rather you didn't go back to that city. Why don't you settle down here? You could have a great life here."

"I already have a great life." Jenna moved the mayonnaise to the side, and considered some leftover pudding. The chocolate dish blurred in her vision.

Did she really have such a great life? For years, she'd told herself she loved living in New York. After all, she'd dreamed of nothing else for as long as she could remember. Living in the city, surrounded by the sights, smells, sounds, hundreds of miles from small-town America…that was what she'd thought she wanted.

Until she actually had it and she found herself lying in her bed at night, wishing the traffic would die long enough to give her a taste of the near silence of Riverbend nights. She'd walk the streets, and miss the expansive views of the sky, the fresh scent of a spring breeze. She'd visit the same coffee shop three times in one week, and every time be treated like just one more customer, rather than walking into the deli in downtown Riverbend and hearing someone call out her name, even if she hadn't been there in a month or a year.

But living in Riverbend hadn't been all Utopia, either, and she needed to remember that.

"I have a great life," she repeated. "And when this is over, I'm going back."

Aunt Mabel sighed. "Well, you can't blame me for trying to convince you to stay here and put down some roots."

Jenna shut the refrigerator door and leaned against it. "What roots do I have in this town, Aunt Mabel? Besides you?"

"More than you think, my dear." Aunt Mabel looked as if she wanted to say something more, but didn't.

Jenna withdrew the chocolate pudding from the fridge. She retrieved a spoon from the drawer and returned to the kitchen table. The first bite of pudding hit her palate with a smooth, cold sweetness. Exactly the antidote she needed for the topsy-turvy day she'd had. After a while, she got up, and had a second bowl of pudding, topping it with a squirt of whipped cream.

It had been one of those days. And then some.

CHAPTER SIX

THE COLD AIR HIT STOCKTON like a punch to his jaw. He loved winter, but not when the temperature dipped below zero. He hurried down the sidewalk toward Samantha's bakery, his coat drawn up against his neck, and wondered idly if Rustica would succeed as well in Florida as it had in Indiana. If winter kept its icy grip on Riverbend, he'd be sorely tempted to try a Gulf Coast relocation.

As he rounded the corner, he nearly collided with a tall figure in a thick wool coat. "Jenna."

Surprise lit the notes of his voice. Sure, she'd been here for a few days already, but every time he saw her, it caught him off guard. It had to be because he'd gotten so used to not seeing her. Not because every time they were together she had him asking himself questions he tried never to ask.

"Stockton. What are you doing out in this cold?" The fur-trimmed hood of Jenna's coat concealed her lithe figure, and made her seem more fragile, not that Jenna was ever vulnerable. The wind blew at her, but she didn't seem affected.

"Heading to Samantha's bakery. I wanted to talk to her about orders for next week."

"Oh." She thumbed in the opposite direction. "Listen, I'm on my way to Betsy's for another meeting, but I'm a bit early. Do you want to grab a cup of coffee and talk about the plans for your anniversary party?"

"You don't have to do that, Jenna. If anything, I owe you for working for me last night. I'm sure you have plenty to do with Eunice's party coming up."

"As do you." She cocked her head and studied him. "You know, it's not a crime to ask for help, Stockton."

"I do—" He cut off the sentence. "Okay, maybe I don't. But this time I am asking."

"Why?"

He couldn't tell her the truth. That something had been awakened in him last night when they'd had that moment over the potatoes, and he'd been thinking about it ever since. That he had stayed up late last night, running through a thousand what-ifs, and always, always, coming back to the same destination. She lived a life apart from his, and always would.

"Because I'm terrible at planning parties," he said, and offered her a grin.

"And I'm terrible at white sauces." Her grin echoed his. "All right. Let's get out of this cold, and see what we can come up with."

They headed into the diner, and took seats in a booth in the back. A waitress brought them coffee, and Jenna wrapped her hands around the hot mug. He noticed Jenna was wearing a tailored white button-down shirt with a close-fitted jacket and matching slacks today. He didn't know designers—couldn't have told a Gucci from a garbage bag—but he could tell an expensive cut and fabric when he saw one.

"I had a lot of ideas for your party," Jenna said. "I've spent a lot of time in Rustica lately and I was thinking if—"

"Jenna Pearson?" The voice cut through the diner, sharp and high-pitched. "Mary Pearson's daughter?"

Tension stiffened Jenna's spine. But she planted a smile on her face and turned in her seat. "Mrs. Richardson. So nice to see you again."

Gertrude Richardson. All towns had a woman like her, someone who thought keeping her opinions to herself was a waste of perfectly good opinions. Stockton wondered how old Gertrude was now—she had to be somewhere in her eighties—and wondered if she'd ever slow down on her one-woman crusade to tell people her version of the truth.

Gertrude propped a fist on her hip. "I hear you're in charge of Eunice's birthday party."

"I am."

"Well, consider this my RSVP. I will not be attending."

"I'm sorry to hear that, Mrs. Richardson. I'm sure Eunice will be disappointed."

Gertrude waved a dismissive hand. "Eunice won't care two whits if I'm there or not. I'm staying away out of protest."

"Protest?" Jenna arched a brow. "Of what?"

"Of her letting you, of all people, be in charge. My goodness, you should be ashamed of yourself, coming back to this town and trying to act like you're some uppity businesswoman, going to show us country folk how it's done." The older woman leaned in closer, sending a wave of floral perfume into the space. "I know you, Jenna. Know where you come from, and it's no fancy city."

Fury raged inside of Stockton. He had lived in this town all his life, and never seen anyone think they could treat another townsperson that way. "Mrs. Richardson, where

Jenna comes from or what she wears has nothing to do with the quality of her work."

"I disagree." Gertrude straightened and a haughty look filled her features. "People are where they come from. Why, their roots form the very foundation of who they are."

"My roots are just fine, Mrs. Richardson," Jenna said. Her voice was firm, but Stockton could read Jenna's face. All her life, the whispers of her childhood had followed her around. He couldn't imagine being the constant topic of gossip and knew it had affected her. Maybe in more ways than he had realized.

"You ask me," Stockton said, eyeing Mrs. Richardson, "we all have roots we aren't too proud of or that we wish were attached to a different tree. Wasn't it your granddaddy, Mrs. Richardson, who was arrested for selling moonshine during Prohibition?"

Gertrude's face paled, then reddened. "That's not the same thing."

"I don't know. Back in those days, I think that was quite the scandal. Seems to me, if we all did a little less judging and a lot more understanding, the world would be a better place."

Gertrude drew herself up. "Well, I never," she said, then huffed and puffed and turned away.

After Gertrude had stomped out of the diner, Jenna turned back to Stockton. "Thank you, but you didn't have to stand up for me."

Stockton's gaze met hers across the table. "I think it's about time someone did, Jenna. And told the people of this town that you're not their personal gossip punching bag."

"I'm…" Her voice trailed off. "Okay, maybe I have been."

"I should have said something sooner. Years ago. But

I was young back then and hell, half those women in the quilting club scared the life out of me."

Jenna laughed, the sound sweet music to his ears. "You and me both."

The moment extended between them for another few seconds. Stockton knew he should say something, should jerk them both out of this connection and back to reality, but he didn't.

Finally, Jenna looked at her watch. "Oh, I'm late for my meeting with Betsy. I really hate to say this, but I have to go." She scrambled out of the booth, swinging her tote bag over her shoulder as she did.

Stockton dropped a few bills on the table and followed after her. They both exited at the same time, and the cold slammed into them, hard. "About the anniversary party," he began.

"I can set up another meeting with you later today or maybe early tomorrow. Or—"

He waved her off. "I trust you, Jenna. Do what you think is best."

"You trust me?" Her gaze narrowed.

He nodded and his gaze met hers. The green in her eyes seemed to deepen, become a storm of its own. "I do."

She glanced away for a second, then nibbled on her lower lip. "What are we talking about, Stockton? A party or something else?"

He took another step, and saw her inhale. Her eyes widened. The cold seemed to disappear, replaced by a growing heat deep inside him. Every time he thought he was putting distance between them, he seemed to do the opposite. What was he thinking? He didn't have time for a relationship, especially one he knew would be complicated. "I don't know. Because last I checked, we were over."

She nodded, but the gesture was short, barely a movement.

"Aren't we?"

"What?"

"Over?"

"What does it matter? You live here, and I live in New York."

"Don't dodge the question, Jenna."

Her gaze darted away from his face and she worried her bottom lip again, wearing off her lipstick and revealing her soft pink mouth. "Of course we're over." The words escaped in a frosty cloud.

"Good. I'm glad we have that settled," he said. "Because the last thing I'd want to do is to repeat past mistakes." He was so close, the sweet scent of her perfume filled his senses, and he could see the slight tick of her pulse in her throat. The wind ruffled the fur around her face, danced across her features. The urge to kiss her rose in him, a force so strong, he had to take a step back to resist the desire. "And I suspect neither would you."

Then he said goodbye to her and headed down the sidewalk, before he did something he knew he'd regret.

"You're doing a good job avoiding him," Livia said later that afternoon when Jenna called her friend using the video camera on her laptop. Jenna had a plan for Eunice's party, but thought it wouldn't hurt to get a second opinion. And, she'd wanted someone other than Aunt Mabel to talk to about the confusing rush of emotions she'd been feeling for Stockton. She'd told Livia the whole story—about dating Stockton in high school, breaking up before she went to college and about thinking she was over him—

Until she saw him and realized she wasn't.

"I'm not avoiding anyone. I'm working," Jenna replied. The stack of notes before her was proof of that. So what if she'd barely accomplished anything since returning from her meeting at Betsy's? So what if her mind had been on Stockton, and on the question he'd asked her, the entire time she sat in Betsy's kitschy Christmas-gone-wild parlor? "In fact, I think I should head over to the party store and check out the options for centerpieces. I was thinking of doing different ones for each table, to symbolize the passing of the decades since Eunice was born. Betsy and I discussed the idea earlier today, and she seemed really excited about it." Jenna flipped the pages and turned a series of sketches toward Livia. "An antique tea cup and a string of pearls here, a set of toy Model T cars here and maybe a tiny disco ball and platform heels here."

Livia nodded her approval, her movements made slow and jerky by the internet connection. "What about the menu?"

"I'm working on that, too." If she could call adding "call caterer to work on menu" to her To Do list working on it. So far, all she'd done was a whole lot of thinking about the caterer.

"Sounds like you've got it all under control."

Jenna laughed. "I think so." The only way to get back on top of her business was to make this work. Between Stockton's party and Eunice's event, she had two opportunities to prove her mettle. A flicker of doubt ran through her, but she ignored it. What was *with* her lately? Why did she keep on faltering?

"Good," Livia said. "I have to go. I'll see you in a few days and in the meantime—" Livia grinned "—call that caterer."

Jenna sighed. "Okay. I will."

Livia leaned in close to the computer monitor, as if she could see inside Jenna's thoughts. "Do you still have feelings for him?"

"Of course not." She toyed with the pen, then clicked it off. "Maybe. A little."

"I'd be surprised if you didn't, honestly. For one, from what you've said, he's a hunk, and for another, you two clearly have a history. How long did you guys date?"

"It seemed like we always did." Jenna took a sip of coffee. The hot liquid seared her throat, good and rich and dark. She'd sent the grounds to Aunt Mabel as a Christmas present, because her aunt had complained about the lack of good coffee in the little town. Right now, though, she barely tasted the Kona blend. "I've known Stockton most of my life, and we just...gravitated toward each other. He was my first friend in elementary school, the one who showed me the ropes, sat with me at lunch and made the new girl feel welcome. I don't know when it became something more. It just did."

"High school sweethearts, huh?"

"And elementary school, and middle school." She ran a finger over the rim of the mug, circling the white porcelain again and again. "I guess it was just expected that we'd end up together. By everyone who knew us, by his parents, my aunt and, I guess, by him and I."

"And yet you didn't. Jenna, that happens to millions of high school couples."

"True." She shrugged, but it seemed such a small gesture for a decision that had changed both their lives. "We went away one weekend, and I realized that Stockton wanted a completely different life than I did. I mean, he'd always said he wanted to wander the world and learn how to cook, but I hadn't thought he was serious, you know? I thought he'd hear about my plans for New York, and go with me. But—" she bit her lip "—he didn't want that at all. Heck, I think he was always halfway to the airport in his mind. I couldn't wait for a man who never knew when, or if, he'd return. I had my own dreams and plans. I had told him a hundred times, but I just think he...didn't listen."

Livia laughed. "He's a guy. I think not listening comes with the testosterone."

"Maybe. But to me, this was huge. If he couldn't listen about the big stuff, how could I be sure he'd hear me on the little stuff? So I went to New York."

An understanding smile filled Livia's face. "And thought he'd follow you."

"No, of course not." Jenna worried her bottom lip again, then let out a breath. "Okay, maybe a part of me thought he would."

"And now you're wondering what might have been, had you stayed in Riverbend?"

"What's done is done," Jenna said. But was it? After that moment in the kitchen at Rustica and on the sidewalk today? Was everything as over as she'd thought?

How could five seconds of conversation in the wintery cold with a man she no longer loved leave her so discombobulated? Since she'd gotten back to her aunt's house, she'd done the only sane thing—and thrown herself into the planning of Eunice's party. "I guess I didn't expect to still be affected by being around him."

"Well, if you're not careful, all those moon-eyed meetings with him will start to make people think you're still interested in him."

"I'm not."

"I know. I heard your many and varied protests." Livia

grinned. "What's that Shakespeare quote? 'The lady doth protest too much'?"

"This time it's true," Jenna said. She got to her feet, gathering the remaining paperwork and stuffing it into her tote. "And on that note, I have a caterer to see, and a party to plan."

Mabel Pearson sat at a corner booth in Stockton's restaurant, sipping a cup of tea while she nibbled at a slice of tiramisu. Stockton watched her for a moment from behind the oval window in the kitchen doors, and grinned.

He wasn't fooled, not one bit. He knew Mabel as well as he knew his own aunts. Heck, he'd spent so much time at her house as a child she was practically family to him, and that meant she often acted like family—by delving into his personal life and then telling him what she thought he should do with his life. Stockton chuckled. Clearly, Aunt Mabel had come here to offer her two cents.

Armed with a fresh cup of tea, Stockton left the kitchen and crossed to Mabel. He slid into the seat opposite her, and laid the steaming mug before her. "A refill for you."

Mabel smiled. "How thoughtful. You were always such a nice boy."

"It's all part of the service here."

Mabel pushed her empty cup aside and took a sip from the new one, eyeing Stockton over the rim. "I hear you're catering Eunice's birthday party. She'll be delighted."

"I hope so. But that isn't what you came here for, I suspect."

"Oh, I'm here for the tea. And cake." Mabel took another sip.

"Aunt Mabel," he said, reverting to the familiar term he'd always called her by, the name she'd insisted on after setting a place for him at the dinner table for the third time in a week, "I know my desserts are great, but I don't think you'd brave this cold for a little cake."

"I've been wondering how long it would take a boy your age to gain some sense."

He laughed. "I'm hardly a boy anymore."

"True. But you can still act like one." Mabel forked off a piece of tiramisu and put it in her mouth. Stockton waited, knowing there was more to come after she swallowed. "You know you broke my niece's heart when you and she broke up."

"She's the one that ended it, Aunt Mabel. Not me."

"If you ask me, a woman doesn't end a relationship unless she has a damned good reason."

He arched a brow at the curse. "Well, either way, it's over."

"You know—" she forked off another piece "—for a long time, I was very unhappy with you for letting her get away."

He scowled. "She left. I didn't let anyone get away."

"Then why didn't you go after her?"

It was the one question he had never asked himself. Eight years ago, he had stood in the Indianapolis airport, credit card in hand, staring at the list of departing flights. There'd been one to New York that morning, and one to Italy. He could have chosen New York.

He hadn't.

"Aunt Mabel," Stockton said, as firmly as he could, "maybe once upon a time it seemed like we should end up together, but it's not going to work. Jenna and I tried it, and found out we're beyond wrong for each other."

"Why?"

"We want different things out of life. We always did."

Aunt Mabel pushed her plate aside, then folded her hands on top of each other. "Are you sure about that? Because if you ask me, the Jenna Pearson who left Riverbend, and the one who returned, are two very different women. And the same goes for you." Her older, wiser gaze met his. "Maybe now you two are the people you should have been back then."

CHAPTER SEVEN

Jenna hated to admit that Livia had been right. That Jenna had indeed been avoiding Stockton, and the hour or two she'd have to spend with him, discussing his upcoming event and planning the menu for Eunice's party. After all, they'd worked together the other night and never come close to repeating any of their past mistakes. And on the street earlier—he'd come close enough to her to kiss her, and hadn't.

Clearly, he was over her. She was glad. She didn't need to muddle things by getting wrapped up in Stockton again.

Then why did Jenna hesitate before pushing on the door? Why had she spent a little extra time on her hair, her makeup and changed her outfit twice?

She shook off the thoughts of Stockton, and entered Rustica. It took a moment for her eyes to adjust to the dimmer interior of the restaurant. The scent of fresh-baked bread, followed by the sweet scent of chocolate, swept over her as she made her way farther into the restaurant. Soft jazz music played on the sound system, and the waitstaff moved about the room almost soundlessly as they took the last of the lunch orders, refilled drinks and delivered plates. The entire atmosphere of the restaurant was relaxed, but homey, as if someone had filled a single room with the best Italy had to offer.

Truly, Stockton had done an amazing job. The restaurant held the kind of atmosphere that begged you to linger, to have another glass of wine, a little slice of dessert. It was quiet enough to encourage conversation, and dim enough to drop a veil of privacy over each of the tables without making it impossible to see the food.

She headed for the bar, deciding it would be best to wait until the restaurant died down a little and Stockton had a chance to breathe.

"What can I get you?" The bartender, a rotund man with a goatee and a receding hairline, gave her a smile.

"Just a diet soda, please."

"You got it." He filled a glass with ice and soda, then placed it before her and moved down the bar to tend to the other customers.

Jenna glanced at the banner draped over the bar, announcing the one-year anniversary party in a couple of days. Holding it on New Year's Eve was a brilliant move. People would be looking for a venue to bring in the new year at, and Rustica would be one of the only ones in Riverbend. Already, a slew of ideas ran through her head for the party. Something simple, she decided, that wouldn't overpower the atmosphere or the food.

"Just can't stay away, huh?"

She spun around on the seat. Stockton stood beside the bar, his white chef's uniform nearly pristine—unlike her own from last night. "I came by to talk to you about the menu for the party and the ideas I had for your event, but I can wait until you're done serving lunch."

"We're almost finished. And, Larry is finally all recovered from the flu, so he's back at the stove. The kitchen is under control. More or less." Stockton grinned, then put out his hand. "Come on, let's get out of here for a while."

"Are you sure? I don't mind waiting."

"I'm a hundred percent sure. Sometimes whole weeks go by before I realize I've been here since sunrise, and not left until long into the night. That's why I walked to work today instead of driving. I got to see the world a little bit. And now, that little taste of being outside has whetted my appetite for more."

She laughed. "More? But it's snowing."

He retrieved her coat from the stool beside her, then slipped it on her shoulders. "I hear it's the magical kind of snow, though."

"Magical, huh? I don't know about that. More like cold and miserable. But if you want to go for a walk while we talk, I'm all about keeping my vendors happy." Jenna slid her arms into the wool coat, then waited while Stockton retrieved his own.

A moment later, they were outside. The temperature had warmed to just over freezing, enough to allow the snow to fall, but not so cold to make being outdoors unbearable. Jenna was glad she'd opted to change into the jeans she'd bought the other day, and had pulled on a pair of Aunt Mabel's winter boots. If she'd been outside in one of the designer outfits she'd brought with her, she'd be freezing to death, and in those high heels, not able to walk that far. The sidewalks were quiet, with most of Riverbend's residents avoiding the outdoors, and choosing to drive to their destinations instead. The snow fell in thick, fluffy flakes, covering her coat, her hood, the ground. "I haven't been back in this town forever," she said, glancing around the downtown area with its cute little shops and brightly covered awnings, the decorated street poles, the benches waiting for warmer weather. "Nothing's really changed, has it?"

"That's what I love about Riverbend. You can depend on it."

Jenna snorted. "And that's what I hated most."

"You know, sometimes dependability can be a good thing."

She let out a breath, watched it form a frosty cloud. "Maybe it is. And maybe it's just an excuse not to take a chance."

"What do you mean?"

"Nothing. Nothing at all." She'd let that slip without thinking twice. Before she left the house this morning, she'd vowed not to revisit the past with Stockton. She was leaving in a few days. Leaving him behind.

They walked for a while, not saying anything, their hands in their pockets. "Do you remember that spring that was ridiculously warm?"

She nodded. "It was like summer in April."

"Do you remember what we did?"

"Oh, goodness, of course I do." She put a hand to her mouth, covering the laugh. "We skipped school. Ran down to the deli, grabbed some sandwiches and had a picnic in the park."

"And, I might add, caught hell with the principal the next day."

"You did."

"Because I was the one who was failing Algebra—"

"And I was the one with straight A's."

"You were a bad influence on me," he said.

Jenna laughed. "If I remember right, it was your idea to skip school."

"It was indeed. But you could have stopped me."

"What, and miss one of the best days of my life?" She shook her head. "I don't think so."

"Was it?" Stockton asked softly.

"Was it what?"

"One of the best days of your life?"

What was it about him that made her forget her best intentions and say the very thing she didn't want to say? Try as she might to put the past aside, it came roaring back in Technicolor images. Her and Stockton, laughing as they ran out the back of the school building, dashing down to the diner and laughing so hard they could barely place their order. Then grabbing a blanket and heading to the park, setting up a picnic beneath a gracious maple tree with new leaves still curled onto the branches.

He'd held her hand while the warm sun draped over them, and kissed her a hundred times, a thousand. The entire day had been...

Magical.

Today, she was sure, would not be a repeat of that afternoon. A part of her longed to return to that spring afternoon and wondered where she and Stockton would be today if they'd managed to stay together. Would they still be strolling down those park paths, happy and kissing, or would they be walking separate paths, miserable and lonely?

"Yes, Stockton, it was," she said quietly.

"It was for me, too." His voice was tender, edged with a gentleness that surprised her.

She could have caved to that tone, could have continued this reminiscence. She knew where it would lead—she'd already treaded dangerously close to that path in the last couple of days. Instead, she retreated to the safest subject she knew—work. Because in the end, Stockton was still the man who couldn't be tied down too long. Back then, it had been to a desk in school, later to an address. But really, Jenna was sure, it was always about being tied down to her. "Anyway, I wanted to talk to you about your anniversary party—"

He put up a hand. "Stop right there. I already told you I

trust you to do a great job. You know me well enough, and I'm sure whatever you put together will be fabulous."

"You don't want me to run everything by you first?"

He grinned. "Nope. Surprise me, Jenna."

For a second, she was transported back to the days when they'd been dating. She'd told him she wanted to plan a special evening out for them—a sort of trial run at what would later become her career—and Stockton had said the same thing. *Surprise me.*

And she had. Stockton had talked often about wanting to get away for a beach vacation—something neither of them could afford during their high school years—so she brought the beach to him for his birthday that summer. Carting in sand to the patio at his house, adding beach blankets, a CD player with ocean sounds, and even ordering a clambake from a local seafood place. Stockton had been surprised, and touched, and showed his appreciation. Many times over.

If Stockton remembered that night, he didn't mention it. She told herself she was glad.

"Come on, I want to show you something." Stockton motioned to the left, and she followed as they skirted a drugstore and headed down a side street. As they moved away from downtown and emerged into a less densely populated area, Stockton's steps slowed. "Now tell me that isn't magical." He pointed at a spot ahead of them. "And what's more…fun."

They'd emerged at the back of the town park, beside the small pond that had been converted into an outdoor ice skating rink for the season. A dozen or so people circled the pond, their skates making a sharp swish-swish sound with each scrape of the blade. Snow fell onto the skaters and the pond like fat white confetti, and as the skaters passed the fresh flakes, it swirled into fluffy clouds that danced along the ice.

Jenna inhaled the fresh, clean air, scented with nothing but Mother Nature, and held the breath for a long time. She pressed a hand to her chest, closed her eyes and let the snow drop wet kisses on her cheeks. It snowed in New York, it got cold in New York, but never, ever like this. Maybe because the city was so close, everything so compacted, there wasn't any room to breathe or feel that natural world.

Had she ever taken the time to really *be* when she'd lived in Riverbend? Appreciate that tranquility and beauty or had she always been too busy concentrating on escaping small-town life and running from the ugliness she'd encountered to see the beauty this town offered, too? Had she pushed down her happy memories, choosing instead to believe the worst about Riverbend and its people?

"It's...different from what I remember," she said finally.

"Come on," he said, taking her hand and tugging her down the hill.

Even through her gloves, she felt his touch. Heat surged through her veins, and even though she knew she should let go—

She didn't.

"Where are we going?"

Stockton turned to her and grinned. "Ice skating."

She started to sputter a protest, but Stockton silenced it with a finger on her lips. Suddenly, she couldn't breathe, couldn't think.

"Do you remember when we were little, we went ice skating every winter as soon as the ice was hard enough?" he said. "We skated until your aunt came and dragged us off the ice and back home."

The memories came back to her in a rush. Her and

Stockton, the wind in their faces, laughing and speeding around the icy circle. When they'd been little, they'd never noticed the cold. There'd only been the next adventure to try, the next snow pile to climb. "I remember," Jenna said. "And when we were done, Aunt Mabel would fill us with hot cocoa until our bellies sloshed."

He laughed. "That she did." Then he sobered and met her gaze. "We had fun, Jenna, the kind of fun where you don't worry about today, or tomorrow or yesterday. You just *are*. When was the last time you had that kind of fun?"

"The problem with that is that tomorrow always comes, Stockton. The principal calls you down to his office and reminds you to get back on track. The bills come due, and you have no choice but to go back to work."

"All work and no play, Jenna Pearson, can make you grumpy."

"All play and no work can get you in trouble." She turned away from the pond. "Now, about Eunice's party…"

"No. I'm not going to talk about that right now. I might be all grown up and responsible ninety-nine percent of the time, but for today, I want to be that kid I used to be." His blue eyes met hers. "The one you used to be."

The man knew her too well, shared too many memories, and it showed in the way he repeated her own thoughts back at her. The knot of tension in her shoulders that had been a constant companion for the past months seemed to tighten, as if in defiance against his words. She glanced at the ice skaters, at their laughing, happy, cold-reddened faces, then back at Stockton. "I don't think we should."

"I've poured my whole self into that restaurant for the past year, and I know you've done the same with your business. I think—" his gaze returned to the skaters "—if anyone deserves a few moments to just be, it's you and me."

She should have disagreed, should have told him they

were here to discuss business and nothing more. But she didn't.

She just nodded, then headed the rest of the way down the hill with the only man who had ever been able to talk her into doing something completely and totally insane. The only man with whom she'd ever been just Jenna.

And that was a scarier prospect than trying to navigate a frozen pond on two lethally sharp stainless steel blades.

They rented skates from a vendor who had set up shop in a small red shed sitting on the banks of the pond. The snow had dissipated, with the occasional flake drifting on the slight breeze. Crisp, clean air gave a bite to every breath they took.

"I don't know about this," Jenna repeated, lingering on the bank. She gave the ice a dubious look. "I haven't skated in so long, I'll probably fall flat on my face."

Stockton put out his hand to her. "I'll catch you. I promise."

The words were meant to be nothing more than a friendly offer. But for a second, Stockton wondered if Jenna would read more into his sentences.

Of course she wouldn't. They were both mature adults, who knew where things stood between them.

But as her hand slipped into his, and she flashed a trusting smile at him, he realized something. Things were shifting between them, and if he wasn't careful, they'd shift down a path he didn't want to journey.

He'd meant only to show her a good time, to ease the lines of worry etched between her brows. He got the feeling it was becoming something more. Very quickly. Already, he could feel the constricting reins of a relationship. The *expectations*. Something he'd never been good at fulfilling for other people.

Stockton skated backward a few steps as Jenna came onto the ice. She kept her gloved hand in his, fingers curling tightly as she took her first steps. They stayed that way for a while—him moving backward, her skating tentatively toward him.

It was like old times, but with a new, spicier edge brought on by their entry into adulthood. Holding her hand then had been the act of a supportive friend. Holding it now ignited a fire in him, and as her hips swayed with the motion of skating, his thoughts traveled down decidedly adult paths.

They were just skating. Nothing more.

"You've got it," he said, as her movements became more confident.

"That's only because you're holding me up." Jenna laughed. "I'm too old for this."

"If you are, then what about them?" He gestured toward an elderly couple, gliding across the ice, hand in hand. They were smiling and laughing as they moved, clearly enjoying the experience—and each other.

"They're the exception to the rule," Jenna said softly.

"Yeah."

Jenna and him started moving along the ice, sticking to the far outside of the rushing circle of skaters. Some people shot them annoyed glances at their slow movements, but most offered encouraging smiles, a camaraderie that seemed to come part and parcel with small-town life. A few people paused to say hello to Jenna. A few others, Stockton saw, noticed Jenna and began to whisper.

No wonder she wanted to avoid this town. Every time she was here, people wanted to gossip about the real-life scandal in Riverbend. The blatant love affair, which ultimately left an orphan in its wake when her mother tried to run off with the other man. Stockton wanted to go to every single person who was talking behind her back and confront them.

"Don't," she said softly.

"Don't what?"

"I can see it in your face. You want to go over there and set those people straight, like you did with Gertrude."

"They shouldn't do that."

She shrugged. "I'm the town scandal. When I leave, they'll stop."

He eyed the people again, and reined in the urge to do something. Jenna was right. He couldn't battle every person in this town. "You know what they need here?"

"Railings for the bad skaters?" Her light tone said she was glad for the change of subject.

He laughed. "No, though that might work." He glanced down at their still-clasped hands, and thought if there were railings, he'd have no reason to hold her hand. "A coffee and hot chocolate stand. Somebody could really make a killing at that."

"I think a coffee shop in general would do well in Riverbend. A retreat kind of place, with big leather couches and coffee tables and live music in the evenings." Jenna glanced in the direction of town, as if picturing such a place. "There's one down the street from my apartment in New York. I love going there."

"Sounds like a great place."

"It is." Her skates swooshed as she turned to the left. "Why don't you open something like that?"

He laughed. "Me? Rustica keeps me insanely busy. I barely have a life. I couldn't add another business onto that load." He glanced over at her. "Hey, you should do it."

"Me? But I don't even live here anymore."

"You could always move."

Jenna's hand slid out of his and she skated forward,

wobbling a bit as she did. The cold hit her face and reddened her cheeks, made her breath escape in frosty clouds. The heightened color accented her beauty and made Stockton want to wrap her in his arms and warm her up. The silence between them was broken by the laughter of a child, the quiet conversation of a passing couple.

"This is nice," Stockton said. Maybe if he established common ground again with Jenna he could get her to open up, because despite everything, he wondered about what was shadowing her deep green eyes. "I work so many hours at the restaurant that I never get time to do this sort of thing."

"Everybody deserves time off."

"True. But not everybody remembers that, especially when today is busier than yesterday." He swung around her, skating backward so he could face her while they spoke. "When was the last time you took a vacation?"

She snorted. "I could ask you the same thing."

"The month before I opened the restaurant, I spent a week on a beach. The entire experience of finding the location for Rustica, stocking the kitchen, choosing the décor, had reached a boiling point in me and I knew I'd be no good to the place if I didn't take a few days off to just chill."

The mention of the beach made him think back to the night Jenna had set up a mini beach on his patio. He'd been to real beaches a half dozen times since that night—and none of them had been as special as that one.

"Did you go with someone?" Jenna asked.

She didn't look at him when she asked the question and he couldn't read what was going on in her mind. "Do I detect jealousy?"

"Of course not."

He didn't believe that for a second. "You didn't answer my question."

Her gaze returned to his, and the fire he knew so well flamed in her emerald eyes. "And you didn't answer mine," she said.

He bit back a grin. "No, I didn't go with anyone. I went alone."

She nodded, but he thought he detected a flash of a smile on her face. Again he wondered why and whether he was reading something that wasn't really there.

"I haven't taken a vacation since I moved to New York," she said after a while. "I kept meaning to, but the business sucked up all my time."

They were speaking the same language. How odd, he thought, that they'd ended up leading parallel lives, hundreds of miles apart. "And now? Isn't this time in Riverbend a vacation?"

She laughed. "Riverbend is not exactly a prime destination spot."

"Depends on who you talk to. Some people love small Indiana towns in the wintertime."

She arched a brow.

"Okay, maybe not a lot of people, but some. And those who live here love this town."

"Not everyone does."

"Some people used to love it, and maybe if they give it a chance, they'll love it again."

Was he talking about the town? He'd damned well better be, because he didn't want to fall in love with Jenna again, and vice versa. No matter what Aunt Mabel had said, he didn't see a huge change in Jenna. A lot more tension in her shoulders, yes, and stress in the lines of her face, but that could all be because her business was struggling. What he didn't see—what he'd never seen—was a desire in her for the same things it had turned out he wanted. Like a place to call home and put down some roots. They might be leading parallel lives, but they were living them on two different planets—and with two different ultimate goals.

"Are you trying to sell Riverbend to me?" she said.

"You used to like living here."

"I never did, Stockton. I always wanted to leave."

He shook his head, and pivoted until he was beside her again on the ice. "No, you always wanted to run away. That's what you're good at, Jenna, running."

She let out a gust. "Me? You're the runner, Stockton Grisham. The man who couldn't plant his feet in one place for more than five minutes."

"I'm planted here."

"Are you?"

"Of course I am. I have a business, employees who depend on me, customers who—"

"But what about *you*, Stockton? Has that wanderlust gone away? Are you any more ready to settle down now than you were all those years ago?"

"I'm settled, Jenna." But even as he said the words, he wondered how true they were. He lived in a barely decorated house. Spent so much of his day at work he rarely saw the sun. Couldn't remember the last serious relationship he'd had. "But what about you? You come back here, supposedly to plan a party, but there's more involved."

"It's just a party."

He shook his head again. "I know you, Jenna. And I know there's something you're leaving out. I think half the reason you're here is because you're running away from something in New York."

"No." She whispered the denial and looked away fast. Her eyes shimmered, with the cold? Or unshed tears?

What was Jenna hiding? What was bothering her?

Even now, anxiety knotted her shoulders, set in her jaw. He wanted to take it away, to find a way to coax that smile back to her face. "Do you want to talk about it?"

"Maybe I ran away from us all those years ago," she said. "But I only did it because you let me go."

"I asked you to go with me."

"No, Stockton, you didn't." Her gaze met his. "You assumed I'd go with you. And when I didn't, you assumed I'd wait for you. You never once realized that maybe I had my own dreams, and they didn't match yours." She looked off in the distance. "Either way, it doesn't matter. All that was years ago. We can't go back in time."

"No, we can't." He let out a breath. "And maybe it's a good idea if we don't."

In the center of the ice, a group of teenagers formed a line and held hands. The one closest to the center held his position, while the others skated around, creating a whip effect for those on the outside. It was a dangerous, but common, game among kids. Stockton had done it himself more than once. As the kids picked up speed, the farthest child at the end of the line lost his grip and spun off, arms windmilling, feet reaching for traction on the slippery surface.

Stockton glanced over at Jenna. Her gaze was off on the park, not on the ice action.

Just before the kid reached them, Stockton grabbed Jenna, hauled her to him and out of the way. She let out a surprised grunt when she hit his chest, and the skater slipped past them to skid to a stop at the edge.

"Sorry," Stockton said. "Just trying to avoid a collision."

"Thank you." Her face was upturned to his, her cheeks and lips red from the cold. He could almost feel her heart beat against his, even through the thick wool of their coats.

He should let go, push her away, and even better, get off this ice and get back to work. But Jenna was warm in his arms, and all the reasons he kept coming up with for why he should stay away from her seemed a million miles away. He had missed her, and as much as he just said he didn't want to revisit the past, a part of him really did. He reached up, brushed a tendril of hair off her forehead, and watched her eyes widen in surprise at the touch. "What are you running from now?" he asked softly.

She shook her head, and unshed tears shimmered in her emerald gaze. Damn it all. His heart softened, and he bent down, and brushed his lips against hers. A soft kiss, nothing more than one to tell her he was here, if she needed him, despite their past.

She let out a mew, and the soft kiss lingered, until Stockton forgot about being friendly, about keeping this light and casual, and he opened his mouth against hers. She tasted like she always had—sweet as cookies and milk, and yet also something dark and forbidden. Her arms went around his neck, and he crushed her to him, his mouth covering hers, taking all of her that he could get out here in public.

Stockton heard laughter. Conversation. The swish-swish of skates gliding past them. And he came to his senses.

"I'm sorry." He pulled back, and released Jenna. "That shouldn't have happened."

"It was insanity." She brushed at her face, as if trying to erase his kiss. "We were both, uh, probably caught up in the past or something."

"Yeah. I'm sure that was it."

She hadn't wanted him at all. She'd merely been reacting out of some long held memory. "I've had enough of the cold," Stockton said. "Let's get off the ice."

He waited for her, but she didn't even look at him as they skated across the pond and back to the rental shed. Neither of them said anything as they exchanged their skates for their shoes, and slid back into their winter boots.

"I'm sure you need to get back to work. I'll stop by tonight after the dinner rush at Rustica is over," Jenna said, "and we can go over the menu for Eunice's party then."

"It'll be easier for us to talk somewhere quiet. How about I stop over at Aunt Mabel's and come to you? If it's not too late by then."

"That'll be fine. I'm a night owl."

He remembered, and remembered all the late-night conversations they'd had, each of them sneaking a phone into their rooms, or, a few times, when they'd snuck out of their houses and taken a midnight walk. But he didn't say that. "I'll see you then."

Jenna nodded, then strode across the park. They didn't need to meet later; they could have handled their business now. Stockton had time before the restaurant needed him, but he sensed she needed time away from him as much as he needed time away from her. To regroup. To figure out what the hell had just happened.

And how he was going to deal with it the next time he saw her.

CHAPTER EIGHT

JENNA WASHED THE dinner dishes, leaving them to dry in the strainer, then realized she had nothing else left to detract her from having a conversation with Aunt Mabel, who had waited patiently at the kitchen table, pretending to do a crossword puzzle. Jenna stretched her arms over her head, and stifled a yawn. Beneath the table, she flexed her legs. Every muscle in her body ached. Who knew ice skating could be such a workout?

And not just for her arms and legs. Her mind rocketed back to Stockton's kiss, and she touched her lips, reliving the moment. Insanity, that's what that had been. Some kind of rekindling of old feelings that were better left buried.

It wouldn't happen again.

She had already made sure of that. She'd laid out her plans for Eunice's party on the table, along with a notepad and pen, a clear signal when he arrived that they would be talking business and nothing else.

"Are you going to tell me what happened today?" Aunt Mabel said. "You've been awfully quiet ever since you got home."

The old wooden chair let out a creaking protest when Jenna sat down and leaned back. She thought about not telling her aunt anything, then realized half the town had probably seen her skating with Stockton today. If she didn't already know, she'd know before the sun rose tomorrow. "I went ice skating with Stockton."

Aunt Mabel smiled. "Ice skating? You two used to love doing that when you were kids."

"It was his idea, to give us both a little break in the day. He was right. It was really fun until…"

Her aunt waited.

Jenna let out a breath. "Until he kissed me."

"And did you kiss him back?"

"Aunt Mabel!"

"It's a legitimate question, my dear. And don't think I got to be this age without kissing a few boys myself."

Jenna ran a hand through her hair. "I don't know what happened. You know me, I like to have everything under control, all the time, and this whole thing with Stockton is so far out of my control now, I'm not even sure what I'm doing from one minute to the next. I should never have agreed to use him as the caterer."

"Well, perhaps, dear, it's not just Stockton that has you out of sorts. You haven't been yourself in a long time."

"I'll be back at it soon. I've got a plan and everything."

"I know you will be. But I wonder if that's what you really want."

"What do you mean? Of course it is."

Her aunt's gaze softened. "This last year, when we've talked on the phone, you've seemed like…" She paused. "Well, like you're not as happy as you once were."

"I'm fine." Jenna's gaze went to the quartet of cow-shaped canisters on Aunt Mabel's kitchen counter. The containers had been Jenna's mother's—a bridal shower gift ages ago—and one of the many things that had made the journey from the farmhouse in the country to Aunt Mabel's house in Riverbend. After her parents died, Aunt Mabel had wanted to get her niece out of the isolated country farmhouse and into the city so she could have friends and community to help her deal with the tragic loss of both her parents. To make the transition easier, Aunt Mabel had brought along as many of Jenna's childhood home's furnishings and décor as she could, so the new home would feel something like the one she'd had to leave. And, Jenna was sure, so that Mabel could still feel close to the sister she had lost. For that and many other reasons, Jenna loved her Aunt Mabel dearly.

"Okay, maybe not so fine," Jenna admitted, not just to her aunt, but to herself, as well. "I don't know why I'm making all these mistakes. It's like I'm sabotaging my own career."

She thought of all the appointments she'd missed, the dates she'd mis-scheduled, the meetings she'd forgotten. It seemed like her brain had become a sieve, and she hadn't been able to find a way to plug the holes before her business slipped through, too.

"Maybe it's your mind's way of sending a message."

"What message is that?"

"That you made a wrong choice."

Jenna got to her feet, the chair screeching in protest. "I'll be fine. A few good parties and things will go back to normal."

Aunt Mabel heaved a sigh, and got to her feet, too. "Maybe yes, maybe no. And maybe you just need to get quiet and listen to your heart." She placed a hand on her niece's shoulder. "All the answers you need are there, Jenna. You just have to listen for them."

Aunt Mabel headed out of the room and up to bed, leaving behind the truth Jenna had been trying to avoid. She'd heard the same message twice in one day from two different people—when things got tough, or scary, or she just plain didn't like the situation, Jenna Pearson ran.

A soft rapping sounded on the glass of the back door. Stockton, here as promised. The man had terrible timing. He seemed to arrive when she was at her most vulnerable. She should have told him she'd meet him tomorrow, in the light of day, but truly, they were running out of time to plan this party and a professional businesswoman would get her work in order as early as possible.

She opened the door and Stockton came in, stomping snow onto the mat. "I think winter is never leaving," he said, offering her a grin.

He hadn't worn a hat and a fine dusting of snow coated his dark hair. Her hand reached out, fingers flexing, half ready to brush it away, but then she pulled back and reminded herself that she wasn't the woman who did that for him anymore.

"Do you want some coffee?" she said instead.

"That would be great. Decaf if you have it, or I'll never get to sleep."

"No problem." Jenna busied herself filling the coffeepot, avoiding Stockton's gaze. She'd thought time and distance would ease the heat simmering between them, but if anything, the attraction seemed to be building, as if now that her body had had a taste of him, the only thing it could do was want more.

She would serve him coffee, talk about the menu and keep her distance. Even if being near him again had stirred up a hornet's nest in her gut, swarming through her veins. Making her question her resolve before she even fully put it into place.

A moment later, she laid a steaming cup of coffee before him and sat down opposite his seat.

He grinned. "This is familiar."

"What?"

"Sitting at this table." He smoothed a hand over the maple surface, his fingers skipping over the decades of scuffs and scratches. "Late at night. Talking."

"Knowing Aunt Mabel was in the living room, listening for a break in conversation so she could yell at us to stop kissing." As soon as she said the words, she thought about that kiss on the ice, the heat against the cold, and how much she had missed kissing Stockton Grisham, whether it was right or wrong. And yes, she had missed talking to him, having his quiet, calming presence nearby.

Stockton chuckled. "Your aunt was quite the watchdog."

"She always liked you, though."

"There was a time when she didn't." He wrapped his hands around the warm mug, but didn't sip. His face sobered, and after a moment, he looked up and met her gaze. "Back when we were in high school, she once told me she thought we would end up together."

"We did. For a while."

"I think your aunt meant something a little more permanent. And when I went one way and you went another, your aunt crossed me off her favorite people list."

Jenna shifted in her seat, wishing she'd opted to have coffee, too, just to have something to do. She glanced at Stockton's hands—long, defined fingers, strong, broad palms, and her mind traveled back to the afternoon, to his touch against her face when he'd brushed her hair back. Why had he touched her, kissed her, if he was as sure as she was that there was no chance of them getting back together?

And why did everything inside her want him to do it again?

Didn't matter. After this, she was returning to New York,

and Stockton was staying here. Each of them was going back to the lives they'd had before Eunice's party dropped into their laps.

Jenna reached out, hauled the pile of papers and the notepad across the table and clicked on a pen. "Let's, ah, let's discuss the menu."

If Stockton was surprised by the change in topic, he didn't show it. Instead, he pushed his half-empty mug to the side and pulled a slip of paper out of his back pocket. "Eunice and Betsy are simple people," he said, unwittingly echoing Betsy's words from a few days ago. "And if you ask me, the best meals are those they know well." He unfolded the paper, revealing a copy of the restaurant's menu. As he talked, he pointed to items in the entrée listings, dishes that Jenna recognized from her night working the kitchen. "If you want my suggestions, I'd go for the sausage lasagna with a béchamel sauce, the house salad with a balsamic vinaigrette on the side and lots and lots of garlic bread." He grinned. "Eunice orders a basket of bread every Saturday to go with her supper, and makes Betsy trot on down to the restaurant to get it for her."

She pretended his smile didn't still affect her. That when that grin had broken across his features, she hadn't felt a quiver deep in her gut. That she didn't stare at his mouth and wonder if he would kiss her again.

"That all sounds, uh, wonderful," Jenna said, writing down his suggestions on the paper. Not because she might forget but because it gave her something to focus on besides him.

They finalized the rest of the menu, a process that took just a few minutes. Stockton had clearly done this before, and moreover, knew Eunice's favorite meals at Rustica. He proposed a selection of two desserts besides the birthday cake, "because Eunice has a bit of a sweet tooth," and the fried ravioli appetizer, because it was the one meal Eunice ordered without fail, every time she came into Rustica. Already, Jenna could see the tables, the settings, the colors in the room. She'd echo the hues used by Stockton's restaurant and make Eunice feel even more at home.

"I'm not surprised your business is doing so well," Jenna said. "A chef who knows his customers that well can't help but succeed."

"I've lived here so long, everyone in town is almost like family." Stockton leaned forward, and the table that had seemed like a big enough gulf between them five seconds ago suddenly shrank into nothing. "You know, this town isn't so bad. Sure, there are a few bad apples, just as there are anywhere, but if you gave Riverbend a chance, you might find it grows on you."

"That's easy for you to say," Jenna said quietly. "It isn't you, or your family, that they talk about. And no matter what other things people might have done, it was their words that spoke the truth."

He waited until she'd lifted her gaze to his, until he had her full attention. "How long are you going to let those few idiotic people dictate your life?"

She shook her head. The back of her eyes burned but she refused to cry. She didn't want to think about those days again, but it seemed they were determined to push themselves to the surface.

"They blame me," she said quietly. "I was only seven years old, Stockton."

"I know, Jenna, I know."

She could still hear the whispers. She'd been so little, people probably thought she wouldn't know what they were talking about, or understand that she was the topic. "Do you know what someone said to me once in the grocery store? That it was a blessing my mother had died. A blessing. Because she'd caused so much turmoil in everyone's lives."

"There are some people who are too ignorant to have mouths," Stockton said.

"Those people," she said, her voice hoarse, "God, all they did was talk about it every time they saw me. About how tragic it was that the little Pearson girl had lost everything. How her mother had been running around with another man. How her parents would still be alive if they hadn't had that argument. How—" Her voice caught on a sob and she shook her head.

Stockton reached out, his hand covering hers. His touch held the comfort of a longtime friend, someone who had been there through the good days and the bad, who knew her as well as she knew herself. Holding his hand was like falling into home.

Why had they ever let their friendship go? Had the end really been that bad, that neither of them wanted to hold on as friends?

"Nothing was ever your fault, Jenna," Stockton said. "And the few people who thought that were just stupid."

She shook her head, keeping the tears in check. Barely.

"It wasn't your fault," Stockton repeated. "You must know that."

"I do, but…" She bit her lip. "But other people think differently. They think if my mother had never met that man, never had me, then maybe she wouldn't have been in that accident. And they blame her for my father's death. If she hadn't been hurt, he wouldn't have been rushing to the hospital." She shook her head. "People loved Joe Pearson. Thought he was the salt of the earth, and when he died, it was like they took out their grief on me, because my mother wasn't there to blame anymore."

"People change, Jenna."

Not everyone, she thought, thinking back to the whispers she'd overheard. Sure, there'd been people in town who had offered a helping hand here and there. Some who had donated clothes, others who had dropped off food at Aunt Mabel's. But none of that made up for the whispers. "If I stay here, I'll always be that girl," she said. "And all I ever wanted to do was get away from being her."

Stockton's fingers grasped hers, and his deep blue gaze connected with her own. "You are always going to be Jenna Pearson from Riverbend, Indiana. And if you ask me, that's a good thing. It means you have a history, a heritage and a hell of a lot of people here who would help you—if you'd just learn to ask."

She shook her head. "You love this town. I don't. So stop trying to sell me on how great Riverbend is."

He was quiet, the moment stretching tight between them as a new elastic. "What are you doing tomorrow morning?"

Gratitude washed over her at the change in topic. Clearly, Stockton could see that holding Riverbend up as some Nirvana was never going to work with her. "Picking out decorations for the party. Meeting with the banquet hall to go over the linens and serveware choices—"

He waved off the tasks. "It can wait an hour or two. I want to show you something."

"I shouldn't—"

"You should. I have something I'd like you to see." He grinned. "And no, it doesn't involve ice skating."

Jenna felt an answering smile curve up her face. Stockton had deftly moved the subject area away from disappointments. And back into something that coaxed along the fringes of her better judgment. "If I take any more time off, I won't have a job."

"One morning more, that's all I ask."

Damn, he was tempting. *Everything* about him was a temptation she should avoid because he came with strings, connections. Jenna didn't want or need any of those, especially not in the short window she'd be in town.

She hadn't intended to spend any time at all with Stockton, and she'd ended up cooking with him, ice skating with him, and now, making more plans. She wanted to say no, knew she should say no, but then her gaze strayed to his mouth, to his deep blue eyes that held real concern for someone he'd known for years, and she couldn't seem to voice the right word. "What time?"

"Eight-thirty, on the dot."

"I'll be there," she promised, though she had no idea what she was promising to do. But she had a bad feeling all she was doing was further derailing her plans. They may have gotten the menu planned tonight, but something far more intoxicating was cooking up between Jenna and Stockton.

Something she would put a stop to—at eight-thirty tomorrow morning.

CHAPTER NINE

STOCKTON HALF EXPECTED Jenna not to show up. He let himself into the restaurant a little after eight, drank his fourth cup of coffee of the morning, and waited for the caffeine to take away the sleepless night he'd had last night. He'd tossed and turned for hours, replaying that kiss they'd shared on the ice in his mind, over and over.

Hell, even now, the memory tingled down his spine. Kissing Jenna had been...wonderful. Sweet. Delicious.

It was the aftermath that fit a whole other category of adjectives. He should have thought it through first. Except, when it came to getting involved with Jenna Pearson, smart thinking had never seemed to be part of the equation.

He knew better. And still, he'd gotten wrapped up in her smile, her eyes, her touch. And then last night, he'd been drawn in by her vulnerability. They'd connected in that quiet moment, just like they had in the old days and for a while Stockton had thought they could go back. Be what they were before everything fell apart when she left for New York.

Except, if he was really honest with himself, he'd admit that things between them had been eroding day by day long before Jenna packed her bags. They'd had a lot of fun during those high school years, but they'd never really built anything solid. One big test—and wham, their relationship was over. And he'd chosen the flight to Italy.

If he'd needed a clear-cut sign that they weren't destined to be together, that was it.

Then why did he keep on stirring up a hornet's nest that had been dormant for eight years?

The front door opened, and Jenna walked in, bringing with her a gust of winter. "Good morning." She might as well have been greeting the paperboy for all the warmth in her tone.

Clearly, he wasn't the only one trying to avoid a repeat of what had happened on the ice. And trying to put last night behind them. The best way to do that, he figured, was to get right to the reason he had called her here today. The more he lingered, the more tempting it was to kiss her again.

Stockton grabbed his coat, and motioned to Jenna. "Come on in the back. We have some things to get before we leave."

"Where are we going?"

"To see another side of Riverbend." When she'd said all that about the town last night, his heart had gone out to her. He remembered those days, remembered the people who had talked about Jenna as if she wasn't in the room. Hell, people still talked about the accidents that had claimed her parents' lives, whenever Jenna's name came up. He could understand her wanting to escape the mantle of being "that girl" but she needed to see the whole picture. Remember the other dimensions to Riverbend that existed then, and now.

He held the kitchen door for her, then directed her to take several foil-wrapped containers out of the walk-in refrigerator and put them into a box. She did as he asked, with only a confused glance in his direction. He added a bag of loose dinner rolls, then hefted the box into his arms and headed out the back door, with Jenna right behind him. Stockton loaded the box into the back of his Jeep, then held Jenna's door before coming around to the driver's side and starting the SUV. A few seconds later, they were pulling out of the restaurant's parking lot and heading down Riverbend's main street. The day was clear and crisp, giving the snow still on the ground a hard, crunchy shine.

"Your one-year anniversary party is tomorrow, you know," she said.

"Yep."

"I know I have a lot to finish up for that, and you probably have plenty to do for the meal, not to mention tonight's dinner service. Whatever this is that you want to show me, can surely wait for another day. I hate to take up any more of your time."

"I have time for this," Stockton said. "I always have time for this."

It took about ten minutes to get to their destination, an old ornate church on the corner of the east end of downtown. Stockton parked the Jeep, hopped out and headed for the back of the truck.

He thought she'd be surprised. Ask a few questions. Instead, she sat quietly in the truck and stared at the tall white spire. "They still run that here."

It was a statement, not a question, but he answered it anyway. Still, he was surprised she recognized their destination. Had she been there before? "Yes."

She got out of the truck, and went around to the back, waiting while Stockton opened the door and pulled out the containers. He hefted most of them into his arms, leaving Jenna with one small container and the bag of rolls. She held the door for him as they headed inside the warm, cavernous building.

As soon as the heavy oak door shut behind them, an older, heavy-set man strode down the aisle and toward them. He wore jeans, a black long-sleeved shirt with a white tab at the collar, and a broad, friendly smile.

Stockton balanced the box on one arm and shook the man's hand. "Father Michael, nice to see you again."

"Always good to see you, too," the other man said. He gestured toward the large box filled with several containers of food. "Ah, Stockton, you bless this place so much."

"It's nothing, really." Stockton shrugged, then nodded toward Jenna. "I brought along a friend today." Before he could introduce her, Jenna was stepping forward and wrapping the priest in a warm hug.

"Father Michael. It's been years since I've seen you."

"And I you." He leaned back and gifted her with a smile. "How are you?"

"Fine, just fine."

Father Michael nodded. "I'm glad to hear that. Come, let's bring this food downstairs. We're still serving breakfast, but we can get this stored for lunch and then start service."

As they headed down the aisle and toward a small door at the back of the church, Stockton turned to Jenna. "How do you know Father Michael?" As far as he knew, Jenna wasn't Catholic and he'd never heard her mention attending this church.

"I've been here before."

"To church?"

A small smile whispered across her face. "No. To the soup kitchen. Well, I don't think they called it that back when I was young, but yes, my family has been here." Her gaze drifted over the murals on the walls, the long rows of pews, the velvet tufted kneelers. "I think I told you we were poor."

He nodded. "Your dad's farm struggled, and you had it tough."

"*Tough* doesn't describe it." She let out a long breath. "We had many dinners here, when I was little. Before we left, Father Michael always pulled my parents aside to ask them how they were doing. And if there was ever anything our family needed, it seemed to just appear, without us ever asking."

Father Michael paused, his hand on the knob for the door that led to the basement hall. "I'm glad we were able to do what we could, Jenna. Your parents worked awfully hard out there, bless their hearts. You know farming. It can be a difficult field to make a living. There are times when the harvest is bountiful, and other times when it's…lean."

Jenna's mind rocketed back, to the days in that low-slung white house far from downtown Riverbend. Surrounded by cornfields and to the rear, a herd of cattle that had dwindled more each year. Her father, working so many hours most days she didn't even see him. Her mother, who went gray before she was thirty-five, worrying her days away. There'd been nights when dinner had been nothing more than a thin soup of root vegetables, and mornings when breakfast was a leftover heel of bread. Jenna had been young, and barely noticed anything except a rumbly stomach, but she remembered the worry, the tears, the long, long days without her father.

Was that what had driven her mother, over and over again, into the arms of another man? The constant struggle, the scrabble for the leanest of existences? Had that been enough to turn her from her family and to someone else she thought had loved her?

She could tell from the surprise on Stockton's face that he had thought he knew everything about her. He knew almost everything—except the parts that she had pushed aside, because they were days she didn't want to remember. She didn't say anything more as they went through the side door and down the staircase to the basement of the church. Voices carried up the stairs.

When Jenna reached the bottom step and she took in the people around her—clad in layers and layers of worn clothing, their faces marred by dirt and their smiles filled with gratitude—her heart clenched. "It hasn't changed that much."

"Well, we have new furniture and a bigger kitchen," Father Michael said with a smile, then sobered. "But sadly, no, the need hasn't changed. It's ebbed and flowed over the years, but there are always gaps that the government can't fill. We have a few beds here now, not nearly enough, but still, we try to fill everyone's needs in some way or another," Father Michael said. "Whatever they need, and whenever they need it."

Stockton excused himself from the group and headed over to the tiny kitchen to unload the food he had brought and store it in the refrigerator for later. The rest of the volunteers were busy setting up for breakfast.

"This place has also become a haven for some," Father Michael went on. "A place for others who are down on their luck and need a way to fill their bellies, or their kids'."

A dozen children sat at one table together, others huddled shyly against their parents. A few babies sat in carriers perched on overturned chairs being used as makeshift stands. There was a combined air of desperation and hope hanging in the air. But still, she heard laughter, joking, and saw more smiles than frowns.

She saw herself, so young her feet didn't hit the floor. Her parents on either side of her, urging her to eat more. She remembered a much younger Father Michael, stopping by their table with a kind word for her father, a bag of groceries for her mother. But most of all, she remembered the people, the community that had sprung up here among the neediest of Riverbend.

She glanced at Stockton across the room and he flashed her a quick smile. He'd read her mind, and taken her to the one place that would remind her that there were good people in this town, too. Very good people.

"You were kind to my family," Jenna said to Father Michael.

"Being kind is part of being Christian," he said, laying a comforting hand on her shoulder. Then he smiled. "And speaking of being kind, I better say grace so people can eat."

She chuckled, and watched him walk to the center of the room. As he said grace, Jenna glanced around once more and realized those who were helping—everything from setting up the buffet line to handing out bags filled with what she assumed were toiletries—were people she recognized from town. Samantha's aunt, who often worked with her niece in the bakery. Mrs. Richards, Jenna's third-grade teacher. The husband and wife who lived in the little blue house across the street from Aunt Mabel. So many familiar faces, all working together in their efforts to help the less fortunate.

And not one of them—not the people here to help or the people here who needed help—looked at Jenna Pearson and whispered. Here, she was merely a welcome set of hands.

When the prayer was done, people rose, crossed to the buffet line and began loading up their plates with scrambled eggs, toast, fried potatoes and bacon. Stockton was on the other side of the line, serving eggs with a smile. Jenna slipped into place behind him, donning the apron and latex gloves another volunteer handed her, then took up the tongs for the toast and dispensed slices to the people passing her station. A few who knew her greeted her, asked why she was in town. She kept the conversation simple and the line moving.

This place had filled her when she was hungry, supported her parents when they were in need. Had Stockton been right? Had she purposely forgotten the other side of Riverbend because she'd been too busy nursing a hurt caused by a few bad apples?

"T'ank you," said a little girl in a pink floral jumper that was too short for her skinny frame. She picked up the piece of toast Jenna had just laid on her paper plate and took a big bite, then smiled. "I love toast."

Jenna smiled and added a second piece of toast to the girl's plate. "Me, too."

Her mother rubbed a gentle hand over her daughter's blond locks, then the two of them moved down the line. The woman looked about Jenna's age and Jenna wondered if perhaps she had known her back in school. As the line moved along, Jenna realized several of the people looked familiar, and that fact disturbed her even more. It was so easy to forget, to push aside the signs of those in need.

For so long, she'd been concentrating on her own business, on her own problems, never thinking about the others who had it worse. She'd forgotten that there was a bigger world outside her own, and that world had once supported her, and her family, with food and hugs.

And without judgment.

"Oh, my goodness. Is that you, Jenna Pearson?"

The woman's soft voice seemed to be a blast from the past. Jenna paused in handing out toast and focused on the woman's face. It took a moment before recognition made it past the worn, tired face devoid of makeup, the plain brown hair pulled back into a ponytail, the faded, gray jeans and sweatshirt. "Tammy?"

"Yep, that's me." She waved a hand over her thin frame. "Had a few tough times as you can see, but I'm glad this place is here."

"Me, too," Jenna said, and meant it. For people like Tammy Winchester, for the others in the room, and for her parents, having a refuge like this, even in a town as small as Riverbend, meant no one had to go without a meal.

"Things are looking up, though," Tammy said, as she held her plate toward Stockton so he could add a serving of eggs. "I have a job interview next Tuesday." She smiled. "Wish me luck."

"Really? What are you interviewing for?"

Tammy smiled. "Anything they'll hire me to do. I'm not picky."

In high school, Tammy had been a part of student council, a member of the cheerleading squad, one of those women who had a ready smile all the time. The same smile was there, and Jenna was sure, so were the same talents. "I'm sure you'll do fine. If I remember right, you were the star student on the debate team."

A pleased look filled Tammy's face. "You remember that?"

"Of course. You were the one the rest of the team relied on whenever we needed a quick, smart response." Jenna smiled.

Worry creased Tammy's brow. She picked at the edge of her toast. "Well, it won't matter what I say unless I find something to wear. The church donates clothing items, but there's really not a lot of businesswoman kind of clothes. Know what I mean? I'd love to wow them at this interview." She glanced over her shoulder, saw the line backing up, and gave Jenna a little wave. "Well, I better get going. Talk to you later, Jenna."

"Good luck at your interview." Tammy moved down, and as the line progressed, and Jenna caught snippets of conversations, she realized Father Michael's refuge was doing more than just feeding people. There was discussion about available jobs, tips on writing a resume, a mention of a class to show one woman how to use a computer.

"This is amazing," Jenna said to Stockton as the line dwindled and the workers began cleaning up from the meal. "So much more than what I remembered."

"The reach of this place expands every year," Stockton said. "Father Michael really wants to make it about much more than food. He wants people to see this place as a resource. He and his team help people with everything, from finding affordable apartments to interviewing for a job. There's not a lot of need in a town as small as Riverbend, at least compared to a city, but he makes sure that whatever need there is, it gets met."

Jenna took the leftover toast and began storing it in plastic wrap. She thought of the Stockton she used to know, a boy who had been too concentrated on having fun to ever do anything practical or serious, or sacrificial. And here he was, clearly a regular behind the buffet line, and also a generous donor of food. Food that came from a restaurant he had opened up in this town, yet one more way he'd set down roots and also boosted the local economy. Stockton had changed, she realized, in more ways than one. "Why are you here?"

"Because it makes me feel good. I'm sure it would be easier to let the leftover food go to waste, but this is rewarding. I found something here," he said, pausing as he loaded the empty chafing dish into the sink, "something that I hadn't realized I'd been looking for until I came across it."

Yes, Stockton had changed—become calmer, more centered. A man who knew what he wanted, and even more, had it.

She envied that peace. For as long as she could remember, she had felt a constant churning in her gut. She'd called it need for a change of her life, and for a while there in New York, the churning had been quieted by success. But then over the past few months, heck, maybe Aunt Mabel was right and it had been more than a year, the churning had returned, becoming a full-blown whirlpool threatening to take her down into its vortex.

And so she had begun to screw up. At first, she had attributed it to her business growing too fast, being too busy to mind the details, but was there more to her actions, as her aunt had said? Was it some subconscious fight to find what Stockton clearly had?

"What did you find here?" she asked Stockton. Maybe if she knew, she'd understand better and be able to find the same.

He thought a moment. Beside them, soap bubbles popped and disappeared in the hot dishwater. The bustle of the kitchen cleanup continued, and out at the dining tables, the low, happy hum of conversation rolled. "That when we help other people, it reminds us of the goodness in others, and in ourselves. And reminds us that there is good everywhere, including this town."

Jenna's gaze took in the people in the room, their faces content, filled by more than just a meal. "You're right," she said softly. "I guess I got too wrapped up in the bad to focus on the good. It was easier, I guess, that way."

Stockton stopped cleaning for a moment, and met her gaze. "I think people do that a lot. About more than just what's happening behind closed doors—about themselves and who they really are."

Jenna loaded the last of the dishes into the dishwasher and thought about Stockton's words. She'd come here with him this morning, sure she'd prove him wrong. Sure she'd find one more argument in the case against Riverbend. Instead, she'd been reminded that this town did, as Stockton said, have another side. One that helped without judging, without asking anything in return. A side that had helped first her family, and later her, when she'd needed it.

She'd returned to Riverbend, so sure this town could never grow on her again. Confident that Stockton Grisham hadn't changed at all. After today, she could no longer deny the truth—

She'd been wrong. There was only one person she didn't really know anymore.

Herself.

CHAPTER TEN

"Don't tell me that's what you're wearing tonight."

Jenna turned, the simple black dress she'd been considering pressed to her chest. "I might. If I even go."

"It's New Year's Eve, Jenna. You have to go out, it's a tradition. And you have to look sexy. That's a rule." Livia grinned. Her plane had arrived that afternoon, and in the few hours since, Jenna had caught her friend and former employee up on all the party plans. Not so much on the personal events. Jenna's mind was still processing how Stockton had surprised her in the past few days.

Livia entered the room and took a seat on the quilted comforter. "Aren't you supposed to go? I mean, you planned this party."

"I'm sure Stockton will have it all under control." Jenna draped the black sheath dress over the chair beside the vanity she'd sat at for so many years, it seemed like it was part of her. The scarred white furniture had been one of the first things Aunt Mabel bought her when they moved to the house in the city, and the first time Jenna had ever owned a matched bedroom set. Even though she'd long ago outgrown the scalloped edged pieces with their painted on pink flowers, she loved every bit of it, from the twin bed to the long, low dresser.

"Maybe. Maybe not. Either way, you should go, if only

to have an excuse to wear a great dress." Livia picked up a second dress lying on the bed. The red jersey fabric hugged Jenna's curves, while the low V-neck offered a tantalizing glimpse of what lay beneath. When Jenna had packed it, she'd been sure it was a waste of valuable suitcase space, but now she wondered if maybe Livia had a point.

How would Stockton react if she walked into the room, wearing this dress? Would he smile and take her in his arms? Or would he be so wrapped up in his party that he barely even noticed her presence?

She glanced at her luggage. In a few days, she'd be packing and heading back to New York. And Stockton would once again be a piece of her past. He had changed in many ways, but not in the ways that were most fundamental to a relationship. He'd danced around them being together again, but hadn't done anything more than that. Just like in years past, Stockton had one foot toward the door even as he said he wanted to stay.

She sighed. "I have so much to do for Eunice's birthday party that I don't really have time to go out tonight. I already made sure the restaurant was all set up for the party tonight. I don't have to be there to host it." She rehung the dress in the closet, then reached for her robe.

"It's New Year's Eve," Livia said, retrieving the red dress and pressing it into Jenna's hands. "A time for new beginnings." She closed Jenna's hands over the plastic hanger. "And if anyone needs a new beginning, it's you."

"I don't—"

"You do. You've been in this rut for too long, Jenna. Get out tonight, have some fun. And maybe you'll find what it is you've been searching for."

Was that why she had returned to Riverbend? She'd been searching for something, something to fill that yawning hole in her life?

Jenna took the dress and turned toward the mirror, holding the crimson dress to her chest. She flipped her black hair over her shoulders, giving her a preview of how she'd look. "And what do I do when I find it?"

Livia smiled, and pressed her cheek to Jenna's. "Grab it with both hands. And never let go."

A local oldies band was setting up on the temporary stage erected by the bar. In the center of Rustica hung a glittery strobe light on a retractable chain, waiting to be lowered at midnight. Streamers shouting "Happy New Year!" and "Happy Anniversary, Rustica!" hung from one end of the restaurant to the other, while hundreds of silver and white helium balloons bobbed along the ceiling. The decorations were classy and echoed the festive, hopeful mood Stockton had wanted for this combination anniversary/New Year's Eve party.

It was exactly what he'd envisioned. He should have been thrilled. Instead, a nagging sense that he was missing something hung heavy on his spirits.

A buffet of dinner selections had been set up along one wall, an appetizer station along the other, and in the center of Rustica—a massive cake baked by Samantha and offering congratulations on a first year's success. All the staff had arrived for the evening—some grumbling about working New Year's Eve, but most happy to be there to celebrate the momentous occasion. Everything was perfect—and hopefully would be well enjoyed by the hundreds of people who had RSVP'd to the party invitation.

Jenna had outdone herself. She'd created a fun environment, but not one that overshadowed the restaurant itself. He knew when he put the party in her hands that everything would be taken care of, and in a way that defied his expectations—not to mention anything he could have put together. The only thing he had to worry about was the food, and even that had Jenna's thoughtful touch. He glanced at the hand-lettered signs posted along the buffet line: AULD LANG SYNE MINESTRONE; CELEBRATION CONCHIGLIEI; NEW BEGINNINGS ANTIPASTO.

It was clever, without being cutesy. He'd been right to trust her with the party, to simply hand over the reins and let her do her job.

Stockton straightened his tie. Damned thing felt like it was going to strangle him. No wonder he never wore the stupid things. He was far more comfortable in the white cotton chef's shirt, or a simple T-shirt and jeans, and being behind the stove instead of on display. But tonight he was spending his time in the front of the house, greeting his guests and thanking each of them for the business. Without these customers, he wouldn't be where he was today— standing in the center of his own restaurant, enjoying the success he had always dreamed of having.

He thought of his father, and wondered if there would ever come a day when Hank Grisham would sample his son's success. Stockton had called Hank the day he opened Rustica, and a couple of times since, and although his father had congratulated him, he'd held firm to the belief that no one could make a successful restaurant in the town Hank had seen as a little pocket of hell.

Stockton glanced around the room again and wondered if perhaps it was more that his father didn't want to admit that his son had done what he himself had never been able to do. Before Stockton was born, Hank had toyed with the idea of a restaurant in Riverbend, even went to work at one in a nearby town to learn the business from the inside out. But when that restaurant failed, Hank had given up on small towns, and pretty much given up on his marriage, and headed out on a cross-country, then cross-world journey with his knife and apron.

Stockton knew he *should* be enjoying his success, celebrating a great year in business. But the emptiness that had plagued him in recent weeks returned with a roar. He told himself it was merely the inevitable letdown that came with reaching a milestone.

Yeah, right.

Nine o'clock arrived. Stockton opened the restaurant's doors, cued the band and started the party. For the next two and a half hours, he was able to forget the emptiness, and concentrate on his customers. Still, his concentration was a fragile thread, and after the twelfth time he glanced toward the door, he knew why.

Jenna.

She hadn't come to the party. Why?

A little before midnight, the front door opened, and Stockton's heart leapt, then dropped again when he realized it was only Betsy and Earl stopping by. "The place looks great," Earl said. "Where's the food?"

Stockton laughed, and gestured toward the buffet tables. "Already have a plate with your name on it over there, Earl."

Earl grinned and rubbed his belly. "Glad to hear that, Stockton. Your cooking is the best—" he glanced at Betsy who shot him a warning glare "—the best, second to Betsy's, of course."

Betsy gave him a tender pat on the shoulder, then turned back to Stockton. "You've done a good job," she said. "I think these decorations are wonderful."

"It wasn't me. This was all Jenna's doing."

Betsy glanced around the room again, reassessing the décor. "Well. She did a mighty fine job. Let's hope she'll do just as good a one with my sister's party."

"She will. You can count on her." Though as he said the words, and watched Betsy and Earl cross to the buffet, he found himself glancing at the door again.

He was about to turn away when he saw a familiar pair of green eyes framed by soft ebony curls behind the glass. *Jenna.*

She entered the restaurant, at first not seeing him, but rather looking past him as her gaze scanned the crowd. Another woman stood beside her, a tall blonde in a blue dress. Her friend Livia, Stockton guessed, the one arriving today. Livia whispered something to Jenna, then headed down the stairs and over to the bar. Stockton waited, and watched, as Jenna's gaze swept around, then came back to center.

To him.

A smile broke across her face as bright and sweet as spring sunshine. He felt something stir deep inside his gut, and wondered what it would take to keep that smile permanently on her face. Wondered what it would be like to see that smile every single day.

The year was starting anew. Maybe they could, too.

"Hi," she said, the word soft and quiet amid the noise of the full restaurant.

"Hi." Stockton took two steps forward. For some reason, he felt nervous and awkward, like he was a teenager again. "Let me, uh, take your coat."

She grinned. "You're not in the kitchen tonight?"

"Nope. Tonight I'm part of the…entertainment." He chuckled. "Though some people might ask for their money back after they spend enough time with a chef who would rather be in the kitchen than playing the small-talk game."

"Oh, I doubt that."

"I have to thank you," Stockton said. "The restaurant

looks incredible. When I walked in here today, I hardly recognized the place."

A flush filled her cheeks. "I should be thanking you. It's not often that I have a client just hand over the keys and say he trusts me."

"I do trust you, Jenna."

She shook her head, as if trying to head off words she didn't want to hear. "I'm glad you're pleased with the results. Anyway, I just came by to check on things and make sure it all went off without a hitch." She started to button her coat again, but Stockton put a hand on hers.

"Stay. Enjoy the fruits of your labor. Have some pasta and sauce. I think that might be a bit more appetizing than your aunt's black-eyed peas and lentils."

Jenna laughed. "How'd you know she's got those ready?"

"I know your aunt Mabel, and if there's one person who's got superstition down to an art form, it's her."

"When I left, she had a broom beside the back door. Said she was going to stay up until midnight, then sweep all the bad luck out the door. And she's also one of the reasons I'm wearing red." She let her hand fall away, and the coat fell open, revealing a red dress that hugged her curves. An incredible, stop-his-heart-for-a-second dress. Holy cow.

"You look great in that color," Stockton said. Understatement, he realized. She looked amazing.

"Thanks. Though I'll have you know, Aunt Mabel's superstitions extend beyond dresses and into underwear." Jenna leaned forward and her voice dropped to a whisper. "She wouldn't let me leave the house unless I was wearing *all* red."

A surge ran through him, and his mind pictured what surprises might be beneath the red dress. Holy cow times ten. For a second, he imagine himself unzipping the dress, watching it fall to the floor, revealing the scraps of red beneath. "You're wearing red underwear, too?"

The flush returned to her cheeks. "I can't believe I told you that. I just...well..."

"We used to tell each other everything," he finished for her. Then he quirked a grin at her. "Hey, anytime you want to tell me about what's under your dress, I'm all ears."

Jenna swatted him, and in that moment, Stockton could believe they were back to how they used to be, years ago. He wanted to hold on to this moment, bottle it, and bring it out after Jenna had left.

"Your aunt's led a pretty charmed life," Stockton said. "Maybe there's something to all that superstition stuff."

"Maybe." Her gaze connected with his. "And...maybe I can stay for a little while."

"That'd be nice," he said softly.

She slipped off her coat. Stockton's gaze drifted down her lithe frame, over the V-necked red dress, past her trim waist, lingering on her bare legs, enhanced by strappy red heels. Desire surged in his veins, pounded in his head, compounded every time he looked at her lips and thought about what she'd feel like in his arms again.

Damn. This was dangerous.

He should turn around, go back to the party and stop letting himself get wrapped up with this woman. Instead, he took her winter jacket, handed it to the coat-room attendant, then put out his hand. "Do you want to dance?"

She hesitated, and for a second he thought she'd say no, but then the smile curved across her face again, and she nodded. "Though I warn you, I'm no Ginger Rogers."

He chuckled. "That's okay. My dancing skills are pretty much limited to slow dances. Anything else, and I look like a chicken flopping on the floor."

"I remember. You were my prom date."

He groaned. "I still can't believe you let me wear that light blue tux."

"It wasn't so bad, Stockton." A soft smile filled her face, and again he got the feeling that if they could somehow hold on to this moment, everything would be okay between them.

"Do we dare a repeat?" he asked.

"Yes. We do." Her hand slipped into his as they threaded their way through the crowd and onto the small dance floor set up to the right of the bar. As they reached the parquet, the band segued from the fast pop song they'd been playing to a slow country ballad. "Did you plan that?" Jenna asked.

"I wish I was that clever, but no, I didn't." He put out his arm, and she stepped into the space, then he took her opposite hand, and they began to step to the side, their bodies not quite touching, but close, very, very close. "Do you remember our first dance?"

She nodded. "Eighth grade. We were all pimples and gangly bodies, and for half the dance all the boys hugged the walls—"

"Too nervous to talk to the girls." He shook his head at the memory. "I sat beside you for seven years in school, and talked to you every day, but you add in some music and dimmed lights, and I was as nervous as an actor before the curtain rises."

"And are you nervous now?"

"Hell, yes."

She laughed. "Good. Because I am, too."

"Don't be nervous, Jenna. It's just me." He brought his face closer to her hair, inhaling the light vanilla-cinnamon fragrance. For a moment, he was lost, in the feel of Jenna in his arms, the scent of her teasing his senses. His gaze drifted along her delicate jaw line, and his body tensed as the desire to kiss her there, to trail kisses all the way down her body, rose inside him. His mouth hovered over her skin, so close his breath made little paths in the fine hairs along her neck. He pressed Jenna closer, until her body and his merged, their steps becoming one and the same. He ran a hand down her back, the dress hitching a little with his touch.

"What are we doing?" Jenna whispered. He could feel the words against his shoulder, and more, feel her tremble as she spoke them.

"I don't know."

It was the truth. He didn't know what he was doing. Or why. All he knew was the sound of this insistent need, pounding inside him, telling him he couldn't let her get away again. Even as he knew they hadn't settled a thing, and as far as he knew, the life she wanted was the same one she'd wanted when they'd broken up.

One that would not include him.

"We shouldn't..." she said, but didn't finish the sentence.

"We've already made this mistake," he said, and still his lips hovered over her neck, and the pounding kept pace with his heartbeat.

"Yeah," Jenna said, then she turned her head just enough so that her mouth was under his.

The band had stopped playing, and around him, the sound of cheering and counting finally infiltrated Stockton's brain. Midnight—they'd reached midnight and everyone was counting down those last few seconds. A sense of magic filled the air, highlighted by the shiny decorations, the sparkling confetti littering the tables. It seemed, at that moment, as if anything was possible.

As if anything he wanted could be his.

The crowd laughed, glasses raised, an air of happy

anticipation filling the room, but still Stockton's attention was riveted on Jenna. Her mouth, her touch. Simply... her.

People chanted the numbers together. "Ten...nine... eight..."

"We could get hurt again," he said.

"Five...four...three..."

"Very hurt," she whispered, and her gaze locked on his. The heat that had been building between them reached a fever pitch. His gut tightened with desire, and he realized that the most magical thing in the room was Jenna.

"Two...one...Happy New Year!" Cheers erupted around them, horns blew, glasses clinked and the band launched into "Auld Lang Syne."

They were old acquaintances, just as the song said, and if they were really honest with each other, they'd admit the truth. They'd never forgotten, not for a moment. And right now, all Stockton wanted to do was remember her, remember this.

"Happy New Year, Jenna," Stockton whispered, then he closed the gap between them and kissed her.

Jenna melted into Stockton's arms, her resistance gone the second he'd lowered his lips to hers. Heck, she'd been unable to resist that man from the day she met him. She'd always been attracted to Stockton, truth be told.

And kissing a man who had known her as long as Stockton had meant he knew every nuance of her mouth, every touch that would drive her wild. His lips claimed hers with a heat that built and built, a sweetness flavored by reunion and second chances. His hands ranged up and down her back, playing a tune that only he knew.

Electricity charged her body, and she leaned into him, craving more of his touch, his kiss, simply craving him. Her mind emptied of every thought except the feel of Stockton against her. He tasted of coffee and red wine, like a special dessert just for her. His tongue swept inside her mouth, and she echoed the gesture, dancing with him. A groan built in her throat and escaped in a soft mew. "Stockton."

He drew back, pressing his cheek to her hair. The tender move nearly brought her to tears. "Aw, Jenna, I've missed you."

She shook her head, and backed up. "We can't do this. I'm going back to New York, and you're staying here."

He caught her hand. "Stay. Don't leave. You can run a business here as easily as there."

"I can't, Stockton. You don't understand. I'd never be happy here."

"Because you hate Riverbend so much or because you never allowed yourself to love it?"

"I...I can't do this." *Can't answer your question. Can't stand here and fall for you all over again.* Jenna spun away before Stockton could stop her.

And before he could see the tears forcing their way to the surface.

The red dress hadn't brought her luck at all. In the end, all Aunt Mabel's superstitions had done was turn her into a bigger fool than she already was. And raised her hopes for a new-year beginning that was impossible to have.

CHAPTER ELEVEN

"You've done my family proud," Betsy Williams said. She spun a slow circle in the middle of the Riverbend Banquet Hall and beamed. The room wasn't entirely done—the finishing touches would come tomorrow, shortly before the party—but Livia and Jenna had made a good start on the setup, thanks to Livia's persuasive abilities with the owner of the venue. Jenna was pretty sure Edward Graham had given them the extra day just to score some brownie points with Livia, whom he seemed to have taken a liking to, but whatever the reason, the bonus hours made for a much more relaxed party-planning experience, something Jenna rarely had.

It had been five days since New Year's Eve. Five days where Jenna avoided Rustica and Stockton, and concentrated solely on Eunice's party. There'd been hundreds of photos to sift through for the memory display, and Jenna had let that task consume her. Rather than deal with what had happened on that dance floor and Stockton's repeated attempts to contact her and explain.

Every time she refused to take his call, Aunt Mabel got this pained look on her face and shook her head. Livia had tried to broach the subject twice—and gotten nowhere. Stockton wanted the impossible out of her.

He wanted her to stay in Riverbend. And trust that the

man who had never been able to commit to her was serious about a commitment now. She knew Stockton—too well—and knew better than to put her faith in the impossible.

"Isn't this just amazing, Earl?" Betsy said, drawing Jenna's attention back to the hall. "It's like something out of a TV show."

"It's something, all right." Earl scowled. "Something fancy."

Betsy slugged him. "Now, Earl, it won't hurt you to put on a tie and your best shirt."

"I'm wearing my best shirt." He patted his Mechanics Know How to Make It Work T-shirt.

"You will not wear that filthy thing to my sister's birthday party. I bought you a nice button-down. You'll look handsome."

"More like a man going to his execution," Earl mumbled.

Betsy rolled her eyes, but bit back any additional comments about Earl's attire. "I'm going home to wrap Eunice's present and get the bed-and-breakfast ready for all her relatives that are arriving today. Lordy, it's going to be busy at my place. I'll see you at the party tomorrow. Me and Earl." She patted Jenna on the back. "I never should have doubted you." She held Jenna's gaze for a long time. "I'm sorry."

Warmth spread through Jenna. "Thank you. That means a lot."

Betsy headed out of the building, oohing and aaahing over the decorations as she left. Earl stayed behind, twirling his ball cap in his hands. "I seen your face earlier," he said to Jenna when the door shut.

Jenna bent over to straighten a display of photographs from Eunice's childhood. "What about my face?"

"Every time my Betsy calls you a local, you look like you want to run off the closest cliff."

Jenna laughed. "Considering we're in one of the flattest states in the nation, I'd say that's pretty hard to do."

"You know what I mean, Jenna Pearson, and don't pretend you don't." He wagged a finger at her. "I've known you all your life. Why, you used to sit in my garage on that stool I got, and watch me work on your father's truck. You'd hand me a wrench when I asked for a screwdriver, and be just a general pain in the neck, like most kids are, but…" He shrugged and his gaze dropped to the floor. "I didn't mind much."

"I remember that. The smell of the oil, the country music you were always playing."

"Nothing can make the day go by faster than a little Travis Tritt." Earl grinned, then sobered. "And I remember when you came to live with your aunt Mabel. After your parents were gone, she moved you on into town, and brought you up right."

"My aunt's a wonderful woman." Jenna switched one frame for another, then shifted another a little to the right, perfecting the display.

Earl nodded. "Yep, she is. Quite the woman." He twirled the ball cap some more. "So was your momma."

"She was a good mother," Jenna said. "Who didn't always make good choices."

"No, I reckon she didn't. But in the end she did the right thing." He ran his thumb along the ball cap's brim. "That man, he asked her to run off with him. Your momma turned him down flat. Made him madder than a hornet, let me tell you. He was in my shop, getting some new tires before he blew out of town, spouting off like Old Faithful." Earl leaned in closer. "She told that so-and-so that her family was more important to her than any plans he had. That she'd been a fool, and she was staying right here to make things work."

"But I thought—"

"What you thought is wrong. Bunch of nonsense made up by people who didn't know any better. I think that day—" his face softened and his voice lowered "—that day we lost your momma and your daddy, your momma had decided to make her marriage work. She was here in town, picking up wine and flowers and all kinds of romantic notions. People say it was for him, but I know better. That man was long gone, off to ruin someone else's life. Your momma was headed home that day, Jenna. *Home.*"

She thought of the intersection where the accident had happened. It was one of those where you could go either way—toward the farm or toward another city. Everyone had assumed that Mary had been going away from the farm, from her family. But what if Earl was right, and she had been going home?

All these years, Aunt Mabel had been trying to tell her that there was more to the story than what Jenna had heard from the gossips, but Jenna hadn't wanted to hear it. She'd simply believed the worst about her mother, because she'd felt so betrayed, so hurt. Sure that her mother was leaving not just Joe Pearson, but her own daughter, too.

"I hated her," Jenna said softly.

"Your life turned upside down. You're allowed a little anger."

"But I should have understood, I should have—"

"Jenna, you were, what, seven when your parents died? Ain't no kid I know that age who can make sense out of the whys and wherefores of the stupid things adults do. Sometimes, you just need a little time to see the whole picture."

"And there were so many people telling me only the worst."

"Don't you listen to people talk," Earl said. "They don't know your mother like you know her. You make up your own mind about her, and you shut those other busybodies out."

"I barely remember my parents."

Earl smiled. "You come over to my garage sometime. Sit on the stool, and hand me the wrench when I need it, and I'll tell you all about him."

Gratitude flooded Jenna, and she reached for Earl, giving his hand a squeeze. "Thank you, Earl."

He shrugged, crimson spotting his cheeks. "You know me, I like to talk." He glanced at the clock. "I have to get going back to the garage. Got a dead Taurus sitting on my lift that needs a new alternator."

"Thanks again. I guess I forgot that there were people like you in this town."

"I ain't nobody but a good neighbor, and you've always had plenty of those."

She thought back, to when she was a child, after her parents had died. She'd been so poor, with so few belongings, and then one day, bags and bags of clothing and toys had arrived on Aunt Mabel's doorstep. "That clothing drive. I remember that. No one ever told us who did that."

"It was Betsy. She ain't never had no kids of her own, and I guess she just thought you were one she could kinda adopt, know what I mean?"

"*Betsy* did that? But I thought..."

Earl waved off her sentence. "Betsy's nicer than she'd like people to think."

And then Jenna remembered. Betsy calling Jenna over when she was riding by on her bike, giving her a stern lecture about road safety. But it had always been followed by a peanut butter cookie. The meals she used to dread at the bed-and-breakfast—Betsy had invited them over at least once a week—and leaving with armloads of leftovers. Abrasive Betsy doing her best to help her neighbor. "That was so nice of her."

"Yeah, well, don't tell her I told you. It'll spoil her reputation. I know my Betsy's got an ornery streak sometimes, but at heart, she's just a protective old goat." He chuckled. "And Pauline Detrich, God rest her soul, she was the principal at Riverbend Elementary, and she used to tell me she'd stop by every day in your classroom and make sure you were catching up to the other kids."

Jenna remembered the older woman making appearances in her classroom, but had never known why. She'd thought it was because the principal was friends with her teacher, or had been sent by Aunt Mabel to check on Jenna. "She's the reason I got in that special tutoring program."

Earl nodded. "You needed a little TLC when you were a kid, and there were plenty of people here who made sure you got it. And your aunt, well, she had it tough, too. Not a lot of money, and a kid she had to feed and clothe. People stepped in, Jenna. Brought you just what you needed, when you needed it."

It was almost the same words she'd heard Father Michael use the other day. All these years, she'd concentrated only on the negative experiences in this town, using them to fuel her leaving when she'd graduated. How easy it was, she realized, to do that instead of think of the good in the people around her.

"This is a town that takes care of its own," Earl said. "And you were always one of its own, regardless of what a few idiots without a stop sign for their mouths ever said." Earl lay a hand on her shoulder. "I've been watching you since you came back here. You've been lost, I think, and coming home, you've been found again. You just don't know it yet. This place is home for you, Jenna Pearson. It always was." Then he left, leaving Jenna alone in the banquet hall, surrounded by pictures of a woman who had spent a hundred years in this very town.

Jenna wandered the hall, for the first time really studying the pictures of Eunice. There were tiny black-and-whites from when she was a child, standing on the front stoop of a low-slung bungalow-style house, eating an ice cream at the summer fair, standing in the woods beside the Christmas tree her father had just cut down. And then, later in her life, pictures of Eunice doing charity work for the local church, accepting a blue ribbon at the pie table, serving hot cocoa at the Winterfest. Happy memories, every one of them.

It wasn't Eunice that left an impression on Jenna. It was the people around her. Members of the town where she had lived nearly all her life. For years, she'd been telling herself that she didn't belong here, that she wasn't a small-town girl at all.

And yet, Riverbend had been there for her, in more ways than she could count. The thought warmed her heart, and made her wonder if she could ever repay that kindness.

She tried to concentrate on finishing the centerpieces, and gave up. Her mind was racing, hundreds of thoughts from the past two weeks crowding her. She grabbed her coat, and headed out the door of the hall, just as Livia was coming in.

"Hey, where you going in such a rush?"

"I just need some air."

Concern knitted Livia's brows together. "Are you okay?"

"Yes." Jenna paused. "No. I just need a little time to think."

"Okay, sure. But if you want to talk, I'm here."

"Thanks, Livia." Jenna drew her friend into a tight hug, then headed out into the bright sunshine. The winter storms had finally passed, and the temperatures were edging into the high thirties. After the cold of the past few days, it almost felt like a heat wave. The snow had turned to slush, forming gray puddles on the sidewalks.

Jenna's boots made sloshing sounds as she walked, slowly at first, then her pace increasing as her feet made the destination decision for her. She cut down a side street, then another, avoiding the main downtown area.

An expanse of green opened up before her, dotted with piles here and there of leftover snow. Most of the Winterfest decorations had been removed from the park, leaving it in its natural state, a little barer because of winter, but still a quiet, peaceful haven.

She'd come here hundreds of times when she'd been a little girl, and even into her teen years. Maybe it was because the open space reminded her so much of the farm she'd lived on when she'd been younger, or maybe it was just that the Riverbend park, with its lush green trees and winding paths, offered a quiet refuge from the hundreds of changes in one little girl's life.

The paths had been plowed, which made walking along the nearly clean pavement much easier. Jenna took her time, not really looking at her surroundings, but breathing them in, letting the crisp air fill her lungs.

But it wasn't enough. She walked farther, and still the knot of tension that had come with her from New York nagged at her neck. She kept heading down the paths, as if distance would change everything.

This place is home for you, Jenna. It always was, Earl had said. Was he right? Had all these past few months of feeling misdirected, and bringing that misdirection to work, mean she was fighting, as Aunt Mabel told her, against what her subconscious really wanted?

Did a part of her want to be back here?

And call Riverbend home?

The thought chafed at her, like a new scab on an old wound. She danced around it in her mind, not sure if it was right, or just the cold muddling her thoughts.

The trees surrounded her like quiet sentries. Far in the distance, she heard the happy laughter of skaters on the pond, the crackle of melting snow falling to the ground, the titters of squirrels enjoying the warmer weather.

She increased her pace, letting the cold air and the long cement paths take her mind off the past few days. She walked fast, intent only on the road ahead, the next curve, the tree at the end where the road turned toward the playground.

"Jenna!"

The shout caught her by surprise and she stumbled, her foot hitting a patch of ice. Just as she was about to meet the pavement, a strong pair of arms scooped her up and righted her again. Stockton.

"Thanks." She shot him a smile.

"Just doing my gentlemanly duty, ma'am." He swept forward into a quick bow, which made her laugh. The tense knot in her neck eased, and a lightness filled her chest.

"Stockton Grisham, always to the rescue."

"I've been saving you ever since second grade," Stockton said, "when you fell on the playground—"

"And you carried me all the way to the nurse's office." She smiled at the memory, then dug her hands into her coat pockets, and started walking again. Stockton kept pace beside her, and for a second, it felt like old times, when they used to walk to and from school together. In the days when she could confide anything to him, and know that he would support, not judge.

"So tomorrow you go back to New York," he said. "Back to business as usual."

"I hope it's not business as usual. That's the last thing I need." She saw his quizzical glance. "In the last few months, I've been...off my game, I guess you'd say. I've started forgetting appointments, and doing stupid things like scheduling DJs and caterers for the wrong dates."

"Maybe you're just burned out."

"Maybe." The thought of going back to her apartment, back to the city, didn't fill her with the same anticipation as always. She glanced around the park, at the trees dusted with white, the rolling hills that would be green in the spring, and the circular beds that would bloom with flowers in a few months. It was quiet and peaceful, the kind of environment where someone could get lost in their thoughts. Where she lived was so busy, with the constant hum of traffic and construction. Still, New York was where her business was, where her things were...and where she belonged. Wasn't it? "I've got a lot waiting for me back there."

"You have a lot here, too."

She stopped walking and looked at him. "Like what, Stockton? You? We keep dancing around this, and neither one of us is really saying anything."

"What is it that I'm supposed to say?" He let out a gust of frustration and his gaze went past her, to the bare trees, their tall skinny trunks vulnerable and stark against the white snowy backdrop. "What are you expecting out of these few days? Because from what I see, all you want to do is get out of town again."

"And all you want to do is escape with your heart intact, like in the old days," she said.

"That's not true."

"It isn't?" In that moment, the years of distance between them was erased, and the old hurt roared to the surface. "Eight years ago, you let me go. Watched me get on that plane and let me leave. Because you were too scared to take a risk, and go with me. To stay in one place with one person."

"And what, watch you bury yourself in your work? Maybe you don't remember, Jenna, but you had only one setting in your mind. Forward."

"There's nothing wrong with ambition. You're ambitious, too. It's what has made your restaurant a success. And yet you criticize me for having the same goals?"

"Yeah, when it's at the expense of relationships with people who care about you."

His words were cold, sharp. But she noticed one thing lacking in them. The word *I*. He hadn't said relationships with him, or that he cared about her. He'd kept it vague, unconnected. "I could say the same for you," she said.

"Is that what you think I'm doing? Because last I checked, I was the one who was staying here in town and you were the one getting on the first plane out of here."

She sighed. "You know, you keep telling me I should change my life. What about you? You spend virtually all your waking hours in this restaurant, so you don't have to risk having a real, in-depth relationship. You're as much of a wanderer today as you were before. Taking the easy way out instead of sticking around."

"Is that what you think, Jenna? That I took the easy way out?"

She arched a brow. "Didn't you? With us?"

"You're wrong. Watching you go to New York was the hard way." He let out a breath that formed a soft cloud around his lips. "The easy route would have been to follow you and pretend we could make it work. Done what everyone expected me to do." He paused a beat. "And marry you."

The last two words hung in the air for a long, long time. "Well, at least you avoided that mistake," Jenna said after a moment.

"Yeah." The word was short, curt and devoid of any inflection that could tell Jenna if Stockton was regretful or grateful. "I didn't go to New York, Jenna, because I wanted…" He shook his head. "I wanted more."

"What more?"

"A way to fill the emptiness," he said after a moment, and an alarm sounded in Jenna's head. Was that what she'd been feeling in these past few months? An emptiness that she needed to fill in a new way?

"I traveled for a while," Stockton went on, "exploring new cuisines, new customs. All the while, I was thinking it wasn't the place that had felt wrong, it was…" He shrugged. "Me. In the end, the only place I wanted to serve a meal was right here, in my hometown. Riverbend is my home, and always has been. I just didn't know it until I left. So I came home. And stayed."

Stockton had a physical address that wasn't changing, but in all these days together, she still hadn't heard what she needed to hear from him—that his emotional address was locked, too. That he was ready to settle down with one person and take a risk on love. That had always been the problem between them—she was looking for more from him than he was willing to give. In the end, nothing had changed between them. Nothing at all.

She drew her coat tighter, even though the outdoor temperature hadn't changed. The chill in the air was entirely between her and Stockton. "Eunice's party is tomorrow," she said, avoiding the conversational powderkeg that

Stockton seemed determined to light. "Are you all set with the menu?"

Disappointment dropped a shadow over his face. "I guess that's it then. There's really nothing else for us to discuss." He gave her one quick, short nod. "I'll see you tomorrow."

And then he was gone, leaving her alone in a park that had once seemed peaceful and wonderful had become cold and empty.

CHAPTER TWELVE

WHEN GRACE, THE HOSTESS, had come to Stockton and said there was a woman waiting to see him, his first thought was Jenna. He smoothed his shirt, ran a hand through his hair and pushed through the kitchen's doors, a smile ready on his face.

But Livia, not Jenna, stood by the hostess station, an envelope in her hands and a sympathetic look in her eyes. "I came by to give you the balance for the catering for Eunice's party." She held up the envelope.

"Oh." Stockton took it, then stuffed it into his back pocket. "Thanks."

"For what it's worth, I told her that avoiding a problem didn't make it go away. Jenna's pretty good at that, you know. Avoiding." Livia started to walk off, then turned back. "And hey, one thing about Jenna that you should know—she's a tough cookie, but inside, she's a bunch of crumbs."

"She's made it clear that she's going back to New York, Livia."

"If you ask me, she keeps saying that because she's waiting for someone to give her a reason to stay."

"You're leaving? Now?" Livia's eyes widened. Behind her, the staff of the banquet hall was busy ironing the tablecloths and setting out silverware. Across the room, Edward was ostensibly watching his staff, but more, Jenna suspected, waiting for Livia to be free.

"I'll be back before you know it. I have an errand to run. It won't take long, I promise." Jenna handed the event folder over to Livia. In it was the detailed plan for Eunice's party, not that Livia, who was a stickler for detail, would have forgotten any of the necessary components. "We've got everything pretty much all set up. The florist should be here in the next half hour, and I'll be back in time to set up the arrangements." Then she grabbed her purse, headed out the door and into the winter sunshine. She drove to Aunt Mabel's house, ran upstairs and grabbed her suitcase. It took a couple of minutes to gather what she wanted, put the items into another bag, then head back out to her rental car.

A few minutes later, she pulled up in front of the church. The vestry was empty when she stepped inside, and the quiet of the ornate room enveloped her like a blanket. It seemed everywhere she went in Riverbend, she found peace and quiet.

Which came with the dual-edged sword of space to think. She'd spent the past two days doing nothing but thinking, it seemed. She'd done a mental dance around the answers she sought, and every time, come back to this. To the people and place that had reminded her of what was important.

Jenna strode down the carpeted aisle of the St. Francis church, then detoured through a pew to reach the side door. The community room at the bottom of the stairs was empty, tables and chairs neatly stacked against the wall, the floor gleaming and freshly mopped. Jenna followed the sound of voices into a small room with a television and a trio of sofas.

"Jenna!" The priest greeted her when she stepped into the room, striding forward with an outstretched hand. "So nice to see you again."

"Same to you." She smiled.

"You just missed Stockton."

"Oh." The sound of his name hit her hard, but she forced herself to keep that smile on her face. A few more hours and she'd be gone, far from Stockton.

Since yesterday, Jenna had made sure to avoid him. She'd had Livia deliver the final payment for the catering, and begged off when Aunt Mabel invited her to Rustica for dinner last night. She'd pled a headache, and tried not to cry when Aunt Mabel brought her back a takeout order of lasagna with a side of béchamel sauce.

Why drag out the inevitable? She was leaving, and he was staying.

"If you stay around a while," Father Michael said, "you can get a listen of the band that's setting up." He gestured toward the main hall, where several men were assembling musical equipment. Jenna recognized two of them from the day she'd been here serving breakfast.

"Band? What for?"

"We're going to have a fundraiser in the spring. To raise money for the shelter." Father Michael tapped her arm. "I heard you handled one of those before."

"I did. It raised four hundred thousand dollars for breast cancer research."

Father Michael let out a low whistle. "That's amazing."

She nodded. "It was one of the most rewarding moments of my career."

"Perhaps you should consider giving us a hand, then," Father Michael said. "Since you are the pro at this."

She shook her head. "I'm sorry, but I'm leaving tonight. I have to get back to New York."

"Of course. I understand." Father Michael looked as if he wanted to say more, but one of the band members called him over to the stage.

As he walked away, Jenna's mind began rolling down the road the priest had presented. She thought of how she'd handle such a fundraiser. How she'd organize the promotion, create a theme that would get people talking, and do it all with a budget that gave maximum dollars to the shelter.

She glanced to her right and saw Tammy in the kitchen, working on a potato salad. She remembered the bundle in her arms, and headed into the gleaming galley-style space. "Hey, Tammy."

"Oh, hi, Jenna. What are you doing here?"

"I brought these for you." She held up two of her business suits. When she'd pulled them out of her suitcase, she'd been sure the dark blue one would be the best for Tammy's complexion, and now, holding it up and near Tammy's peach skin, she saw she was right. "I think this color would look great on you."

Tammy beamed, and the joy in her features sent warmth spreading through Jenna. She thought of her overstuffed closet in her apartment, brimming with clothes she'd stopped wearing or didn't need, and realized she could make a small, very small difference, here in Riverbend. How many suits did one woman need anyway?

It wouldn't be enough to repay those people who had made a difference in her life, but it would be a start. And for the first time since she arrived in Riverbend, Jenna felt a sense of connection to the town. The knot of tension in her neck that had seemed a constant companion slowly loosened.

"Oh, my goodness. Thank you so much," Tammy said,

running a gentle hand over the soft wool fabric. "These are wonderful. I really appreciate it."

Jenna glanced out to the front room again, where the men had gathered with the priest, presumably to discuss the upcoming fundraising event. Once again, a list of ideas danced in Jenna's mind. She could feel the familiar buzz of anticipation in her gut, the same feeling that she'd once had when she'd opened her business.

Was that what had caused her to lose her touch? Was that why she couldn't seem to get back on track? Because all the engagement parties and birthday parties and corporate dinners had seemed so...empty?

Fundraising. Making a difference. The knot of tension disappeared completely as the idea formed in Jenna's mind. She turned back to Tammy. "Listen, I know you're interviewing for another job, but I was wondering if you'd like to work with me on a project here."

"Work with you? On what?"

"Father Michael wants to hold a fundraiser for the shelter. I'd offer to organize it, but since I live in New York, I'll need a local contact to handle a lot of the details." She thought of the gregarious, organized woman she'd known in high school. What better person could she call on for help? "I think you'd be great at that."

"Really?" Tammy's eyes widened, first with shock, then with hope. "You think so?"

Jenna nodded. "I do."

Tammy stepped forward and enveloped Jenna in a tight, earnest hug. "Thank you. Thank you so much. You've changed more than just my outfit today, Jenna."

As Jenna returned Tammy's embrace, she thought about the circle of life. Twenty-plus years ago, her family had been the one in need. In this very basement, people had filled that need, receiving gratitude in return. She saw now why people helped others—the return on investment was far greater than the work involved. This, she realized, was exactly what she had been searching for.

The only problem was that she was returning to New York, to the same world that had drained her. And leaving all this behind.

The room was ready. After returning from dropping off her suits at the church, Jenna had spent the rest of the day at the banquet hall with Livia, putting the finishing touches on the tables, adding the rest of the photos, and setting up the flowers. Livia had left to go back to Aunt Mabel's and change, while Jenna slipped into the hall's ladies' room and switched from jeans and a T-shirt to a little black dress with heels that she'd bought yesterday.

She checked her reflection, smoothed her hair and touched up her makeup. She was ready, too. She stepped out of the ladies' room and took in the ballroom one more time. Everything was in its place, as it should be. A multi-tiered cake in yellow and pink—Eunice's favorite colors—sat against one wall, while two long tables lined with photographs sat against the other. The centerpieces representing each decade anchored the tables and provided a visual history of the past hundred years. Helium-filled pink and yellow balloons stood in massive bouquets throughout the room while a giant banner congratulating Eunice on her hundredth birthday dominated the wall behind the head table.

For a second, she thought of the party she'd helped plan at Stockton's restaurant. New Year's Eve, supposed to be the night of new beginnings, new resolutions. And all she'd done that night was complicate her life by kissing him.

And worse, falling for him again.

In the past two weeks, Stockton Grisham, with his sexy

smile and patient approach to everything, had done the one thing Jenna swore he'd never do again—infiltrated her heart. She didn't know when, but somewhere between the ice skating and the kiss on the dance floor, he'd reawakened feelings she'd thought no longer existed.

But it was no fun to travel a relationship road by herself. She might be ready to settle down, but she hadn't seen one sign that Stockton was any more ready now than he had been eight years ago.

She checked her watch. In an hour, Eunice's birthday party would begin. And in five hours, she would be gone, on her way to the airport with Livia. Returning to her city life, and leaving this small town behind for good. For Jenna, it wasn't soon enough.

The side door opened, spilling bright light into the hall. A silhouette of a man filled the doorway and Jenna's heart tripped.

Stockton.

It didn't matter how often her brain told her that they were over, the rest of her didn't seem to listen. And now, with her departure so near, an ache began to build in her chest. Telling Jenna Pearson that leaving Riverbend was going to be harder than she'd thought.

"I've got the food," Stockton said. "I'll need to set up in the kitchen. Shouldn't take very long."

Nothing personal in his statement. All business.

Exactly the way she wanted it. After all, hadn't she made it clear to him that she was leaving? That after today, they would go back to where they had been—living in separate states, no longer together. Still, a persistent feeling of disappointment hung heavy in her stomach. She pushed it away. *Get through this party, and everything will be okay.*

Stockton hefted a large insulated container into his arms, then entered the hall. Jenna hurried over to the doors leading to the kitchen, holding them open for him to pass through. It wasn't until he reached her, and the gap between them closed from feet to inches that she realized her mistake. Holding the doors put her almost skin to skin with him. She caught the woodsy notes of his cologne, noticed the way his dark hair curled a little along the edge of his neck, the warmth emanating from his body. Everything inside her ignored common sense, and sent a hot surge of desire through her veins.

"Thanks," Stockton said, as if he'd been completely unaffected.

"No problem." Once he was in the kitchen, she stepped away, letting the door shut on her hormones.

But not her emotions.

Hurt bubbled over inside her, and as much as she tried to ignore it, told herself she was over him, that the kisses they had shared had been nothing more than a crazy indulgence in old feelings, still the pain of his coldness stuck. That once again, he was letting her leave.

He carried in a half-dozen containers, all without much more than exchanging a few pleasantries with her. *Hasn't this weather been nice? How long do you think the higher temperatures will last? Surely, Eunice will love the food...*

Things like that, all impersonal. Nothing about their conversations over the last few days, nothing about the kisses they had exchanged. It was as if she was dealing with an ordinary vendor, not a man she had a personal, complicated history with. Not a man she was about to say goodbye to for the second time in her life, in just a few hours.

After the last container was loaded into the kitchen, Stockton called out to Jenna. "Would you mind giving me a hand for a second? I've got some of the waitstaff coming over but I hate to waste even a second when it comes to hot food."

She glanced around the room one more time, ensuring the flowers were in place, the centerpieces laid out according to her plan, the linens neat and pressed. Livia would be arriving any minute to give the room a second set of eyes. Every time she planned a party, Jenna felt as if she couldn't go over the details enough. She'd fret and stew, and pace and straighten—

She'd be better off in the kitchen, keeping busy, so she wouldn't get too obsessive over a simple birthday party.

"I have a few minutes," she said, then entered the kitchen and donned an apron. Surely she could spend these few minutes with Stockton and stay immune to his charm.

"A little bit of déjà vu, isn't it?" Stockton said, as he slipped on an apron emblazoned with Rustica's name and logo. "You and me, working together. Just like two weeks ago, when you helped in the restaurant."

"And burned a sauce, if you remember right. I'm not exactly sous chef material." She started pouring hot water into the chafing dish bases, so they would keep the food warm and moist once the burners underneath were lit. "You know, we worked together in a kitchen once before."

Stockton paused in the middle of pouring rolls into a huge glass bowl. "We did? When?"

"Home ec. Tenth grade. We were kitchen partners for cooking class."

He laughed, and the light sound eased the worries in Jenna's chest. Stockton had always been able to do that with her—make her forget her troubles and find something sweet to celebrate about her day. His lighthearted approach to things had been the perfect antidote to a girl who wanted to forget the heavy past that dogged her. "I forgot about that. Probably because it was such a disaster."

She wagged a finger at him. "*You* burned the cookies."

"I was distracted." He reached for another bag of rolls.

"That wasn't it at all. You weren't much of a baker, admit it."

He crossed to her, and for a second, she thought he was going to kiss her again. Instead, he reached past her for a container of butter. Disappointment fell like a stone in her stomach. God, she was a mess. Didn't know what she wanted from one minute to the next. "I wasn't much of a baker. And I was distracted." He paused a second, his gaze locking on hers. "I still am."

Jenna swallowed hard. "By what?"

"By you." Then he backed away, and laid the butter beside the rolls.

Her laughter shook a little. She went back to filling the pitcher with hot water and transferring it to the chafing dishes. "It looks like we'll have close to two hundred people here tonight. A lot of people from town are coming, and Eunice's cousin from Pennsylvania is—"

"Are we going to talk about it or not?"

"Talk about what?"

"About you leaving. Every time I bring it up, you change the subject."

The last of the dishes had been filled. Jenna put the pitcher into the sink, then turned around and faced Stockton. She crossed her arms over her chest, as if that was any kind of barrier between them. "I'm better off in New York, Stockton."

"Are you?"

She threw up her hands. "What's that supposed to mean?"

"Are you happy? With your life? Your job?"

"Of course I am." But just as it had with Stockton, Jenna could hear the answer coming too fast, too pat.

He shook his head and studied her. "I've known you almost all your life, and I'm telling you, you aren't happy. You can go back to New York, go back to your business, and tell yourself this is exactly what you wanted, but I think you're going to find the same thing I did."

"What's that?"

"That there's a hole in your life that no amount of distance can fill."

It was as if he'd read her mind, and still, she resisted. She kept thinking how he was just letting her go. It was eight years ago, all over again, and Jenna could barely stand to watch the inevitable conclusion unfold. "There is no hole, Stockton. And if I seem off or whatever you think, it's stress, nothing more." She waved toward the room set up for the party. "Out in that room, that's my job—" and then she thumbed in an easterly direction "—and there's my life, several states away."

He shrugged. "Okay, if that's the way you want it." He closed the emptied insulated containers, and carried them out the door and back to his truck.

"It is," she said, but Stockton was no longer in the room, and the only person she was telling was herself.

CHAPTER THIRTEEN

STOCKTON HOVERED NEAR the buffet table, greeting the people he knew and refilling the dishes as needed. He could have hidden in the kitchen, but some masochistic urge kept him out here, with Jenna only feet away. The guests talked among themselves, filling in the silence because the band was late. Jenna had been on the phone, trying to reach them, her face flushed with frustration.

"Stockton! Come on over here, young man." Betsy waved at him from the head table.

He crossed to Betsy, Earl, Jenna's aunt Mabel, and Eunice, and several other members of Eunice's family that he didn't recognize. "Yes, ma'am?"

"Thank you for making my birthday meal," Eunice said. "You know how I love those toasted raviolis."

"I do indeed." He cupped a hand around his mouth. "And I made sure to put extras aside for you to take home."

Eunice giggled like a girl. "Thank you, Stockton."

"Anything for you, Mrs. Dresden." He pressed a kiss to her L'Air du Temps scented cheek and wished her a happy birthday.

"Enough about the meal," Betsy said. "When are you going to do something about our Jenna?"

"Excuse me?"

"You aren't seriously going to let her go back to New York, are you?"

"I don't think I get a vote."

"Of course you do," Aunt Mabel cut in. "If you ask me, yours is the only vote that matters."

"There's Jenna's."

Aunt Mabel waved a hand. "That girl doesn't know what's good for her when it's standing ten feet away. Come to think of it, neither do you."

He chuckled. "Aunt Mabel, I most certainly know what's good for me."

She shooed at him. "Then go get it, and quit standing around this table, moping like a puppy that's lost his tennis ball."

Jenna's aunt couldn't have been more obvious if she'd hung up a sign ordering Stockton to propose to her niece. "Aunt Mabel, you are a terrible matchmaker."

"I don't know about that," Earl cut in. "She told me I should call on Miss Betsy here, that it'd be the best thing I ever did. And what do you know? Mabel was right."

"Oh, Earl," Betsy said, feigning annoyance, but her cheeks colored with pleasure.

Aunt Mabel frowned at Stockton. "I'm too old to have my remaining family scattered to the four corners of the world."

"New York is hardly the other side of the universe."

"It is to me, and it will be to you if you don't get smart, young man." Aunt Mabel pushed a box across the table to him. "Inside that box is Jenna's grandmother's engagement ring. Her father put it on her mother's finger, and her mother promised her that when she was ready to get married, it would be hers. I've kept it all these years, waiting for the right man to come along for my Jenna."

"Aunt Mabel—"

"You keep it, Stockton. Even if I was mad as heck at you for letting her get away the first time, I've always known you were the right man for her. Now it's just time you and Jenna realized that."

Stockton put the ring in his pocket. Later, he'd return it to Aunt Mabel. For now, it seemed easier just to keep it and appease everyone. But as he walked away and felt the heft of the ring box, he wondered if maybe this was a case of his elders knowing better than he did.

Jenna watched the exchange between her aunt and Stockton, but didn't hear what they'd said. She thought she saw her aunt give something to Stockton, but what it was, she didn't know. Whatever that had been about, it was all classic Aunt Mabel—interfering for the sweetest of reasons, and over the objections of the niece she had raised.

Right now, Jenna had more important things to worry about, like MIA musicians. She dialed her phone again, and once again, there was no answer.

Livia crossed to Jenna's side, and handed her a revised schedule for the day. "Things seem to be going pretty well."

"Except for the band not showing up. Where are they? Do you think they got lost?"

"I faxed the directions myself," Livia said. "And it's not like this town is so huge you can't find your way around."

Jenna laid a hand on her friend's shoulder. "I don't think I ever thanked you enough for flying down here and helping me with this party."

"I didn't do much. I was more moral support than anything else."

Jenna laughed. Gratitude for friends like Livia washed over her. "Well, either way, you're getting a paycheck at the end of this. And hopefully, the success of this party will turn into more when we get back to New York."

Livia toed at the floor, her bell-shaped skirt making a soft swish. "About New York..." She glanced up at Jenna and grimaced. "I don't think I'm going back tonight."

"Do you want to take a later flight? I can change our reservation."

"I meant I don't think I'm going back...ever." Livia's gaze swept over the room and settled on one person. A smile curved up her face as her gaze lingered on Edward Graham's tall, lean frame. "Seems I've been offered a job."

"A job? Where?"

"Here." The smile widened. "Edward said he needs someone to run the Riverbend Banquet Hall for him. And..." she let out a deep breath "...he's asked me to do it."

Edward caught Livia looking at him, and he tossed her a smile back. Livia practically hummed with joy.

A whisper of envy ran through Jenna. "That's wonderful, Livia. Though I think he has an ulterior motive for offering you the job."

"And I have an ulterior motive for accepting." Livia laughed, then sobered. "I'm sorry, Jenna. I really love working with you, but this town kind of grew on me in the last few days and I think this will be a great opportunity for me."

"I think it will, too," Jenna said, then drew Livia into a hug.

"You're going to do great when you get back home. I know you will."

Home. The word didn't seem to hold the same meaning it once did. Jenna told herself it was only because she'd been away from her apartment for so many days. That once she stepped back into the busy city, everything would be fine.

Wouldn't it?

She looked around the banquet hall, filled to brimming with a lifetime's worth of friends in Eunice's life. It took living in the same place, year after year, to build up this kind of close circle. In her neighborhood in New York, there were people who had known each other for decades, and surely, some of the same kind of relationships as Eunice had here.

The difference? Eunice had lived in Riverbend all her life. She was the quintessential small-town girl. As Jenna watched Eunice laugh and chat with person after person, she realized their memories wrapped around Eunice like a blanket. A part of Jenna, a part she had always shushed, craved that blanket for herself. Her mind went back to Tammy, to Father Michael, to the people she had seen working together for the common good, and wondered if maybe she was looking in the wrong place.

Her cell phone rang, jarring her out of her reverie. In a halting, apologetic voice, the drummer of the missing band confirmed Jenna's worst nightmare. She sighed and hung up the phone, then turned to Livia. "The band isn't going to make it." God, this was just like all the mistakes she'd made in New York. Was she ever going to get out of this rut?

"I thought you had them booked."

"They were, but apparently the band double-booked. The band leader didn't tell the guitarist that they had other plans already, and the guitarist went ahead and made an agreement with someone else. Right now, they're in Indianapolis, playing at someone's wedding."

"Oh, no. That stinks."

Jenna paced in a circle. "I can't believe I did this again.

I double-checked with them, but I should have triple-checked. Quadruple-checked."

"This one's not your fault. They double-booked, not you."

Jenna waved toward the head table, where Eunice sat with her closest friends and family members, waiting for the music to start and her birthday party to get fully underway. "Tell that to Betsy. She's just been waiting for me to screw up. She told me this was the most important day of Eunice's life and I had to get it right."

"But you did. Everything is arranged as it should be, and it all looks great."

"Except it's a bit quiet in here." Jenna paced again, tapping her phone against her chin. "I need to fix this. Now."

"In a town this size, where are you going to find a band on such short notice?"

Jenna flipped out her phone, and dialed another number. "I have an idea."

Ten minutes later, Betsy was marching across the room, her face a mask of anger. "Why is there no music?"

"I'm taking care of it. Give me fifteen minutes."

Betsy let out a frustrated gust. "I hired you to provide a perfect party for my sister's birthday. And now..." She threw up her hands.

"It will be perfect, I promise."

"Your aunt said you were the best. If you ask me, this is far from best."

"Now, Miss Betsy, not all of us can meet your high expectations." Stockton's voice was quiet, cajoling. "Everyone in Riverbend knows if they want someone who goes above and beyond, they need to stay at Betsy's Bed and Breakfast."

Her chin jutted up. "Of course. I run my business very efficiently."

Jenna glanced at Stockton and wondered where he was going with this. "That you do," Jenna agreed.

"And yet, I'm sure even you have had days when things didn't go as planned," Stockton went on. "Guests who arrived unexpectedly or a dinner that didn't turn out quite as you expected."

"Or the plumbing breaking at the worst possible time," Betsy said with a frown at the memory. "Right in the middle of a family reunion, too. Goodness, what a stink. Literally."

"Exactly," Jenna chimed in, with a grateful smile for Stockton. "And I'm sure all you wanted your guests to do was relax, enjoy themselves and give you a minute to rectify the situation. Like call another band to come in and replace the one that couldn't make it."

It took a moment, but the anger washed from Betsy's features, replaced by understanding. She nodded. "I'll go back to the table. Get Eunice to share her top five memories with the guests. That should be enough time until the music arrives."

"Thank you," Jenna said. "That's all I need."

Betsy patted Jenna's arm, and in her eyes, she read something more than agreement. She saw acceptance, warmth. "We all have little glitches," Betsy said.

"We do. And in the end, I think it will all work out fine."

Betsy considered Jenna again for a long time, then nodded and smiled. "I have no doubt it will. No doubt at all."

Twenty minutes later, the band was on the stage and launching into a bluesy-jazz mix of oldies but goodies. Across the room, Jenna saw Eunice nodding with the music, clearly pleased with the choices. The guests chatted and laughed, and she overheard several comments about the excellence of the food, the cool factor of the decorations, and the memories seeing Eunice's photographs had evoked.

The party was a success. She'd done it—and she'd done it well. It was going to take some hard work, but she could bring her business back from the brink of disaster. In her pocket, she patted her plane ticket, and told herself she'd be back on top in no time.

As she made her way through the room, checking and double-checking that the food was still hot, the photographs still in the right order and the guests happy and fed, an odd sense that she was missing something filled Jenna. At first, she thought she'd overlooked something for the party. Forgotten a place setting or the guest book or some other detail.

No, that wasn't it. Everything was where it should be. Still, she couldn't shake the feeling.

Father Michael walked over to Jenna, and shook her hand. "Thank you," she said. "You really pulled off a miracle for me at the last minute."

He waved off her gratitude. "I didn't do anything but drive the van that got the band here. You did something much bigger."

"What's that?"

"You gave them a second chance." He waved toward the band. "And that's something that can't be bought. You did it for Tammy, too. Goodness, Jenna, you're making changes all over this town. People will miss you when you leave, that's for sure."

"Oh, I don't know about that."

Father Michael's gaze swept the room, then came back to Jenna's face. "I think you need to have a closer look at all the friendly faces here. This is your home, Jenna. It always was." Then he walked off toward the band.

Her home. Hadn't Earl said pretty much the same thing? For so long, she'd resisted that thought, sure that she could never feel truly at home in a town where the whispers about her parents were a constant hum around her. She'd been too busy listening to that hum to appreciate the rest of the town. To realize it offered a connection, one she had foolishly left behind.

And then, she knew. What she had been looking for all along wasn't success, or a great party, but this—

This people connection that showed she had made a difference. She'd handled dozens and dozens of parties, but after all the flowers were dead and the decorations taken down, what had she been left with? A sense that she'd thrown a great party, sure, but there'd always been that little sense of *is this it?*

She brushed off the questions. She didn't have time to deal with them now—she needed to keep her focus until Eunice's party ended. She headed over to the buffet line, and a moment later, Stockton joined her. "Thank you for what you did with Betsy."

"No problem. You know her as well as I do. She can have a temper, but she can also be fair and understanding."

Jenna nodded her agreement. She gestured toward the head table, where the group with Eunice was chatting, laughing and eating their second helping of Rustica's entrées. "So what was that all about with my aunt and Betsy?"

"The food." He grinned. "And you."

Jenna groaned. "Do I want to ask?"

He chuckled. "No, you really don't."

Undoubtedly, her aunt was playing matchmaker, one of the roles she liked best. Jenna decided to stay far, far away from that topic. Stockton had dropped the subject of her staying in Riverbend, and seemed fine with the fact that she was leaving for good in a few hours.

She tried not to let the disappointment swell in her chest, but it did all the same.

With all the guests served, Stockton began cleaning up the buffet while the waitstaff carried in the empty plates and dirty silverware. Stockton hefted the massive, and nearly empty, bowl of salad into his arms and headed for the kitchen. Jenna grabbed the container of rolls and followed after him.

She found him in the kitchen, busy scraping the leftovers into a small container, then loading the dirty bowl into the sink. Silence extended between them, while outside the double doors the room's chatter continued at a happy hum, set to the beat of the band's soft rock tunes.

She watched him work, watched the movements of his lean frame, the way his jaw set in concentration. She knew Stockton better than she knew anyone else. Could have drawn his features in her sleep. And she had loved him nearly all that time.

How was she going to leave this town? Leave him again? It had been so hard for her to get on the plane to New York the first time. She'd told herself at the time that she was making the right decision, the one that was best for both of them. Eight years ago, it had felt right.

But now… Now it hurt.

The kitchen doors swung open and Livia strode into the small space. "Hey, sorry to interrupt, but it's time to sing happy birthday to Eunice and let her blow out the candles."

"Great," Jenna said, although she was feeling far from festive. Birthday cake meant the end of the party was nearly here, and she'd be that much closer to putting Riverbend and Stockton far behind her.

Jenna left the kitchen, then signaled to the band. As they launched into "Happy Birthday," Jenna and Livia wheeled the cake in front of the head table. Jenna lit the three numeral-shaped candles spelling out the number one hundred—much better than the overwhelming option of a full hundred candles—while Eunice came around to stand before her cake. "It's beautiful," she said. "Goodness gracious. I can't believe I'm a hundred years old. I still feel ninety." She laughed.

Someone called "speech, speech" from across the room. Another voice asked, "What's your advice for living to be one hundred?"

Eunice thought a second, her hands clasped at her waist. "Find what truly makes you happy, and living to an old age will be easy."

The ballroom erupted in applause, the band launched into "Happy Birthday" and the crowd began to sing to Eunice. She leaned forward, paused, as if she was making a wish, then she blew out all three candles. There was another, more enthusiastic round of applause, then Jenna and Livia took the cake back to the kitchen to cut it into serving pieces.

"I can do this with Jenna," Stockton said to Livia. "You go keep Edward company."

"I'm not turning that offer down," Livia said. She thanked Stockton, then left the kitchen, a wide smile of anticipation on her face. Jenna suspected it'd be a long time before that smile disappeared, given the way things were going between Livia and the owner of the banquet hall.

"Looks like Eunice's party was a success," Stockton said to Jenna as he dipped a long cake knife into hot water and began slicing through the dessert. With deft movements, he cut off squares and loaded them onto plates that the waitstaff then put onto trays. As he did, Jenna added dessert forks to each serving. The waitstaff moved in and out of the kitchen, delivering the cake to the guests before returning for more.

"Things did go very well, even with that little glitch with the band," Jenna said. "I'm pleased, not just for my company, but for Eunice. And for you. This should help spread the word that Rustica is one of the best restaurants in Indiana."

Stockton sliced the last piece, then put the knife down. "You know, I didn't take on this job because it would help my business, Jenna." He considered his words for a second. "Maybe I did at first, but then it became something more."

Jenna propped a fork onto the small plate, set it on the tray, then faced Stockton. There was nothing left to do, not really, except finally deal with what they had been dancing around for days. "What do you mean?"

"I did this because I wanted answers." He leaned back against the stainless steel countertop. He wore his white chef jacket and dress pants, but to Jenna, he had never looked more handsome. She wanted to reach out and touch him, to kiss him just one more time before she left.

She stayed where she was. Trying to be wise, not rash.

"Answers about us," he said.

"Us?" Her heart beat faster, and her breath caught in her throat.

"You asked me why I didn't come after you when you went to New York." His blue gaze met hers, so direct she was sure he could see inside her.

She shrugged, as if the topic didn't send a sword through her heart. As if bringing up those awful days didn't still hurt like hell. "I just assumed if you wanted to be with me, you would have come after me. You didn't, so…" A long breath escaped her. "So that was it."

He pushed off from the countertop and closed the gap between them. Her pulse began to race, and as she looked over his face, her mind repeated one phrase over and over again.

This is the last time you're going to see him.

Because even if she returned to Riverbend after this, to visit with her aunt, or to see Livia, she knew, deep in her heart, that she would not be with Stockton again. They had reached some kind of pivotal moment in their relationship, a door that had been opened by the catering job, and she was about to let that door shut.

Once it did, she sensed whatever feelings might have remained between them would die. It would be over. For good.

"I always wondered why you left so abruptly."

"It was the end of the summer. I had a job offer at a party planning company, and there was an opening at the college there for the hospitality program—"

"Which meant you'd planned this, at least a little."

She bit her lip. "I just couldn't find the right time to tell you."

"Was it really that?" he asked quietly. "Or did you drop that bombshell and hop on the next plane so you could leave me before I left you?"

"I…" Her protest died on her lips. She thought of those last few months when they'd been dating. Stockton had talked about traveling the world, then coming back to Riverbend. All she heard, though, was "leaving town." She was so sure—so, so sure—that he'd never return. That he'd find someone else in another city.

"People are going to leave you, people are going to disappoint you. So why not force that process along a little bit?"

"I didn't…" She sighed and shook her head as tears worked their way to the surface. She thought of all the people who had left her, or let her down. Her parents dying, her world turning upside-down. Had she done that to Stockton, too? Been so ready for someone else to leave her that she did it to them first? "Okay, maybe I did. But how can you blame me for a little self-preservation? By the time we graduated high school, I realized all your talk about traveling the world was so you could get away from the one thing you've always avoided like the plague. Commitment."

"My schedule is insane, Jenna. Even if I wanted to have a family—"

"If you want something bad enough, you get it, Stockton. You did it with your restaurant. You bucked all the odds, silenced the naysayers. You did it. But when it comes to your personal life…you don't take that same risk. And you know why?" She didn't wait for an answer. "Because you're guarding something, too. That's the part you've given to your restaurant instead of to other people." Her hand flattened against the left side of his chest. "The one thing I could never have, no matter how hard I tried. Your heart."

She stepped away and headed for the swinging door of the kitchen. "That's why I'm going back to New York, Stockton. Because I know better than to wait around for something I'm never going to have."

CHAPTER FOURTEEN

NIGHT HAD FALLEN, bathing Riverbend in a nearly silent darkness. Like most small towns, everything buttoned down once the sun went down. Most of the shops were closed, the traffic disappeared and even the neighbor's dogs seemed to quiet their barks. Jenna stood in the bedroom she had lived in since she was seven years old and added the last of her sweaters to her suitcase. "I'm all packed."

Aunt Mabel sighed. "I wish you wouldn't go."

Jenna turned and drew her aunt into a tight hug. "I'll be back soon, I promise."

"I'm going to hold you to that," Aunt Mabel said. "And please, don't let so much time go by next time."

Jenna laughed, then went back to her suitcase while Aunt Mabel took a seat on the bed. "You could always come to New York and visit me, Aunt Mabel."

"I could. And while I was there, I could stock up on that coffee you're always sending me." Aunt Mabel smoothed a hand over the quilt at the end of Jenna's bed. "Or…you could call Percival Mullins."

Jenna glanced around the room, but didn't see anything she'd left behind. The bathroom, had she gotten everything in there? Either way, if she forgot anything, her aunt would send it to her. Still, the persistent feeling that she was leaving something behind nagged at her. "Percival who?"

"The Realtor. I saw his sign on a tiny little storefront on Main Street yesterday. It's a sweet little shop. Used to be an antiques shop, until Lucy Higgins retired and moved to Florida."

"I remember her. She gave me a lace handkerchief once. Told me every young lady needs a handkerchief."

"Well, her store is empty now." Aunt Mabel traced over the triangles that formed a starburst on the quilt's panels. "It's a really nice place, too. The kind of place that would make a great office for a party planner."

Jenna zipped her suitcase shut, then slid it onto the floor. It was a little lighter than when she'd first arrived, because her suits were now with Tammy, but still the Samsonite hit the floor with a soft thud. "Gee, is that a hint?"

Aunt Mabel shrugged. "Call it a suggestion."

"A pretty obvious one." Jenna laughed.

Aunt Mabel's light blue eyes met her niece's. "Don't you want to live to be a hundred?"

"What's that got to do with Lucy Higgins's store?"

"Lucy retired at eighty-five. You know why she kept that shop open as long as she did? Working long past the age most people retire?"

"Because she needed the money?"

"Because running that little shop made her happy. Didn't make her rich, but sure made her happy." Aunt Mabel rose. She cupped Jenna's jaw in the same tender way she had when Jenna had been a little girl. "What you're doing now isn't making you happy, my dear. You keep telling yourself it is, but I know you as well as I know my own self, and you are searching for something, something that you already have here."

Jenna opened her mouth to argue back. The sentences formed on her tongue, but refused to leave her mouth.

Aunt Mabel was right. Jenna had been telling herself

that once her business was back on track, she'd be happy. She'd find that missing ingredient that had been plaguing her for months, no, years. But she hadn't, even as she'd stood in the middle of Eunice Dresden's birthday party, surrounded by happy, content guests.

She had, however, felt that sense of satisfaction earlier today. When she'd stood in the basement of the church and promised to help Father Michael plan the shelter's fundraiser.

"Running a business like that out of a town this small would be tough," Jenna said. "I mean, I'm sure I'd draw a lot from nearby cities, like Indianapolis, but still, it would take time to spread the word."

Aunt Mabel smiled. "Good thing you have a whole town to rally behind you. Who better to spread the word than your friends and neighbors?"

Jenna thought of what Earl had said, and what people like Father Michael and Betsy had done, and what they were still doing to help the people of the community. Riverbend truly was a family, complete with the quirky uncles and overbearing aunts.

The kind of family that had always been here, waiting for her. She'd let what a couple of people said ruin this town for her. No more. She realized what had bothered her all these days about going back to New York—

Her heart wasn't in the big city. It never had been. It had always been right here, in Riverbend's center.

"Friends and neighbors," Jenna repeated softly, then hefted the suitcase back onto the bed, unzipped it and began to unload everything she had just put inside. While Aunt Mabel stood beside her and cried.

Stockton had been a fool.

He stared at the ring box sitting on his dresser and

wondered how it was possible for a man to make the same mistake twice in one lifetime. He'd woken up this morning, and for a second he'd thought it was the day of Eunice's birthday party again. That he had a second chance to make things right between himself and Jenna. Then he saw the ring box and realized that day had already passed.

His cell phone rang. Stockton yanked it up, flipped it open and barked a greeting. "Yeah?"

"Yo, Stockton, this is Larry. You sick or something? Everyone's here waiting for you, for the staff meeting."

Stockton glanced at his watch and let out a low curse. In the year Rustica had been open, he had never been late. Never called in sick. And here he was, daydreaming and running a half hour behind. "I'll be right—" His gaze lighted on the ring box again. He thought of Jenna's words yesterday, accusing him of using his business as a way to avoid his fears. To avoid going after what he really wanted. To avoid committing to another person.

Damn. She was right. He *had* done that for the past two weeks—always, coming back to work instead of going after the thing he wanted most in life. Only a fool would keep doing something that wasn't working, and sure as hell wasn't making him happy.

"I'm, uh, not coming in today."

"You're…what?" Larry sputtered. "I think we have a bad connection because I thought I just heard you say you're not coming in today."

"You can handle the meeting and service today, Larry. I've got some…personal things to take care of." Larry spouted a few more objections, but Stockton cut him off. "You'll be fine. I'll see you tomorrow." Then he hung up the phone, grabbed his jacket and headed out the door.

* * *

Aunt Mabel had swept the front parlor twice already. Mopped the kitchen before the sun finished rising, and had fluffed the pillows on the parlor loveseat so many times, Jenna was surprised there was any pouf left in them. "Aunt Mabel, what are you doing?"

"Preparing for the first footer. A few days late, I might point out, but better late than never." She grabbed a dust rag and a bottle of furniture polish and set to work on the bookshelves.

"The first...what?" Jenna took the rag from her aunt's hands. "Here, let me do that."

"Goodness gracious, Jenna. I swear you never pay attention." Aunt Mabel handed over the cleaning products, then faced her niece. "The first footer is the first visitor of the new year."

"Aunt Mabel, the new year is already almost a week old. Surely—"

"We haven't had any visitors since the clock struck midnight on New Year's Eve. But we will today." She smiled, then fluffed the pillows. Again.

Jenna sighed and finished dusting. There was no arguing with her aunt when it came to her superstitions. Most days, they were just a funny quirk, but every once in a while, they drove Jenna crazy.

"You know the rules about first footers, don't you?" Aunt Mabel asked when Jenna finished the bookcase.

"Uh, no, not particularly. And really, I think—"

"In order to have good luck for the year, the first footer must be a man. Preferably a dark-haired man." Aunt Mabel grinned. "And he can't be cross-eyed or flat-footed. Both of those are bad signs."

Jenna laughed. "Well, I think you just crossed poor Earl off your list. That man's got the flattest feet in Indiana."

Aunt Mabel gave her niece a gentle swat. "Earl is not

coming to visit today. At least," she put a finger to her lips, "I don't think he is."

"How do you know anyone at all is coming by?"

"I dropped the tea towel this morning when I was making my coffee. It fell clear on the floor, right past my fingertips." Aunt Mabel wagged a finger. "That, my dear, is a sure sign a visitor is on his or her way."

Jenna shook her head, but didn't argue the point. Aunt Mabel almost always had someone stopping by for tea, so the tea towel theory could apply to about any day of the week. "I have to run out for a little while. I have a meeting with Percival over at the shop." She held up a hand. "I'm not making any promises, Aunt Mabel. I'm just going to check it out as a possible location." If her memories of the little antiques store were right, though, the shop would make an excellent location for an event planning business, particularly one that focused on philanthropic events. It was long and narrow, with two wide plate glass windows at the front. Great visibility, and plenty of room for small tables and displays.

"I'm glad you decided to stay in Riverbend," Aunt Mabel said.

"I am, too." Jenna sighed.

Aunt Mabel reached for her niece, her voice and her touch gentle, filled with concern. "You're thinking about Stockton, aren't you?"

"I have to go," she said, instead of dealing with a subject that would bring her nothing but heartbreak. She'd half expected him to come running after her when she'd left Eunice's party last night, but no, he had let her go. Again. Her heart wrenched at the memory, but she told herself it was all for the best. What best she couldn't quite see right now.

"If you're going to live in this town, you're going to see

him," Aunt Mabel said. "Maybe every day. So why don't you just go talk to him this morning and see where the two of you stand?"

Jenna laughed. "If you had your way, Aunt Mabel, the preacher would be standing in the front parlor by the end of the day."

Aunt Mabel arched a brow and grinned.

Jenna wagged a finger at her. "Don't get any ideas."

"Well, goodness gracious, somebody better get some ideas. Lord knows the two of you are moving slow as snails."

Those words made her think of their time on the ice, the push-pull of their attraction as they circled the ice. And that kiss…

No matter what happened, she was never going to forget that kiss. Or the one on New Year's Eve. Or any of the hundreds of times he'd touched her. That was going to be the hardest part about seeing Stockton from here on out—knowing what it was like to be with him, and knowing she never would again.

Stockton nearly tripped running up the stairs to Aunt Mabel's house. Had Jenna said her flight was last night? Or this morning? Damn, his brain was a muddled mess. He leaned hard on the doorbell.

The front door opened, sending a gust of warm air out into the winter chill. "Well, well, if it isn't Stockton Grisham." Aunt Mabel smiled. "Young man, you are as foolish as a squirrel trying to cross the highway. Come on inside, before you catch your death of a cold."

"I just want to know where Jenna is, Aunt Mabel."

"Nope, you have to come in to do that. Because you, Stockton, are the first footer." Aunt Mabel grinned and made a sweeping gesture of greeting. "The first guest to enter my house in the new year. And you are a man, and not flat-footed or cross-eyed."

He crossed the threshold and shot the older woman a curious glance. "The what?"

"First footer. A lucky omen, if you ask me." Aunt Mabel paused and tapped her chin. "Hmm…the only thing that would make this luckier would be if—"

"I brought a lump of coal with me?" Stockton held out his hand and dropped a shiny black rock into Aunt Mabel's palm.

Jenna's aunt beamed. "Exactly! A little coal to bring some warmth to the new year." She patted his cheek, then kissed his face. "Thank you, Stockton."

"Gee, Aunt Mabel, you wouldn't have tried to set that up by leaving that rock on the steps, would you?"

She grinned again. "Of course not. Well, maybe I nudged Lady Luck…a little."

"Maybe that's a good thing, because I think I need some luck today." He glanced into the house, up the stairs, down the hall to the kitchen. "I need to see Jenna. Is she here?"

"Oh, my, you just missed her. She's—"

But Stockton was already gone, racing back down the stairs and climbing into his car. As he put it into gear and navigated the downtown streets of Riverbend, he dialed the number for the local travel agency, run by one of the women in his mother's bible study. "Paula? It's Stockton Grisham. Listen, I need a ticket to New York—"

He stepped on the brakes. The Jeep screeched in protest. Was that…?

"When do you want to leave?" Paula asked.

A grin curved up Stockton's face. "I don't think I need to. Thanks, Paula." He tossed the phone to the side, parked the Jeep and climbed out. He crossed the street, ignoring the blare of someone's horn, and stopped outside the dark and closed shop that used to house an antiques store. "Jenna. You're still here. I thought you went to New York."

She pivoted toward him, a key in her hand. "I changed my mind."

His heart hammered in his chest. "Changed your mind?"

She held up the key and smiled. "It looks like Riverbend's population is going to grow by one more."

"You're...you're staying here?"

"I'm relocating my business here. And changing directions. From party planning to charitable events." She glanced back at the storefront and peace filled her features. "That's what I was missing all this time. A purpose to my work."

"I think that's the perfect combination for you."

"Me, too." Jenna's gaze traveled over the rows of businesses that lined Main Street. One of Aunt Mabel's neighbors came out of the corner bookstore. She raised a hand in greeting, and Jenna waved back. It was a small moment, the kind that happened every day in towns all across America, but it filled Jenna with a sense of belonging.

Something she hadn't even known she wanted until she had it.

"When you plan a party," she went on, "it's all over once the decorations are down. I wanted something that had more lasting power. Something that...made a difference. And when Father Michael started talking about the fundraiser for the shelter, I realized that was exactly the kind of business I wanted."

Stockton smiled, and her heart fluttered. "Good."

"Good that I'm staying in town or good that I'm starting a charitable events business?"

"Both." He took a step closer and the cold air that had hovered between them seemed to disappear.

As much as Jenna wanted to stay in this circle of her and Stockton forever, she realized she was torturing herself, standing here and talking to him, wishing he'd say something he was never going to say. "Well, I better get going. I have a meeting with Percival—"

"You're always trying to escape, Jenna Pearson, and I'm always trying to catch you." He reached out and put a hand on her arm. Even through the wool, she could feel the heat of his grip. "And I really want to catch you."

Her heart trilled, her pulse skipped, but still she held back from hoping. She couldn't let herself do that, and be let down again. Because she'd fallen for Stockton all over again, and fallen even harder the second time, because she knew what she had given up eight years ago and didn't want to do it again.

He took a step closer. She caught the woodsy notes of his cologne. She could live to be a thousand and she'd never forget that scent. Everything about Stockton Grisham was implanted in her memory and she held her breath as she waited for him to speak again.

"I was coming after you, Jenna," he said. "I should have done it last night, but instead I went back to the restaurant and worked. Doing exactly what you said I always do. Retreating into work, and avoiding relationships. It's what my father did, and I was too stupid to realize what it cost him. Until I almost made the same mistake."

Her breath was still caught in her chest, and her pulse thundered in her veins. "What…what mistake is that?"

"My father buried himself in his work. He used it as a way to distance himself from his family, his own son. He did it literally and figuratively by working as a traveling chef, until finally, my mother filed for divorce. And even when I saw him in Italy, I realized he wasn't any happier there than he had been here. You know why?"

Jenna shook her head.

"Because he didn't have this." Stockton placed a hand on Jenna's heart, then placed hers on his. She could feel the steady thump-thump of his heart beneath her palm. It was a comforting, steady sound. Something she could depend on, for a long time to come. "I let you get away once, Jenna, because I thought it was easier to stay uncommitted than to connect. You were right. I might be living here, but in my heart, I was still wandering, looking for something that I already had. You."

Stockton's words echoed in her head, and joy swelled inside her chest. His smile seemed to fill her, and she finally allowed hope to spring to life. "Really?"

He nodded. "Really and truly. I was on the phone, buying a ticket to New York, when I saw you outside the shop. I was going to find you, no matter where you were. I would have taken a spaceship, if necessary."

She looked at his handsome face, and knew there was more than one reason she hadn't gotten on that plane last night. "I stayed because…you were right. I have been afraid to change. Afraid to take a risk. Most of all, afraid to return to Riverbend." She gestured toward the town that she had grown to care about in a way she never had before, because she had finally seen past the few negative people and into the heart of the town. "It was easier to run than to trust."

"Trust that people would be there when you needed them."

She nodded, and tears sprang to her eyes. This time, she let them come, let them fall. Let Stockton see inside her heart. "That's what small towns are all about, aren't they? Community. It was what I was searching for, and I didn't even know I wanted or needed it, until I found it."

She shook her head. "All these months, I thought I was struggling in my business because I had lost my touch. For years, I had been too consumed with building the business to notice anything other than the bottom line. Then, after I hired Livia, I had more time. Time to think, look around me, and when I did, I felt unsettled. Like I had made a mistake. I kept thinking if I moved to another apartment, or I landed another corporate account, everything would start to feel right. But it never did. It took coming here for me to realize that was because I left my heart..." She paused a moment and caught Stockton's deep blue gaze. "Right here."

"If you had left, you would have taken my heart with you. Which would have been an awful shame." He held her face in his hands, so gentle and sweet. "Because I love you, Jenna. I always have. I wish I'd been smart enough to tell you years ago."

He loved her. Not the silly infatuation love they'd had when they'd been in high school. Not the love between two lifelong friends. But the kind of love people built lives on. Started families with. Bought a house and lived a life with. "Oh, Stockton, I love you, too."

His smile lit his eyes. He reached up, whisked away her tears, and placed a gentle kiss on her cheek. "Ah, Jenna, you have no idea how long I've waited to hear you say you love me."

"As long as I've waited to hear you say it back," she whispered.

"Too long," he said softly, then drew back and the smile widened. "Well, after all that, I guess there's only one thing left to do."

She cocked her head. "One thing?"

He dropped to one knee and fished a box out of his

pocket. "Get married." He thumbed back the lid of the box, revealing the diamond ring inside.

Jenna gasped, and the tears that had stopped began anew. "Is that…my mother's ring?"

"Yes. And now, it's yours, thanks to your aunt Mabel." Stockton grinned. "Marry me, Jenna. Marry me because you love me. Marry me because you never want to say goodbye again. Marry me because—" he let out a sigh that touched the deepest places in her heart "—because I didn't know what I was giving up when you walked out of my life eight years ago, and now that I do, I'm damned grateful to have a second chance to get it back."

Marry him. Take that final step in trust and commitment, with Stockton Grisham. She could see it already—his hand in hers, the two of them standing at the end of the church aisle, promising to stay together forever. To settle down in this little town and build a life. And maybe someday, sit in a banquet hall surrounded by all their friends and family, celebrating decades together.

Her hand closed over the ring box, and with it, Stockton's fingers. "I told myself today that I could live in Riverbend, open up a business here and be happy for the rest of my life, but…I was wrong."

He swallowed hard. "Wrong?"

She nodded. The velvet of the box kissed against her fingertips, a waiting promise. "In my heart, I'm a small-town girl, after all. And a small-town girl can never be truly happy unless she marries the boy next door."

He grinned. "I lived two blocks away from you."

She drew him to her, and placed a soft, sweet kiss on his lips. "Close enough, Stockton Grisham. Close enough."

He was still kissing her as he slid the ring onto her finger. It nestled against her skin, as if it was always meant to be there. The same way she and Stockton fit together, like two pieces of a puzzle.

There was a sound behind them, of a car door shutting. Jenna and Stockton broke apart, and turned at the same time. Aunt Mabel stood on the sidewalk, beaming at them. "She said yes?"

Stockton nodded. "Guess I'll be calling you Aunt Mabel for real from here on out."

"Well, my goodness, it's about time. I was worried I'd be celebrating *my* hundredth birthday before you two got smart. So I came down here myself to make sure you did the right thing. And…goodness, you did." She drew both of them to her in a hug that nearly took Jenna's breath away. Then Aunt Mabel stepped back, and reached into the big front pocket of her long wool coat to withdraw a shiny U-shaped object. "To the new couple," she said, holding out what Jenna now saw was a horseshoe. "And always be sure the tines are pointing up, to hold in all that good luck."

Jenna's gaze met Stockton's. His blue eyes seemed to go on forever, like an ocean she would spend a lifetime exploring. "I don't think we're going to need the horseshoe, Aunt Mabel," she said, slipping her hand into Stockton's. He gave her fingers a squeeze, then wrapped his arm around her waist. "Because we're already lucky enough."

Stockton nodded. His fingers grazed over the diamond that promised a new beginning for both of them. "We found everything we wanted and needed, right here in Riverbend."

Jenna rose on her toes and pressed a kiss to Stockton's lips. "A new year, a new beginning—"

"For old loves who never forgot each other."

Jenna curved into Stockton's arms, and pressed her head to his chest. His heart beat steady, right in time with her own. "And never will."